HIS FINGERS BEGA̶N̶... ...̶D̶O̶W̶N̶
HER ARMS, STROKING HER SENSITIVE SKIN.

"Do you know why I left that day, princess?" Brady asked.

"I think I know, my lord," Regina answered. "And I think I'm glad you left."

"Why were you glad I left? Were you as frightened as I was?"

"I'm frightened now, my lord," she said.

"Oh good, I'm not the only one . . ." he said, breathing the words against her lips, then covering her mouth with his own.

White hot lightning streaked behind Regina's eyes and shot through her body. Brady's mouth moved on hers and she felt the tip of his tongue along the soft, moist flesh of her bottom lip. She vaguely felt his hands slide down her back, to her waist, rising across her midriff, sliding up and over her breasts. It was wrong, it was right. It was what she wanted . . .

∽ ∽ ∽

"Kasey Michaels never fails to entertain us! She has an amazing talent for creating realistic and memorable characters!" —*Literary Times*

"Kasey Michaels creates characters who stick with you long after her wonderful stories are told. Her books are always on my nightstand."
—Kay Hooper, bestselling author of *Out of the Shadows*

*Please turn the page for more praise
for Kasey Michaels and her delightful romances . . .*

"Michaels has written the most thought-provoking sensual romance I have ever read. . . . A heart-grabbing story."
—*Under the Covers*

❧ *ESCAPADE* ❧

"Vintage Michaels. A wonderful romp with all of her deft touches of high wit and striking humor."
—*Belles and Beaux of Romance*

"A delightful novel. . . . Michaels creates a great cast of characters."
—*Southern Pines Pilot* (NC)

"Escapade is the perfect choice for those who enjoy madcap romantic comedy."
—*Bookbug on the Web*

❧ *INDISCREET* ❧

"A lively romp . . . a well-plotted, humorous story filled with a bevy of delightful supporting characters. . . . This story will not disappoint."
—*Library Journal*

"Kasey Michaels returns with all the hallmarks that have made her a romance treasure: humor, unforgettable characters, and a take on the Regency era few others possess. Sheer reading pleasure!"
—*Romantic Times*

OTHER BOOKS BY KASEY MICHAELS

Someone to Love

Waiting for You

Come Near Me

Escapade

Indiscreet

Then Comes Marriage

KASEY MICHAELS

WARNER BOOKS

An AOL Time Warner Company

WARNER BOOKS EDITION

Copyright © 2002 by Kasey Michaels
All rights reserved. No part of this book may be reproduced in any form or by any electronic or mechanical means, including information storage and retrieval systems, without permission in writing from the publisher, except by a reviewer who may quote brief passages in a review.

Cover design by Diane Luger
Cover illustration by Tsukushi Kainuma

Warner Books, Inc.
1271 Avenue of the Americas
New York, NY 10020

Visit our Web site at
www.twbookmark.com.

For information on Time Warner Trade Publishing's online publishing program, visit www.ipublish.com.

W An AOL Time Warner Company

Printed in the United States of America

First Printing: January 2002

10 9 8 7 6 5 4 3 2 1

To Michael Seidick and his wife, Susan,
two halves that make a perfect whole.

When my love swears that she is made of truth,
I do believe her, though I know she lies.

—William Shakespeare

Chapter One

"Bored, Brady, old friend?" Bramwell Seaton, Duke of Selbourne, asked as he snagged two glasses from a passing servant. He handed one to his friend, who was just now leaning against a marble post in the overheated ballroom, stifling a yawn behind his hand.

"Obviously you haven't been paying attention, Bram. I passed beyond bored more than a year ago," Brady James, Earl of Singleton, told him, gratefully accepting the glass. "What you see before you now is stultified. Damn near mummified. Tell me again why society finds this endless parade of opulence necessary."

Bram took a sip of his wine, smiled as his beautiful wife waltzed by in the arms of a half-pay officer whose expression told the world he felt as if he'd just died and gone to Heaven. "But that's precisely the point, Brady. Parading opulence. Look at me everybody, I've got more hothouse flowers at my ball than Lady Whoever had at hers. Look at me everybody, I have more diamonds in my tiara. Look at me everybody, I can afford the best tailor to swathe my corpulence in the finest satin. Look at me, look at me. Please, everybody, look at me."

"Your Sophie doesn't act like that," Brady told him, waving to the duchess of Selbourne, who was at that moment delightedly waggling her gloved fingers at him. "She enjoys herself, no matter where she is. I think she genuinely likes people, all sorts of people." He pushed himself away from the post, grinned wryly. "I mean, she seems to like you."

"Correction, my friend. Sophie *adores* me. She tells me so just often enough to keep me from thinking too long about the times she *doesn't* adore me."

"Her aim improving?" Brady asked, as the two men made their way to the anteroom where, Brady hoped, he could find himself a card game and a quiet corner.

"Thankfully, no. Although she never quite forgives me when I step out of the line of fire. She'd much rather I catch whatever she throws. Remember that god-awful vase Prinny gave us as a wedding gift? The big blue one with the naked nymphs and prancing centaurs? Missed that one entirely when it came my way the day I forgot to show my face at Sophie's little tea party for Lady Sefton. Made quite a mess, I tell you. Broke into a thousand pieces."

"It would have been a bad influence on your children in the long run," Brady said, smiling. "I looked closely at it one night, you know, while waiting for you and Sophie to appear. I truly believe a few of those prancing nymphs and centaurs were . . . copulating."

Bram grinned. "Sophie said they were just being extremely friendly when I tried to point out that fact to her. But she did cross nearly the entire room to pick the thing up and wing it at me, so I think she knew. Oh, by the bye, Sophie's found another one for you."

"Another vase? What in God's name would I want with one? Please don't tell me I so forgot myself as to compliment the damn thing. Our dear Prince Regent has the pocketbook of a pauper and all the taste and refinement of a whorehouse madam."

"No, not another vase, as well you know. Another female. A Miss Sutton, I believe. Good family, sweet girl, and very biddable."

"Lord save me," Brady said, shaking his head. "That would be the fourth one this week, and the last one hadn't even cut her second teeth yet, I swear it, Bram. I never should have told Sophie I was feeling left out now that you and Sophie, and Kipp and Abby, and seemingly all my friends are so happy, so . . . so *married*."

"Relax, the Small Season will be over soon, and you can escape to the country."

Brady looked around the card room, saw that every chair was filled. Not that he wanted to play for the tame stakes his hostess allowed anyway. "Maybe sooner than later, Bram," he said, turning on his heel. "But stay or go, I'm definitely fleeing this insipid ball before Sophie sics Miss Sutton on me. I'll stop round tomorrow, to apologize to your dear, meddling wife."

"You'd better," Bram called after him. "And, being a good friend, I won't tell her you're coming. Otherwise, I can see myself helping to amuse Miss Sutton until you appear. Do you think she'd like a rousing game of snakes and ladders?"

Chuckling under his breath, Brady made his way to his hostess, bid her a good evening, gathered his hat, gloves, cane, and cloak, and stepped out onto the wide marble porch.

He cut quite a handsome figure in the rather garish light from the flambeaux affixed to the facade on either side of the door. Tall, over six feet, and with the build of a man who enjoyed physical exercise, he tapped his tall hat down on his golden brown hair at a rakish angle that shaded his bright brown eyes. His tanned skin contrasted well with the pure white of his linen and his black-as-ebony evening clothes and cloak.

He took a deep breath of the never wonderfully perfumed London night air, pulled on his gloves, and tucked his cane under his arm. It wasn't past midnight yet, which meant that parts of fashionable Mayfair were just now coming alive, and he could feel the excitement in the air. An excitement he, unfortunately, didn't share, as he knew he had somehow lost his interest in the social whirl.

And yet, what else was there? No wars to fight at the moment. No large scandals, although one would probably be along any moment, for this was, after all, London. Even the government seemed to be running itself smoothly, an oddity in itself, but just one more reminder that, other than visiting his tailor or whiling away the hours in some gaming hell, there was precious little for him to do. Precious little he *wanted* to do.

Perhaps he would leave the city and return to his property in Sussex. He could throw himself into riding his fields, checking the estate books, and spending some long, quiet evenings by the fire with a snifter of brandy, his favorite hounds sleeping in front of the hearth.

He made a mental note to have someone hunt up some dogs for him. Preferably big, tongue-lolling, sleep-on-your-feet dogs.

Mostly, he needed to clear his head. He flipped a coin in the direction of the nearest footman, telling him to find his coachman in the crush of coaches lining Berkeley Square and inform him that his master would find his own way home this evening.

The air was warm for this late in the fall, with a hint of fog whispering at his feet, and he really didn't need his cloak. Using his cane, he deftly swept back the cloak, flipping the ends over his shoulders, revealing the fine cut of his evening clothes, and started off toward his mansion in Portman Square.

The flagways were still fairly well populated, what with members of the *ton* still hieing here and there, and the streets clogged with coaches either surrounded by other coach traffic or parked wherever possible, awaiting their owners. As usual, the pungent odor of horse manure overrode the essence of the high-class, perfumed, ofttimes unwashed bodies heading to or from yet another party, yet another ball.

Only after he'd walked for a few blocks did Brady at last feel some small, satisfied solitude. He enjoyed the night, the sounds of it, the smell of it, the now more thick, silent fog, the hint of danger that was ever in the London air, even here, in the rarefied air of Mayfair.

He smiled in the darkness as he thought about his

friends. Bram and his adorable Sophie, now the parents of two, and yet still very obviously lovers. About Kipp Rutland, the Viscount Willoughby, and his bride, Abby, already gone from London, on an extended honeymoon at the Willoughby estates. They'd sent out notes to Bram, Brady, and others, thanking them very much for *not* visiting.

Three confirmed bachelors, and two of them now wed, leaving Brady feeling very much alone, very much on the outside, looking in at his friends' happiness. Not that he wanted a wife, needed a wife, or could even picture himself dandling a drooling infant on his knee. Just turned thirty, he was too young, he was having too much fun, he was . . . *fun*? He was bored. Damn it all to hell, he was bored.

He had to be bored. Otherwise, why would he have taken the time to go haring off to a benighted village like Little Woodcote with the silly notion of discovering information about the waif Kipp and Abby had recently rescued from the London streets?

"Because she lied," he said out loud as he turned yet another corner, still meandering aimlessly, chafing slightly because Regina Bliss's secrets were still safe, his trip having been a total waste. "Because she has the strangest way of looking straight through you with those wonderful grey eyes. Because she's beautiful, and you can't get the image of her face out of your head. Because you can't stand secrets. And, face it, man, because you had nothing else to do. Not one damn other thing to do but go riding off to find out why a servant girl is a near master of the English tongue and uses that tongue to tell whopping great fibs."

Brady winced, embarrassed to be talking to himself, and looked around, hoping no one had overheard him. "Well, damme," he said, marveling at the absence of people, of hacks, of coaches, taking in the fact that the fog had turned from romantic to oppressive, and figuratively kicked himself.

That's where meandering will get you. It will get you lost.

Brady stood still, hoping to get his bearings in the fog, closing his eyes as he mentally tried to retrace his steps. He'd left Berkeley Square, turned north. Walked a few blocks, then turned west, heading in the general direction of Portman Square. Except he should have turned north again a few blocks earlier.

Damn! Damn and blast! He should have just walked over to the park and kept to the main thoroughfares. That's what he should have done. But the main thoroughfares were just that, the main arteries for the *ton* and their coaches and their noise and congestion, and even horse manure. He'd wanted peace and quiet. He'd wanted to be alone.

And now he was alone, in spades.

Flipping back the edges of his cloak even farther, to free his arms, he took hold of his cane by the knob, secure in the knowledge that the decorative piece also held a hidden rapier beneath its ebony-wood casing.

It wasn't so much that he feared attack. It was that he didn't want to be found in a gutter the next morning, with everyone knowing he was stupid enough to have gotten himself robbed in the middle of Mayfair. Pride. Unreasonable at times, unfathomable, he was sure, to the weaker sex, but there it was. He didn't worry about stumbling across some opportunistic cutthroats; he just wouldn't want anyone to know he'd been such a clunch as to unwittingly put himself in danger's path.

His mind now concentrated on his surroundings, every slight noise, every cough that could have come from the next alleyway, Brady turned to retrace his steps to a more populated street.

"Now!"

The hoarsely whispered word that seemed to come from nowhere and everywhere—blast this fog!—had Brady whirling about, his blade already exposed to the faint yellow glow of a faraway streetlamp. He positioned himself for battle, evenly distributing his weight on the balls of his feet, holding up the blade, raising his other arm for balance.

Nothing. There was nobody there. Nothing but the night and the fog and his overworked imagination.

Wasn't that above everything wonderful? First he'd been talking to himself. Now he was hearing things. Feeling silly, stupid, and wondering when he'd turned into a nervous old woman, Brady bent to retrieve the casing for his blade, and then kept going facedown on the wet flagway under the blow from a club that smashed into his shoulder.

His battered, bleeding nose already giving him hell, Brady shook off the force of the blow and quickly rolled to his left, hoping to regain his feet.

He got to his knees before another blow broke his right

arm—he could feel the snap. He could hear it. The blade fell from his suddenly nerveless hand.

"Bastard!" he shouted, climbing to his knees once more, using his left arm to brace himself until he could get to his feet, determined at least to see the face of his attacker.

Attackers. There were three of them, all masked, all of them holding wicked-looking wooden clubs. And, his brain registered before the blows came raining down on him and his consciousness faded, they were the best-dressed street thieves he'd ever seen.

The next thing Brady thought, when he could think again, was that if he wasn't dead yet, he was going to be in the next few minutes. Because he could feel the rough burlap around him. He could smell the rotting vegetables the sack had held before it held him, held him stuffed up inside the sack like a baby in a very inhospitable womb.

He could feel the sway of a vehicle as it rumbled through the streets. Local cutthroats would have killed him, taken his purse, possibly even stripped him of his valuable clothing, then left him in the gutter—all in the space of a minute. This was different. He was being taken somewhere. That wasn't good. That couldn't possibly be good.

Brady bit his bottom lip nearly through when one of the sets of boots propped on him as if he were some human footstool lifted for a moment, then slammed heel first into his side; once, twice, a third time. It was almost an absent-minded violence, the sort of violence committed by a man who hurt people just because he could.

Brady lay very still, hoping the man would lose interest in a target that didn't moan, didn't cry out, didn't try to fight back. God, he hurt. He hurt everywhere. His stomach was close to turning with the sick pain of broken bones, the crush of his headache. How many times had they hit him? Had Caesar suffered a dozen stab wounds? Would those have hurt less than the blows from those three vicious clubs?

"He moved. God, he moved," a voice said from somewhere above him.

That same boot slammed into Brady's back. Once. Twice. "Don't be such a woman. It's just the coach that's moving. He's dead."

"Or he will be in a few minutes," yet a third voice said. Or was it the first one, speaking again? Brady couldn't tell. The heavy burlap kept him from distinguishing more than a few words at a time, and nobody was saying more than a few words at a time.

Well, at least they weren't having tea and crumpets as they drove him to wherever they were taking him. That would be lowering, wouldn't it?

Brady was getting giddy, and he knew it. He couldn't move. Not for the pain. Not for the confines of the sack. Not unless he wanted another kick, and he certainly didn't want another kick.

The coach turned onto a much rougher road, one that couldn't have been cobbled in a dozen years, and then slowed, stopped.

Brady could hear the cry of gulls, smell the murky water of the Thames . . . and he knew. Things weren't about to get any better for him. They were about to get a lot worse. But why? Why?

A door opened, hands grabbed at him, and Brady could hear the chink of heavy chains as he was half-lifted, half-dragged out of the coach and unceremoniously dropped onto the ground. He fought to keep himself from blacking out, although the pain that shot through him made him wish for blessed unconsciousness. Every second bone in his body must be broken.

"Is that enough weight, do you think? We could find more chains, I suppose. Wouldn't want him floating back up."

"Oh, he'll come back up sooner or later. After the fishes get through the bag and nibble on him for a while. Now, come on. One less nosy bastard and still time to get in a few hands at faro."

It was true. Everything he thought was true. The sons of bitches were going to drown him. Worse, they were going to drown him, then go play cards.

Brady tried to kick out with his feet, arch his back inside the heavy burlap. Useless, painful, but necessary, because he'd be damned if he'd just let them drown him, let them kill him without putting up a fight, throw him into the Thames like some unwanted puppy.

A well-placed kick to his head that set his ears to ringing reminded Brady that he was only wasting his strength and gathering himself another injury. He didn't want to go into the water, that was for sure, but he damn well didn't want to go into the water unconscious.

So he moaned once—no need to fake the heartfeltness of that moan—and purposely went limp. Moments later, he was lifted up and carried, chains rattling, his every bone and muscle screaming in silent protest, then dropped at least four feet into the rough bottom of what had to be a small boat.

God. This was it. This really was it. He was completely powerless. He was being rowed to the center of the Thames, to be dropped overboard. To die. For Christ's sake—to die. To feel the cold water closing over his head, to feel himself being dragged to the bottom, to hold his breath until his brain buzzed and his lungs burned.

To at last give in to the uncontrollable urge to breathe.

And without knowing. Without knowing why, who. That was even worse than the dying. The not knowing.

Brady opened his eyes, finally realizing he had shut them tight. The burlap was coarse enough that he could breathe through the rancid-smelling material, even see the light of the small lantern hung on the bow of the boat. But he couldn't see his killers; he couldn't see their faces.

Dancing. Two hours ago, he'd been dancing. An hour ago, he'd been talking to Bram, joking with Bram. An hour ago, he'd been bored.

He wasn't bored now. Good God, he wasn't bored now.

"Far enough," he heard one of the men say, and Brady heard the oars being lifted, could hear the slap of the water against the sides of the boat. This was it. This was the end. This was where he would die.

A wave of despair swept over him, defeating him, allowing all the physical pain to batter at him, tell him that he had no defenses, no recourse, no way out of what these three strangers intended for him.

He would die. Fish would eat him. And only a few friends would cry. No family, no heirs, no widow. Not even a loyal hound. Just a nice ceremony if they found his body, a well-prepared luncheon after the interment, and then everyone would go home to their own families, their own lives.

He had lived for thirty years, and he would leave nothing behind. The knowledge rocked Brady, sickened him.

And then he got mad.

With his body broken, with his spirit badly mangled, with his whole self stuck inside a smelly burlap sack wrapped with chains and a watery grave awaiting him, Brady James, soon to be the late Earl of Singleton, got really, really *mad*.

Half-lifted, half-rolled, Brady felt himself being hefted over the side. He took a deep breath even as his injured ribs protested, and braced himself for the cold sting of the water that rapidly closed over his head.

The shock of the cold water roused him even further, delivering a sharp shock to his brain, clearing away the last of his despair so that he could think. So that he could remember the stiletto hidden inside a specially made leather-bottomed sleeve inside his waistcoat.

How had he forgotten it? He always carried a knife hidden in his top boots. But evening dress didn't call for top boots, and left him feeling naked, so that he'd ordered his tailor to fashion the pocket. Kipp had teased him at the time, reminding him that most men were content with watch pockets, but now Brady thanked his forward-thinking self for indulging what anyone else would call an affectation.

The stiletto was inside the left side of the waistcoat, easily accessible with his right hand. Except that, now, his right hand was pretty well next to useless, so that Brady had to struggle to unbutton the tight-fitting waist-coat with only his left hand.

Years. It took years. To lift his left arm. To untie his cloak and rid himself of that dangerous weight. To fumble with the buttons of his waistcoat. To, as he sank deeper into the dark water, twist himself about until—eureka!—he caught the hilt in his hand.

The wet burlap was the devil to cut, but as panic wouldn't help him, Brady stabbed the stiletto into the rough fabric and then sawed it back and forth, back and forth, conserving his strength, his breath, until the sack opened enough to push it back, over his head, out of the way.

Fools. The fools had put chains on the sack, but they had left Brady's hands and feet free, hadn't weighted his body with more chains. Thank God for amateurs.

With a last kick of his legs, Brady was free. Free, thirty feet below the surface of the water, with only one good arm and lungs that burned for air. Kicking his feet like scissors, his evening slippers long gone, he put his head back as if he could actually see light above the surface, and headed up. Up.

His body was going numb, maybe from lack of air, maybe from the temperature of the water. But that was all right, because he couldn't feel the pain in his right arm and ribs anymore. Just the pressure building in his chest. The burning, the returning panic, the god-awful urge to breathe . . . just to breathe.

His head broke the surface of the water just as Brady had begun thinking he'd fought the good fight, but lost.

He kept his head tipped, trying to float on his back as he gulped in air; sweet, life-sustaining air.

He had two good legs. Well, one good leg at least. The left one didn't seem to be working quite right. He had one good arm. His head hurt like a bitch, and one eye was definitely swollen shut.

But he was alive. As he floated on the current, his good arm slowly waving beneath the surface, Brady did the oddest thing. At least he thought it was the oddest thing.

He began to cry.

Anger. Pain. Panic. Relief. Who knew why he cried; Brady certainly did not. He just gave himself over to the emotion, out in the middle of the Thames, all alone in the dark, and slowly making his way closer to the nearest shore, he cried as he hadn't done since he'd been a child.

They'd pay. Whoever had done this to him. Oh, yes, they would pay. His helpless tears infuriated him, took him beyond anger, took him all the way to a cold-blooded hate that sustained him, gave him the strength to pull himself, one-handed, onto the smooth rocks along the shore.

He lay there for long moments, gasping for breath.

He'd find them.

He tried to move, get to his feet, and fell back onto the rocks.

He'd find them all.

Cursing, stumbling, cradling his useless right arm in his left, he made it up the embankment and began limping away from the docks.

He'd find them, and he'd learn the reason behind the attack if he had to beat that reason out of them.

He'd prefer beating it out of them.

Leaning against dank stone walls, moving from shadow to shadow so that no casual cutthroat would see him and recognize an easy target, he lurched and stumbled and made his way toward streetlamps in the distance.

He'd destroy them, whoever they were. Take them down, one by one, and destroy them.

A hack. Brady couldn't believe his luck. He'd actually found a hack. He had to let go of his right arm in order to fish—damn, he didn't want to think about fish!—his purse out of his pocket.

"Portman Square, and there's another fifty pounds in it for you when we get there. Hurry," he managed to get out as he tossed the entire purse at the goggling driver.

Moving his jaw to speak sent lightning-hot shafts of pain through Brady's face, nearly dropping him to his knees. Somehow, he climbed onto the greasy leather seat, grateful even for the smell of moldy straw on the floor of the hack. "The mews behind Number Twenty-one. For God's sakes, man, hurry."

Oh God. They'd pay.

Chapter Two

The duke of Selbourne had really outdone himself, with the help of his wife, and his good friends, Kipp and Abby.

Singleton Chase was draped in black bunting, from the ebony-silk swags over the mirrors to the black crepe wreath on the front door.

There were over eighty mourners, a fine turnout, considering those attending had to travel all the way to Sussex. The invited guests tiptoed down the hallways to their rooms, shaking their heads as they passed by the late earl's bedchamber door and the crepe wreath that hung there.

They sipped wine and port in the late earl's drawing room, ate a substantial luncheon and funeral cakes in the late earl's dining room, and bowed their heads in the late earl's small private chapel as the local vicar read the words over a black-bunting-draped casket.

Then, just as Brady had supposed, they had watched as

the late earl's body was committed to the marble mausoleum before heading back to the drawing room and stuffing their faces all over again. Drinking his best wine, ordering his servants about, speculating about who might have murdered poor old Singleton, making plans for a card party that night before everyone headed back to their own homes in the morning.

There was even laughter, and Sir Roger had spent the night in Lady Bledsoe's chamber while Lord Bledsoe snored off his liquor in a chair in the late earl's private study.

Made a person really glad to be alive, it did, watching how his mourners mourned.

"You look like bloody hell, you know," Bram said, turning away from the window, where he stood the day after the funeral, watching the last of the traveling coaches moving off down the drive.

Brady tried to smile, but the pain in his face turned the smile into more of a grimace. His jaw hadn't been broken, thank God, but his nose had, and the skin around his eyes was still badly bruised. He looked very much what he was, the loser of the fight that had ended with him stuffed in that damn, dark sack. "Are you saying I'm not pretty anymore, old friend?"

"I'm *saying* that you don't look ready to do anything more than lie there and let Wadsworth mother you. Are you still feverish?"

"Feverish? Swallow enough of the Thames, Bram, and you get more than feverish. I was sick as two dogs. For a while there, I thought you might not have to go scaring up another body to stick in that coffin."

"Yes, there is that," Bram said, shooting his cuffs. "Have I told you yet how very much I did not appreciate your note? Let's see, how did it go? Oh, yes. Something like this, Kipp, if you're taking notes. 'Bram, old friend, I need a small favor. You have three days in which to find a body, dress it in evening clothes, have it tossed in the Thames, then claim it when it is found, hopefully after the fish get at it. Use the ring I've enclosed as proof the body is mine, make sure it's on the body when it goes into the water. Have the funeral at Singleton Chase within a fortnight of this letter. Everything will be explained later.' I appreciated Wadsworth's rather elegant script much more than I did the note's contents, in case anyone is wondering. And, old boy, I think it is now *later*, and I'm waiting for that explanation."

"That makes two of us," Kipp Rutland said from his chair near the fire. "Four, if we count the ladies. And if you don't soon let my Abby in here to fuss over you, I do believe she and Sophie will find a way to break down the door."

Brady attempted to shift himself in the bed, as one of the pillows Wadsworth had propped behind him had fallen sideways. He pressed his good leg against the mattress, pushed with his good left arm, then winced, falling back on the bed. "Damn. I'm about as helpless as an infant."

"And twice as cranky," Kipp said, saluting Brady with his wineglass before taking a sip. "Oh, I forgot to tell you. As Bram seems to have already supposed, yes, I'm going to use this in my next novel. Aramintha Zane has never written about a man coming back from the dead. Although it has been done." He looked at Bram. "Is that blasphemous? I wouldn't want to be blasphemous."

"I'm still trying to figure out why you want to be Aramintha Zane," Bram teased, helping Brady with the pillows. "Byron seems to do well enough with the ladies swooning all over him because of his scribblings."

"I prefer anonymity," Kipp said, wincing. "Or do you truly believe I'd want a gaggle of giggling females tagging after me, talking about my books as if they were anything more than my private amusement?"

Brady sighed, relaxing as Bram shifted a pillow so that his right shoulder was more supported. "Excuse me, please, and a thousand pardons for the interruption, but I think we were talking about *me*?"

"Actually, I'd rather talk about the poor fellow we just buried out there," Kipp said. "In the name of research for my novel, you understand. Bram, just how does one procure a body?"

"I was prepared to buy one, actually, just as our medical students do, when luck turned my way and a body did wash up below the South Docks. One of London's ambitious fledgling surgeons was about to cut into it when I arrived, quickly identified the body as Brady's, then palmed the ring, pretending to take it from the man's hand. The fellow had been in the water for some time, and his own mother wouldn't have recognized him, or dared to doubt a gentleman come to claim his friend's body. Being a duke has its advantages, although I'd never considered using my rank in this way before, I must admit."

"That couldn't have been enjoyable," Brady said,

wishing Wadsworth would come in, bring him something cool to drink. The damn fevers kept coming and going, and right now one was burning up his insides. "You have my eternal gratitude, for that, for organizing this spectacle. There isn't a person in London who doesn't believe the earl of Singleton good and dead."

"And celebrating that fact, at least three of them, right? You're still sure they weren't ordinary cutthroats?"

Brady looked at Kipp. "Their speech was educated, their evening dress certainly ruled out any notion I had been set upon by street thieves. And remember, they didn't rob me. They just wanted me dead. I'm not sure, but I think I remember something about me being nosy. I'm not nosy, am I?"

Bram and Kipp exchanged looks, smiled. "Not at all," they said in unison, and then laughed.

"Do you remember, Brady, how you couldn't rest until you found out the name of Fanley's latest mistress? As I recall, you camped outside his house in Grosvenor Square for three nights, just so you could follow him."

"It was a bet, Kipp," Brady said, suddenly embarrassed. "It was a bet with Freddie Roberts as to who could figure it out first. I was new to London, and young, green as grass. And I won the bet, if you'll recall."

"Young," Bram repeated. "Green as grass. Just youthful high spirits, Kipp, that's all. Of course, that doesn't explain why our good friend here devoted several weeks to an investigation of Baron Chalmers just last year, sure the man was hiding something about the facts surrounding his wife's unfortunate, fatal fall down the stairs."

"He confessed, didn't he?" Brady asked, glaring at Bram.

"Oh, he did, he did. He didn't have much choice, considering you'd bribed several servants into telling you about their argument that last night, then confronted the man at Lady Hertford's ball." Bram paused, held up a finger. "Do you suppose?"

"No, I do *not* suppose. Chalmers was hanged six months past, and nobody liked him enough to come after me for revenge. I have no enemies, Bram. I've had time to think about this. I have no enemies."

"Speaking as your friend, Brady," Kipp said, rising from his chair to stretch his legs, "I'd say you have to have at least three. Either that, or a jolly trio of your friends tied you up in a sack and tossed you in the Thames. I rather doubt that."

"So do I," Brady admitted. "Which is why I expressly asked you to bring Regina Bliss with you for the funeral."

"Because you went to Little Woodcote and asked about her? I thought you said you'd been discreet?"

"Apparently not as discreet as he'd like to believe," Bram said, rubbing at his chin as he thought. "So, if I'm understanding this correctly, you feel you have no enemies, but you think perhaps Miss Bliss does?"

"That's ridiculous," Kipp said, dismissing Bram's words. "Regina is a child—"

"Not quite a child, Kipp," Bram interrupted. "She seems to grow older every day, the better fed and clothed she becomes under Abby's care. I'd say your little rag doll seller has aged to at least seventeen, perhaps even more. She is a tiny thing, but her eyes are wiser than her years would indicate. Then there's her speech, also not the sort of diction learned on the streets. You have to admit, Kipp, she is a bit of a mystery. At least enough of a mystery to have intrigued our bored yet nosy friend."

"Now who's going to be writing fanciful stories?" Kipp asked, obviously flustered. "Oh, all right, all right. Even Abby says Regina is probably closer to nineteen than she is sixteen. She says I haven't seen the child undressed, and she has, and so she should know. Don't ask me *how* she'd know, because when my wife tells me things like that I usually try to find something important to do elsewhere."

"She has a secret," Brady interrupted, tiring fast, so that he wanted to get this interview over with and take a nap. Like an old man, he needed his naps. Just another reason to want revenge on whoever had tried to kill him. But not the main one, not by a long chalk. They had unmanned him, terrified him, turned him into a blubbering baby. He still had nightmares. Terrible nightmares in which the blade of the stiletto broke before he could slice his way out of the sack. Nightmares in which he just kept sinking, sinking into the blackness of the Thames, the blackness of eternal night.

"We all have secrets, Brady," Kipp said. "Or we used to, until you ferreted them all out. I'm still trying to figure out how you knew I'm Aramintha Zane."

Brady tried to smile, nearly succeeded. "Brilliant, educated guess?" he said, which was all he'd ever say on the matter. The truth was he'd been waiting for Kipp in his study one day, decided he needed to write a note and leave for an appointment with his vintner, went searching in the desk for writing paper—and found a letter from Kipp's publisher. But that was much too mundane a story; he'd rather appear brilliant than just lucky.

"Shall we get back to Regina?" Kipp asked. "You already know her story. She was in terrible straits, fresh out of the country, and found work making and selling rag dolls under the tutelage of a not-quite-sterling old besom named Cast-iron Gert. When Abby and I found her outside Covent Garden, Regina was bent over like a hunchback, fake sores stuck to her, and pretending to be blind. Abby thought she was no more than ten or twelve years old, until I told her otherwise."

"An old street beggar's trick, but an effective one, especially for soft hearts such as your wife's. And the girl pulled it off? Blind as well as hunchbacked?" Bram asked. "Quite the actress, I'd say."

"Quite the liar," Brady said, sighing as Wadsworth appeared, carrying a tray holding a single glass and a pitcher of lemonade. "Ah, my savior and boon companion. Thank you."

Wadsworth, a tall, spare man of indeterminate age, set down the tray, then poured a glass of the cool liquid for his employer. "I am going to have to ask Your Lordships to leave. His Lordship needs his rest," he then said, straightening, his startlingly blue eyes shifting from Bram to Kipp to let them know his request was, in reality, an order.

"Just a few more minutes, Wadsworth," Brady said. "We're nearly done here."

"Very well, sir. But when you're weak as a kitten and

cursing your fever, don't look for pity from this quarter, for there will be none."

Brady watched Wadsworth's departing back until the butler had left the room, quietly closing the door behind him. "The man fair dotes on me," he said, as Bram and Kipp broke into laughter. "And he saved my life," Brady added, sobering both men.

"It was pretty bad, wasn't it?" Bram asked, subsiding into a chair.

"About as bad as you can imagine," Brady told him tightly, remembering the fear, the blind panic, the humiliating tears. Each day he hoped the memories would lessen, and each night he awoke in stark panic, desperately clawing at the burlap shroud until Wadsworth, who still slept on a cot beside him, could wake him, calm him. "But I'm going to get my own back, Bram, I promise you that. I'm going to find those men, and I'm going to discover the reason behind their attack on me."

"And you think the reason has something to do with Regina," Kipp said, nodding. "I'd already told you I'd sent someone to Little Woodcote to investigate her story about her aunt and uncle—the vicar and his wife—being killed in a carriage accident, so that she was turned out into the world, penniless."

"I know you did, and I know you told me your man found the vicar and his wife enjoying quite good health. But that's all that your man did," Brady pointed out reasonably. "I, on the other hand, spoke to the vicar, spoke to several people in the village. I also made the idiotic mistake of leaving my card with several of those I'd spoken to, asking them to contact me if they remembered anything about a small, redheaded girl with big grey eyes and a smart mouth. A month later, I'm beaten to flinders, tied up in a sack, and tossed in the Thames. That's not a coincidence, gentlemen. It can't be."

"I always said you were too nosy for your own good," Bram said, sighing.

"Always knew that nose of his would get him into trouble some day," Kipp added.

"Oh, wonderful," Brady grumbled, trying to sip his lemonade without spilling any of it on the bedclothes. He was damnable clumsy with his left hand, and the passing of time hadn't added to his proficiency. "Just what I most need and desire at a time like this. The comforting words of my best friends."

Kipp shook his head, made a move toward the door. "I'm imagining that you want me to bring Regina to you now, so you can question her some more, perhaps discover that she's some long-lost heiress or something equally fanciful? But be warned—she thinks you're dead, as we decided that the fewer people who know about this sham of yours, the less chance for discovery."

"Don't go after her, Kipp," Brady said. "I've got time enough to talk with her, as she's going to be staying here, with me, at least until the Spring Season."

"Pardon me?" Kipp asked, turning back to look at Brady. "I thought Wadsworth said you'd passed beyond delirium days ago. You can't be serious."

"Oh, I'm very serious, Kipp," Brady said, carefully setting down the empty glass. "My first thought was simply to have everyone believe me dead, so that I could be free to sneak around London, discovering the names of my supposed killers. It was a good idea, considering the state I was in, but I've since thought up a better one. A much better one."

"And you're going to tell us about that idea?" Bram prompted, pulling a cheroot from his pocket, lighting it with a taper from the fire. "My, Kipp, aren't we the lucky ones?"

Regina Bliss sat over a tambour frame, making perfect, infinitesimally small stitches in her latest project. That project was making herself useful, making herself as near to invisible as possible. Sweet, biddable, helpful. That was Regina Bliss. A perfect paragon.

She ought to know. She worked at it hard enough.

She kept her head bent, hiding the expression in her eyes, the sunlight coming through the mullioned window haloing her shiny auburn hair with brighter red and even golden highlights.

"Please go on, my lady," she prompted respectfully as Lady Willoughby paused in an increasingly halting explanation that had staggered Regina to her center. "You were saying that the earl is not deceased after all? How strange. I could have sworn you all attended services for the man just two days ago."

"We attended services for *some* poor unfortunate man, Lord rest his soul," Abby told her. "But it's true, Regina, the earl is very much alive. Battered and broken in body, but alive. And he needs your help."

That brought Regina's head up, and she looked at

Abby in mingled shock and curiosity. "*My* help? I don't understand."

"Neither do we," Sophie put in, walking past Regina, patting her on the shoulder before sitting down in a nearby chair, arranging her skirts about her with a grace that was nearly an art. "But His Lordship is ill, and we must humor him, yes?"

Regina looked at the duchess. What a beautiful woman. Beautiful and pure and good, and much wiser than she'd want the world to believe. Regina secretly studied her, picking apart her mannerisms, aping them when alone in her room, trying out the pert sideways tipping of Sophie's head, the way she looked down, then up, as if trying to hide some delicious secret that would show in her eyes. Oh, the woman was a piece of work, and somebody had trained her well, until her every move had gone from practiced to natural. Regina admired her very much.

"Begging your pardon, Your Grace, my lady, but you may have to humor the earl. I, however, do not. He is nothing to me."

"Ah, but you are not nothing to him, my dear," Sophie explained. "In fact, he very much believes that you are the reason he was nearly murdered."

"Me?" Regina pressed both hands to her chest, goggling at the two women. "That's ridiculous! Why would I want the man dead? I barely know him."

"Oh, no, no," Abby protested quickly. "It's not like that. It's not like that at all. It's just that you were so secretive about your past, my dear, and that piqued His Lordship's interest enough for him to make inquiries about you in Little Woodcote. He's like that, His Lordship, never content until he discovers everyone's secrets." She colored prettily, a woman whose attractiveness seemed to bloom and blossom more and more ever since her marriage. "Then he goes about settling everyone as he thinks best."

"And a lovely job of playing Cupid he did for you and Kipp, yes?" Sophie said, smiling. "Although I did help."

Oh, wonderful. Now the two women were smiling and dreamy-eyed, remembering something that must have been quite lovely for them but had nothing to do with Regina. "I remember now," she said, in an attempt to get the women back to the subject at hand. "His Lordship was there the day Lord Willoughby confronted me about my fib concerning Little Woodcote."

"Yes," Abby said, "that small fib about being the orphaned niece of the vicar. A story you then very neatly amended to describe yourself as the runaway stepdaughter of a vile, wicked man who took over your father's business and then treated you as less than the lowliest laborer in that business once your mother died. We didn't believe that one, either, if you recall, although you *did* tell it rather well. We really should have spoken to you more, asked more questions, but . . . well, there were other problems at the time that occupied us, I'm afraid."

Regina stood up, began to pace. "I was surprised that you didn't press me for more information."

"More fibs," Sophie put in. "You would just have told another fib, yes? And another, and another?"

"Story, Your Grace," Regina corrected. "I would have told another story. There's a difference. But you knew, my lady, you and Lord Willoughby both. You knew that I had a good reason for those stories, and you trusted me enough to take me on, keep me with you, allow me my privacy. This time serving you and His Lordship has been a slice of Heaven after my sojourn with Cast-iron Gert."

"You've never disappointed us, Regina, and have become more of my friend and companion than a servant," Abby said. "Between us, my husband and I agreed you were entitled to keep your own counsel. Lord Singleton, however, made no such promise. He traveled to Little Woodcote, made some inquiries, left his card with a few people, and shortly afterward found himself sinking into the Thames, trussed up in chains and burlap. He does not consider that a coincidence."

"No," Regina agreed, hanging her head. "I suppose he wouldn't." She took a deep breath, lifted her eyes to Abby, and said, "What does he want from me?"

Sophie clapped her hands. "Ah, now we get down to cases, yes? What he wants, my dear, what he requires, is for you to stay here, at Singleton Chase, until he is recovered from his injuries. Months, my dear, this will take months. And then, when he is healed, and the Spring Season is upon us, he wishes for you to accompany him to London."

Regina shook her head, confused, but also very much intrigued, definitely excited by the prospect. London! How she longed to return to London, and Her Ladyship had already told her that she and His Lordship would not be going back to the city in the spring. "Why? To what purpose?"

"Why, to discover his murderers, of course," Abby

said. "Although I'm still not quite sure on the how of it, to tell you the truth."

Regina bit at her bottom lip as she looked from Abby to Sophie, seeing the concern in Abby's eyes, the twinkle in Sophie's. "But *you* know, don't you, Your Grace? You said you don't, but you do. You wouldn't have it any other way."

"My dear, I make it a point to know everything, yes," Sophie told her. "Wadsworth and I have struck up a friendship, you see. It always amazes me how very *open* men are to compliments. So, yes, even if the gentlemen believe we don't need to know more than they have chosen to tell us, I already know *everything*."

"And you'll tell me?" Regina asked, looking around the beautifully appointed drawing room, trying to imagine herself residing here. Although she wouldn't exactly be here, in the drawing room. She'd be in the servants' quarters. Still, she'd be warm, and safe, and she'd be returning to London, which was where she needed to be. She kept her expression carefully blank even as, inside herself, she was doing handsprings.

"I'll tell you what His Lordship told Lady Willoughby and myself when we met with him earlier. You will be well cared for, probably beyond your wildest imaginings. This is what matters most, yes?"

"Will I still receive my quarterly wages?" This was very important to Regina, that she receive her wages, for she had plans of her own, plans she saw no reason to share with anyone.

"*Double* your quarterly wages, Regina," Abby told her

with a smile. "His Lordship is very desirous of having you here."

"To wait for his recovery and then return to London with him so that I can tell him who tried to murder him?" Regina stood, walked to the window overlooking the well-manicured grounds. She turned, braced her hands behind her, on the sill. "But how would I know that?"

"That," Abby told her, "is a question only you can answer, my dear. But His Lordship is certain you have that answer. Do you?"

Regina looked straight into Abby's eyes. She was very good at staring other people down, and she knew it. And then she blinked, the first to look away, because she owed this woman so much. She owed her the truth, or as near to the truth as she felt it possible to say. "I might."

Chapter Three

The duke and his duchess departed Singleton Chase only an hour after Sophie's talk with Regina, anxious to get on the road, heading back to London and their children.

The next morning, Regina stood on the wide marble steps outside the huge country house and waved goodbye to Lord and Lady Willoughby, Abby shy and smiling, but Kipp patently pleased to be on the way to resuming their very private honeymoon.

Regina walked down the steps and along the crushed-stone drive, kicking at the odd pebble, holding her hands clasped behind her as she breathed in the cool country air.

Alone. Once again, she was alone. Or as alone as she could be in a house with forty bedrooms and at least as many staff. As alone as she could be with the lord of the manor lying injured in his rooms, hiding from the world.

There would be no guests, that was certain. Nobody visited an empty house of mourning.

Regina stopped, turned, looked back at the house. Fashioned of dull orange brick, the main structure was actually a huge square, with a square center court at its middle. Two stories high, and with immense attics, every room had a window, every room possessed its own view, either of the grounds or the square center garden.

Regina knew that there was a second, smaller square at the rear of the house, surrounding yet another garden, an entire other, yet attached building housing the ballroom, the kitchens, and even the chapel they had all prayed in the other morning.

So much roof, so many chimneys. The windows magnificent in their size, and in the symmetry with which they marched along the structure. An entire village could be housed within these walls, and yet only one man lived here. One man, and more than forty servants.

What did people do with so much space? Why did they find it necessary?

And yet, Regina knew, Singleton Chase was far from the largest estate in England. She knew there were homes boasting over one hundred bedrooms, estates so vast it took a small army of servants to keep the fires stoked, the silver polished.

Perhaps it was a competition among the peers. If so, it was a silly one, to Regina's mind.

She stood, rocking slightly on her heels, trying to imagine herself as mistress of a place like this, mistress of Singleton Chase. After all, if she was to dream, it was much better to be the mistress than the maid who scrubs the hearth.

She'd serve tea in the main drawing room, sit at the

bottom of the table when the ballroom was rearranged for huge dinner parties, gazing down the endless length of the table to her lord and master, who was hidden by the dozen braces of candles and a floral centerpiece that stood a good three feet high. She would laugh—ha-ha-ha!—as her guests entertained her, and entertain them in turn. Diamonds at her throat, diamonds in her ears, her ivory gown of softest silk, she would be the envy of every woman present, the secret dream of every man.

And then, after the guests were gone, she and her adoring—slavishly adoring—husband would mount the wide, curving staircase, arm in arm, and disappear behind the closed doors of the master's chamber.

To do what? Regina frowned, her daydream stopping at that point. Oh, she knew what came next. She wasn't such a looby that she didn't know what came next. She'd just never seen the attraction, the point of the thing. She knew the eventual outcome—a child, an heir—but the method of procreation seemed, to her, to be very limited in imagination. And esthetics.

Not that she'd have to worry about that. She had other things to do than to daydream, other plans that had little to do with finding herself a man.

She needed to find three men.

How long, she wondered, before His Lordship, the earl of Singleton, would be able to help her?

Regina turned back toward the house, knowing she should be making herself useful in some way, fitting herself into the ebb and flow of Singleton Chase, disappearing yet again into the woodwork, unremarkable, unnoticed. Safe.

But when she mounted the rear staircase to the servants' quarters, it was to see a maid emerging from her attic room, carrying the small portmanteau that held all of Regina's worldly belongings.

"Ah, there you are, miss," the maid chirped. She was a red-cheeked, full-figured woman with wisps of blond hair sticking out from under an enormous white mobcap, the sort of woman who instinctively mothers everyone she sees.

"Um, yes . . . here I am," Regina said, pointing to the portmanteau. "But not for long?"

"Oh, this?" the maid asked, hefting the portmanteau as if it weighed no more than a feather. "I'm just taking it all downstairs for you, miss, as the master requested. We don't ask why, not here at Singleton Chase, not from the earl, and not from his father before him. Good men, both, and you don't question good men, now do you? Especially since His Lordship is much too battered for anything havey-cavey, if you take my meaning. I'm Maude, by the way, and pleased to serve you, miss," she ended with a bobbing curtsy.

Regina pressed a hand to her forehead, rubbed at her temples with fingers and thumb. "Well . . ." She sought the proper words, knowing there were none. "Well, yes, thank you, Maude. Shall . . . shall I just follow along behind you?"

"As you wish, miss," Maude said, and Regina stepped back to allow the maid to pass, then trudged along behind her, back down the staircase, turning right along the main hallway leading past His Lordship's apartments, then left

along another hallway, finally stopping outside one of the
forty bedrooms.

"Here?" Regina looked around, expecting someone,
anyone, to pop up from behind a chair and rudely tell her
to go back where she came from and take the mending
with her as she went. "But . . . but this is the chamber my
lord and lady Willoughby used when they were here."

"Yes, I know, but it's all ready, including clean linens,
so that Mrs. Gaines, that's the housekeeper, well, she
thought you wouldn't mind, miss. It's ever so much easier than taking yet another set of rooms out of dust sheets.
There's also the rooms the duke and his duchess were in,
but that hasn't been made up yet, considering the maids
are all still busy cleaning up after that gaggle of London-
ers who made such a mess. Spilled powder and bootblack
and ripped sheets. Think they were all raised in barns,
that's what."

The chamber behind the door, Regina knew, included
a huge bedroom combined with a large area just for sitting, relaxing. There was a dressing room, a small room
fitted with a cot in case either the guest's maid or valet
was wanted close by. And there was a water closet. A
truly lovely water closet, complete with a darling, hand-
painted tub.

She was going to stay *here*? For the months and
months it would take Lord Singleton to recover—she was
going to be allowed to stay *here*?

"Um, well . . . yes . . . *yes*, Maude," Regina said, gathering herself, slipping into the role of grand but kind
dame, lady of the manor, mistress of her own affairs. It
was a stretch, considering Maude knew full well she had

come here as one of Lady Willoughby's maids, but she could do it. "I think this will be . . . adequate. Thank you."

Maude depressed the handle, threw open the door. "Think nothing of it, miss. Now, I'll just put away these few things. Don't have much, do you, miss? I suppose that will change."

Regina mentally reviewed her wardrobe, which didn't take long. How long could it take to count the dress on her back and two others that looked as alike as peas in a pod—all three of them a dark midnight blue that she covered with one of her three huge white aprons? "Do you . . . do you suppose so?" she asked Maude, wondering if she should pinch herself, wondering how much she dared dream.

"Considering that Mrs. Waters from the village has already been summoned, and considering that she's a seamstress, I'd have to say I most certainly do suppose. Not that I'm the sort to mix in anyone else's business, mind you. No one can say Maude pokes her nose in where it don't belong. Now, would you be wanting luncheon in your room or would you be kind enough to come downstairs?"

Regina took the hint Maude had laid for her and agreed to come downstairs for her midday meal. "But, please, don't bother serving me in the dining hall," she said, remembering her daydream. The only thing sillier than her daydream would be to see herself alone at such a large table, nibbling bread and making conversation with herself. "I really don't want anyone to fuss. Can't I please just eat with all of you?"

"Mrs. Gaines might not approve, miss," Maude said, looking unsure for the first time. "You are a guest in this house, you understand. His Lordship's guest. Best if you show the staff who you are, first thing. They'll soon forget you slept in the attic with the rest of us these past few nights."

"Forget, Maude? Or conveniently not remember?"

"They'll do as Mr. Wadsworth says, miss. Everyone does, even His Lordship. Mr. Wadsworth is a formidable man."

And yet Sophie had wrapped that formidable man right around her little finger. Well, what Sophie could do, Regina could do. It might take longer, but she could do it.

Regina followed Maude into the room, then perched on the high, wide bed, watching as her meager belongings were folded into drawers, placed in the huge cherry clothespress. "Do you happen to know how His Lordship is feeling today?" she asked before the maid could take her leave. "I'd really like to see him. Thank him for all he's done."

"I really couldn't say, miss. None of us has seen His Lordship. Mr. Wadsworth drove him down himself, late at night, and we were none of us aware he was here until the next morning, when Mr. Wadsworth swore us all to secrecy. Formidable, Miss. Mr. Wadsworth is formidable."

"Yes, you did say that," Regina mumbled, gnawing on the side of her thumbnail, then quickly stopping once she realized what she was doing. Ladies didn't chew on their nails. "Well, then, could you please ask Mr. Wadsworth if

I might see His Lordship sometime today. Or tomorrow," she added hastily, not wanting to appear pushy.

"I'll do that, miss. Oh, and you must call him Wadsworth. It's only other staff that calls him Mr. Wadsworth. But you knew that, didn't you, miss?"

Regina lowered her eyes to her hands, which were twisting in her lap. Good Lord, she must look like someone who had just escaped from an asylum. Biting her nails, wringing her hands. Soon she'd be howling at the moon. "Oh, yes, of course. I knew that."

Maude curtsied once more, turned to leave.

"Maude?" Regina called after her, suddenly frightened to be alone. She slipped off the bed, approached the motherly woman, placed a hand on her arm. "Maude, this is all very nice, but all very frightening. I don't have to tell you that I'm not a lady, that I don't know the first thing about being someone's house guest. I don't know what to do, what to say. How to act, how to fill the days. Can you help me?"

Maude looked at her, her broad, plain country face softening, then gathered Regina into her arms. "Oh, you dear, dear miss. Of course I'll help you. We'll all help you. You're going to be fine, just fine. You'll see."

CR

Regina was well fed. She had left off her aprons and soon would have three new gowns—one pink, one white, one a delicate light green. She had new kid shoes on her feet and a soft cotton nightgown Maude had unearthed from the earl's late mother's trunks in the attic.

The foray into the attic had also produced four lovely shawls, two pair of gloves that fit her small, thin hands remarkably well, and a pleasing assortment of hair ribbons. There had also been a dove grey woolen cloak with a fur lining Mrs. Gaines had told her was sable, from somewhere in the wilds of Russia. Regina loved the cloak, almost as much as the matching sable muff, but she didn't think she'd ever dare to wear either piece.

Regina walked outside most days, either in the courtyard or outside the square, in the gardens. She spent one rainy day walking the length of the one-hundred-foot-long (she'd paced it out) portrait gallery, inspecting all the James family ancestors, finding one she felt certain had the current earl's same twinkling brown eyes. Brown eyes were ordinary, she thought, but there was something about the earl's eyes that was memorable. The twinkle. It had to be the twinkle.

She read. Wadsworth brought her painting materials and had a footman set up an easel on the south lawn so that she could paint whatever struck her fancy. She painted a bumblebee, and gave it Lord Singleton's face.

She knew every room of the immense house, having peeked into every bedroom, trailed her fingers over the piano in the music room, even tried strumming the harp, cutting her fingertip in the process. She found a billiards room tucked away toward the rear of the second square, but wasn't sure if ladies were allowed to play at such a game, and wondered if there was a chessboard anywhere about. Wondered who would be her opponent if she did find the board.

Maude came to her in the evenings, in her rooms, and

the two of them darned sheets and sipped tea and ate cookies the maid brought upstairs in her apron pockets. They laughed, and Maude brushed Regina's hair after her bath, and Regina read to the maid from books she'd found in the huge library.

By the time two weeks had passed, Regina knew every member of the staff by name, and every member of the staff had been, à la the duchess of Selbourne, neatly wrapped around her little finger. It wasn't difficult, for Regina was by nature a friendly person, and the Single-ton staff were all unfailingly friendly.

Save one.

Regina could not get around Wadsworth. She'd tried, Lord how she'd tried. She'd thanked him politely each time he did her a service, which was rare, and she never failed to say hello when he passed her in the halls. She complimented his proficiency as he stood to one side of the table, supervising the delivery and removal of food courses, told him each meal was the most delicious she'd ever had, including the green peas she choked down just because he was looking at her.

She minded her manners, having found a book in the library that explained the intricacies of all the cutlery she found beside her plate three times a day.

She had, in a word, been exemplary. Sweet. Biddable. Careful to smile, eager to please.

And if she didn't soon find something else to occupy her mind she was going to go stark, staring mad!

She walked past His Lordship's chambers at least a dozen times a day, varying the times, hoping to, just once, find the door unlocked, or not hear voices from inside that told her Wadsworth was with the earl.

She'd asked Wadsworth nicely if she might visit the earl. She'd smiled, she'd wheedled. She'd dropped her eyelids, then looked up at the man with an innocence that should have melted the sternest heart.

This morning, she had stamped her foot and yelled at him, *demanded* to be allowed five minutes with His Lordship, who was keeping her prisoner here against her will.

Nothing had worked.

His Lordship was resting. His Lordship was recuperating. His Lordship could not be disturbed. *Would* not be disturbed.

So now Regina was sneaking, in stockinged feet, along the narrow corridor that ran between the kitchens and the butler's quarters, heading for the rack of keys that hung from hooks in the wall.

While the cook stirred her pots, and the scullery maid peeled prawns, and a footman worked in a small room, polishing boots, Regina tiptoed, stopped, listened, tiptoed again, making her way down the hall.

Each key had its own hook, and each hook was placed just below a hand-printed label affixed to a long bar of wood. Regina ran her eyes across row after row of differently shaped keys, her mind boggling at the sheer number of them, considering that Mrs. Gaines only carried about twenty on a fat metal ring hung from her waist.

Finally, on the very bottom row, she read "Master's Bedchamber." Her eyebrows raised, her lips formed what she knew was an evil smile. She would, if she were not such a "lady," smack her lips in satisfaction.

She lifted the key, then looked at the other hooks. None were bare, so these must be duplicates of keys Mrs. Gaines held, along with seldom-used keys. One bare hook would be noticeable. And Lord knew Wadsworth noticed *everything*.

What to do, what to do. Then Regina saw it; the hook holding a set of two keys. She quickly lifted off one, and hung it on the empty hook. Perfect. She might just want to consider a career in crime, as she was rather good at it, if she had to say so herself.

The key and its small ring safely stuffed in her pocket, Regina tiptoed back down the hallway, slipped back into her shoes, then turned into the kitchen, bade everyone a cheery hello, and asked if it would be possible to have a second slice of the lovely apple pie Cook had served that night at dinner.

Oh, she was a cool one. A thief with an appetite. And her hands barely shook as she lifted the first bite of pie to her mouth.

She drank the glass of cold, fresh milk Cook offered her, daintily patted her lips with a linen serviette, then made a great business out of being tired, ready for an early night.

Maude followed her upstairs after a few minutes, her duties now fairly confined to serving as lady's maid, and offered to help Regina out of her gown.

"Oh, no need, Maude. I thought we'd read a bit. Or don't you want to know what happens next to the rich and handsome Mr. Darcy?"

"Do you think Miss Elizabeth Bennett will accept him? He's been naughty, but Miss Jane Austen explained all of that, didn't she? Miss Elizabeth certainly seems to understand. But, oh, that little scapegrace, Miss Lydia, running off like that with Mr. Wickham. Shame, shame on her! Ladies don't do that, you know. You want to know what ladies do, miss, and they don't do that."

"I'll remember, Maude, next time someone asks me to elope with them," Regina said dryly, motioning for Maude to take a seat by the freshly laid fire, then sitting down across from her and opening the book to the page she'd marked.

An hour later, with the house quiet, and Maude snoring by the fire, Regina closed the book, slipped out of her shoes, and tiptoed to her door, opening it slowly, peeking left, then right, to make sure the hallway was empty.

The mantel clock in her room had just chimed out the hour of ten. Regina already knew where Wadsworth was at ten each evening, for the man, bless his starchy hide, was very much a creature of habit. At nine he tucked His Lordship in for the night, and at ten he had a glass of port with Mrs. Gaines in his own sitting room.

Right about now, Wadsworth was taking his first sip of port, and Mrs. Gaines was reciting tomorrow's menus and, ever hopeful, batting her eyelashes at the determinedly oblivious butler. According to Maude, the two had been dancing around each other for years, neither of them taking the first step that could lead to a deeper relationship.

"That's because Wadsworth doesn't have a heart," Regina whispered now, under her breath, as she sidled along the wall, slipped around tables, pulled a face at a suit of armor that never failed to startle her in the dark.

She made her way to the corner of the hallway, peeked down the next hallway, congratulated herself for making it this far without being discovered, wished she could dare to extinguish the few lights in this brighter hallway.

Now came the really hard part. She reached into her pocket, pulling out the key, held it tightly in her hand. So tightly, it pressed painfully into the soft flesh of her palm.

Still on tiptoe, Regina headed toward the double doors leading to the master chamber, stopped in front of them, took a deep, shuddering breath, and inserted the key in the lock.

Click.

Was that loud? Could a *click* have been that loud? It had sounded like a cannon going off in the hallway.

"Stop it," Regina whispered, ordering herself to relax, to stop being missish. She was simply going to visit with His Lordship. In his bedchamber. After dark. Just the two of them. Alone together.

Nothing wrong with that. Not a single, solitary thing.

The door opened without a sound, without so much as a squeak. Good old Wadsworth, keeping everything shipshape, in apple-pie order and all of those good things.

She closed the door behind her, holding her breath as the latch engaged, then turned around and stood very still. She waited for her eyes to become accustomed to the dark, as only a few candles burned inside their holders beside the bed, on a small table placed in front of a mirror, the mirror lending the candle twice the light.

Puddles of light, that's all, along with the glow from the fireplace. Certainly not enough light to read by, so His Lordship could only be lying in his bed, sound asleep, totally unaware that Miss Regina Bliss had come calling. Unaware that she had come to demand some answers about this "plan" he had supposedly hatched, this "plan" that included her participation and cooperation.

Neither of which he would get unless he told her everything she wanted to know.

Her vision had adjusted enough that she could see some outlines in the room, see the bed almost clearly, thanks to the candle burning on the bedside table. So why wasn't she moving? Why wasn't she crossing the floor, stopping beside the bed, and waking up the lord of the manor?

And that was the problem. How did one wake up the lord of the manor?

Regina grimaced, angry with herself. She'd put all her plans into getting here, getting into the room, and hadn't thought much beyond that point. Now she was here, and she didn't know how to wake the man? How ridiculous.

She wondered how much time had passed since she'd last heard the clock. Surely no more than a few minutes. She had plenty of time before Wadsworth returned at midnight.

"Come on, come on," she urged her reluctant feet under her breath, her hands balled at her sides. "You didn't come this far just to have a fit of the vapors. Just move, will you, please?"

She moved. She walked, very slowly, carefully placing one foot down, then the other, until she was standing next to the bed. She'd done it. She was actually standing next to the bed.

The empty bed.

By the time that knowledge dawned on her, even before her stomach could drop to her toes, Regina heard a voice behind her say coolly, "Good evening, Miss Bliss. I wonder, do you know how close you just came to having your very pretty head blown off your shoulders?"

Chapter Four

*B*rady had been lying in his bed, his prison, kept awake by his various aches and pains, longing for sleep and yet fearing the nightmare. He'd tried to concentrate on his plan, weigh the risks, consider the possibilities. Even savor the victory, if everything went as he hoped.

And then he'd heard it. A slight *click*. A sound not all that obvious, but echoing like a gunshot in his quiet chamber. It couldn't be Wadsworth; the man had gone an hour earlier, promising to be back at midnight.

Instinct took over, instinct and a flash of panic that turned to anger, giving Brady the strength to move and the ability to ignore the pain of moving.

Hobbling, trying to cradle his injured arm, he picked up the loaded pistol he insisted upon having next to the bed and slipped into the shadows. Waited.

The door opened, sending a wedge of light from the hallway into the room before quickly being closed. He lowered the pistol. Idiot girl! Did she think he wouldn't see her?

He waited until she crossed the room, approached the bed, then spoke to her from the shadows, enjoying the startled look on her face as she whirled about, hunting for him in the darkness.

"Well?" he prompted her, as she remained silent. "Have you nothing to say? Perhaps you'll want to tell me you mistakenly entered quite the wrong chamber? No, it would have to be something more inventive than that, wouldn't it, Miss Bliss? You are a quite inventive liar, after all."

Still she said nothing. She just picked up the candle and held it high as she walked toward him. He turned from the light, but not before she'd seen his face.

"You're really injured," she said with some surprise, pointing out the obvious. "Your face . . . your arm . . ."

"My arm, my knee, my once-pretty nose, my ribs. My pride. I think that pretty much covers it," Brady finished for her, feeling his strength beginning to lag. Just holding the pistol was almost too much for him. God, how he hated being weak!

Regina took the pistol from him, laid both it and the candle on the table, then stepped beside him, put an arm around his waist. "Here, let me help you. Just lean on me, and I'll get you back into bed, take care of you."

"What a lovely invitation, my dear," Brady said sarcastically, "but I'm afraid I can't take you up on it just now."

"Don't be brave, as I must tell you that it isn't the least bit becoming," Regina said sharply, giving him a slight push at the small of his back, urging him toward the bed. "You must be a mass of pain, and you're burning up. What is Wadsworth giving you for the fever?"

Half-hopping, and leaning on the small, slight girl more than he'd like, Brady somehow got back into the bed, and Regina arranged the covers around him as his teeth began to chatter. He was sure it was the fever that had him looking at Regina, seeing an angel where a very real girl stood in the candlelight. "What is he giving me? Something. I don't know. Something vile."

"Oh, well, if it's vile, it must be good," Regina told him, smiling down at him. "But I doubt it would hurt if I were to wipe you down with some cloths dipped in cool water."

Brady's head was buzzing as if an entire hive of bees had taken up residence between his ears. "What?" he asked, looking up at her.

"Never mind," she said, patting the covers, tucking them more closely around him. "In any event, we'll wait until you're feeling warmer."

"Any . . . any minute now." Damn. His teeth were chattering again. So sick. He'd been so damnably sick and weak these past two weeks. He'd been feeling better before the funeral. Far from cured, but better. Wadsworth had warned him that he'd been exerting himself too much, during the days his friends were there, and after, when he'd demanded pen and paper, and spent hours each day going over his plans, refining those plans.

If he died, Wadsworth would probably stand over his body, wagging a finger, and saying, "I *did* warn you, sir." Hell, the man would probably have those words chiseled into the stone outside his space in the mausoleum. Except that space was already occupied, wasn't it?

"Probably just stuff and mount me, prop me in a dark corner," he said, speaking out loud, unaware that he had spoken out loud.

"Now that's a pretty picture," Regina said, lifting his head with one hand as she held a glass to his lips. "But what would we stuff you with, my lord? I don't know you very well, but I believe it would be safe to say you're already quite full of yourself."

"Funny," Brady bit out, then choked on the cool water, winced as he coughed, setting every broken bone in his arm and ribs to rattling. "Damn. Damn, damn, damn!"

Regina wiped at his chin with a soft cloth, patted his lips. "I'm going to have to be considerably kinder to Wadsworth, I see. The man must be a saint, to put up with such a fractious patient."

"Fractious! I'm not . . ." Brady threw off the covers, no longer freezing, but suddenly hot as fire. "Not fractious. God, I'm burning up."

"The cool cloths," Regina said, nodding. "I'll fetch them. You just stay here, all right?"

Even in his agony, Brady saw the humor in her statement. "Madam, where would I go?"

He closed his eyes, and it seemed that only a moment later Regina was back, carrying a basin she placed on the table beside him. "Here we go, my lord," she said, lifting a cloth from the basin and wringing it out before folding it, placing it across his brow. "There, that's a good start. Now we'll do the rest. If I might just push up your sleeve? And

I'll unbutton the top of your nightshirt, so that I can bathe your neck and chest."

"I—I beg your pardon?"

"Oh, don't look at me like that. I'm not going to ravish you or anything. I'm simply trying to break this fever. You can't go on like this, you know. My father had a terrible fever a few years ago, and my mother and I worked day and night to break it. So, yes, I've seen a man's chest before, my lord. I promise not to swoon, or to take advantage."

"I'm not your father, Miss Bliss."

"Yes, I know. He was a *much* better patient. Now, just lie there, and let me work."

Did he have a choice? No, he didn't. He certainly couldn't call for help, have Wadsworth come rescue him from this impudent slip of a girl. Wouldn't that be above everything wonderful?

Besides, it felt good. The coolness of the cloth on his brow, the way she held his hand as she patted his arm with another cool, wet cloth.

His eyes opened when she moved down on the bed, raised his nightshirt to his knees, lifted his foot and began to wipe his leg. "What . . . what are you doing?"

"That's a nasty bruise, isn't it, here, on your knee. Even worse than the bruising on your face, although both appear to be fading. There's some quite lovely yellow and magenta. I'd ask you to tell me all that happened, but I don't want you to think about that now. Just lie there and let me cool your fever. We'll talk when you're stronger."

This was insane! A young girl, alone with him in his

bedchamber, his body exposed to her, her hands on him, touching him . . . soothing him.

Brady closed his eyes. He felt the cloth being lifted from his forehead, to be replaced some moments later, cool again against his hot skin. He felt his good left hand being wrapped in another cool cloth, his left arm being lifted, washed. How could he ask her to stop, when he didn't know what he longed for more, the cool cloths or her gentle touch.

He must have slept, he might be dreaming. He heard Regina's voice, singing to him softly, the words making no sense, yet pleasing to his ear.

He heard Wadsworth, but couldn't open his eyes, his eyelids were too heavy.

"Very well, miss," the butler was saying. "I'll leave you to it."

He heard himself sigh, knowing that Regina wasn't going to leave him to Wadsworth's efficient but none too gentle ministrations.

Brady slipped more deeply into sleep, Regina's hand in his.

And the nightmare didn't come. For the first time in weeks, the nightmare didn't come.

Brady woke the next morning, blinking himself awake to another day of pain, of frustration, of fever and more pain. Except that he didn't feel feverish; he just felt weak. Weak as a kitten, foolishly weak, maddeningly weak. And yet better, somehow better.

He lifted his head on the pillows and his eyes went wide as he saw Regina. She had pulled up a chair sometime during the night, and was now sound asleep, her head bent onto the mattress, still holding his hand.

Brady looked at her, slowly remembering, marveling at the fact that she was still there, that she had come to him at all, and then stayed.

What a pretty child, with her dark copper curls haloed with gold in the morning sun that crept across the bed, her long black sweep of lashes, the soft pink roses in her cheeks. Seventeen, Kipp had said, or perhaps nineteen. Yet so much older in some ways, so much younger in others.

And a mystery. More than anything, he believed himself attracted to the mystery of her, the secrets she carried.

He couldn't blame her for what had happened to him, but he was sure his attack was connected to the questions he'd asked about Regina in Little Woodcote. Yes, the little princess had secrets, dangerous secrets, and it was possible she needed him as much as he needed her.

Brady moved on the bed, trying to stretch out some of the morning stiffness in his knee and still not disturb the sleeping girl.

"You're awake."

So much for trying not to disturb her. Regina straightened her back, moaned softly as she pressed a hand to her spine, then smiled up at him.

"Now we both ache," she told him, rising from the chair, still holding his hand. With her other hand, she pressed at his brow, his cheeks. "Fever's gone," she told him, smiling. "Are you hungry?"

Surprisingly, amazingly, he was. "But no more broth," he warned her. "Wadsworth has me drowning in broth. I'm very much an opponent of drowning."

"Yes, I can imagine you are. But I didn't know water to be so hard. How did you get all those bruises, and that broken arm?"

"Let's just say that I took exception to being attacked by three men and fought back. Unfortunately, I don't think I inflicted a quarter of the damage I sustained."

"Three?" Regina broke eye contact, slipped her hand out of his. "Well, that's hardly fair, is it? I was only told that you were subdued, tied into a sack, and tossed into the Thames. I didn't realize you'd also been beaten. To tell you the truth—"

"You do that? Ever?" Brady interrupted, and just saying the words made him realize how much better he felt, how much more *alive* he felt this morning.

"Occasionally," Regina told him, rolling her eyes, and not the least bit insulted. "Anyway, as I was *trying* to say, I feel I should apologize for . . . well, for breaking in here last night. I had begun to believe you'd just been avoiding me. Avoiding my questions."

"And you must have dozens," Brady answered, his smile rather lopsided, but it still felt good. "Do you suppose they could wait a little longer? Until I'm vertical?"

"You hate feeling weak, don't you? Vulnerable?"

"That couldn't have been one of your questions, little princess."

"No, but now that I have agreed—I do agree, you know—not to press you about your plans for me at this very moment, I have a host of other questions just bubbling inside me. For instance, is your nose always going to look like that? Not bruised, of course, but with that little bit of crookedness to it? I think it's quite dashing. After all, a man shouldn't look *too* pretty."

"Dashing," Brady repeated, lightly touching his nose. "Does it alter my appearance that much?"

She tipped her head to one side, as if considering the question. "Yes. And no. I still know you, but you're not quite you anymore. You could be your own brother, I suppose. And dashing," she added, wagging a finger at him. "I mean that, truly. Of course, you haven't been shaved yet this morning, and that also changes your appearance."

Now Brady rubbed at his chin, at the morning stubble of his always thick, fast-growing beard. "Changes me, does it? For good or ill?"

Regina shook her head. "Are you really so vain? Or is there another reason for these questions?"

"Never mind that now," Brady said, carefully boosting himself higher on the pillows. "A well-trimmed beard? A mustache? Longer sideburns? What would most change me?"

"Oh, I understand now. Lady Willoughby told me you plan to take me to London with you in the spring. As you're dead, you certainly can't appear as yourself, now can you? Is that it? You don't just plan to be in London, you plan to be *seen* in London. Am I right?"

Brady was saved from answering by Wadsworth's entrance, the man carrying yet another covered silver tray that doubtless contained a pot of weak tea and some sort of watery gruel. "Eggs, Wadsworth!" Brady called out, figuring it was time to assert himself once more as master of his own household. "Eggs, and ham, and a small mountain of toast."

"And with me having to hold your head over the bucket when you bring it all back? No, sir. I won't allow it."

Brady opened his mouth to protest, but Regina beat him to it. "Wadsworth, your master has made a request, which *you* are to consider an order. Now, you start His Lordship off with some tea, and I'll go downstairs and ask Cook to make up a proper breakfast. And, if anyone has to hold his head over a bucket, it will be I, because I take full responsibility for any possible repercussions. Do we understand each other, Wadsworth?"

Brady pulled the blankets up to cover his grinning mouth as Wadsworth stood up very straight, looked down at Regina, who was looking right back up at him from the far side of the bed.

Wadsworth's nostrils flared.

Brady slid his eyes toward Regina.

Her nostrils flared.

He looked back to Wadsworth . . . and watched, amazed, as the man blinked. "Very good, miss," the butler said, putting down the tray and going about the business of pouring out a cup of tea.

Regina looked at Brady, winked, and all but danced out of the room, as if she had won a long, hard-fought battle. Knowing Wadsworth, Brady supposed she had. Or else Wadsworth wanted her to believe she had. There was always that . . .

∽

Brady's door was never locked after that first morning when Regina had hand-fed him his first bites of solid food in weeks. It had hurt to chew the ham, but Brady persisted, and Regina had cut the ham into such small pieces that at last he managed it.

The whole time she had been feeding him, Regina kept up a constant chatter about what she had been doing during the days since she'd arrived. He learned about her daily walks, the books she had found in the library, the fact that a maid by the name of Maude had become "my very good friend and companion."

He'd known what she'd been about. She'd been talking just to keep his mind off the fact that he was sitting propped up in his bed like some damn invalid, while she spoon-fed him as if he were an infant.

He would never be able adequately to express his gratitude to this wise child.

His warm and fuzzy feelings faded, however, in the next few days, as Regina had taken over the role of caretaker with a vengeance. Wadsworth's no-nonsense care began to be seen as a treasured memory as Regina pulled the covers from the bed and insisted His Lordship get washed, get dressed, and sit in a chair at least for a few hours each day.

He didn't want to. He really, really didn't want to. It hurt to move. Didn't she know it hurt to move? Hadn't she seen his fading bruises? Was she so blind she didn't see the sling on his arm?

But when he tried to point all of this out to her, she'd simply tossed her head, called him a "baby," and warned him that if he didn't have his valet come help him dress, *she'd* dress him herself.

"Gratitude only goes so far, madam," Brady had told her, skewering her with his slitted eyes.

"Yes, yes, I'm *so* frightened. Look at me, shaking in my shoes. Now, come on. I'll just look through your wardrobe to find something easy for you to put on."

"You will kindly stay *out* of my wardrobe, Miss Bliss," Brady had warned, then looked down, surprised to see himself actually sliding toward the floor, moving out of the bed in his anger, his desire to stop her from pawing through his clothes, ruining his neckcloths . . . seeing his unmentionables.

"Aha!" she'd all but shouted, pointing at him, just in case he hadn't noticed that he was standing up on his own two almost steady legs. She ran to the door to the dressing room, pulled it open, and Rogers, his valet, was standing there, already holding a pitcher of water and a shaving blade. "It worked, just as I thought it would. He's ready for you now, Rogers. I'll be back in an hour. Please don't tire him."

She was a minx. A sneaky, interfering, maddening little minx.

And yet, for the past week he'd been getting dressed each day, staying out in his chair longer, although he still hadn't tried the stairs. His strength had begun to return, his aches had lessened, and the fever seemed gone for good.

Only the nightmares remained, but even those had become less frequent.

He owed Regina Bliss. He owed her mightily.

But he couldn't forget his belief that, if it weren't for her, he'd never have been attacked at all. His own curiosity, and his blundered investigation in Little Woodcote aside, his entire recent near tragedy was, quite simply, all her fault.

That thought soothed his battered pride, although he knew he could never look into a mirror and still believe it all true. She hadn't sent him to Little Woodcote. He'd done that on his own.

But he did enjoy her. She played chess with him every afternoon, and had bested him at least twice, showing herself to be a fair strategist, with an endearing way of gnawing on her lower lip when lost in thought.

She surprised him by quoting Shakespeare, and a few lines from Richard Sheridan's latest play that had opened in London two seasons ago.

He tried out a few French phrases on her, and she answered him immediately, in that same language.

And she asked questions, sat at his feet and asked questions.

By the end of a week, she knew all about his childhood, his late parents, his likes and dislikes, his hopes and his dreams. She had a way of cocking her head to one side, giving him her whole attention, prompting him at just the right time, in just the right way, to keep him talking, saying things he hadn't shared with anyone, or even thought about for years.

It was only when she was gone, flitting off to read to

Maude, or to take a walk in the brisk fall air, that Brady realized that he still knew nothing about her. Nothing.

℘

The weather turned colder, and Regina at last gave in to both her desires and the cold, donning the grey cloak and muff for her daily walks. The cloak's hood was also lined with sable, and she felt positively cosseted, surrounded by all that softness, all that warmth.

His Lordship's mother must also have been a small woman, for the cloak was only a little too long, just long enough that Regina could kick at it as she walked, watch as it swirled in front of her. She kept her head down as she retraced her steps through the gardens, heading for the French doors that entered into the drawing room.

It was only after she'd climbed the few steps to the small brick patio that she looked up, and saw His Lordship sitting in a chair, a cloak around his shoulders, a blue-and-green-plaid woolen blanket wrapped around his legs.

"Well, my goodness, look at you," she said, surprised. "Not only downstairs, but outside. Have you been sitting there long?"

"Long enough to watch you dancing in my mother's cloak," he told her, but he smiled as he said the words, and his eyes were soft and warm. "It was always her favorite."

Regina reached up a hand, stroked the fur edging the hood. "I shouldn't be wearing it . . ."

"Don't be ridiculous. I'm happy to see it. But it does

remind me. I'd only arranged for a few additions to your wardrobe, just to tide you over these few months. You'll need much more before we go to London. Gowns, dancing slippers, shawls, gloves. A riding habit, if you ride. Do you ride?"

"Only if the horse doesn't move," she told him, smiling secretly. He couldn't understand her answer, she knew, but she certainly had sat her share of wooden horses with straw for manes. She'd also sailed storm-tossed seas in a few ships, without ever leaving a port. All that was needed were a few props, and an audience willing to use their imaginations.

"Do you want to ride?" Brady asked after a moment. "I can't be of much use as your teacher, not with my arm still like this, but I could find someone to teach you."

Regina shook her head. "No, I don't think so, thank you. But . . ."

"But?" Brady asked, as she felt her cheeks grow warm.

"I'd like to learn to drive. I can control a wagon, I know that, but it would be so wonderful to sit behind a spirited team, up high, wearing driving gloves, and perhaps with a feather in my hat."

"Ah, yes, with a feather in your hat. I can see the attraction," he said. "All right. We'll wait until my arm is better. That way, when you take a corner too fast and throw me into a ditch I can break a new bone, rather than the same old bone."

"I'd be very good," Regina said, lifting her chin. "I'd be *excellent*."

"Yes, I believe you will, little princess. Now, how about you help this decrepit old invalid up and we'll go inside before your nose freezes off? Wadsworth tells me you've been playing at the piano, and even singing. Perhaps, as I plan to stay downstairs until bedtime, you'll agree to serenade me after dinner."

She held out her arm, helped him to his feet. He really didn't need her support anymore, but he had found that he enjoyed it. He liked the fresh smell of her hair, her skin. He liked the softness of her body as she urged him to lean into her. She was small and slight, the top of her head only rising as high as his shoulders, but if she wanted to help support him, he was willing to allow her the fantasy.

"I'd be happy to play for you, my lord," she said as she held open the door for him. "For a price."

"Oh, really. And what would that be?"

"Tonight you tell me just why I'll be needing gowns and slippers and the rest. Tonight, my lord, you tell me your plans. Otherwise, I will leave for Willoughby Hall in the morning. Unless I'm a prisoner here?"

"Do you feel like a prisoner, Miss Bliss?"

She stopped, looked up at him. "No," she said softly. "I feel exactly like what you called me. I feel like a princess."

Chapter Five

$\mathscr{R}$egina sang for Brady, knowing her voice wasn't particularly strong, although it was pure, and heartfelt. Her mother had told her that. "You could make a hardened soldier weep, my dearest," her mother had said.

Blinking back tears at the thought of her mother, Regina slipped into another piece of music, one for which there was no vocal accompaniment, then finished with a flourish once she'd regained control over herself, stood up from the cushioned bench, and looked at His Lordship.

"*Brava*, Miss Bliss, *brava*," he said. "Excuse me for not applauding, but believe me when I say Wadsworth's compliments weren't effusive enough."

"Thank you, my lord," Regina said, dropping into a curtsy even as she grinned. "And my thanks to Wadsworth. We're rubbing along splendidly now, you know."

"Don't be smug. Wadsworth does only what he wishes.

And, since soon he'll be wishing me back upstairs in *my* prison, I suggest we get on with it."

"Definitely," Regina said, sitting down beside him on the small couch. How strange that not so long ago she had bathed him, fed him, and not thought a thing about it. Now she had to stiffen her spine in order to will herself to sit down beside him, too aware that he was a man, she was a woman, and nothing could come of their association . . . outside of her dreams. Her foolish dreams. "Now, to begin. You'll want to know why asking questions about me got you beaten and dumped into the Thames. Correct?"

"Succinctly put, Miss Bliss. Yes, that is exactly what I want to know."

"I haven't the faintest idea," Regina said brightly, looking him square in the eyes, knowing he probably felt tempted to throttle her.

Her words appeared to stop him, but only for the space of two heartbeats; her two heartbeats. "I am a gentleman, Miss Bliss. I pride myself on being a gentleman. And still I must call you a liar."

Regina shrugged. This was better. She could handle him, and her own thoughts, much better when they were sparring. "Oh, all right. I thought I'd try at least, but I can sense that you are going to steadfastly refuse to see your inquiries at Little Woodcote and your . . . your *dunking*, as mere coincidence."

Brady looked at her closely. "You don't ruffle easily, do you, princess? Couldn't you at least *pretend* to be afraid of me? Even a little in awe?"

Regina grinned. Now she was completely comfortable.

She didn't know why, but she was. "I've seen your knees, my lord," she reminded him, and then laughed as the man blushed. He actually *blushed*!

"Miss Bliss, I'm losing my patience."

"Losing it? First, my lord, I believe you'd have to *find* it. Oh, all right. But has it not occurred to you that my story might be as personally painful as your own?"

"No," he said after a moment. "No, I'm ashamed to say that it has not. I've been much too busy feeling sorry for myself. Please, Miss Bliss, forgive me."

"And then tell you?"

He reached out his good hand, squeezed her fingers. "Yes. I'm sorry, but I really must know."

Regina took a deep breath, let it out in a sigh. "Very well. I'm an actress, my lord," she said baldly, getting as much of the truth out as quickly as she could, knowing she'd reserve some of it until she trusted him more. If she ever trusted him more. Because there was a world of difference between liking the man and trusting him. Now, with the knowledge she'd just given him, she'd be better able to judge the man.

Brady let go of her hand, slapped his against his forehead. "Of course! Bram even said it. Why didn't I see it? The farce with Cast-iron Gert that Kipp and Abby told me about when they found you. Easily slipping into the role of a crippled, blind child and wringing tears from the gentle Abby. And then the clear diction, the Shakespeare, the chameleon who changes her colors to fit wherever she is put, each new situation. You're an *actress*!"

"You would have thought of it eventually," Regina told him kindly. And, so far, so good. He didn't seem to look down on her because of her occupation, as many would. Why he even seemed to be happy about it.

"Perhaps," he agreed. "But you're so young. I wouldn't have thought you'd be so accomplished. And yet my first guesses, that you'd been someone's companion or lady's maid didn't quite fit, also because of your age." He narrowed his eyes at her, leaned toward her, grinning. "Or are we all still wrong there, as well, little princess? Perhaps you're really an old crone of five-and-twenty, pretending to be younger?"

"Does it matter?"

He sobered immediately. "It shouldn't."

Her own smile vanished. "No, it shouldn't, should it? But I will tell you anyway. I will be twenty years old the day before Christmas. A woman grown."

"'A woman grown? Hardly, Miss Bliss," he said, his tone light as he seemed to move away from her, even without moving. "But, to get back to the rest of it, if you please. You are an actress. In Little Woodcote?"

"Hardly, my lord," Regina said, mimicking his words and tone. "We traveled all of England." There, that was truth. Not the entire truth, but enough for now.

"We? Your troupe?"

"A very small troupe," Regina said, a warm rush of memories, both good and bad, rolling over her. "I was born in the back of the wagon my parents used to travel across the country, stopping at fairs and small towns, to bring cultural enlightenment to the natives, as my father would say. There were six of us, all together. Two wagons."

With only one wagon stopping at Little Woodcote twice each year for these past three years.

"And you appeared with your parents and the others?"

Regina pushed away her sad thoughts, delaying the inevitable. "I understand I made my debut in swaddling clothes, playing the baby Jesus, the very next day." She sat back, sighed. "It was a good life."

She'd given him an opening, and he leapt at it, just as she knew he must do. "But that good life ended in Little Woodcote. When?"

Closing her eyes and leaning her head against the high back of the couch, Regina whispered, "A lifetime ago. Months and months ago, before I made my way to London, to be found and saved by Cast-iron Gert. I could sew, you understand, having helped with the costumes, and I could paint, as I'd always helped with the scenery as well. It was easy enough for me to make the dolls we sold."

She turned her head on the back of the couch, smiled at Brady. "And I could act. You should have seen me. I made a very creditable street urchin. Watch."

She hopped up from her seat, shook herself slightly, and then slowly sank toward the floor, bending her knees awkwardly, dropping one shoulder, lifting the other. She raised her light grey eyes toward the ceiling, so that her already pale eyes appeared to be almost completely white, tipped her head awkwardly. "Buy me dollie fer yore laidie, guv'nor?" she said in an extremely credible, high-pitched cockney, holding out one hand blindly, as if holding one of the dolls. "Jist a bitty one?"

"Jesus," Brady said.

Regina straightened, shook herself again, and rejoined him on the couch. "I'm small, and that helped. But you'd believe me, if you saw me, wouldn't you? Remembering that Cast-iron Gert had also slapped some very remarkable oozing sores on my face and hands. Trust me in this, my lord, there are far fewer blind and crippled in Londontown than you might believe."

Brady shook his head. "But how? How did you sink to such a state? Let's travel back to Little Woodcote, shall we? Because that's where it all started, isn't it?"

She bit her bottom lip, nodded, wanting to get the rest of her story—parts of it true, some of it false and fanciful, much of it hidden—over quickly, then just as quickly turn His Lordship's attention back to his own problem. "We were set upon by thieves, late one night. Fortunately, as it turned out, I had been so tired I lay down in my clothes. I woke to hear my father calling out in his most threatening, carrying tone. 'Run, my baby. Run like the wind.' I didn't understand, and peeked through the curtain hung around my cot, to see my mother and father hard in the clutches of the thieves. They would have had me, but my father . . . he went rather *wild*, kicking and fighting, sacrificing himself so that I could break free, run off into the woods."

"They were all killed? The entire troupe."

Regina nodded. Lying became more difficult now, but she owed His Lordship as much truth as he needed, that she needed so that he would help her. Or did he truly believe she had remained here, at Singleton Chase, just because everyone had expected her to stay?

"And you saw their killers?"

"'I saw them. Three of them." She wiped away a tear with the back of her hand. "Three men attacked you, my lord. Do you think they are the same three men?"

"I believe it's more than possible. Except that I can't understand why your parents and the others were murdered. Who would bother to murder simple traveling players? Certainly not to rob them, not if they were the same men who attacked me. They were dressed as gentlemen."

"Yes."

"Yes? The men you saw? They were also dressed as gentlemen?"

Regina lifted her hands, scrubbed at her cheeks. She had to stop now, before she tripped over her own tongue. "Please, I don't want to think about this anymore tonight. My parents are gone. I don't know why. Truly I don't. I just know I was told to run, and I did. I ran and I ran and I ran, not stopping until I couldn't run anymore. I didn't stay, I didn't try to help . . ."

Brady took her hand again. She felt so good, so safe, when he held her hand. "You had no choice, princess. Your father told you to save yourself, sacrificed himself for you. It was what he wanted."

"I know," Regina said, looking away, toward the night outside the large windows. "I know."

"These men—did they see you?"

Regina shook her head. Her father had made sure they'd never seen her, not in all the years they'd traveled to Little Woodcote. "I don't think so. I had just sort of peeked through the curtains. But there was a lantern in the wagon, so that I could see them. Not as clearly as I might have, as I was looking at my mother, my father. But I have a fairly good idea who one of them must be. It's why I came to London. To find him, except that I spent most of my time just trying to survive. I had so hoped, when Lord and Lady Singleton took me in . . . but we left London so quickly. I went with them, as there wasn't much else I could do, and I felt I needed money—my wages, you understand—in order to return to London."

"I see. And now you're here, with me. You must have considered the attack on me to be in the way of a gift from the gods. Once you realized that I fully intend to discover the identity of those three men."

"I hope you kill them all," Regina said, suddenly fierce, her hands drawn up into fists. "I hope you kill them, and let me watch."

Brady lay in his bed, weary, but his mind was too active to allow him to rest.

There were holes in Regina's story, huge gaping holes, but Brady hadn't wanted to point that out to her, not once she'd at last confided at least part of her story to him.

He hadn't even pressed her for the name of the man she suspected, mostly because he now felt sure he already knew it himself. The troupe had been in Little Woodcote. There was nothing there, not even a population large enough to warrant a visit from a small traveling troupe.

Especially since she'd said the murders occurred "months and months" ago. Months and months ago would have been at the height of the season for traveling players. They would have been stopping in market towns, small cities. Not benighted villages like Little Woodcote.

No, Regina's troupe had been there for another reason, not to perform. Miss Regina Bliss might be an accomplished actress, and a truly inventive liar, but her nervousness had betrayed her tonight, as her memories caused her pain, as her feelings of guilt over leaving her parents had taken precedence, if only for a few moments, over her desire to hide some other truth from him.

Why? Why, now that she knew he would help her—for his own selfish reasons, yes, but he *would* help her— would she continue to lie, carefully sidestep a truth she felt necessary to keep hidden?

What else did her parents do, besides travel the country, bringing culture to the hinterlands?

The war was over; there was no more need for spies.

Smugglers? They could be smugglers, he supposed, as there were always smugglers, and buyers for the goods slipped across the channel from France. It would be an easy thing for the troupe to stop at port cities, conceal French silks and brandy in their wagons, then deliver them to eager buyers along their yearly route through the southern half of England.

That was possible, but not profitable. Not if there were only two wagons.

Unless what they smuggled, moved about the country, was something small. What was small, yet valuable? Diamonds? Jewelry? Secrets?

Secrets. Everyone had secrets. Everyone. Brady knew that, and had made a hobby out of discovering as many of them as possible. But he had never used the secrets he discovered for his own personal gain.

Had Regina's parents been dabbling in secrets? Trading those secrets for money, promising protection from revelation of those secrets in exchange for purses of gold?

Regina would know. But Regina wouldn't tell him. That would be betraying her parents, her dead parents. But she'd know. She'd have to know.

Was he right? It was possible. No wonder she lied.

Wadsworth entered the room, tiptoed to the side of the bed. "You are supposed to be asleep, my lord. Keep pushing yourself as you did today, and you'll be right back where you started. Sick, feverish, weak as a puppy, and the bane of my existence. I would hope for more consideration, sir, I really would."

"Is that why you allowed Miss Bliss to stay with me that first night, Wadsworth?" Brady asked, looking up at the man who was frowning down at him. "She is now thoroughly compromised, you know."

"It is a known fact that a gentleman cannot compromise a servant or an actress, my lord," Wadsworth reminded him, as Brady had told him all he'd learned about Regina as the butler had first helped him into bed.

Brady felt a shaft of anger shoot through him, but refused to consider why it had appeared. "And is that how you see her? As a servant? An actress?"

"I see her as many things, my lord. At the moment, I see her as my salvation. I have other things to do, you know, than to fetch and carry for an uncooperative patient. Now, if you would just take this medicine, I will be able to return to my bed and rest my aching bones. Weeks of sleeping in here with you have aged me. I long for my own bed."

"I exist only to please you and your aching bones, Wadsworth. Tomorrow I tell her my plan, or at least most of it. I think she'll be receptive. More than receptive. It will take very little to pass her off as my ward. The little princess even speaks French."

"My compliments, sir, to both you and the little princess," Wadsworth said, spooning a vile liquid into a half glass of water, then recorking a small dark bottle and placing it on the table. "You are a very lucky man. Miss Bliss could have been a fishmonger."

"Give her a few moments, and she could probably convince you that she is," Brady said, diverted. He drank the water, then frowned as he realized what he'd just done. "What did you just give me?"

"Laudanum, sir. To help you sleep."

"Don't do that again, Wadsworth," Brady said tightly. "I need my wits about me."

"And the nightmares, sir? Do you need those as well?"

"I'll rid myself of those soon enough, Wadsworth. Once I'm healed and in London, ferreting out those three men. The nightmares will stop then."

"Yes, my lord," Wadsworth said, turning away from the bed, only to stop, hesitate, and turn back once more. "I . . . I wish to tell you . . . that is, I have been with the family since before you were breeched, my lord."

"I know. Is there more? I hesitate to point this out, but you did wish for me to rest."

"Yes, my lord, there is more, and then perhaps we both

might rest. I've watched you grow, endured your pranks, even lied to protect you a time or two, in order to save you from your mother's anger, your father's disappointment. You were a rare handful, my lord, a rare handful. Never mean, but always mischievous, always a delight to my lord and his sweet lady. And you have never been anything but unfailingly kind to me. What I am trying to say is that there . . . there is a certain *fondness* I feel for you, sir. That night, when you appeared at the door with that hack driver barely able to support you, and I saw you . . . how you were . . . well, sir, I would not wish to see you put yourself in danger again."

"Thank you, Wadsworth," Brady said, amazed, humbled. "I promise to be very careful."

"Yes, well . . . good. I just thought I'd mention that. Good night, my lord. Sleep well."

"And you. Good night, Wadsworth," Brady answered, watching the butler go, his back straight, his step steady. The door closed. "Well, I'll be damned . . ." he said, smiling in the near dark.

"Gawain Caradoc? What sort of name is that?"

Brady sat behind the chair in his private study, amused to see Regina's eyes widen as she repeated the name he'd just told her.

"I haven't the faintest idea. I made it up. Gawain Caradoc, twelfth Earl of Singleton. I think it has a certain *ring* to it, don't you?"

"More of a *clang,* I would say." Regina shrugged,

leaning forward in her chair, resting her elbows on the desk. "So, what's my name to be?"

"Is Regina Bliss your true name?"

She sat back again, shook her head. "What do you think?"

"I think we'll be safe in leaving it alone, that's what I think. Am I right?"

"I don't think I like how smug you can be, that's what I think," she told him, crossing her arms over her chest. "I could have told Her Ladyship my true name."

"I doubt that you could. Constitutionally, Miss Bliss, you were not born for truth. I've decided to consider it a failing of your chosen profession. Playing roles, and all that sort of thing. Now, do you think you can play the role of Gawain Caradoc's ward?"

Regina bent her head, thought about it. Being presented in society as the ward of the new earl, a man just back from years spent on the Continent, a distant cousin who had never before even seen London. Going to balls, dancing, being invited to tea parties, going to the theater . . .

"I could do it," she said at last, raising her head to look at Brady levelly. "But it might be less risky if I were to be your page, or perhaps your valet? I've played Romeo a time or two, you know, and know how to prance about in men's clothes."

"Men do not *prance*, Miss Bliss. And, no, I will not have you masquerading as my page, or my valet. You're too small, for one thing, and only a dolt would ever believe you to be anything but a female. My ward, Miss Bliss. You will be my ward. It's only being out in society that you will be able to look at faces, perhaps remember one . . . or two or three. Besides, I can't keep you in sight if you travel with me as a servant, and I believe I'll be safer if I can see you."

"Oh, very well," Regina agreed unhappily. "But I believe we might alter my surname a little more. Just to be safe, your understand."

"Bliss is too close to your real name? Really? How about you tell me your real name, and let me judge."

"How about I tell you the name of the man I think we're after?"

"George Kenward, Earl of Allerton," Brady shot right back at her. "Allerton being less than a stone's toss from Little Woodcote. Oh, don't look so surprised, Miss Bliss. I've had time and enough to think these past weeks. So, am I right?"

Regina nodded. "I can't be sure. But I think it must be him. I really didn't get a very good look at any of them. When morning came, and I dared to sneak back to where we were camped, everything was gone. Everything. I followed the wagon tracks to Allerton Manor. The gates were locked, so I couldn't get inside, and then the sun came up, and people were on the grounds . . . and I ran away again."

"There was nothing else you could do, princess," Brady told her. Then he sighed. "You do have a way of distracting me, don't you? Making me feel sorry for you, in sympathy with you. All right, I won't press you further. Pick a name."

"Felicity," Regina said promptly. "In French, bliss is

félicité. Regina Felicity. Yes, that's perfect. Isn't that romantic?"

"It's horrible," Brady told her flatly.

"Oh? Really? And Gawain Caradoc is a thing of beauty? Just sort of *rolls* off the tongue? I think not, sir!"

Brady held up his good hand, signaling surrender. "All right, all right. We have more important things to discuss. For instance, tell me again about my face. Is the nose enough, or should we discuss beards, mustaches?"

"Always straight back to you, my lord. How unsurprising," Regina said, but she smiled as she said it. She understood his concern. He had to look enough like himself to pass for his cousin, but not so much as to excite too much curiosity. "If you were just to allow your hair to grow?" she suggested, thinking it a shame to cover such a handsome face with a beard. "I've seen drawings, of the *Incroyables* in France . . ."

"Old drawings, I'm afraid. Shoulder-length hair is no longer fashionable."

"Then you will *make* it fashionable again, my lord," Regina said, feeling herself leaping headfirst into the thrill of Brady's plans. "You cannot go into society with only a name. You have to be different from yourself. Almost the exact opposite of yourself, to really fool everyone."

Brady frowned. "I had thought I'd be dark, and brooding. The nose, you understand. Rogers tells me it makes me look rather more fierce than before."

Regina shook her head, got up, began to pace. "No, no. That's not good. Being dark and fierce would bring you entirely the wrong sort of attention, especially if you began asking questions about your late cousin. You have to be . . . harmless." She whirled about, pointed a finger at him. "That's it! You have to be harmless!"

Brady propped his good elbow on the arm of the chair, dropped his chin into his hand, obviously appreciating the sight of Regina in full creative spate. And Regina knew why. No one could accuse him of forcing her into this charade, making her an unwilling accomplice to his plans, not with her so eager cooperation. "Go on."

"Harmless," she repeated once again. "The sort of man who fades into the background. Not at all memorable, or at all dangerous. No!" she exclaimed, raising her hands in front of her and mentally erasing that idea. "You'll never learn anything, being a milksop, hiding behind pillars, being shy and unremarkable. You have to stand out! Be noticed! And yet not be taken seriously. Yes, yes! That's it. Definitely."

Brady grinned. "Do you even *listen* to yourself? You're making no sense."

Regina waved him away, because she was still thinking, the ideas fairly tumbling over themselves inside her head. "I have it!" she said at last, going over to the desk and pressing her palms against the surface. "You have to be a fop. A dandy. Mad for clothes, tottering around on red heels, waving your lace handkerchief, taking snuff. Writing horrible poetry, reciting it in public at the drop of a hint. All of that. Just like the fops and dandies in the farces—I know you must have seen farces in Covent Garden. Just like that, my lord. You must be just too silly for words."

"I'd rather jump back into the Thames, with a brick tied around my neck," Brady told her, his jaw hardening.

She fought down her exasperation. "But don't you see? It's perfect. You've been on the Continent. You traveled, avoiding the war, wining and dancing and romancing your way across Europe, frittering away the years. And now, by some stroke of luck, you're the new earl. You're amazed. You're overjoyed. You're *ecstatic*!" She leaned closer, narrowed her eyelids. "Can you giggle?"

"Giggle?" Brady sat up in his chair. "I most certainly can *not*."

She stood back, crossed her arms beneath her breasts. "That's all right. I'll teach you."

"I don't think so," Brady said, pushing himself out of his chair. "Dark and brooding, Miss Bliss. I've decided. And with a mustache."

She glared at him. "Light and silly and even foolish. Unconcerned about anything more than your own good luck and enjoying the Season to the top of your bent. And with hair to your shoulders."

"Never," Brady told her, standing up, turning toward the window. "I'd die first."

"No, my lord, you wouldn't," Regina said, definitely serious now. "But, remember. They've killed before, these men we're after. They wouldn't balk at killing again." She went to Brady, put her hands on his good arm. "Please, remember this, too, my lord. *I'm* the actress, *I'm* the one who knows the power of a role done right, the effect a lifted brow, a dangled wrist—and, yes, a giggle, has on an audience. I know what I'm saying, and I know how to teach you."

"You're positive?" Brady asked, turning to look down at her, and she relaxed, sure she had him.

"I'm positive, my lord."

"I'll feel like the world's greatest idiot, and Bram and Sophie will be witness to all of it. I'll never hear the end of their jokes and jibes. I'd rather—no, I won't say that again, will I? Oh . . . very well. If you're sure. A fop. Good God, a fop." He shook his head. "But no giggles. I absolutely refuse to giggle."

"Yes, my lord," Regina said, content to be humble in victory. "We'll begin our lessons this afternoon. Let's just hope you're as good a pupil as I am a teacher."

"You know, princess, you really have to try harder to believe in yourself. You're too modest by half."

Regina giggled.

Chapter Six

Six weeks later, Brady stood in the center of the room, shaking his head as he looked at his reflection in the mirror. "Satin. Violet satin."

"Embroidered violet satin," Regina amended, sitting in a nearby chair, sipping tea. "And I especially like the buttons. Do you think anyone will believe they're real amethyst?"

"The real question, princess," Brady told her cuttingly, "is do I care?"

"You will notice, my lord, that the lining is also satin, but white, to match your—excuse me, madam—your breeches, my lord. The waistcoat, while also white, was specially embroidered to match that edging the frock coat. I put three girls working on the pieces for a week."

"And they did a marvelous, job, Mr. Watkins," Regina said as Brady turned around, winced as he looked at the back of himself over his shoulder. All he needed was a posy tucked behind his ear and he could outshine any farmer's pig dressed up for the village fair.

"Must there be gold buckles on these shoes?" Brady asked. "They're damn gaudy, that's what they are."

Regina laughed. "Dearest cousin Gawain, with the violet, and the embroidery, I doubt anyone will even *see* the shoes. How is the neckcloth? Does it make your collar too high?"

"Any higher and I'd slice off my ears when I turn my head—if I *could* turn my head, which I can't. What else? I know there has to be more."

"Yes, my lord, I have devoted myself to nothing but your requests since I first received your note last month. And may I say, my lord, that I am both delighted to find you well and honored to have been brought into your confidence."

"You've been my tailor for years, Watkins," Brady told him. "I knew I could trust you, and, whether you know it or not, you helped save my life with one of your less exotic and yet unique creations. Added to which, you already had my measurements, which made all of this easier. What did you tell your workers?"

"That I had been commissioned to outfit the new earl of Singleton, my lord, following your most strict instructions as to fabric and . . . and style. I admit to being amazed, my lord. These clothes are well out of the ordinary for you. Now, Lord Cummings, he fair dotes on satins and bright colors, as do various other of my patrons, although I do believe I have outdone myself with your new wardrobe, my lord. You will be the talk of Mayfair this coming Season."

"I'll be the laughingstock of Mayfair, you mean," Brady said, trying to shrug out of the close-fitting frock coat with little success. His arm had only been out of the sling for two weeks, and he was still stiff, sore. "I don't think we'll need to see any more, Watkins, as I'm sure everything will fit. Now, if we could see Miss Felicity's new gowns? It was a stroke of luck that your sister is a seamstress. She traveled here with you, I understand?"

"Yes, my lord. Bessie—that is, Madame Elizabeth—is awaiting Miss Felicity in her chamber now for her fittings."

Brady looked at Regina, who was still sipping her tea. "Well? Aren't you eager to see your new wardrobe?"

Regina put down her cup. "I didn't wish to appear overly anxious, cousin. It wouldn't be ladylike. However, if I might have your permission to retire to my chamber . . ."

"Oh, go, for pity's sake," he told her, and she was out of her chair and fairly running to the door a moment later. "Her costumes will be suitable for a young ward, Watkins? Nothing too daring, you understand."

"She will not outshine you, my lord," Watkins told him, holding up yet another frock coat, this one in robin's-egg blue satin.

"That wasn't what I—oh, hang it, Watkins, is there nothing *normal* in that great trunk you brought with you?"

"I don't think so, my lord, no."

"No," Brady said, eyeing the blue frock coat. "I didn't think so, either."

Regina wore one of her new gowns to dinner that night, a simple pale yellow gown with a cut velvet bodice and long sleeves. She walked into the drawing room, where His Lordship awaited her, and held out her skirts as she twirled around in front of him, then sank into a low curtsy. "My lord Singleton, how good to see you again."

Brady felt a sudden urge to rip one of the drapes from the window and cover Regina's bosoms, that were half-exposed above the low neckline of the dress. Damn Watkins, and damn his sister Bessie! Did the two of them think French also meant *naked*? Where in blue blazes had Regina hidden those breasts when she'd so successfully played the urchin?

It didn't bear thinking about. Just as the look of her now didn't bear thinking about. He didn't dare think about it, which was going to be difficult, because he had to look at her.

Look, but never, never ever touch. Not if he wanted to be able to live with himself once this little adventure was over and done, and Regina Bliss was free to leave, leaving him free to get on with his own life. That was what he wanted, to gain his revenge, then get back to his former life.

Of course that was what he wanted. How could he possibly want anything else?

Brady ordered himself to calmness, then walked over to Regina, held out his hand, and she placed hers in it as she rose. He bent over her hand, his lips stopped a mere inch above her skin, and then stood back, still holding her hand. "Perfect," he said, looking somewhere slightly above her left ear. "Absolutely perfect. But I must ask you something. Are they all this . . . um . . . lovely?"

"Oh, no," Regina told him, smoothing down her skirts, touching her fingertips to that damnable neckline. "Each one is better than the next. And most are expressly for the Season, you understand. Lighter muslins and some silks." Her eyes lit with delight. "And the gowns for the balls! Madame Elizabeth said she wanted everything to look as if it had all come here expressly from the Continent on your orders. Different, without being too daring, I believe she said, although I have to tell you, my lord, it took some convincing for me to believe the necklines aren't too low."

Brady bit the inside of his cheek. "Really. How very odd that you'd think any such thing. But you're convinced now that the necklines are fine?"

"Oh, yes. Madame Elizabeth promised that I shall set a new fashion and make her fortune for her into the bargain, because I've promised to order more gowns from her once we're in London, and then tell everyone that she is my modiste. Isn't that nice? My lord, you will be *amazed* to see my wardrobe."

"I'm sure I will," Brady said, his voice solemn as he began to tell her that her necklines, well, they just wouldn't suit. "Miss Bliss, I don't think I can carry this off. You do look splendid, truly, and I have no qualms about your performance, but as for—"

"You hate your new clothing," Regina interrupted, nodding. "I could see you weren't overjoyed with Mr.

Watkins's creations. But they are necessary, you know. I barely recognized you myself. Your hair is growing rapidly, which is also good, and once you've agreed to apply yourself and mastered your lessons I'm sure your own very good friends won't recognize you."

Brady was momentarily diverted. "Recognize me? They'll be too busy rolling on the floor, clutching their middles as they roar in laughter even to acknowledge me."

"But they'll know you have good reason for the deception," Regina reminded him. "What does Wadsworth say about your new wardrobe? And Rogers?"

Brady went over to the drinks table, pouring himself a glass of wine, smiling when he held up the decanter of ratafia and Regina pulled a face, having already told him she thought the stuff "vile." This was good. She might have bosoms to tempt a saint, but she was still Regina. He had to remember that she was still Regina. No one more than Regina. And her virtue was as safe as houses, just as he'd promised his friend Kipp.

"Wadsworth, that good and loyal retainer, told me I look like a ninny," Brady said conversationally, downing his wine. "And I left Rogers weeping in my dressing room. I think that just about says it all, don't you?"

"Yes, it does. It says that we've done it just right. But now we'll have to get down to cases, won't we? You've been putting it off long enough. It's time you learned to be the fop in earnest. The clothes will help, I believe, but if you cannot put your entire heart and soul into your lessons I fear we'll soon be found out for the impostors we are."

The thought of more intensified daily lessons with Regina, with his new awareness of Regina, put Brady immediately on the defensive. "It's not quite Christmas, Miss Bliss. There's still time. We don't move to London until April."

Regina sat down on one of the couches, looked up at him through her lashes, just as the duchess of Selbourne did to such great effect. The minx had probably watched Sophie, then copied her. God, was the whole world conspiring against him?

"You're afraid," she said, then smiled.

Her statement shook him, until he realized she couldn't read his mind. She didn't know what he was thinking, just what she *supposed* he was thinking. "Afraid? Afraid! Of what, Miss Bliss? Of London? Of unmasking Allerton and his companions?"

"No, my lord, not that. You're afraid to be seen in public as anything less than yourself. You're afraid of being a laughingstock, a figure of fun. And yet that's just what you need to be in order for your plan to work."

"I do have my pride," Brady said, turning away as he sipped his wine. He had to get himself back under control, stop looking at Regina, stop thinking about her as a desirable woman.

"Yes, you do, my lord," Regina agreed. "And you have your life. Now, what is it worth to you to find out just who tried to take both from you?"

Brady turned again, looked at her. Stared at her, for long moments. Well, this was better. It was difficult to have romantic thoughts about a woman you suddenly felt a strong urge to strangle. "You know just where to put the knife, don't you, Miss Bliss?" he said coldly. "Just how did you come to this conclusion?"

"I've heard about the nightmares, my lord," she said quietly. "I have them, too. Nights when I'm running, running, and calling out for my parents. They're alone, and helpless, and they need me. Yet I can't find them, I'm afraid to find them, afraid of what I'll see when I do. I wake, hating myself for my weakness, hating myself for having deserted them."

She picked up the ends of the ribbon tied under her bodice, wrapped them around her fingers. "If I had to play the blind beggar child in the middle of a ballroom as I asked the Prince Regent himself for the next dance, I would do it, my lord. I would do *anything*, if just to stop the nightmares, rid myself of some of the guilt I feel. I'm even responsible for *your* nightmares, my lord, at the bottom of it."

Here he went again, round and round. Exasperation. Curiosity. Humor. Pity. Desire. How could one small female elicit so many emotions from him, and all in the space of a moment? He asked her gently, "And that's why you're so eager to help? Because of the guilt?"

Regina looked up at him, her eyes flat and hard, her pointed chin raised. She suddenly looked all of her nineteen years, plus ten. "I want them punished, my lord. I need them punished. Exposed, condemned. I'm helping you because you're helping me, but I'd be in league with the Devil himself if I thought he could help me."

Brady ran a hand through his too-long hair, cupped that hand behind his neck as he looked at Regina, sighed. Why did he even bother to fight? He understood her because he had the same feelings. They had the same mission, and that's what he had to remember. They were allies. "All right, Miss Felicity. We begin lessons in earnest tomorrow morning."

Christmas Day dawned with a brilliant sun reflecting off the three inches of new snow that had fallen overnight, and Regina had already donned her new boots and Lady Singleton's cloak before racing out into the snow.

She went out onto the south lawn, stamping her feet as she applied herself to spelling out her name in the snow, jumping from letter to letter as she completed each one, nearly falling as she completed the "A" and tried to leap clear without making any more marks.

She tipped her head, narrowed her eyes, and decided she'd done a fine job. A fine job. If His Lordship looked out his window he would see her name, the letters ten feet high at least, stamped into the snow.

So now what?

She could lie down, move her arms to make wings as she fashioned a snow angel, but that would mean getting snow on her cloak, which she was loath to do.

Perhaps she'd take a walk. They couldn't go to church in the village, as nobody knew they were in residence. There wasn't even a Yule log burning in the fireplace, or any decorations on the mantel. This was a house of mourning, manned only by servants, servants sworn to secrecy about their master and his "companion."

But Cook had promised a feast, later today, and the

whole house smelled of roasting goose and pastries. And she'd made a present for His Lordship, a pair of black-velvet slippers she'd embroidered in red-and-green thread, as well as embroidering handkerchiefs for all of the staff. Except for Wadsworth. She'd found some moss green velvet in the attics and made him a small pillow to place at his back when he sat in his rocker.

Regina kept her mind concentrated on the beauty of the snow hanging heavy on bush and branch, on the coming feast, on the joy she would feel when everyone opened their presents.

It kept her from thinking about her parents, at least a little bit. It kept her from thinking about all the Christmases she'd shared with them, with the whole troupe. The laughing, the games and songs, the general silliness as her father dressed as Father Christmas, wrapped himself in the red-velvet robe he wore onstage, and with a holly wreath on his head.

"Oh, I miss you so much," she said, looking up at the bluer-than-blue sky, blinking away tears. "Why did you do it? Why, Papa?"

The snowball took her by surprise, smacking against her hood, knocking it off her head.

She whirled about, searching for her attacker, but couldn't see anyone.

Another snowball, this one missing her by inches. She quickly pulled up her hood again, to protect herself. But now at least she knew where to look; toward the trees to her right. Squinting against the sun even as she bent, picking up some of the heavy snow and forming it into a ball, she could just see a figure darting between the trees.

"I've got you!" she yelled, taking careful aim, then unleashing the snowball. It hit a tree just as her attacker ducked behind it. "Coward! Come out and fight fair!" she yelled, already gathering more snow.

She stopped in the midst of drawing back her arm to throw another cold, wet missile as Brady stepped out from the trees, one hand behind his back.

"I surrender, Miss Felicity," he called out, purposefully walking toward her, not stopping until he was only ten feet away from her.

"Too late! No quarter, no mercy!" she cried out, and loosed the snowball, grinning and hooting as it caught him in the middle of his chest.

She watched as he looked down, wiped the melting snow from his cloak, then squeaked, and began to run, as he started toward her, holding a snowball of his own in his now good right hand.

She ran, looking back over her shoulder, unaware that she had just raced across her earlier handiwork, ruining it. She laughed as she ran. She laughed when the first snowball passed harmlessly by her, and even laughed when the second one caught her flush between her shoulder blades.

She even laughed as her toe caught on a hidden rock and she went tumbling, facefirst, to the ground, lying there, turned onto her back, looking up at His Lordship's concerned face.

"You're all right?" he asked.

"Per-perfect!" she said between giggles, then shot out her leg, catching him at the ankle, so that he, too, tumbled down into the snow. Before he'd completely hit the ground she was at him, both gloved hands filled with snow, rubbing the cold confection into his face, trying to force it down inside his collar.

Together, they rolled over and over, down the slight incline, mashing snow into each other's faces, laughing like children just set loose from the nursery.

"Stop! Stop!" Regina called out at last, her long lashes caked with wet snow. Snow in her hair, her ears, her mouth. Snow everywhere. "I surrender!"

Brady rolled onto his back, taking her with him, so that the hood of her cloak fell forward, nearly obscuring her face. "Are you all right?" he asked, his hands on her shoulders as she half sprawled across his body.

"Are *you* all right?" she responded, suddenly coming to her senses. "I'm not the one who's been injured."

"I haven't felt this good in months," Brady told her. "Years."

"Me too." She looked down at him, at the way his long wet hair plastered to his head, the way his eyes twinkled, at the laugh lines around both those eyes and his wide, grinning mouth. She felt herself growing oddly warm, right in the pit of her stomach, and realized she wanted to reach out her hand, wipe the hair from his face, smooth it back on his forehead.

"I'm freezing," she said instead, pushing herself away from him even as she watched the smile fade from his face, the delight in his eyes dimming as he suddenly seemed to realize who they were, where they were, *how* they were.

"Yes, of course," he said, helping her to her feet. "We'd better go back."

"Yes, go back," Regina said, shivering. They should go

back, go all the way back to the beginning, because there was no future in going forward on this particular path. She knew it, he knew it. "Definitely."

Neither of them spoke all the way back to the house.

⁓

Brady thought up and then discarded three separate excuses not to go downstairs to Christmas dinner. He could claim fatigue. He could claim a relapse. He could tuck a white feather behind his ear and call himself the coward that he was.

Was he out of his mind? What did he think he'd been *doing*, rolling around in the snow with Regina Bliss?

She wasn't a child. He knew she wasn't a child.

But she was an innocent. Damn it, he knew that as well as he knew his own name . . . not that he called himself by his own name anymore. He was Gawain Caradoc. Fake. Impostor.

And guardian to Regina, as surely as if her parents had personally entrusted her to his care.

He had to remember that. If he forgot all else, he had to remember that.

It was proximity, that's what it was. They were here, together, day in, day out. They were each other's only real companions, and they shared a history, even if that history was only that they had both been victims of the same three men.

If Brady lately felt himself attracted to Regina, it was simply because of these things. They, again simply, were just too much together, thrown together for the sake of their plan, locked here together as they waited, in secrecy, for the Spring Season.

Of course he was attracted to her. He'd soon be attracted to anything in skirts, for he was a healthy, virile man, and he enjoyed the company of pretty females.

Willing females.

Females about as distant from Regina Bliss as the moon.

Brady went downstairs only when the last gong had rung, avoiding Wadsworth's disapproving look and merely following after Regina as she headed for the small dining room that had been set with the usual two settings, one at either end of the longish table.

Their meal, course after course, as Cook had really outdone herself, probably in preparation for the servants' own feast tomorrow, was eaten in silence, Regina obviously in no more mood to talk than he.

It wasn't a comfortable silence.

For the first time since the night she had bathed him through his fever, he felt uncomfortable around her, and she, obviously, around him. It was as if she knew he was now aware of her as a female, and Lord knew how she now saw him.

Was it too late to send her away? Send her back to Kipp and Abby? Out of sight? Hopefully out of mind?

"You wouldn't go, would you?" he asked, even before he could think the thing through.

"I beg your pardon," Regina said, leaning to her left, to be able to look down the table at him, past the huge centerpiece he'd been grateful to hide behind through six interminable courses. "I wouldn't go where, my lord?"

"Back to the Willoughbys," he said, standing up, walking down the length of the table and holding out his hand to her, helping her to rise. "You wouldn't go, would you? You'd just follow me to London and probably ruin everything by popping up just when and where I didn't want you, doing whatever you thought best. I doubt anything you think *best* would be helpful to me."

"Well, if I wouldn't help you by following you to London, I suppose I should just go with you," Regina said, as they reentered the drawing room. "It seems easier."

"Yes, I suppose it does," Brady said, leading her to one of the couches, waiting while she sat down. The neckline of her powder blue gown was more modest than most of her new creations, and he didn't know if he should be happy or sad. No, that wasn't true. He should be happy. But it made him sad. "I suppose that's settled then? We continue with our plan?"

"I have never considered *not* continuing with our plan, my lord," Regina said, picking at the lace at her cuff.

Brady smiled, just slightly, ruefully. It appeared that Miss Bliss didn't lie quite so convincingly this evening. Could it be that she had *hopes* for him? That would be too bad, that would. That would, in fact, be a damn pity. It was bad enough that he was using her. He certainly would never *use* her.

Was that distinction plain in his mind? He certainly hoped so.

"I've a present for you, Miss Felicity," he said now, stepping back and gifting her with an elegant, rather florid bow, one more in keeping with the "costumes" tucked away upstairs in his clothespress. He straightened, reached into his pocket, and pulled out a string of perfect pearls that had once belonged to his mother. "For you. Your beauty surpasses these pearls, indeed any jewel, but as I had no time to compose an ode to your eyelashes, I hope this paltry gift will keep me in your good graces."

Regina looked up at him, gave herself that slight, unconscious shake he'd noticed before she slipped into a role, and then pressed both hands to her cheeks. "La, sir, but they are lovely. Nearly as lovely as that grand compliment. Were I still with Cast-iron Gert I might snatch them up and rub them across my teeth, to satisfy my greedy self that they are real. But I will just thank you, dear uncle, and allow you to fasten them around my unworthy neck."

"Imp," Brady said, and dropped them unceremoniously over her head, for the strand was long and he did not need to open the clasp. "There will be other baubles, lesser pieces from my late mother's collection, to complete your other outfits. Do you like them, princess?"

Regina gave another small shiver, obviously coming out of her role, then touched her fingertips to the pearls. "I like them very much, and promise to take very good care of anything you might lend me, my lord."

"The other jewelry may be necessary to our plans, Miss Bliss, but those pearls are now yours, my birthday gift to you, unless you thought I had forgotten it," Brady said, unhappy to hear the stiffness that had come into his voice. God, he hadn't been this clumsy since his first days in society. Something had to change, and change quickly, or else they'd never make it from now until it was time to move to London. Not without killing each other, or worse.

Regina looked up at him oddly, as if trying to gauge his mood, something she rarely did, as she seemed more prone to just trampling willy-nilly all over him whenever another idea or the fancy struck her. "Thank you, my lord. I shall treasure them always." And then she hopped to her feet. "I've got something for you, too, but nothing quite as grand, I'm afraid."

She reached behind a pillow on the couch and pulled out a pair of black-velvet slippers, handing them to him.

"You embroidered them yourself?" he asked, impressed, running a fingertip over the intricate swirls of bright red-and-green threads.

"*Made* them and embroidered them," Regina told him, her hands behind her back as she rocked on her heels. "I was hoping to make you a dressing gown, but I couldn't find enough material in the attic. I told you, I'm very good with a needle. So you shouldn't feel the need to worry about me, once we've accomplished what we plan to do in London. I will always be able to fend for myself, even if I've already decided I couldn't return to the stage. Not without my parents and the troupe."

He shot her a look that should, if she were at all sensible, have sent her whimpering from the room. But hard looks were all but lost on Regina Bliss, and Brady knew that. Still, she had this ability to make him *so* angry. It was almost as if she worked at it.

"Why are you looking at me as if I just said something terrible? That does concern you, my lord, does it not? What will happen to me once this is all over? Once we've found and punished the guilty, and you are once more free to be yourself?"

"I hadn't thought that far ahead, Miss Bliss," he said tightly, knowing that he lied. He'd been thinking ahead, entirely too much, about entirely the wrong things. Like how Regina would look with her head on the pillow next to his, and how she'd feel in his arms.

"Oh, yes you have. You've been thinking about it all afternoon, as a matter of fact," Regina told him, her chin raised as she looked him full in the face. "And now you know. You don't have to worry about me. I'll land on my feet. I have so far, haven't I?"

And then, before he could answer her—even hope to come up with an answer for her—she left the room, and all he could do was to watch her go.

Early the next morning, secure inside an unmarked coach and with the shades lifted so that he could not see the rapidly melting snow drip from the trees, Brady was on his way to his hunting box in Lincolnshire.

He left behind the trusty Wadsworth, who would inform Regina that His Lordship would return the last week of March, to prepare for their removal to Portman Square.

It wasn't the best solution Brady could find, or the most heroic, but it was the only one.

Chapter Seven

"Maude? Have you seen my yellow-kid gloves? I know they must be around here somewhere . . ."

"In your hand, Miss Felicity," Maude told Regina, who looked down at her hand, then giggled.

"I guess you might think I'm a little nervous," Regina said, wrapping the gloves in tissue paper and placing them in the nearest portmanteau. "And I guess you might be right."

"I'm all aflutter myself, miss, going to Londontown and all, after these long months with the master gone. But now he's coming back, and we're off. Is it true there's sin on every corner? Cook vows there is sin on every corner."

"Even in the middle of the block, Maude," Regina told her, carefully layering more of her new wardrobe into the trunk sitting on the floor. "But, as Mr. Samuel Johnson wrote, 'When a man is tired of London, he is tired of life, for there is in London all that life can afford.' Not that I could afford very much of it when I was there," she added with a grin. "Besides, Maude, we'll be in Mayfair, where it is fairly safe. I doubt there are more than two or three devils per corner."

"Now you're funning with me, aren't you, miss? Shame on you. But I have Cook's best hatpin already tucked up in my reticule, so Heaven help the devil who tries to be cozy with me! Here you go, miss, you'll be wanting to take all your handkerchiefs."

"How many handkerchiefs have I embroidered these past three months, Maude? I imagine everyone here will be glad to see me gone, so they don't have to thank me for yet another one." Regina took the pile of lace-edged handkerchiefs and placed them in the trunk, then stood up, pressing her hands against each side of her spine and stretching. "Do we have it all now, Maude? I think we do. Oh! My pearls!"

She ran to the small table beside her bed and took out the string of pearls. Maude had wanted her to keep them in the locked drawer of the writing desk in the room, but Regina wanted them always close to her. At night, once she was alone, she'd take them out, hold them, sometimes even fall asleep with the strand clutched in her hand. She told herself she longed to strangle the earl of Singleton with them, for having deserted her. She told herself that, but she knew it wasn't true.

"I'm going to wear them, beneath my traveling jacket," she said, dropping them over her head. "And Lord help the robber who tries to take them from me."

Maude's eyes went wide. "Robber? Mr. Wadsworth never mentioned robbers."

Regina put her arm around the maid's shoulders. "Don't worry, Maude. We'll be three coaches, Wadsworth told me, and Lord knows how many outriders, bringing His Lordship's mounts and curricle to town with us. We'll be safe as houses. If the earl ever gets here, that is. Wadsworth thought he'd arrive yesterday."

Maude considered all of this for a moment. "I'm still taking Cook's hatpin."

Laughing, Regina kissed the maid on the cheek, then called out "Enter" to whoever was knocking at her door.

Her mouth dropped open before she could recover herself as the earl of Singleton entered. The *new* earl of Singleton, in all his glory.

She'd longed to see him again, even as she'd variously cursed him and missed him, and she'd been nervous as a long-tailed cat in a room full of rocking chairs ever since word had come that he was expected back at Singleton Chase. She'd wondered if she'd fall on his neck like some lovesick ninny or pretend to shun him, or if she'd take one look at him and realize that she'd been weaving romantic dreams around a man who, after his absence, had no power to move her at all.

And now he was here. And she barely recognized him.

In three months his thick, sandy-colored hair had grown almost to his shoulders, and he wore it combed straight back from his forehead, with one thick lock falling forward at the moment so that he gave his head a quick toss, sending it sailing obediently back into place.

He held his head high, his posture almost ridiculously correct as he walked into the room, then halted a good ten feet away as he dropped into an elegant leg, a move accompanied by a grand sweep of his right arm. In his right hand was a fine white-linen handkerchief with at least four inches of lace dripping from it, lace that matched the intricate jabot at his throat.

He was dressed in traveling clothes, if anyone could consider such absurd finery as mere traveling clothes. His pantaloons were dove grey, his waistcoat embroidered pink satin. A darker grey frock coat with lapels at least eight inches wide was decorated in platter-sized ivory buttons, and was so wasp-waisted that Regina wondered if the man could take a deep breath.

He looked silly. He looked completely at ease in his silliness, as if he'd spent the last three months practicing his new role in a room full of mirrors.

Finally, just as his silliness relaxed her somewhat, the twinkle in his eyes reminded her of how much she had missed him. She was nervous suddenly, and that angered her.

"My dearest Regina," Brady purred as she stood there, still unable to speak, "please tell me you're not still lollygagging here while we lose the first of the most delightful morning hours. I am assured you were informed of my return last night, and my wish to be on our way this morning? Come, come, my dear, do hurry. I hope to make the Lion Head Inn before two, so that my man can commandeer the kitchens to prepare our afternoon meal. We could, of course, dare the fare at the Lion Head," he added, shuddering delicately, "but I am afraid my spirit might then be so broken as to make it impossible to go on to our next stop."

"My God," Regina said, finally able to move, to speak.

She walked up to Brady, then circled around him as he turned with her, the gilt quizzing glass hung on a dove grey grosgrain ribbon around his neck stuck to one eye as he dabbed the handkerchief at first one corner of his mouth, then the other. "My God, you've done it."

"Done it? Done it? Pray, Regina dearest, explain. What have I done? Have I been naughty? I vow, I have no recollection of being . . . *naughty*, in at least a fortnight. Egad, I must have been in my cups. Tell me, did I enjoy myself?"

Even the cadence of his speech had changed, from a crisp, clear English to a faintly bored, lazy drawl. Regina held up her hands. "Stop, stop! You need to save something for London. Too much rehearsal, Papa always said, can make an actor stale, his performance lackluster. Although I will say that you are far from lackluster, my lord."

"Uncle Gawain," Brady corrected her. "That's Ga-*wain*. Please do have a care to pronounce it correctly. Now, if you're finished here, the footmen I have waiting outside—such obedient servants my late cousin had, a true credit to him, I'm sure—will remove all these trunks and such and we will be on our way. Do you have a vinaigrette with you, my dear? I often feel faint, even queasy, during long coach rides, and am never without one, myself."

Regina looked at Maude, who clearly didn't realize that she was looking at her employer, and then shrugged. "Remember, Maude, from this moment on, I am Miss Regina Felicity. And this, as I'm sure you know, is the new earl of Singleton. He's a vision, isn't he?"

"Uh-huh, a pure treat," Maude said in a rather hollow voice, and then tottered to the nearest chair and sat down with a thump.

⚘

Brady helped Regina into the first coach, then climbed in behind her, grateful to unbutton his frock coat as he sat down across from her after carefully splitting his coattails and removing his curly-brimmed beaver.

So far, so good. He'd been right to leave, right to re- move himself from temptation born, he felt sure, of the enforced intimacy he and Regina had shared at Singleton Chase. He felt more himself now—stronger, with a clearer head, with no lingering physical or even mental weakness to cloud his mind, befuddle his judgment.

She was Regina Bliss, female and coconspirator. Noth- ing more. The only thing they had in common was their common enemy.

This was going to work. It really was going to work. Either that, or he was so busy hiding behind Gawain Caradoc and his practiced silliness that he was able to convince himself of just about anything.

"Christ, Watkins didn't leave me room to take a deep breath. No wonder all those dandies prance about town as if they had a poker stuck up their—well, never mind." He lifted his cane, sharply tapping it on the roof of the coach, and called out, "To London, my good man, to London! And for God's sake, mind the ruts!"

He then smiled at Regina. "Rooster—that's my coach- man—will now probably gift his lily-livered new employer with a tour of every rut and deep puddle in the road. Still, I'd like to think he misses me very much."

"Aren't . . . aren't we going to wait for the other coaches? I think they're still loading them."

"They know the way, and will follow along soon enough. I never was one for wanting to lead a parade." He ran a finger between his collar and neck. "I thought I was used to this ridiculousness, but I'm not. And this coat is so tight, I'm lucky to be able to raise my arms at all."

He looked at her, much as he had been trying to avoid doing so, even as he'd told himself he felt no great need to look at her, no great desire to look at her.

She wore her dark red hair up in curls, as befit a debutante making her entry into society, and her long slim neck and impertinent chin were both shown to great advantage by the more sophisticated style. She wore her new clothes as if born to them, and moved with even more grace than before, and she had always been graceful.

In short, she looked all of her twenty years now, and gloriously so. Not that he cared, for he most certainly did not care. He cared for nothing except keeping his eye on the prize—unmasking and punishing the three men who had tried to kill him. "So, Miss Bliss," he said now, hopefully keeping his tone light, "Wadsworth informs me that you've also been busy?"

"Don't call me Miss Bliss, *cousin*, even in private," she warned him. "I am your ward, so you might easily call me Regina, as you did earlier. It's easier, and leaves less room for mistakes in public."

"Still the teacher, I see. But also the pupil, if Wadsworth is to be believed."

Regina nodded. "Wadsworth was quite helpful. I've perfected my table manners, he promises, and I've been tutored in all of the dances. Harry, the head footman, was my partner for the waltz, and all the servants joined in as I learned the dances that required a full complement of dancers. You, my lord, may have the only staff in all of England that can perform the quadrille and several Scottish reels."

"It sounds as if you didn't have time to miss me," Brady said, his tongue unguarded for that one moment, and Regina's head jerked up as she looked into his eyes, her lips drawn into a tight line.

In her company again for less than an hour, and already he'd made a mistake, said something entirely too personal. If he was smart, he'd stay safely inside the role of the inane, harmless Gawain Caradoc. Brady James, a man who had, it seemed, learned only how to lie to himself over the past months, couldn't seem to speak to her without first making sure he could get his foot into his mouth.

"Have you been able to find out if the earl of Allerton will be in town for the Season?" she asked, rather clumsily attempting to change the subject.

Still, Brady was more than happy to oblige her. But first he opened a concealed compartment next to him and pulled out a silver flask and a small glass. "Foppery is thirsty work," he said, as she watched him pour some burgundy into the glass, then toss the liquid back in one swallow. "Ah, that's better. Oh, don't look at me like that.

I haven't turned into a sot as well as a dashed dandy. But it would do me well, I believe, to have the smell of strong spirits on my breath at all times. No one is more harmless than a man who drinks his breakfast. Now, what did you ask me?"

"I asked, Uncle Ga-*wain*, if you had discovered whether or not the earl of Allerton will be in London when we arrive. He is the reason behind this entire masquerade, if you'll remember. Allerton, and whoever else was involved in murdering my parents, trying to murder you."

"Oh, there was no need of that. Allerton is always in town for the Season. He and his son and daughter. Have I told you about them?"

Regina shook her head. "It was three men, Uncle Gawain. I'm sure there was no woman with them. Still, I suppose I should know anything you know."

"All right then, we'll pass some of the time between here and the Lion Head familiarizing you with the Allerton family. There is, of course, the earl himself. The family is a fine one, or was, until he took over the reins. A dedicated gamester, you understand, and his heir, the viscount, is truly his father's son. Boothe Kenward, the Viscount Allerton. At least a half dozen years my junior, but already jogging along quite happily on the road to dissipation."

"Could he be one of the other two?" Regina asked. "What does he look like? Can you describe him?"

Brady closed his eyes, rubbed at his forehead. "Tall. Very tall. Very thin as well. He wouldn't strip to advantage, even if he'd dare to climb through the ropes at Gentleman Jackson's. That's a boxing saloon, you understand. Very pale blond hair. Dresses all in black, pretends to be a turf-and-table sort, a sportsman, but a cow-handed driver with no eye for horseflesh. He's tried for the Four-in-Hand Club several times, until he was laughed away the last time he applied."

"You don't like him."

"I don't dislike him," Brady said honestly. "But his opinion of himself is so high, I doubt he'd be broken-hearted to learn that I feel quite indifferent to him. Unless he's one of them. That would pique my interest."

"Then I suppose the viscount is safe, for your description does not fit any of the three men. There were no blonds, and all three of the men were older than I suppose the Viscount to be. What are you planning? I mean, I know we're going to try to see who the earl's friends are, and then unmask them in some way—but how? Knowing isn't enough. We have to be able to *prove* that these are the men."

"I've thought about that," Brady told her, attempting to cross his legs and belatedly realizing that the snugness of his pantaloons prohibited it. "And, yes, I intend more than just to appear in London and hope Allerton throws himself at my feet, eager to confess, a victim of his own guilty conscience. But we'll leave that for now, as we've left so much still to be discussed, haven't we, while I tell you about the sister. Do yourself a favor and banish any idea you might have of making her your very good friend."

"Why would I want to do that?"

Brady lifted a single eyebrow. "Oh, I don't know. Suffice it to say, I think you're going to *help* me, whether I want your help or not. Trying to insinuate yourself with Belle in order to be invited into the Allerton household would *not* be helpful to me. Understand?"

"No, I don't," Regina said, sounding a bit mulish. "As soon as you said there was a daughter, I thought it might be a splendid idea to offer her my friendship. I could get into their London mansion, possibly poke around in the earl's private study when no one is looking—"

"Get your head blown off by the earl," Brady ended for her. "No, I think not. Besides, Belle is the only one of them with any brains. Make a dead set at her, and she'll wonder why."

"Why would she wonder why?"

Brady thought about the flask, but then dismissed it as the coward's way out. "All right," he said, hoping to get this over quickly. "Bellinagara Kenward could be a problem. She and I—she and *Brady*—were once romantically involved."

Regina sat back against the squabs. "Oh. *How* romantically involved?"

"Ladies, my dear princess, do not ask that sort of question."

"True, but I do. Are you afraid she'll recognize some mole on some usually unseen part of your body you now plan to expose as Gawain?"

"Now you're being impertinent," Brady warned her, and he did reach for the flask, just to give his hands something to do. "And we were not quite *that* romantically involved. Plus, it was years ago, at least four or five, if I'm not mistaken. I pursued her, she eluded me, and that's the end of it."

"That long ago? She must be ancient," Regina said, and Brady watched her relax her posture slightly.

"Belle is far from ancient, although she must be at least four-and-twenty. And beautiful. And unattainable."

Regina pulled a face. "Oh, bother. Next you're going to tell me she's as pure as the driven snow and the innocent victim of her papa's spendthrift ways. Why, I believe I feel a tear threatening behind my right eye. No, wait. Not a tear. Just you, Uncle, poking me in the eye with a load of rubbish."

Brady glared at her. "I think I liked you better when you were playing the shy and blessedly quiet servant girl."

"And I think I liked you better when you told me the whole truth. Now, is this Belle going to be a problem for you, or isn't she? Because if you're thinking of forgetting the whole thing if her papa is the murderer, just because she's beautiful—well, let me know now, and I'll finish this job on my own. I'd much prefer it that way in any case."

Brady's jaw hardened. "Forget? There's little chance of that, Regina. But I won't use Belle to get to her father, and I won't allow you to use her either. Is that clear?"

"As crystal, my lord," Regina said, shaking her head in disgust. "You're an idiot. It couldn't possibly be clearer than that."

Brady sat forward on his seat, nearly choking on his tight neckcloth. "May I remind you, Miss *Felicity*, that I nearly died?"

Regina folded her arms across her midsection. "And may I remind you that my parents *did* die?"

"Well, that very neatly trumped what I thought was my ace, now didn't it?" Brady sat back, smiled. "Why are we fighting with each other, princess?" he asked, slightly amazed at the way her grey eyes flashed cold fire at him in her anger. "We're allies, remember?"

"So you're not going to go all arsy-varsy over this Belle person, and ruin everything?"

"One, I never did go all—don't use that sort of language, if you please. And two, I see no reason to involve Belle in any of this."

"Yet you warned me against her."

"I was planning ahead," Brady said, and grinned. "Of course, now you can tell me you didn't learn that Belle exists and then immediately begin thinking of ways to get close to her and, through her, close to Allerton."

"I already admitted to that," Regina responded, nearly muttered. "Oh, all right. We'll not discuss this Belle person anymore. Agreed?"

"Agreed," Brady said gratefully, turning to look out the side window at the passing scenery. "We should be at the Lion Head in another hour. I think I'll take a nap."

"Do that," Regina told him, giving him a look he'd rather ignore, then pulling a small book from her reticule, opening it, and very pointedly ignoring him.

He let his head slip slightly to the side, looked at the title of the book through slitted eyes. She was reading a tourist guide to London, one he remembered as having lately resided in his library. The book contained drawings of street maps and locations of major buildings, the homes of many of the *ton*. Clearly Regina had a few plans of her own for how she would go on in London. How wonderful.

Brady kept his eyes closed until they reached the Lion Head, but he did not sleep. With Regina Bliss around, he decided, it might be safest never to sleep again.

They stopped for the night at a coaching inn situated at nearly the exact halfway point between Singleton Chase and London, and Regina sincerely hoped Brady wouldn't make a cake of himself again, as he had at the Lion Head, posturing and prancing and causing one farmer who had been sitting in the common room to choke on his rabbit stew.

"Promise me you won't go too far, this time," she said, as Brady helped her down from the coach. "One or two mentions of 'my good man' should be sufficient, and the quizzing glass is entirely too much."

"Have you definitely decided your role in life is to set yourself up as my critic?" Brady asked, tucking her arm round his elbow and mincing toward the front door of the posting inn. "I remember Byron going on and on about the species, and damning every last one of them to hell."

"I would rather be served dirt for my dinner than to call myself a critic," Regina returned hotly. "I am your *mentor*, my lord. And, as your mentor, I have to tell you that you are overacting horribly. You'd be fine enough on the stage, I suppose, as the highborn idiot in a broad farce, but for the real world you really do have to refine your lunacy. You never should have left Singleton Chase, tried to learn your new role on your own."

Brady stopped in the middle of the inn yard, looking wounded. "Are you calling me a buffoon by any chance, my dear Regina? Because if you are, I believe I must protest. You wanted a fop. A dandy. A silly man as opposite from my *cousin* as possible. I thought I was doing quite well."

"Oh, really?" Regina shot back at him as he touched a hand to that damn quizzing glass yet again. "And you saw nothing wrong, then, in threatening to drop into a swoon when the innkeeper at the Lion Head said we'd have to wait ten minutes for a private room? Half-staggering to a chair, your hand to your forehead? *Whimpering*. I didn't know which I wanted to do more—slap your silly head or go running back to the coach, screaming."

"We got the room immediately, as I recall."

"Yes, we did. Right after the innkeeper tossed that merchant and his nice wife out of it, the poor man still gnawing on a chicken bone. You should have been ashamed."

"I was. Horribly ashamed," Brady told her.

Regina relaxed slightly. "You were?"

"No, my dear, I wasn't. I was thrilled. And do you want to know why? I was thrilled—in case you don't ask—because the innkeeper, and the choking farmer, all fully believed I was who I said I was. I've stopped at the Lion Head at least two hundred times, and everyone there knows me. But today they did *not* know me. I think that says it all, don't you? Why, as a matter of fact, it also proves your point. You should be over the moon, glorying in your triumph—and not critiquing my absolutely *sterling* performance."

Regina looked at him for long moments. "You fell on your head while you were away, didn't you? You've scrambled your brains somehow. It's the only answer."

"It's one answer, but not the right one. Now come along, it's time to practice on these good people. I think I shall flirt with Trudy—I believe I remember her name correctly—and see if she remembers me. Although I'll keep the mole private, of course. Come along, my dear."

"I'd rather eat dirt for dinner," Regina said, pulling her arm free, wondering just when she'd been so lonely or so confused that she'd thought Brady James attractive—in any way.

"Yes, you've already said that. Do try not to be redundant, my dear. It's *so* fatiguing," Brady drawled, sighing theatrically. Then he waved a hand at her—the hand holding the snow-white-linen handkerchief with its five-inch-deep lace edging. "Oh, very well. Run along, run along. If one must insist on an evening constitutional, I suppose the saner one must bow to those wishes. I myself never walk. Be back in an hour, if you please, or I dine without you."

"Do that, as my appetite is truly gone now," Regina said, then turned on her heels and headed toward the center of the village. It was only a small village, one with which Brady was obviously familiar, and one he seemed to consider safe enough for his "ward" to walk down the wooden flagway without coming to grief.

And, my, but it felt so good to be out and about! Unfettered, no longer hidden behind the walls of Singleton

Chase, and free to see the world as she'd done while traveling with her parents. Regina loved small villages, as everyone was nearly always friendly, giving a smile or a nod of the head as they passed by, the children happy and healthy, even the village dog usually well fed.

She would have liked to stop in one of the small stores, purchase a ribbon or a stick of hard candy, or some such thing, just to talk to another person, just to feel normal for a few moments, and not feel as if she must constantly mind her words, play her part. But she had every penny accounted for and reserved for her own purposes, and she might need them if Brady was going to stumble over this Belle person, as she feared he might.

Oh, the man seemed serious enough, and determined enough, but it was obvious to Regina that he retained some silly soft spot for Allerton's daughter. If the beautiful Belle sobbed on his shoulder, begged Brady for mercy, Regina had serious doubts he would still turn the earl over to the hangman. Men were like that. They just couldn't concentrate on the main prize, not when a pretty woman came into the picture.

Not that she, Regina, cared a whit about Brady, or this Belle person. They could marry and have a dozen children for all she cared, bill and coo and slop all over each other all the days of their lives. All she wanted was her revenge.

"Lie to him, Regina, but not to yourself, because you do care about the man, curse him," she muttered, about to turn back to the inn, for she'd also lied to Brady about not being hungry. She was starved. Besides, without her there to keep him on a tight leash, Lord only knew what sort of ridiculousness Brady would start next, acting as Gawain Caradoc, fool extraordinare.

"Gina? Gina—is that you? Wait, oh, wait! It's me, Gina. It is *I*!"

Chapter Eight

Regina halted in the act of turning back toward the inn, her feet frozen to the flagway, her heart lodged halfway up her throat.

"Cosmo?" she asked, her throat tight as she finally turned, saw the wide-as-he-was-high Cosmo, dressed in his brown monk's robes, obviously ready for his role of Friar Tuck. "Cosmo! It *is* you!" she exclaimed, just as the man wrapped her in a bear hug that lifted her a full six inches off the ground.

"Oh, Gina girl, we thought you'd left us. Where are your parents? Off digging up dirt and herbs again?" Cosmo put her down, then hugged her to him once more. "Thomas and David will be over the moon, simply over the moon! Come! Our wagon is just at the edge of town. Let's go find your parents. We'll eat, we'll sing, and Thomas will rejoice that he doesn't have to play Maid Marion tonight."

He lowered his voice to a whisper. "Not that he can,

not half so good as you, my dear. It's these cheek whiskers, you understand. Man won't shave them off, then wonders why everyone sniggers when he comes on-stage. I make the much better woman, but this belly of mine makes it difficult for Sir Robin to lift me in his arms and save me from Prince John."

Regina wiped at her tears, gave a small laugh. "Oh, Cosmo, I can't tell you how good it is to be with you again."

"Then be our Maid Marion. Be our Queen Elizabeth. Be our Juliet. Come with us, Gina. We need you terribly."

Regina shook her head, took a step back. "I can't, Cosmo. And I can't explain, either." She looked at him, sighed. "Oh, Cosmo, I can't tell you how good it is to see you! And you're performing here tonight? Where? I must be there, to cheer you from the audience."

Cosmo looked at her closely, consideringly. "Wearing a mighty fine gown, aren't you, Gina? Something havey-cavey is going on, isn't it? Maybe I'm not so happy to see you, maybe none of us will be so happy to see your mama and papa, either. Left us alone, for days, until we finally figured out you weren't coming back. Neither you nor the wagon. Do you know, Gina, how difficult it is to perform with only half our costumes and scenery? We've been reduced to villages like this, scrabbling for every penny."

"I'm so sorry, Cosmo," Regina told him sincerely. "But I promise you, it was not our intention to leave you. Things . . . well, things happened. Horrible things. Mama and Papa are . . ." She buried her face against Cosmo's broad chest, and began to cry. "Oh, Cosmo, Mama and Papa are gone."

"There, there, sweetings," the actor said, patting her back. "I knew something bad had to have happened, and told Thomas so when he swore you'd joined a larger troupe and deserted us. Gone, are they, you say? I feared as much."

Regina nodded, sobbing. She'd thought she was over the worst of her grief in just trying to survive herself, had channeled that grief into thoughts of revenge. But seeing Cosmo, telling Cosmo, brought the heartache back. "I couldn't come to you, Cosmo, for fear I'd bring the trouble to you."

He held her away from him, then reached into the side pocket of his monk's costume and pulled out a large, only slightly soiled handkerchief. "Here you go, Gina," he said, offering it to her. "Now, since when do we care about trouble, eh? Haven't we been through thick and thin together all these years?" He patted his ample belly. "I'm the thick, Thomas is the thin."

Regina gave a watery laugh. "And David is the pretty one," she said. "I remember. Oh, Cosmo, I have so much to tell you."

"And tell us you will, as soon as I go back to the wagon and rouse Thomas and the pretty boy. Tonight's performance is now hereby officially canceled! We'd only sold a dozen tickets anyway, Now, where will we meet you? Will you come to our wagon?"

Regina thought about that for a few moments, considering Brady's reaction—if she chose to tell him. "I'm not sure, Cosmo. I don't know if—no! He takes me as I am, or not at all, and if he doesn't trust me to trust you, then the devil with him. I never wanted to do this his way in the first place. If the man had to tread the boards for his living, he'd starve in a week."

Cosmo frowned. "I'm sure you know just what you're saying, Gina," he told her. "However, anytime you want to tell me what that is, I'm ready to hear."

"I'm sorry, Cosmo," Regina apologized, handing him back his handkerchief, which he stuffed into his pocket once more. "I'm not making much sense, am I? Tell you what—you go back to the wagon and wait for me there. It may take some time, but I'll join you there, probably after dark. I'll be alone, or I may have someone with me. Be nice to him, Cosmo. He's a good man."

Cosmo's huge cheeks puffed out, then retracted. "Man? You're traveling with a man? Has it come to that, Gina? Oh, your poor parents! They never wanted such a fate for you."

Regina shook her head, pulling a face. "Never! I would *never*—oh, bother. Cosmo, you'll just have to wait for explanations. I promise you, I'll tell you everything. Just, please, don't say anything about Mama and Papa. Nothing about them except that they were players. Nothing else."

"Nothing else? Why?"

"Because this man knows only what I've told him, and I've told him nothing else. Nothing about Papa's little project. Not a word about how we'd gone off on our own, how you were to wait for us to return and we didn't. Just remember this. We were together, Cosmo, all of us, with both wagons, when we were attacked by highwaymen. Your horses bolted with the wagon, and the three of you got away, but when you came back our wagon was gone and there was nothing else for you to do but leave again, mourning your three good friends. Understand?"

"Not at all, my dear Gina, not at all. But as I'm not one to forget my lines, I'll do as you say."

$$\mathcal{C}$$

"You'll love them, you'll see," Regina said, her arm slipped through Brady's as they walked along in the darkness.

"Love them, princess? I'm still trying to remind myself that these three men are alive. Or did you forget telling me that the entire troupe, save you, had perished? I see I must write down your lies, just to keep them straight for you."

"I told you all of this at the inn—I ran away so quickly that terrible night that I could only assume that Cosmo, Thomas, and David had also been killed. After all, they weren't there when I came back. As it turns out, they were able to escape with one of the wagons. Please, Brady, try to keep the facts straight in your head."

"That should be easy enough, considering you've only handed me two or three of them. Not your correct name, precious little about your parents. May I live in hope that your three friends will be able to tell me more?"

"If you were to be rude enough as to ask them. But you won't be. You promised, remember?"

"Ah, but that promise was wrung from me, under duress. You came racing into the inn, your cheeks all flushed, your eyes bright, and said you had a wonderful surprise for me if I agreed not to ask any questions. Fool that I am, I agreed.

Now, here I am, dressed in these silly clothes, risking my ankles as I mince my way through the dark, worrying about the impression I might make on three cowards who ran off, leaving you and your parents to their fates. I can't tell you how pleased I am, princess."

"They did not—oh, never mind. Just please believe me when I tell you that they're totally blameless. And my friends. We have to help them, you know. The . . . the *incident* left them with barely enough scenery and costumes to launch a small production, and I'm sure they need help. I thought we'd take them to London with us."

Brady tripped over a fair-sized stone and nearly pitched forward onto his face. "You thought we'd—oh, I don't think so, princess. I very much do not think so."

"Why not? They could prove helpful. Thomas could teach you how to walk in those ridiculous, high-heeled boots, for one. And David could show you how to act like a dandy and still seem like a man instead of a—"

"I beg your pardon," Brady said, truly affronted. "Are you saying that I—"

"You most certainly do," Regina interrupted, laughing. "That's what I've been trying to tell you. Your actions are too broad, too exaggerated. In short, my lord, you've been overacting. Horribly."

Brady considered this for a moment as they began walking through the dark once more. "And the clothes? They're also too much?" he asked, hopefully.

"Oh, no, the clothes are just right. It's you who are wrong."

"Damn," Brady grumbled, seeing his hopes of banishing at least some of the lace and satin to Perdition, or at least to the back of his clothespress, vanish. "But no more threats about swooning? No more slight screams at the sight of bread without the crusts cut off? Is that what you're saying?"

"Definitely," Regina agreed. "In fact, I think what we need is to slide some of your first idea into my idea."

"Meaning?"

"You need more *teeth*, my lord," Regina explained. "The clothes and hair and this affected drawl you're using are all good. Combined with your unlovely nose, I doubt your own mother would recognize you. You just have to stop being so . . . so *silly*. It's embarrassing."

"Oh, well, then, if I'm *embarrassing* you . . ."

Regina gave him a small slap on the arm, and Brady smiled, because he enjoyed the fact that she seemed to feel so at ease with him. Women didn't feel at ease with gentleman they had romantic designs on, he was sure of that. It was bad enough he kept seeing her as a woman now, a desirable woman. If she were to begin seeing him as a desirable man, well, then there'd be the devil to pay, wouldn't there?

"Thomas is . . . well, you know, and *he* doesn't embarrass me in the slightest. You're still misunderstanding. It's your deplorable overacting that upsets me, positively sets my teeth on edge. Remember, sir, I am an accomplished actress. You are the amateur. Therefore, it is my opinion that counts."

Brady gave a small flip of his head, sending that one errant lock of hair back where it belonged. "I would be quaking in my boots, my dear," he drawled sarcastically, "should your opinion matter a whit to me. As it does not,

I do believe I shall survive unto the morning with little or no ill effects."

"There!" Regina said, turning on him, pointing a finger up into his face. "That's it! *Now* you've got it. That's perfect! The fop, the dandy. Lazy, bored—but always with a sharp, cutting edge to his tongue. Oh," she said, smiling, "I'm *so* good."

She was so entirely pleased with herself. Brady longed to grab her, kiss her smiling mouth. He so forgot himself as to begin to put thought into deed when a loud shout came out of the darkness.

"Gina! I thought the man must be in his cups, drunk and delusional, but it's true! Oh, come here, darling, and let me kiss your cheeks, your hair, your tiny hands and feet. Allow me to prostrate myself before you, where I shall gladly drown in my own happy tears!"

Regina grinned. "That would be Thomas. Remember to study him, Uncle Gawain, for he's perfect," she said, then turned and ran toward the tall, thin man now holding his arms out to her.

"Study him, because he's *perfect*," Brady rather singsonged, knowing he was most probably being petty. But, after all, *look* at the man. Skinny as a stick, his hair a fright, his hose mended in at least four spots. This was who he was supposed to *study*? Hardly.

Well, maybe a little. The man did have a way with his posture. Straight of spine, and yet with his limbs looking so loose, as if they'd float away if they weren't attached at hip and shoulder. Remarkable. Graceful. Brady gritted his teeth. Almost *condescending*, as if he were a king being extremely polite to his most inferior subjects.

"Interesting," Brady said as he watched Thomas approach him, as the man stopped, struck a pose, then gifted him with an elegant bow. "Quite a lovely bow, my good man," he added. "Allow me to introduce myself, if you please. I am Gawain Caradoc, Earl of Singleton. And you are . . . ?"

"I believe that can wait, my lord Singleton," Thomas said, rising once more to his full height, which was a good three inches shorter than Brady, although that didn't seem to stop the man from looking at him down the length of his nose. "I have been told that you and Gina are traveling in company? You have an explanation for this, I'm sure."

Brady opened his mouth to reply, but before he could a blur passed before him, the blur shouting "Gina, my love!" before picking up Regina, planting a kiss full on her mouth.

"David, stop!" Regina protested laughingly as a young man entirely too handsome for his own good (or Brady's) whirled her in a circle, dropping more kisses on her cheeks, her throat.

Brady struck his own pose; one hand on his hip, the other holding his quizzing glass to his right eye. "Yes, David, do stop mauling the girl, if you please," he drawled, wondering why he longed to break David's pretty neck, right after he'd broken the man's legs and arms, and possibly his nose. No, definitely his nose. "It would so fatigue me to have to kill you."

He watched as David looked at him, looked back at Regina. "Who's the flash cove, Gina? Whoever he is, we don't need him. Not now that you're back."

"David, David, David," Thomas said, sighing, "it is just as Cervantes said, 'A closed mouth catches no flies.' I suggest you close yours, before you swallow more than one. This gentlemen, you see, is the earl of Singleton." He turned to Brady. "Forgive him, my lord, he's young. Built like a Greek God, I grant you, but young, and still rather vacant between his ears."

"I apologize, my lord," David said with a grin that, to Brady, seemed to set the boy's perfect, pearly white teeth to twinkling in the moonlight. David then bowed, elegantly, making Brady feel fairly ancient, especially when, his apology completed, he turned back to Regina once more, giving her yet another kiss.

"Shall we adjourn to the wagon with the infants, my lord?" Thomas asked as, hand in hand, Regina and David headed toward a large, looming shape in the darkness. "Cosmo is brewing tea. But if he offers you cakes, decline. I keep telling him we could paint his cakes black and use them for cannon balls."

"Thank you for the warning. Young love, Thomas?" Brady then asked, indicating Regina and David with, he hoped, a languid wave of his arm.

"Young idiot, my lord," Thomas answered, shaking his head. "Gina adores him as she would a puppy, and takes him just as seriously. And our young David kisses his own mirror with much more fervor, and definitely with more of his feelings involved. Does that put you at your ease, my lord?"

Brady was glad for the dark night, for he could feel the heat rising in his cheeks. "It was an idle question, Thomas," he said, reaching into his pocket to take out his snuffbox, intending to hide behind the ridiculous ritual, and the even more ridiculous sneeze. "May I offer you some of my sort?"

He then watched in considerable awe as Thomas took the small golden box, tapped the lid once with his index finger, then opened it with one hand, took a pinch that he placed on the back of his other hand, snorted it delicately, took another pinch, and repeated his graceful action. "Delightful, my lord," he then said, snapping the lid shut and handing the box back to Brady with a flourish before patting at his upper lip with a handkerchief he'd pulled from his pocket. "I must have the name of your chemist."

"You didn't sneeze," Brady said rather accusingly. He hated snuff, but felt certain a dandy would never be without his snuff box.

Thomas laughed. "And I didn't take snuff, my lord," he told him. "Horrid, messy habit, I believe. Plays havoc with the clothes and the nose. But I'm always polite when offered. You just assumed that I'd actually taken some of the stuff."

"I wish I'd thought of that," Brady muttered to himself, stuffing the snuffbox back into his pocket as Thomas led the way to the wagon, circling around it to where an open fire burned and the rest of their party was gathered.

He was introduced to Cosmo in short order, and within moments decided that it was the rather overstuffed man, older than the others, who was in charge of the small troupe, although Thomas was a close second. He sat down in the rickety chair offered to him—the best of a bad bunch set out in a semicircle around the fire— accepted a cup of tepid tea, declined the cake, and waited.

Waited for Regina and her friends to run through their rather bizarre conversation.

"We wintered in Kent, with the Amazing Andersons, who had just toured the area themselves, and to much better effect than our poor troupe. Half our necessary props were in your wagon. Imagine if you will, Gina, staging *Macbeth* with only the scenery drop from *Twelfth Night*. No castle, no ramparts. Just all these *trees*."

"Great Birnam Wood came to Dunsinane in the first act, and never left. Fortunately, no one in the audience noticed. They were too busy laughing at Cosmo, here, when his whalebone snapped. Sounded like a rifle shot, and propelled him halfway across the stage."

"Lady Macbeth had no fears about all that blood on her hands that night. She was much too busy trying to stuff herself back inside her broken corset. Looked like she'd grown another—"

"David, my pet, not in front of the child."

"The Andersons asked us to join them for the traveling season, but we had to decline, of course. They work with acrobats, you know. And a dog that walks about the stage on its hind legs, holding explanatory placards in its mouth. So *declassé*."

"Oh, enough, enough! We must hear from Gina now. Gina, sweetings, tell us *everything*."

Brady leaned forward on his chair. "Yes, *Gina*, do tell us everything," he prompted.

Then he watched as Regina stood, smoothed her skirts, and took center stage, her head high, her hands neatly folded in front of her. "As I told you, my good friends, Mama and Papa perished in the attack from the highwaymen—and I'm still so very overjoyed that you were able to escape. I had no idea that you had, you see, for I'd run into the woods as Papa commanded, and when I returned *both* the wagons were gone."

"Horses bolted. Plunging, tearing, screaming in fright at the sound of gunshots cracking the silence of the night."

"David near wet himself, and did lose the reins."

"I most certainly did not! It was *you* who—"

"Yes, yes, enough of finger pointing, my dear. What matters is that the horses bolted for more than a mile before we overturned in a ditch. It took us hours to get back to the scene, and no one was there. No one. But you are safe, darling Gina, and that's all that matters. Isn't that right, Cosmo?"

"So true, Thomas. Fate, my dearest friends, most often moves in mysterious ways."

"Exactly," Regina said, bowing slightly, obviously acknowledging both the interruption and Dame Fate—and, Brady thought, probably warning the trio to silence.

The men had sounded convincing. Still, Brady looked at the three men, realizing that they were actors, and actors were *supposed* to sound convincing. In addition, there was something in the way Regina had looked at them, especially at David—the youngest and probably the least experienced—that made him wonder if he should be swallowing all of this whole, or applauding a performance.

"But what did you do then, Gina? Where did you go? How did you survive?" Cosmo looked at Brady in a way that made him long to squirm in his chair, perhaps throw himself at Cosmo's feet and beg forgiveness. "You must have been desperate."

"I beg your pardon," Brady said, sticking his quizzing glass to his eye. "Are you saying I resemble the last sad hope of a desperate woman? I believe I'm offended, sir."

"My apologies, my lord," Cosmo said, not looking at all repentant. "But she had to have been desperate. She'd just lost her parents, and us as well."

"Oh, I was desperate, Cosmo, I was," Regina said, drawing everyone's attention back to her. "But I was fortunate enough to make my way to London, where I appeared with the most wonderful Mrs. Gertrude Iron. We had no wagon or access to any stage, but we roamed the city doing impromptu performances, then retired to our quite lovely rooms at night. I was most fortunate, and had the grandest time, truly."

Brady did not groan. He didn't roll his eyes. The mention of Cast-iron Gert and Regina's stint as a beggared, barefoot blind girl selling rag dolls outside Covent Garden did not cause him to choke, spit, or otherwise betray the fact that he was about to swallow his tongue. He decided he was a pretty good actor himself.

Much as he longed to hear the rest of Regina's fanciful story, he decided that he might be better served to interrupt now, and weave his own fairy tale, one that put him in a good light.

"Having seen Regina performing with Mrs. Iron," he said, walking over to stand beside Regina, "I took it into my head to hire her for a small project I've undertaken. Isn't that right, Regina?"

She looked at him quickly, and he winked at her. "Oh,

yes, right. His Lordship has hired me. We're . . . we're . . ."

"We're going to unmask a murderer," Brady finished for her, quickly rummaging through his brain and coming up with one of his friend Kipp's plots from an Aramintha Zane novel, improvising quickly to include himself in the story. "I am new to the earldom, you understand, as my cousin, the late earl, was the victim of foul play some months past. It has come to my attention that another gentleman, and his lady wife and young daughter, were murdered in just such a cruel way years ago, although the daughter's . . . well, how do I put this? Nothing for it but to say it, I suppose. The daughter's *body* was never recovered from the Thames."

"So I'm going to enter society with His Lordship, and he's going to refer to me as his ward, and then let it be known that I just might be that missing daughter."

"Although her memory is quite gone . . ." Brady put in, then stepped back a pace to let Regina keep the plot rolling.

"Oh, gone. *Gone*. But she has this . . . this *mole*—"

"On a rather intimate part of her anatomy . . ." Brady said, putting his handkerchief to his mouth to cover his smile.

Regina glared up at him, her nostrils flaring. "Exactly. And if she recovers her memory, she may be able to recognize the men who murdered her parents. Tying them up in sacks, weighting them with chains, dropping them in the filthy Thames at midnight, so that they went down, down, into the dark water . . ."

"Yes, my dear, I believe they understand," Brady said, wishing Regina weren't quite so good at sparring with him, reminding him of things he'd rather forget. He turned to the three men, who were looking at them intently. "And that's it, gentlemen. So you see, you have nothing to fear from me as far as Miss Regina is concerned. We are business partners, pure and simple."

"But how *exciting*!" David exclaimed, clapping his hands. "Is there a role for me? Perhaps as Gina's ardent suitor? I make a truly splendid Romeo. No, no! Byron! I could be handsome and brooding and have all of London at my feet while you two sneak about with no one paying any attention, finding your murderers. I saw Byron once, and he isn't half so pretty as me."

Brady complimented himself that he did not allow his upper lip to lift in a sneer, knowing it was beneath him to feel jealously over this callow youth. This handsome-as-sin callow youth who had kissed Regina on the mouth. Twice. "Very good, Regina," he then whispered to her. "Now say good night, and I'll leave a purse tucked up somewhere on the wagon early tomorrow as we sneak off for London at the crack of dawn. You can even pen them an emotional farewell note, asking them to meet us at Singleton Chase in two months."

Regina shook her head, whispered right back at him. "No, I don't think so. A mole? Who'd believe that? I went too far, and it's all your fault, too. My lie was *much* better than yours, if you'd only let me tell it."

Thomas took out his handkerchief as Brady and Regina whispered, blew on his quizzing glass, then polished it. "Pack of lies," he told Cosmo, loud enough for Brady to hear. "Better than some of her stories, but still a pack of lies."

"Lies? Then she won't need me to play a role?" David asked, and Thomas cluck-clucked with his tongue a time or two, looking at the younger man in genuine pity for his lack of brainpower.

"Oh, yes, David, quite the pack of lies," Cosmo agreed, shaking his head. "But she'll tell us everything in her own good time. Gina? You *are* going to take us with you to London, are you not? I think you need us."

"Oh, most definitely, dearest Cosmo. His Lordship is all but crying out for our assistance," Thomas said. "The role he's playing is in dire need of refinement."

"See? I told you so, my lord Overactor," Regina said smugly.

Chapter Nine

*R*egina and Brady spent a week at the posting inn, visiting the traveling wagon daily, during which time Thomas taught and Brady dutifully listened and learned.

The truth was out, at last, spoken about during the long evenings spent around the open fire, with only Regina's fib about Madam Gertrude Iron still her own secret. She would always be grateful to Brady for not upsetting her dearest friends with the truth about that unlovely interlude.

As far as Cosmo, Thomas, and David knew, Regina had procured employment as a maid in Viscount Willoughby's London mansion after her time with Madam Iron, and the earl of Singleton had taken an interest in her and her story, which he'd heard from the viscount's bride.

The idea that Regina might have lied to the earl and his lady did not upset her three friends, who had only nodded their understanding when Brady told them how she'd tried to hand them all some farradiddle about being the orphan in the storm, as it were. They hadn't been at all surprised to learn that Brady had then traveled to Little Woodcote, to check on Regina's fanciful tale.

As Cosmo had told Brady, "Once, when she was five, she told us she'd been stolen by gypsies and was, in fact, a princess. She's rather good, was rather good even at that young age. Why, I think she had her own mother doubting that she'd given birth to her there, for a while at least."

In return for the truths Brady and Regina had handed them about Lord Allerton and the murder of the earl of Singleton, the trio felt it necessary to inform Brady that they had never been camped outside Little Woodcote at all. In truth, as Cosmo told him, they had never been to Little Woodcote, although Regina's parents had traveled there twice a year for at least three years.

"And he's not really Gawain Caradoc, the new earl," Regina had put in quickly, just as Brady had been about to ask her a few pertinent questions. "He's Brady James, the man who went poking into my life in the first place—and without me asking him to do so, I might add. He left out that part, didn't he?" She'd then folded her arms across her waist and glared at him. "Just in case you think I'm the only one who has *bent* the truth here."

It had taken that full week for everything to be sorted out, the fibs from the truths, the facts from the fictions, and David had given up trying to understand on the second day, happy enough to know that, yes, he would be traveling to London and, yes, he would get a new suit of clothes.

Thomas, who had offered David in the role of one of my lord Singleton's boon companions from the Continent, had also put forth himself as His Lordship's cousin on His Lordship's mother's side, a shy and retiring gentleman who would not wish to go into society.

But it was Cosmo's role that caused all these wonderful plans to come to a crashing halt, for Cosmo met them at the wagon the morning of their removal to London, dressed as Mrs. Matilda Forrest, Regina's chaperone.

The corset might have been repaired, but it would take more than whalebone and tight lacings to squeeze Cosmo's girth down below the size of a small . . . well, a small whale. A small whale dressed in red-and-white-striped satin, red slippers large enough to stomp out small villages, and a blond wig covered in curls, ringlets, and stuck with two large white ostrich feathers. He also carried a small reticule and a fan, and wore lace mitts, but at that point, they really didn't matter.

"Never!" Brady declared once Cosmo had presented his idea, completely forgetting his lessons in drawling dandyism and reacting with a red face and quite a loud, forceful bellow.

"And why not?" Regina asked, hands on hips. "She— he—doesn't look any more ridiculous than *you* do, my lord. And I think that heart-shaped patch on Cosmo's chin is fascinating."

"I could never remember if it's left cheek for Tory, right cheek for Whig, or the other way round," Cosmo explained, deftly opening the fan and waving it just below his beauty-marked double chin. "So I put it in the middle. Women shouldn't be involved in politics anyway, don't you think, my lord?"

Brady turned on his heels and walked away from the wagon, calling out "Regina! *Now!*" He wasn't sure if she'd follow him, or if he wanted her to follow him, but he knew he had to get away from the wagon and the three actors before he exploded.

He liked the men, all three of them now that he'd finally realized that David was as harmless and silly as any debutante. Maybe they could dress David up as Regina's chaperone? No. That wouldn't work. He was too young, for one, and for two, Brady still didn't like having the kissing, hugging little twit too much in Regina's company—a thought that still plagued him, because he was not at all in charity with Miss Regina Bliss at the moment.

Still, Thomas would be fine. Unobtrusive, yet there, handy in case Brady had a question, and for the most part a stabilizing influence. David would be fine, as his pretty face would keep him trapped behind potted palms as he tried to evade giggling little girls who thought him handsome.

But Cosmo as a woman? Oh no. Oh, most definitely not!

He stopped walking, turned around, and began to talk. Luckily, or else he might look a little foolish, Regina had obeyed, and followed after him.

"I will *not* enter London society with that . . . that . . . that *woman*! My God, Regina, I'd rather we found the Amazing Andersons and their dancing dog, and took *them* to London."

Regina stepped closer, patted his arm. "There, there, my lord, calm yourself. I know what's wrong, you know."

Brady closed his hands into fists, wondered what would happen if he just threw back his head and howled. Probably nothing. These were people who didn't seem to flinch at the unusual, even a howling earl in puce satin.

"What's wrong," Regina went on, clearly unaware that Brady felt close to exploding, "is that you believe we aren't approaching this problem with the seriousness it deserves. And that's nonsense, because we are. We're just as serious as you are, maybe more so. We just . . . well, we just had to find a way to fit ourselves into society, just as you have found a way to insert yourself into society."

"By wearing satin, and red heels, and prancing about like a ninny," Brady gritted out. "I must have been out of my mind. Get hit on the head enough, swallow enough of the Thames, and it spins a person straight out of his mind. But no longer, Miss Bliss, no longer. As of this moment, our plans are changed."

"Oh, really? In what way?"

He narrowed his eyelids, glared at her. "One, we wave good-bye to Thomas, Romeo, and *Matilda* as we ride out of their lives. Two, I take you back to Lord and Lady Willoughby, with the fervently expressed request that they chain you to a bedpost until I tell them it's safe to let you go. Three, I burn these clothes, cut my hair, and enter society as the dark, brooding Gawain Caradoc I wanted to be in the first place."

"You'd have to keep the hair, my lord," Regina pointed out coolly. "Unless you want to delay your arrival in society even more, while you grow hair on your upper lip."

Brady stepped back a pace, more than a little rattled by her quick acceptance of his new plans. "Then it's settled? You agree?"

"Oh, most definitely, my lord, although I hadn't said anything for fear *you* wouldn't agree. It's definitely better this way. Meeting up with Cosmo and Thomas and David only made an already unworkable plan worse. You'd never have been able to pull it off anyway. To be frank, I think I'm relieved."

Brady opened his mouth, pointed his finger at her, closed his mouth again, then slapped both hands against the sides of his face, just to keep his brain from exploding. "I can't stand it," he said, not to Regina, not to himself, but just addressing his comment to the world, in case anyone was listening. "How does she do it? How does she turn everything around as if it was *my* failure? It wouldn't work, she says," he went on, now waving his arms and pacing the dirt path at the end of the grassy area where the wagon sat. "I'm not good enough, not convincing enough. Nothing about that idiot preening peacock with brains to match. Not a word about Thomas and his—oh, hell, Thomas is fine, just fine. But Cosmo? He looks like a tent at the Bartholomew Fair! But no. *No.* They're just fine. It's *me.* I'm the part that doesn't work, the player who can't play."

His harangue done, he whirled back to look at Regina once more. "You're dumping me," he said accusingly. "You've used me, and now you're dumping me, casting me off. You probably dressed Cosmo up like a Christmas pudding just so I'd finally recognize the depths of my folly, tell you the plan won't work. Because you have your own plan now that you've found your friends again, don't you,

Regina? You know the name, you know he's in London, you have the clothes I bought you on your back and my money in your pocket, and you have your own plan that includes those three ninnies, but eliminates *me*. Well, little girl, it won't work. Do you understand? It won't work!"

Regina rolled her eyes. "Oh, all right, all right. I didn't think you'd be so upset. I apologize, although I think it mean-spirited of you to remark on my clothes that you gave me and the wages I honestly earned. Nevertheless, we'll go to London with you if you insist. There. Everything's settled."

She'd turned away from him, heading back to the wagon before Brady let out a low, intense string of curses that would have any real dandy falling into a horrified swoon.

CB

Regina stretched as she heard the knock on the door, then turned onto her side, hoping whoever wanted to disturb her would give up and go away. The coach holding His Lordship and her had arrived in Portman Square after midnight, and she'd been too exhausted to do more than allow herself to be led upstairs to her room. She hadn't done more than look around, realize that she'd gone from one comfortable nest to another, then fall into bed, still dressed in her underclothes because the other coaches hadn't yet arrived.

She and Brady hadn't spoken much on that second long leg of their journey, which had suited Regina down to the ground, for the man had a look in his eye that warned her he wasn't in the mood for idle chatter. Neither was she, for she'd had a stomach-tumbling, scary moment when he'd declared that she would no longer be a part of his plan.

She didn't, and would never, worry about not being able to have her revenge on the earl of Allerton and whoever else had a hand in murdering her parents. One way, someday, that score would be settled. No question, and she was young, she could afford to be patient.

But when she, just for an instant, imagined herself never seeing Brady again? Well, that had been an enlightening moment, and definitely not a pleasant one, for she'd realized at once that having Brady walk out of her life would leave her with a huge, gaping hole where her heart had once resided.

How had that happened? When had that happened? And why would she feel this way about a man who was very openly and honestly using her for his own ends? A man who saw her as she was, an actress. A man who knew her for a whopping great fibber, and was more than aware that she was not of his class, his social level.

When had she begun weaving fanciful, happily ever after daydreams about the man? During the days she'd nursed him back to health and been impressed with his courage and fortitude? After that day they'd spent rolling in the snow at Singleton Chase, when he'd been young and laughing and wonderful? During the months he'd been gone, when she'd fallen asleep holding the pearls he'd given her, missing him?

When had she decided that he was silly, and sweet, and necessary for her happiness? When had she decided that his smile was all she needed to light her day, warm her heart?

Never, that's when! Because anything else was impossible. Because he was playacting a role, she was playing a role, and what they had together was nothing more than lines in a play, a made-up story that had a passably pleasant first act, a fairly rocky second act, and a finale still to be written. And once the curtain rang down, and they'd taken their bows, accepted the applause, Brady would go back to being the real earl of Singleton, and she would head out on the road with her friends.

She'd remember that, keep it always in the forefront of her mind. None of this was real. Not this mansion, not this room, not her fine clothes, not her next weeks of mingling with the shining lights of London society. *He* wasn't real. And her feelings for him certainly weren't real. They couldn't be real.

The knock came again, and Regina groaned, rolled onto her back once more. "Oh, come in, whoever you are, but don't think I'm happy to see you."

She opened one eye as the door opened, then sat up quickly as Wadsworth entered, a man who looked as if he was definitely on some mission that wouldn't carry along with it any great joy for her. "Wadsworth," she said—fairly squeaked. "You've arrived."

"We have *all* of us arrived," the butler told her, stopping a good ten feet from the bottom of the bed, looking at Regina as if he expected her to have some answer for his statement.

She considered it safest to oblige him, at least until she was more awake, and had her wits about her. "Well, good. *Good.* I know you all left earlier than we did yesterday morning, but His Lordship explained that heavy coaches travel more slowly and need to stop more often. I imagine we passed you at some point?"

He looked at her levelly for the count of three, then said, "Wagons loaded with silliness, it seems, travel even slower, miss, and do not arrive until the next morning. Although there are always small silver linings to be found, I suppose, as the wagon was left elsewhere in the city and the silliness and their luggage arrived at the serving entrance in a pair of rented hacks." He took a deep breath, shuddered, probably at the memory of seeing Thomas, Cosmo, and David sitting in the Singleton kitchens, munching breakfast. "Why was I not informed of this arrival?"

"Poor Wadsworth. Didn't you know my friends were coming to London with us?"

Wadsworth's expression told her that he most certainly had not been informed and, that if he had been, the doors and windows to the mansion in Portman Square would all have been nailed shut posthaste before they could arrive. "His Lordship failed to mention it," he said. "I wonder why."

Regina grinned, fully awake. "No you don't, Wadsworth. You know exactly why he didn't tell you. The man's afraid of you. Everyone shakes in their shoes when you so much as look at them—*especially* when you look at them. Except me, of course, which you also know, as well as knowing that I'll give you an answer. Possibly not the correct one, very often one with little truth to it, but definitely an answer. That's because I think you're rather sweet, in a gruff and unlovable way. So tell me, is His Lordship hiding in his rooms, afraid to face you? I don't think so, but that would be funny, wouldn't it?"

"His Lordship did not sleep here last night," Wadsworth told her. "I had hoped that you would know his whereabouts, and if we should be concerned that he is not yet returned. I see now that you are as unaware of his plans as you should be, but I do not appreciate being likewise in the dark concerning the master's comings and goings. I have my reputation to preserve, you understand."

Regina nearly hopped from the bed in a quick sharp mix of anger and fear, but remembered her state of undress in time, pulling the covers up to her chin. "What time is it, Wadsworth?" she asked, longing to find His Lordship, then strangle him.

"It is past ten, miss," Wadsworth told her, and a slight quaver in his voice, not betrayed by his stiff and straight posture, softened Regina's heart toward the man even more. "Do you think I should send a note round to the duke of Selbourne?"

Regina bit her bottom lip, mulling Wadsworth's suggestion. "No, I don't think so. Not yet. I'm sure His Lordship thinks he knows just what he's doing. But if you'd leave, I'll get dressed, and we can all wait for him downstairs. Is there a bellpull in this room? Can I ring for Maude?"

"I'll send in your maid," Wadsworth said, bowing. "And then I will go downstairs, assure myself that none of our three new guests has either pilfered the silver or soiled the furniture, have all their luggage burned, and find them rooms in the attic. Oh, and I suppose I should have Rogers shave your chaperone, as she seems to have been cursed with a morning beard."

"Nothing fazes you for long, does it, Wadsworth?" Regina asked, as the butler turned to leave the room. "Nothing except any thought that the earl might be in some danger. He's not, you know, for I'm sure all he did was to spend the night skulking about outside the earl of Allerton's mansion, making his plans. Besides, we're with him now, and we will protect him. All of us."

Wadsworth's shoulders stiffened, and he turned slowly, ran his gaze up and down Regina as she sat forward in the large bed. "If I were to truly believe that His Lordship's only protection other than myself was comprised of an impertinent chit, a prancing fool, a dimwitted Adonis, and a fat man in gown and beard, I should have to shoot myself. Good day, miss. We'll expect you downstairs in a half hour."

Regina stuffed the covers against her mouth, giggling, until Wadsworth had taken his exquisitely timed exit, then came to herself in an instant, leaping out of bed, anxious to dress and be downstairs before His Lordship came back from spying on Lord Allerton.

Brady posed on the carpet in the drawing room, one hand on his hip, the other holding a lace-edged handkerchief to his lips, waiting for Bramwell Seaton, Duke of Selbourne, to stop laughing.

He'd slipped into his Portman Square rooms before dawn after a night spent inspecting the exterior of Allerton's mansion, counting doors and windows, daring to approach closely enough to test the strength of the ivy growing up the rear of the building. He'd then stripped out of his dark clothing, and Rogers—the valet sworn to secrecy about the whole thing—had helped him into fawn-colored pantaloons with green stripes, a sunshine yellow waistcoat, and a grass green coat cut with wasp waist and heavily buckram-padded shoulders.

He had six fobs hanging from his coat, his buttons were white bone and the size of small dessert plates. His high-heeled boots of black and tan were festooned with tassels that dangled against his shins, his shirt points rose above his chin, and the lace at his wrists and throat gave whole new worlds of meaning to the sartorially descriptive word "waterfall." His hair was slicked back from his forehead and clubbed at the nape with a bright yellow grosgrain ribbon.

It was no wonder Bram was laughing.

"Bram, darling," his wife Sophie scolded, "you shouldn't be embarrassing our dear friend this way. You are embarrassed, aren't you, Brady?" Then she grinned. "Lord knows you *should* be."

Now Brady waited for Bram to stop laughing and for Sophie to stop laughing. What jolly, happy friends he had. Wasn't he a lucky man?

"If you're quite done?" he ventured at last, as Bram wiped at his eyes and Sophie struggled with a bout of hiccups. "I did write to tell you of my plan, you know. It's not as if my appearance comes as a complete surprise."

"Oh, Brady, old friend, trust me in this," Bram said, folding his handkerchief and putting it back in his pocket, "nothing you wrote to us could have prepared us for your appearance here this morning. But it works, it works. I wouldn't have known you if I had passed you in Bond Street."

Brady carefully split his coattails and just as carefully sat down, praying the seams of his pantaloons would hold. "Then at least one thing has gone right since last we spoke," he said, accepting a glass of wine from his friend. "Bram, Sophie, this had better work. It might be easier being dead than having to live as Gawain Caradoc if it doesn't, because that's all that would be left to me otherwise."

"It's a little late for second thoughts, Brady," Bram pointed out, handing a glass of lemonade to his wife, who was still beset by hiccups. "In fact, from the moment I announced that the body we found was you, and we planted that body at Singleton Chase, I'd say the die has been cast. Oh, and forgive me. I should be addressing you as Singleton, shouldn't I, so that I don't slip and call you Brady. Or are we to be close friends, and I can address you as Gawain?" He shuddered, took a sip of wine, grinned. "Lord, I hope not. I do have my own consequence to consider, you understand."

"Planning on cutting me in society, are you, Bram?" Brady asked, attempting to cross his legs, then giving it up as a bad idea. If his pantaloons were an inch tighter at any seam, he was sure he'd end up gelding himself. "I don't blame you. But I thought you'd at least allow Sophie to help introduce Miss Felicity to the *ton*."

"Miss Felicity? Oh, you mean Regina Bliss. Please tell me she isn't rigged out as ridiculously as you, old friend."

Brady felt his lips tighten. "Watkins's sister has designed what she's sure is a very Continental wardrobe for Regina. From the look of the necklines I've seen thus far, and from the sheerness of the materials, I can imagine quite a few French damsels have caught their death of cold these past months."

"Oh, oh," Sophie said, setting down her glass and smiling at her husband. "I do believe our little rag-doll seller and well-behaved maid of all work has cleaned up to advantage, yes? How very interesting. Tell us, *Gawain*, is she ravishing? I'm willing to wager that she is ravishing. That wonderful burnished red hair, those lovely grey eyes that are always so alive with mischief, even when she attempts to be demure. She's really quite unique."

"She's an actress," Brady bit out, wishing Sophie would, just this once, not be so insightful. "I've finally got some of the truth out of her. She and her parents traveled the country in a wagon, putting on performances in small towns, until the parents were killed by Allerton and she escaped to London."

"An actress. Of course!" Sophie said, clapping her hands. "Bram, darling,—didn't you say as much about Regina? I think you did, yes. Oh, you're so brilliant."

Bram lifted his wife's hand to his lips, kissed her fingertips. "Thank you, darling. And at least one question has at last been answered. An actress. But that doesn't explain why her parents were killed—you did say that, too, correct?—especially if you still believe we can lay the blame at Allerton's door. Why would he bother murdering traveling players?"

"That's true, Gawain—you see, I'm practicing myself,

just like an actress," Sophie said, then frowned. "So she really is an orphan, yes? The poor—thing."

Brady sighed. "Why were the parents murdered? A good question, Bram, and one I'm still trying to answer. Which is why I've also acquired Regina's three fellow players, whom we chanced upon on our way here. Asking Regina anything outright only elicits another fanciful story, but I'm hoping one of these men will finally trust me enough to take me fully into his confidence."

"*Four* actors now, Gawain?" Bram asked, looking at him quizzically. "Quite the entourage."

"Yes, and an entourage that did *not* accompany Regina and her parents on their last fateful trip to Little Woodcote. So far, I've learned from the youngest one, David— whom I may still strangle—that twice a year for several years he and the other two, Thomas and Cosmo, waited with the second wagon in another village while Regina and her parents stopped in Little Woodcote. Always, the wagon returned in three days, and the entire troupe then bought new clothes and dined well for several months. Until the last time, when the wagon never returned."

"Because her parents had been murdered and Regina had escaped to London," Sophie said, sighing happily when there were no more hiccups to interrupt her speech. "And, even more interesting, those trips to Little Woodcote seemed to have put money into the pockets of Regina's parents, yes?" She turned to her husband. "Bram? What could Allerton have been paying them for, do you think?"

"Blackmail?" Bram suggested, shrugging. "And, if so, perhaps Allerton wasn't the only victim, and the other two men had joined with him to eliminate Regina's parents and their problem. Did this David tell you there were other villages, other visits in which he and his friends weren't included?"

"I asked, but no. Just Little Woodcote. Twice a year. Other than that, I know nothing. Regina says it's enough that I know that Allerton and two of his cohorts or cronies or whoever killed her parents, then tried to murder me after I went to Little Woodcote to ask questions. She's protecting them of course, and I can't blame her, if they were involved in something illegal."

"Illegal, and dangerous," Bram pointed out. "But then why would they have taken Regina with them? Wouldn't it have been safer to leave her behind, with the others? Unless they didn't believe they *were* in danger. And she's sure it's Allerton? She saw him?"

Brady shook his head. "She didn't really see any of the men too clearly, and she's convinced they never saw her. But she knows the Allerton name, and I'm sure they know of her existence, because she suggested I change her name from Bliss to Felicity. I can see why, because although the paint on the wagon was badly faded, I could make out the words BLISSINGTON WORLD FAMOUS TRAVELING PLAYERS."

"Blissington to Bliss. Interesting," Bram said, nodding. "But what about Regina? I'll assume she made that name up out of whole cloth?"

"No, Regina is her name, I'm sure of that, although it would seem that her parents and the other players have dubbed her Gina. I doubt Allerton ever heard her name, in any case, but we should be safe with Regina Felicity.

God, Bram," Brady said, trying to slump against the cushions while his clothing insisted on keeping his posture uncomfortably straight, "what a mess I've made. I nearly get myself killed, I'm sitting here in lace and satins thanks to an idiotic plan born, I'm sure, of fever, dirty water, and possibly a touch of insanity. Worse, I've involved a maddening but innocent girl—"

"Worse—or better—but definitely interesting to us, you find yourself entirely too *attracted* to this innocent girl . . ." Bram inserted, and Sophie giggled as she gave her husband's arm a slap.

Chapter Ten

*R*egina had considered the many ways in which she could greet Brady when he returned to Portman Square. Anger. Tears. Indifference.

She settled for bored curiosity.

"So? How go the wars, my lord?" she asked, barely looking up from her teacup as Brady entered the drawing room just as the clock on the mantel struck the hour of noon.

"Well enough, if I can ever get the sound of my friends' laughter at my expense out of my head," he answered, heading for the drinks table and a glass of wine. "Do Bram and Sophie think I don't own any mirrors?"

Regina bit back a smile. Poor man, he'd never get used to his new wardrobe, no matter how well he'd learned to carry off the role of fop. "So you've been visiting the duke and duchess of Selbourne. How nice. Tell me, did they recognize you?"

"I sent in my card—my new card—so they already

knew who I was. But, no, I don't think they would have recognized me otherwise. At least His Grace swore he'd pass me on Bond Street without recognizing me, although one could very easily take that as he wouldn't *wish* to recognize me."

He lifted the wineglass to his lips, took a sip. "You know, I may end up drinking in earnest, morning to night, if I have to parade myself around like this for too long."

"You'll get used to it in time," Regina said, hard-pressed not to laugh as Brady gingerly sat himself down on the facing couch. "It's a costume, my lord, just as we wear costumes when on stage. Good to help both the audience and ourselves enter into the play. If you were to consider yourself as playing a role, appearing onstage, I think that would help you enormously."

"Making a bonfire of my new wardrobe in the middle of Portman Square would help me enormously, Regina," he informed her tightly. He stood up once more. "Now, if you're quite ready, I've already asked that my curricle be brought round so that we might begin your driving lessons at a time when the park is fairly empty of targets for you to run down with the horses."

Regina hopped to her feet, instantly diverted. "You remembered? And you're really going to teach me?"

"Actually, we're going to dabble our toes in the waters of society, and having you at the reins of my well-known curricle, with me sitting beside you, will undoubtedly cause us no small attention, no matter how thin the company in the park. I suggest a light cloak and a fairly sturdy pair of gloves, both of which Wadsworth has already sent someone to fetch from your maid."

Regina saw no reason to hide her excitement. "Oh, this is wonderful! We're going into society. I don't think I really believed that until this moment. I hope Maude brings me the yellow straw bonnet."

"The one with the feathers? You had mentioned feathers, I believe," Brady asked, as they walked to the foyer.

"Definitely the one with the feathers. And remember, my lord, you are Gawain Caradoc. From this moment on, whether we are here, alone, or out in the world, you are Gawain Caradoc. This is vitally important."

"Oh, bother," Brady said with an only slightly exaggerated toss of his head, causing Wadsworth to give a delicate shudder as Regina and Gawain passed out into the warm spring air.

Brady handled the reins as they moved through the always congested traffic on the roads leading to the park, and Regina watched his hands as he drove, marveling at the ease with which he handled the pair of midnight black geldings in the traces.

"You're quite good at this, my lord," she said, as he expertly edged the wheels of the curricle past a large carriage with but an inch to spare. "Do we have time to pass by Lord Allerton's mansion in Grosvenor Square, or did you see enough of it last night to suit you?"

Brady slanted her a very un-Gawain-like look. "What makes you think I've been to Grosvenor Square?"

She smiled, folded her hands in her lap. Really, the man had no idea how inventive she could be when she put her mind to it. "Let's just say that Thomas and Rogers seem to be kindred spirits. Rogers told him about your late-night travels as the two of them spent an hour in a comfortable coze. Rogers, by the way, is still lamenting the dirt on your boots and the tear in the knee of one of your finest pairs of black pantaloons. Did you inspect the Allerton mansion on your knees, or just from a mud puddle?"

Brady looked at her for so long that he nearly ran the curricle into a dray wagon that had turned onto the roadway. "I can still send you to Willoughby Hall, you know, princess."

"No, you can't, because I won't stay there, and you need me here."

"Actually, I don't."

"Yes, you do," Regina persisted. "Because, my lord, whether you admit it to yourself or to me, neither of which you've done, I am to be your *bait*."

"Never!" Brady all but shouted, turning through the gates, into the park. "I would never use you as bait, put you in danger—and if you'd just tell me the whole truth, I probably could have this nonsense over in a fortnight and get back to my life."

Regina cocked her head to one side, looked at him closely, seeing the hot color that had come into his face. "You mean that, don't you? But I'm the perfect bait. Surely you've realized that by now. We both even spoke about it when we were first making up fibs to tell Thomas and the others."

"I said I'd never use you that way, Regina. I didn't say I was an idiot. I most certainly did think about it, during the first flush of my anger. And of course it would be simple to wave you under Allerton's nose, making up some story about how—no! You get enough ideas on your own, don't you. But that was never my intention for long, once I'd come to my senses but, unfortunately, too late to change the fact that we'd announced my death, and too late to keep you from being involved in some way. And I do have a very good plan now, you know."

"So you've said. I was beginning to wonder, my lord," Regina told him, looking around the park, marveling at the sight of so many nannies and their charges, the few couples strolling the smaller paths, the tight groupings of well-dressed ladies chattering away under the shade of the trees. "What is your plan?"

Brady touched the brim of his curly-brimmed beaver and gave an almost imperceptible nod as they passed by two matronly ladies standing at the edge of the path. "The one on the left, in the rather ridiculous pink satin, is Lady Jersey. Sharpest eyes and largest mouth in the *ton*. And she didn't recognize me, although I'm quite sure she is now staring at our backs, having recognized the curricle. My confidence, dearest Miss Felicity, grows by leaps and bounds. Oh, and I *plan*, my dear, to become a shadow of my former self," he drawled, then grinned at her, rather vacantly, Regina thought. Why did he only listen to her about remaining inside his role of the silly Gawain when she longed to speak to him as Brady?

Then, belatedly, she thought: Lady Jersey? Really? Well, goodness, she'd just passed by Lady Jersey!

Regina quickly looked back over her shoulder at Her Ladyship, who was now deep in conversation with her companion. She'd heard of Lady Jersey, as had anyone in England with at least one ear, but she'd never thought she'd see her. She certainly never thought she'd be better dressed than the woman if she did see her.

Still, Brady's words repeated themselves inside her head, and at last she turned back to him. "A shadow of your former self? I beg your pardon, cousin, but I don't understand. Your former self is dead, so that I'd say it would be rather impossible to—oh!" She knew she was goggling at him now. *"Really?"*

"Yes, really," Brady told her, pulling the curricle to the side of the path and setting the brake. "Oh, and may I tell you that the quickness of your devious female mind amuses me even as it terrifies me."

"Thank you, my lord. You're going to be your own ghost? How are you going to do that?"

Brady shrugged his heavily padded shoulders. "The sprinkling of a little brackish water from the Thames, some bits of sacking, a few chains—and a low moan. Definitely a low moan. I believe people expect that sort of thing."

"The brackish water is a nice touch, and I now know how to fashion quite believable bruises and running sores, if you want," Regina said, considering the matter purely as she would see the thing performed onstage. "But where?" she asked, once the idea of the stage entered her head. "Where are you going to be Brady's ghost?"

"I'd initially thought about Allerton's mansion," he told her, arranging her hands on the reins. "But the ivy isn't strong enough and the man seems to have let his downspouts fall into sad disrepair. But that's probably a good thing, because the earl may be a killer, but he isn't stupid. He most probably does not believe in ghosts."

"So you're going to abandon the plan? That's probably a good thing, although confronting Allerton as your own ghost was very inventive of you. It wouldn't do to get caught inside the Allerton mansion, dripping water from the Thames."

"Keep your elbows loose and your hands light, but never release the tension," he instructed her, pushing the brake off with his foot. "There you go. And I haven't abandoned the plan, I've just reworked it."

Regina kept her eyes on the bit of roadway visible just beyond the ears of the lively pair. She'd driven her parents' wagon since she was a child, but Portia and Cleopatra had been aged before she'd been born, and wouldn't have known how to bolt, or even remembered that they ever could. These horses were different, and she knew it. She knew it, and she adored Brady for trusting her with them, and likewise trusting her not to upset him onto the roadway, definitely drawing attention to them, but possibly breaking both their necks in the process.

She bit her lip as the horses tried to break from the walk she wanted to hold them to, careful to keep her hands "light" on the reins even as she kept her control firm. "Reworked it how, my lord?" she asked, holding her breath as the curricle entered a turn.

"Ah, brilliant, but not in the league of your uncle Gawain, I see," Brady said teasingly, putting his hand on hers as they entered the turn, guiding her as she pulled back slightly on the reins. "There were three men, remember?"

Regina relaxed as the turn was accomplished without tossing either of them onto the roadway, and her confidence grew. She gave a slight flick of the reins, and the blacks began a smart trot on the long, empty straightaway in front of them. "You're right, my lord. I'm not as brilliant as you are, obviously. But we only know about Allerton. We have no idea who the other two men might be, remember?"

"Process of elimination, my dear," Brady said, chin lifted as he pointedly ignored the openmouthed stares of two young bucks dressed in the first stare of fashion, if one believed the height of fashion to include orange-and-green-striped waistcoats. "Popinjays," he then added, shaking his head as he dabbed a lace-edged handkerchief at each corner of his mouth.

"You cut those gentlemen as if they weren't standing there," Regina said, taking her eyes off the path just long enough to see the two affronted gentlemen looking after them, shaking their heads and talking a mile a minute. "Why did you do that?"

"Why? Must you ask, or did you not see their shirt points? A good quarter inch above the bottom of their earlobes. Any fool knows that to be excessive. A gentleman of fashion draws attention to himself, yes, as we are the more attractive of the sexes, but he does not make himself a picture of fun by going to extremes."

Regina looked at him, her mouth open, and then threw back her head and laughed out loud. "Oh, my lord, that's wonderful. You're going to set yourself up as an arbiter of fashion."

"One does what one must to improve the masses,"

Brady replied, employing his handkerchief once more, this time to polish his quizzing glass. "Deuced fatiguing, but some of us are called to a higher order, you understand."

Regina giggled. "Forgive me," she then said, trying to control her amusement. "I know I've told you to keep to your role, but now I see I am going to have to learn to accept you in that role. You are amazing, you know. Thomas has done a splendid job."

"He had help," Brady said, taking the reins from her as they neared another corner, this one sharper than the last. "I think that's enough for one day, don't you? I shouldn't wish to squander all of my splendor on this one small pocket of humanity. We dine early this evening, and then join the duke and duchess of Selbourne in their box at the theater. Do you enjoy Sheridan, my dear? I understand we're to be entertained by his *The School for Scandal*. An apt title for us, I believe."

"Will Allerton be there?" Regina asked, excited by the chance to see a play performed in a real London theater, but still more interested in the earl.

"My dear, everyone will be there, including, we can only hope, some of Allerton's boon companions. The shade of my former self is, as you may have realized by now, quite interested in His Lordship's boon companions."

Regina thought for a moment, then snapped her fingers. "Of course! I must have been paying too much attention to the horses not to see it all at once. If you can't haunt the Allerton mansion, you'll haunt the home of his friends."

"One by one, princess," Brady told her, as they drove out onto the street once more. "Until one of them goes haring off to set up a meeting with Allerton and the final corner on our deadly triangle. Once we know the identity of all three men, we can decide how best to confront them."

"But what if he has more than two good friends? He probably does, doesn't he? Or do you plan to be haring all over London, wailing and dripping, until you finally pick the right house to haunt?"

Brady sighed. "If you're going to complicate things by being logical, princess, I won't allow you to come along."

"You'd let me come along?" Regina's heart did a small flip in her chest. "Really?"

He turned his head, looked down his nose at her. "With Rogers now a traitor to me, do I have a choice? I'd much rather know where you are than be worried that you were going to pop up when I least expected you."

Regina folded her hands across her midsection. "How nice that we've come to understand each other so well."

"Then you'll tell me why your parents stopped in Little Woodcote twice a year, and why Allerton murdered them?"

Regina instantly bristled, her good feelings toward Brady evaporating in the heat of her anger. "Clearly, my lord, we don't understand each other quite that well."

"You don't trust me, you mean," Brady responded, as they pulled up before the mansion in Portman Square. "Why, Regina? Was what they did so terrible?"

"They did *nothing* terrible! And, if you'd minded your own business instead of sticking your nose into mine, maybe your nose wouldn't be crooked now," Regina told him, hopping down from the seat of the curricle almost before Brady could set the brake.

He was after her in moments, once a groom had run to the heads of the horses. "It has occurred to you, hasn't it, that when we unmask Allerton as the one behind the murder attempt on me, your parents' story will come out as well?"

She stopped so quickly on the steps that he ran into her back. "No," she said, turning to look down at him, because he had retreated to the flagway. "My parents' names will never be brought into this. Not in public. Allerton tried to kill you for quite another reason entirely."

"Really?" Brady drawled, following after her as she turned to enter the mansion. "And what would that reason be?"

She turned on him once more, tears standing in her eyes, tears that maddened her because this man had driven her to them. And she thought he'd captured her heart? How could she have been so stupid? "The reason, my lord? Because you're an ass. What other reason could there be?"

"I'm sorry, Regina," Brady said, walking into her bedchamber two hours later, unannounced. He could have had himself announced, or knocked on the door and begged admittance, but, although he was now an "ass," he wasn't entirely stupid. Announcing his intention to enter her chamber would be the surest way of hearing the key turn in the lock, with himself standing on the wrong side of the door.

He watched as she turned away from her dressing table, a hairbrush still in her hand. Would she throw it at his head? He didn't think so, but still he kept his distance.

"I mean it, princess. I'm truly sorry. And you have every right to wish to preserve your good memories of your parents, and their good names."

"They didn't have good names, Brady," she told him, pulling the brush through her long, burnished curls. "They were players, remember? We don't have good names. We have reputations."

Brady rubbed at his forehead, wishing himself back in time, back to the point where he'd heard there was a mystery about Kipp and Abby's new housemaid. Knowing what he knew now, he'd never have gone to Little Woodcote, never would have asked questions, never would have lifted a finger in order to stick it into Regina Bliss's business.

He looked at her, felt his blood grow hot, even as it had the first time he'd seen her, every time he saw her. "No, that's not true. I would do it all again," he muttered, and Regina stood, walked toward him.

"You said something?" she asked, and he looked at her again, saw the servant girl, saw the woman she'd become. He saw those odd grey eyes that had first captured his interest because of the intelligence in them that she couldn't hide, the mischief always lurking there, peeking out at the world. He saw her hair, unbound and hanging past her shoulders; a living fire that he felt sure would be warm to the touch, if not hot enough to burn him.

Recovering himself and banishing thoughts that led round and round and to nowhere but trouble, Brady struck a pose and drawled, "La, princess, can't a man have a private discussion without interruption?"

"A private discussion?" Regina peeked behind him, smiled. "Oh, hello there," she said to nothing at all. "Please forgive me for not noticing you sooner. What a lovely little man you are, all green of face and blue of hair. Are you His Lordship's new page?"

"Very funny, very droll," Brady said, as Regina straightened, looked up at him again. "However, if you're quite through?"

"It wasn't me who was talking to myself, my lord," Regina pointed out, taking up the heavy length of her hair in both hands, then doing something magical with it so that it was suddenly twisted quite neatly on top of her head. The style showed to advantage the only faintly sharp, very clean line of her chin, the length of her smooth, white throat, tempting him to intimacies that would shock them both, if he were to give in to that temptation.

"Perhaps I was only bucking up my own courage, my dear. I've come to apologize, you see. Yet again. I know you're very protective of the memory of your parents. I know that, and yet I continue to push at you unmercifully, ask for answers I have no right to know."

"But you do have a right," Regina said, surprising him. "You nearly died, remember? And if you don't, I do, for I was with you, felt the heat of your fever, saw your bruises. Still, my first loyalty is to my parents. Mine was to be a private revenge, never made public. You want quite the opposite. If I tell you what Papa did? No, I can't do that to him. Because he never meant any real harm. Really, he didn't. It's just that we needed the money."

"Ah, now we're getting somewhere," Brady said, taking Regina's hand and leading her toward a pair of high-backed chairs arranged in front of the fireplace, urging her to sit down. "I don't want the details, princess, if you can't share them with me, but I need to know if your father made Allerton a victim, or if His Lordship was also up to no good. It's important that I know this, truly. Especially if I have to find another story to tell the world, rather than the real one."

Regina looked down at her fingertips, then folded her hands in her lap, peered up at Brady. Sighed. "His Lordship sold something he didn't actually have, believing he'd soon have it from Papa. His Lordship, believing Papa could deliver that something, also spent money not yet in his hand, went deeply into debt, and became quite . . . angry when Papa told him he needed more time to produce what His Lordship wanted, and more money to produce it. I heard him shouting all of this at Papa, right before Papa yelled to me to run away."

Brady sorted through Regina's words, trying to connect them to blackmail, jewels, secrets—anything that could be sold for profit. He settled on: "Blackmail? Secrets? Your father promised to gather information for Allerton and Allerton sold it—or used it to extort money from others?"

Regina sat back in her chair, her eyes wide. "My goodness, wherever did you get such an idea? Papa? Selling secrets? Don't be ridiculous. It wasn't secrets, it was—"

She shut her mouth with a snap, and Brady longed to reach for her, shake the answer out of her. "I promise not to say anything to anyone. Save Allerton, of course, if I find I need to do so. Just remember this, Regina. He'll be locked up for trying to murder me, but he and his friends would be hanged if we could prove they murdered your parents."

"Is that true? They won't hang for what they did to you?"

Brady wasn't positive, but that did sound reasonable. It took more to hang a peer than it did to swing a horse thief from the gallows. He pressed his advantage. "That's why you're still here with me, Regina. Not as bait, as you thought, but to tell your story when the time is right. I need the world to know Allerton is a murderer. I want the man to hang. I'm not even ashamed to say that I want the man and his two friends dead for what they did, to your parents, to me. Don't you?"

She closed her eyes, nodded. "All three of them deserve to be punished for their crime. But," she said, looking at him again, "not if it means exposing my father's small . . . business indiscretion."

"But then how were you going to punish him?"

"I'd planned to find Allerton and shoot him myself, or at least that's what I thought when I dreamed of revenge while sewing dolls for Cast-iron Gert. In truth, I'd probably be dead or worse by now if Lady Willoughby hadn't bought me, taken me home with her. By then I'd realized I'd need to bide my time, have enough money to live on, and then take my chance when it presented itself. I'd begun to think what I could do would be to become a maid in Allerton's service, and then go on from there. There was no rush, you understand. My parents are gone. If I had to wait years, I'd wait years."

"No, you wouldn't have," Brady said, contradicting her. "You're many things, princess, but I don't think you're patient."

"Perhaps. But once you became involved, well, I truly thought they'd hang for trying to kill you. That's why I agreed to help you. Oh, I'm so confused. Cosmo says—"

"Ah, good. I had hopes for him the moment I met him, which is why your friends are here today. What does Cosmo say?"

"He says I should tell you," Regina said, standing, beginning to pace. "He says we might want to get revenge on our own, and that our plans are wonderful, but that we'd never be able to put them into action. He says I'm too fanciful by half and that I should behave myself. He *says* that you deserve to know why you almost died."

"I knew I liked Cosmo," Brady said, dismissing the mental picture of the rotund man in satin gown and feathers.

Regina stopped pacing, squared her shoulders, lifted her chin.

Brady tried not to look too eager to hear what she had to say. So he lifted his quizzing glass by its riband and began idly swinging it back and forth. The picture of patience . . . while his heart beat at triple its normal speed.

"Tulips," she announced at last. "Papa was growing

tulips for the earl. There, I've told you. Now can we just get on with it?"

The quizzing glass dropped to his waist, unheeded. If Regina had said, "Papa was smuggling diamonds for the earl," Brady would have understood. He would have understood most anything. But *tulips*? He looked around the large room, then stood up, went to the vase on the table in front of the window, picked it up, brought it to Regina. "Tulips? You mean like these tulips? Regina, that makes no sense. Nobody's gone into a dither over tulips in years."

"But they used to," Regina said, touching one of the perfect pink blooms. "Papa told me all about it."

"Tulipmania," Brady said, returning the vase to the table. "I remember reading about it somewhere. Holland produced tulips that were sold all over the known world, bringing in prices for single roots that could beggar a man."

"They even traded in tulip futures, speculating on crops of the roots not yet harvested," Regina said, sitting in the chair in front of the fireplace once more, so that Brady also sat down. "The lowliest farmer dug up his yard and planted tulips, and fortunes were made. In Holland. Papa told me of one English trader he'd read about, a man who paid one-half of his entire fortune for a single root. And all he did was plant it in his conservatory and invite his friends in to see it."

"It was a mad time," Brady agreed. "But that was when—the 1600s? A long time ago, Regina. Now everyone has tulips, as the Dutch couldn't keep the market cornered forever."

"That's true. Although there are still some tulips that bring up to two hundred pounds apiece, for those willing to pay. Papa loved tulips," she said, smiling sadly. "At least half of our wagon was filled with pots of them. When they were in bloom, he'd arrange the pots around the stage while we performed, he was that proud of them."

Her smile faded. "Then the earl of Allerton came to one of our performances about three years ago. He'd been in the country to witness a boxing match, or some such thing, and he and his friends decided to see our performance."

Brady scratched at a spot behind his left ear, unwilling to admit that he still didn't understand much of what Regina was telling him. "Go on," he said at last, when she didn't speak.

She lifted her shoulders, dropped them on a sigh. "After the performance, the earl took Papa to one side and tried to buy his tulips. Papa sold him three or four of his most unusual roots, I forget how many, but then Papa started talking about his hopes for a new tulip, the one that would change the world of tulips forever. His Lordship was very interested and paid Papa so that he could continue his experiments, as long as he, Allerton, would be the one to produce the tulip in quantity and sell it to the world."

"Allerton? Selling posies? No, I'm sorry, Regina. There has to be more to it than that."

"Not if you knew that Papa promised His Lordship a black tulip," Regina said, almost mumbling the words.

At last, Brady understood. "A *black* tulip? Really? But there's no such thing, is there?"

Regina got to her feet once more, so that Brady also had to stand up, follow her as she walked across the room to look out the window overlooking the square. "No, Brady, there isn't. There is no such thing as a black tulip. There never was, and there probably never will be. Except, of course, for the one Papa showed His Lordship two years ago on one of our visits to Little Woodcote to pick up more funds for his experiments."

She turned from the window, tears shining in her eyes, and spoke quickly, as if she wanted to get past her father's duplicity as rapidly as possible. "I don't know what he did. Dipped it in ink—something—but Papa left our wagon carrying what he insisted was a true black tulip and came back two hours later, his purse heavy, and with a smile on his face so huge I thought his cheeks would crack. He was so pleased with himself, telling us how he'd promised to reproduce his miracle a hundredfold by the following spring. We needed a new wagon, you understand, as ours was nearly falling apart after so many years on the road. A larger wagon, to have more space for Papa's experiments. We needed money, and Papa got us money."

"Now I think I'm beginning to understand."

"Oh, Brady, Papa was so happy, right up until the moment when I asked him how sure he was that he could give the earl the hundred black tulips he promised to deliver to him this past spring, every single root to be worth at least the same, if not more than the yield from twenty acres of standing corn. A fortune, Brady, and only the beginning of a greater fortune. He had no answer for me, of course. Papa didn't always plan too far ahead."

At last Brady saw it all, even if what he saw was leagues from anything he'd imagined. In fact, if Regina weren't crying even as she spoke, he'd believe she was handing him another whopping great fairy tale. "So last spring, when you returned to Little Woodcote, the earl was expecting a delivery of one hundred black tulips?"

"Yes, yes, yes," Regina said. "Not just roots, but tulips attached to those roots. They bloom naturally in the spring, you know, just like those over there, on the table. His Lordship wanted to see them in natural bud and bloom, sell them in bud and bloom to the buyers he had waiting in Holland and elsewhere—buyers who had already advanced funds to Allerton—because otherwise no one would believe him. And who would? People had been trying to produce a black tulip for over two hundred years, without success."

"But there were no hundred black tulips to show him, were there? I can see that your father had a problem," Brady said. "How did he intend to handle it? I mean, he could have just not shown up in Little Woodcote. Truth to tell, it seems the easiest way out of a fairly dangerous dilemma, since Allerton had been his banker, plus recklessly spending his own and other people's money all over London in anticipation of recouping a fortune for himself and, I suppose, at least two of his friends."

"Papa didn't know all of that, he didn't know that Allerton had problems of his own. He just thought he could ask for more time, another year to recover from the mysterious blight that had destroyed the roots of all the black tulips he'd been prepared to present to His Lordship. Papa," Regina said, wiping at her tears with the handkerchief Brady handed her, "thought he could talk his way around *anything*. And talking had worked, for nearly three years. I guess he had no reason to think it wouldn't work again. He wouldn't have taken Mama and me with him to Little Woodcote, had he thought otherwise."

"No, of course he wouldn't have done that," Brady said, patting her shoulder. At his touch, she gave out with a small, hiccuping sob, and he pulled her against his chest, rubbed his hands up and down her back as he stared at the pink blossoms in front of the window. "Tulips," he said, trying to digest all he'd learned. "I was beaten up, my bones broken, and damned near drowned—over a bloody bunch of tulips . . ."

"I'm sorry," Regina said against the lapels of his frock coat. "Now that I think about it, I suppose you'd rather it had been secrets?"

"Or diamonds," Brady said consideringly, then snapped himself to attention, because he suddenly realized that he was holding Regina in his arms, and enjoying the sensations that caused very much—or as much as his dratted tight pantaloons would allow. He put his hands on her waist and pushed her away from him a few inches, let his arms fall to his sides.

Regina tipped back her head, and asked, "Brady, are you all right? You're upset, aren't you? I suppose I would be, too, if I thought somebody wanted to kill me because of a flower."

"Well, not to worry," he said, prudently hiding behind

his imaginary cousin, Gawain. He wheeled about smartly on his heels and walked over to pluck a single pink tulip from the vase, break off half its stem, and tuck the flower into his buttonhole. "But I do believe my lord Singleton has discovered just the accessory he needs to become the sartorial darling of the *ton*."

"The sartorial laughingstock, you mean," Regina said, touching a finger to the already drooping flower. "It's too big to wear on your coat. Everyone will laugh at you."

Brady breathed in Regina's delicate perfume, telling himself that the last thing he needed was another complication in his plans, especially not now, when at last he saw some hope of success. "*Au contraire*, princess. Not everyone will laugh. And that's the whole point, isn't it?"

Chapter Eleven

He wore the embroidered violet satin, the same ludicrous rigout Regina had seen on him at Singleton Chase the day Watkins had come to the countryside to present the earl with his new wardrobe.

Only now he wore it . . . better.

It was still ludicrous; white-on-white embroidered-satin waistcoat, amethyst buttons, gold shoe buckles and all. And yet now Brady wore the clothes with a sangfroid that amazed her. He *strolled* now, rather than minced across the room, and his step was steady, with no betraying wobbliness around his ankles as he fought the red heels on his shoes.

He carried his lace handkerchief with a lazy indifference to the thing dangling from his hand, and when he lifted his quizzing glass to his eye he did it with an arrogance that would have anyone he peered at through its horribly magnifying lens wanting either to sink into oblivion or call him out for pistols at dawn.

And the trio of barely opening pink tulips pinned to his lapel with a diamond-studded bar was just the crowning touch he'd needed to make his the unique presence in any room.

That he was still, with his long hair clubbed at his nape with a lilac-satin bow, the most handsome man she'd ever seen, was something Regina preferred not to think about.

He touched a hand to the black-satin band on his upper left arm as Regina walked with him to the carriage that would take them to the theater (Cosmo, in his role of Matilda Forrest, chaperone, brought up the rear in a rather subdued brown gown, but with three small ostrich feathers stuck into his turban). "It has been some months since my dear cousin cocked up his toes, but I am aware of the niceties, you see," he told her.

"Many would say that you should be doing more to remember your cousin, my lord," Regina told him. "It has been some months, as you say, but traditional mourning lasts a year, I believe."

"True, true, although it's rude of you to point out any lapse in my behavior as I am horribly sensitive to insult. By rights, I suppose I should be dressed all in black, but that's such a depressing color, don't you think? Surely this armband is sufficient, especially as I never even knew the fellow. Satin, of course, and made specially for me by Watkins. Good man, Watkins, although I must remind him to be a tad more generous with the material when next I require his services. I cannot imagine straddling a horse in anything now residing in my clothespress, for example, not without shocking the ladies when my seams split, can you?"

"Oh, I don't know," Regina said, arranging her skirts around her and smiling down at her new kid slippers, that were so very comfortable. "I should think you might enjoy shocking the ladies, dear Gawain. And everyone else. Now, if we're done telling you how wonderful you look, do you think you could spare a moment to compliment me on my gown?" she asked, touching a hand to the long strand of pearls around her neck. "Maude says I look splendid."

"And fair Maude would be correct," Brady told her, waving a languid hand as Cosmo heaved himself onto the facing seat, straining even the well-sprung springs of His Lordship's fine carriage, then immediately began to fan himself. "Although if you're truly open to suggestion, you might consider stuffing this handkerchief into the neckline?"

Cosmo snorted, then bowed his head.

Regina put her hands to her chest. "Why? Is it too low? Maude said so, but Madame Elizabeth assured me—oh, you *wretch*! I'm dressed in the height of Continental fashions. Madam Elizabeth showed me the pattern cards she'd received from Paris. Why did you say that to me?"

"I have no idea, my dear. Perhaps I'm a mean, mean man. You should probably just ignore me."

"And I'll ignore the both of you," Cosmo said, looking at them from overtop his fan. "But if any lascivious rascal dares to pinch me, my lord, I expect you to call him out."

"I'll do that, Mrs. Forrest," Brady agreed. "Whalebone swords at twenty paces. Would that be acceptable to you?"

"That would be splendid, my lord," Cosmo agreed.

Regina looked at Brady, still smarting over his remark about her neckline and trying to make out his expression in the dimness of the interior of the carriage. "I'll never understand you. *Either* of you—and, no, Matilda, I don't mean you," she said honestly, then sat back against the squabs, remaining silent until the carriage came to a halt in front of Covent Garden Theater.

The last time Regina had seen this place she had been acting the role of a blind, crippled beggar for Cast-iron Gert, living hand to mouth and rapidly losing hope. Now here she was, clean and well dressed, well fed, and about to enter society. It was mind-boggling.

London citizens without the wherewithal to purchase tickets for the performance, but with their usual inquisitiveness when it came to watching the *ton* at its amusements, lined the flagway as Regina took Brady's hand and stepped down from their carriage.

If there were "oohs!" and "aahs!" for her appearance from an admiring throng of at least thirty bystanders, they were swallowed up by the near raucous—no, definitely raucous—reaction to Brady, who already stood on the flagway in all his lilac splendor.

"Coo, would ya clap yer peepers on that one," Regina heard quite clearly. "Ain't he a treat, now."

"Pretty boy, pretty boy," came another voice from somewhere to Regina's left, followed by the unmistakable sounds of lips being smacked together, kissing the air. "Love a duck, but that's a queer nabs if ever Oi saw one."

"Wot, yer blind? Not wi' that package twixt 'is legs, 'e

ain't," a female voice cried out clearly. "First poke's free fer yer, lovey!"

"Why are you still standing here?" Regina asked, trying to talk without moving her lips. "Let's go inside before you start a riot."

"I must agree, my lord," Cosmo said, straightening his turban after his near tumble from the carriage. "Unless you see an opportunity here, which I believe I might."

"You, too, Mrs. Forrest?" Brady asked, winking at the man. "Gawain Caradoc should not arrive quietly, should he?"

"Definitely not, my lord," Cosmo declared.

"If you'd both just stop talking and move on?" Regina whispered again, feeling nervous. After all, she had lived with denizens such as these. She knew how quickly they could turn from amusement to violence.

"In a moment," Brady whispered back at her, then slipped out of her grip on his arm, stepped forward a single pace. He smiled broadly, held on to the lace-edged handkerchief with two fingers even as he removed his snow-white curly-brimmed beaver (banded with lilac satin, of course), and then delivered an elegant leg first to the group of bystanders to his right, then another to those on his left.

He then took hold of Regina 's hand, squeezing it as he said, "Curtsy, princess. Smile and curtsy to your approving admirers. After all, we didn't come to London to hide under a bushel basket."

"Oh, I give up. All right, I'll do it." Never one to say no to the thought of taking her bows in front of an audience, Regina promptly held out her left arm, holding on to the skirt of her palest pink gown, and dropped into a curtsy fit to honor royalty.

She rose again, just as gracefully, turned, and repeated her curtsy, her head bent low for a moment before grinning straight into the face of—good Lord, Cast-iron Gert! How strange life was. You went round and round, but even when the circles traveled over each other, each circuit proved different than the last. Once she'd been dependent on the quite unlovable and often mean Cast-iron Gert, and now the woman was yelling to her, her hand out, pleading with her to toss a few coppers her way.

"Ladies and gentlemen," Brady called out, his voice immediately silencing his audience. "I appreciate your welcome to the finest city on this earth—London. Allow me to introduce myself. I am Ga-*wain* Caradoc, Earl of Singleton, and this magnificent lady is my ward, Miss Regina Felicity. We love you all, London citizens! And now I shall have my esteemed coachman distribute coins to each and every one of you. Rooster!" he called out as he reached into his pocket. "Come take this purse, if you please."

"I think that's enough," Regina said around her smile as the ragtag crowd broke into loud cheers and began pushing toward poor Rooster from both sides of the flagway. Brady must have agreed, for he led her into the theater, Cosmo following along behind, past the openly disapproving eyes of at least fifty members of the *ton*.

Brady bowed to each of them as they passed by, barely imperceptible inclinations of his head as if these were his subjects and he their ruler.

"Caradoc?" Regina heard someone say. "That's what he said, wasn't it? Never heard of the man."

"The new earl of Singleton, Boothe, old man, ain't you got ears? Heard he was in the park today, with Singleton's horses. Sally Jersey's all a-twitter about it."

"I don't care. Man's a twit. Anybody can see that." The man who had been addressed as Boothe now raised his voice so that everyone could hear. "And who's the doxy with him?"

Regina's blood froze as Brady halted, slowly turned, already raising his quizzing glass to his eye.

"Don't," Regina begged quietly. "I don't care what he said."

"Ah, but I do, princess, I do. I do," Brady told her just as quietly. "Mrs. Forrest? If you would be so good as to locate someone familiar with this establishment, so that Miss Felicity and yourself can then be escorted to the relative sanity of the duke of Selbourne's private box? I fear I must stay behind, to step on a particularly offensive bug."

Regina rolled her eyes. "Your seams are too tight for stepping on bugs, my lord," she told him in a whisper, so that no one else could hear. Then she said, more loudly, "Perhaps this is a good time to take the high road?"

Brady leaned down to whisper in her ear. "The man who spoke, princess, is Boothe Kenward. Allerton's whelp. Opportunities such as this don't come waltzing down the lane all that often."

Regina gave a slight shiver, then lifted her chin, spoke loudly and clearly. "Oh, very well, Uncle Gawain. But it's all so fatiguing. We'll have to burn your evening slippers, and I know how fond of them you are."

"Brava, Regina," Brady said quietly, motioning for her to follow Cosmo, who had already commandeered a young man in livery, obviously a person employed by the theater. "Although, if His Grace is already upstairs, you might want to send him down. I do have a fondness for my back, and would like someone to watch it for me."

Then he turned to face Boothe Kenward, whom Regina recognized immediately from Brady's description. Tall, too thin, blond, and with a look to him of a man who knows he's not quite all he should be but hopes the world might overlook that fact.

She allowed Cosmo to escort her toward the stairs, then stopped. "You go ahead, Matilda, and fetch the duke if he's handy. I'm staying here."

"But—"

"Don't argue, Matilda, or I'll snatch off that silly turban and then no one will even remember that His Lordship was about to get himself killed," Regina said warningly, and Cosmo shrugged, quickly turned, and mounted the wide stairs, following the servant.

Viscount Allerton still stood at the side of the large lobby, but his friend had distanced himself by at least six feet, as had everyone else, although no one had left the crowded lobby, as they'd all sniffed out the possibility of a show to rival that soon to be presented onstage.

As Regina watched, Brady approached the friend. "Excuse me, my good sir. Would you be so kind as to inform your companion that Ga-wain Caradoc, Earl of Singleton, thinks he's a horse's ass? I'd do it myself, but to so much as look at such an ill-favored specimen would most probably upset my delicate stomach. There's a good fellow."

"Why, you—" Viscount Allerton said, stepping forward, his hands clenched into fists.

"Oh, very well," Brady said, sighing deeply even as he turned, struck a pose, his quizzing glass stuck to his eye. He looked the Viscount up and down, then nodded. "Yes, it's just as I feared." He let the quizzing glass drop, turning to face the center of the lobby. "Would anyone have a peppermint? I'd carry my own, save it would ruin the fine cut of my waistcoat. So soothing to the stomach, peppermint, you understand. I'd be most grateful."

"Turn around, Singleton, and face me like a man," the Viscount demanded.

"Oh, *must* I?" Brady drawled, sighing. "I'd much rather you simply apologize, then crawl away to your cave until you learn some manners. Or perhaps you could introduce me to your sire? As the distinguished Robert Burton wrote with such stunning wisdom, 'Diogenes struck the father when the son misbehaved.' "

"That's swore," the Duke of Selbourne said, giving Regina's shoulder a quick pat before walking past her, toward Brady. " 'Diogenes struck the father when the son *swore*.' Forgive me for correcting you, my friend, but I thought I should clarify that. Good evening to you, Kenward. Have you and the earl been introduced?"

"We were just doing that, yes." Brady took out his snuffbox, tapped the lid once with his index finger, then flipped it open, offering it to the viscount. "Some of my private sort, my lord?"

"I wouldn't touch—" the viscount began, only to be cut off by something Brady said to him, something he said so quietly that only the viscount heard.

Still, obviously, he'd heard enough, for after only a moment more of hesitation, he dipped thumb and forefinger into the offered snuff, then lifted it to his nose.

What followed was a string of sneezes so profound that several people began to giggle.

Brady, watching the viscount all but crying into his handkerchief, dipped his own thumb and forefinger into the small box, lifted his fingers to his right nostril, and made quite a business over inhaling the snuff. "Ah," he then said, smiling. "So very mild. A quite innocuous sort, specially mixed for me. Don't you agree, my lord Allerton?"

Boothe Kenward, Viscount Allerton, was now red-faced, tears streaming down his cheeks. "Oh . . . quite," he choked out before sneezing three more times in quick succession.

"We shouldn't keep the ladies waiting, my friend," the duke of Selbourne said then, and he and Brady bowed to the viscount and his companion, then turned and walked toward the stairs, the sound of sneezes . . . and laughter . . . following them.

"Now here's a naughty puss," Brady said, extending his arm so that Regina took it. "I believe you were asked to proceed to His Grace's private box."

"Did you believe that I would?" she countered as she lifted her skirts an inch and started up the stairs.

"Not for a moment," Brady told her.

"What did you say to him, my lord?" Regina asked,

unable to wait until they were seated to hear what had been said. "He turned white, then red, then white again."

Speaking so that only the duke and Regina could hear him, Brady told her, "I pointed out to him that he could either be a very good boy and take snuff with me, or I could slap his ignorant face, publicly challenge him to a duel, and laugh as I then splashed his brains all over the dueling field."

"There were a few other words in that statement, as I recall, rather descriptive words," His Grace said.

"Ah, yes, but none of them for polite company, now were there?" Brady answered with a smile. "In addition, I know that the dear viscount is a coward of the first water. That did help. Now to hope that figuratively boxing the son's ears brings the father out where I can see him. Oh, and Bram? Please allow me to take this moment to remind you never to take me up on an offer of snuff. Not unless you first line your nostrils with lead."

Regina stopped dead on the first landing. "You lined your nostrils with lead?" she asked, peering up at him, trying to look inside his nose. "Is that why you didn't sneeze?"

"Hardly, princess, but Thomas did teach me his tricks on the taking of snuff—or the *not* taking of it, I should say—and then I went a step further in filling my snuff-boxes with the very worst sort Rogers could find. I'm not a nice man, princess. Remember that."

His Grace laughed out loud. "You do know that every idiot in London will be asking to partake of your sort, just to prove that they're as much a man as you are, and won't sneeze."

"That's terrible," Regina said seriously, and then laughed. "Oh, that's really, really terrible! I can only hope the play is half so good."

Leaving Regina behind with Sophie and the softly snoring Matilda Forrest, Brady and His Grace walked along the wide corridor during intermission, Bram introducing the new earl of Singleton to anyone who wished to be presented.

Everyone wanted to be presented.

"That's Ga-Ga-Ga-*wain*," Brady said as he bowed over Sally Jersey's faintly grubby paw after Bram had introduced them. "The Round Table, chivalry, jousting, riding to the rescue of fair damsels in distress—my personal favorite, that. Ga-*wain*. Romantical, ain't it?"

Brady was pleased that Lady Jersey, known as Silence because of her inability to keep silent, just stood there, clearly at a loss for words.

He turned to her companion, Sir Henry Cox, looking at him through his quizzing glass. He had to be careful around Sir Henry, who had known him for years. "My God, man, but you look familiar. Something about the eyes, I think. Do I know you?"

"I was just thinking the same thing, my lord," Sir Henry replied, holding on to Brady's hand just a little too long, in Brady's opinion. "Perhaps during the war?"

Brady lifted a hand to his mouth, delicately coughed into his handkerchief. "The war? Oh, I don't think so, sir. Most of that . . ." he hesitated, waved his hand in a circle as if searching for a word, ". . . that sordid *business* took place in Spain and even Portugal, I believe? Damp there, I've heard. No, that can't be it. I'd never go there."

"But you haven't been here, in England," Sir Henry persisted, and Brady wanted to stuff his handkerchief in the man's mouth, shut him up.

"Not for years, no. It is, you understand, so much more economical for a man of social ambition and little funds to make his splash on the Continent. Have you been to Paris? Perhaps we met there? I do so adore Paris, but when word came that I was now the earl? Well, a man of social ambition and ample funds can do very well in London, can't he?"

"Paris?" Sir Henry persisted. "Even during the war?"

Yes, you inquisitive twit, even during the war, Brady grumbled inside his head. But outside his head, he only smiled, winked, and said quietly, a sudden fierceness in his tone, "There are many ways of fighting a war, good sir." Then he quickly held up his hands. "But, no. We will not discuss that. Will we, Sir Henry? We will discuss the play. Isn't it marvelous? The aim of those wonderful creatures sitting up near the rafters, I mean, as well as that of those standing in the pit. Seldom have I seen fruit and vegetables launched with such stunning accuracy."

When Sir Henry and Lady Jersey had moved along— so many people to see, so many people one wanted to see them—Bram said, "You've got Cox thinking you were a spy. He'll whisper that to Sally, who will whisper it to the world, and by tomorrow you'll be that splendid man in the height of fashion, and you'll have so many invitations you won't know what to do with them."

"Yes, it is working out well, isn't it?" Brady said, stopping to take snuff, neatly flipping open the lid with one hand. He offered the box to the duke.

"I think not," Bram said, laughing. "At least not until you teach me your little trick. I could have sworn you sniffed some of the stuff."

"I'll send Thomas round tomorrow, to instruct you. Two of us not sneezing will have every idiot in town begging some of my sort, and then sneezing themselves into next week. Did it ever occur to you, friend, just how silly our society is?"

"You already knew that, my friend, and I believe we've already had this discussion."

"True, but I never knew it as well as when I thought I was about to die. My life passed before me, and there wasn't much to see, and few to mourn me. It was sobering, to say the least."

"You know what you need, don't you?"

"Other than to go someplace private and pull at a certain pinching seam before my voice rises another octave?"

Bram laughed. "Yes, other than that. You need a wife, my friend, a wife and a few pink-cheeked children running about, calling you Papa."

"You and Kipp," Brady said, shaking his head. "You do know Abby's increasing, don't you?"

"Yes, and don't change the subject. I've seen the way you look at our Miss Felicity. Does she share your feelings?"

Brady felt his jaw tighten. "Now is neither the time nor the place, but, dear friend—are you out of your mind?"

"Why? Because she's an actress? My own Sophie was the daughter of a—well, you know that story. We all of us have titles, *Gawain*, but that doesn't make us particularly laudable, does it? In fact, she might not have you. You are making a bit of a cake of yourself you know, even if it is for the best of reasons."

Brady did his small trick with the snuffbox, just to occupy his hands. "She's the most maddening creature," he said after a moment. "Part child, part woman, part imp, and with this unreasoning belief that the truth is something one tells only if one's back is to the wall and no suitable lie can be found. Plus, she doesn't yet fully trust me."

"Really? That would make it difficult to court her, if she doesn't trust you, that is. Perhaps that's because you've told a few great fibs of your own?"

"Not to *her*, damn it," Brady said with some feeling, surprising himself with his own vehemence. "My God, I must be in love with her. Why else would I care if she's telling me lies?"

"Because you're incurably nosy?" Bram suggested. "That is how you ended up in the Thames, isn't it?"

Brady nodded. "Yes. Yes, of course. I'm incurably nosy. That's all it is. I can't abide secrets. It isn't love at all. What a relief."

"Now who's telling lies?" Bram asked, then stepped forward to greet yet another hopeful member of the *ton* who had come to beg an introduction to the new earl of Singleton.

A moment later Brady was being introduced to three gentlemen he'd played cards with until dawn more than a dozen times, and not one eye flickered with a single hint of anything save curiosity about the new earl. Either, Brady decided, his disguise was excellent, or he'd lived his life surrounded by idiots and not realized that fact.

"So you're the new earl, eh?" the Honorable Richard Simeon said.

"True enough, sir," Brady replied, bowing. "I'm the new earl. It was a wonderful surprise."

"So terrible about your cousin, what?" Baron Triplett said, pumping on Brady's hand.

"Well, yes, that too, of course. Such a sad loss. My gain, you understand, but a sad loss."

"I think it's criminal that his murder was never solved," Mr. William Vimes put in, shaking his head. "It's not safe to walk the streets of our own city."

"Murdered?" Brady said, stepping back a pace in shock. "How dreadful! Why wasn't I told?" He stepped forward once more, quizzing glass stuck to his eye, and glared at Mr. Vimes. "Are you quite convinced then that it wasn't suicide? I'm sure more than one man has tucked himself up inside a sack and tossed himself into the water."

Mr. Vimes, indeed all three men, looked at Brady as if he were insane. "The sack was tied up with chains, and Selbourne here tells us your cousin had been beaten."

"Oh, very well then. But still . . . no, I suppose not." Brady sighed. "There is someone looking into this sad affair, I assume? At least one of you good men, friends of my cousin? You've been working diligently to bring his murderer to justice?"

The three men exchanged glances. "Us?" Baron Triplett asked. "But wouldn't that be up to you?"

Brady pressed both hands against his chest. "Me?" he exclaimed, horrified. "Good gracious, no. Why should I? I didn't even know the man."

The not so Honorable Mr. Richard Simeon shrugged, looked at his friends. "I suppose he's got a point. But why haven't we done anything? Brady was a good enough sort. Maybe we could all chip in some blunt, hire on a Bow Street Runner?"

"Didn't like him that much," Baron Triplett muttered, and Mr. Vimes nodded his agreement.

"I say, Selbourne, what about you?" Mr. Vimes asked. "You and Brady were close as inkleweavers, as I remember it."

"Yes, but I didn't really *like* him," the duke of Selbourne said, holding his expression to one of careful neutrality. "He was more my wife's friend."

"Yes, yes," Mr. Vimes said. "Brady was always one for the ladies. Ah, I don't care what anyone says, I miss him."

"And I'm sure he misses you, in his way," Brady said as the three men wandered off. "Well, that was enlightening, wasn't it? And all three of them ate their heads off at my funeral. You know, Bram, I'm beginning to think I should have done this years ago. I never knew how disliked I am."

"Not disliked, Brady," Bram said, taking his arm and leading him back to the private box. "But we are, as a sex, more caught up in ourselves than we are with the world around us. At least until we're married, that is. I fear I was nearly as shallow until I finally was brought to understand exactly what is important in this world."

"No homilies now, please, my friend," Brady told him. "I'm in the mood for revenge for being half-beaten to death and then thrown into the Thames, nothing more than that."

"Are you sure? Are you sure that's all that's driving you? Because you could have stopped this at any time, long before coming to London dressed up like a Christmas pudding. All it would have taken would be for you to present yourself with some story of being nursed back to health by some kindly soul until you'd regained your wits, and about having had your ring stolen before you were tossed into the Thames. That would explain how I had come to identify quite the wrong body. An idea borne of fever and fear did not have to drag on this long, to put you where you are now. Now tell me you never thought about that."

"Yes, I've thought about it. I was going to send her away, almost immediately, and do pretty much what you've just said. But the sons of bitches murdered her parents, Bram," Brady said through gritted teeth. "She was forced to work as a beggar right here, in Covent Garden, pretending to be blind, living each day wondering if this would be the one in which someone would realize she wasn't the child she pretended to be—not that being a child would protect her from the worst of this city's monsters. If it weren't for Abby and Kipp, God only knows what would have happened to her by now. And all because of Allerton and his friends."

"I see," Bram said quietly.

"Do you? Do you really?" Brady asked. "Do you see how *special* she is? I did. The moment she walked into Kipp's study that first day. I knew instantly. There was something about her, something in her eyes. When Kipp told me she was just a child, I tried to forget what I'd seen and concentrate on learning more about her. Helping her if I could."

"Which got you tossed into the Thames."

"Which was most probably the luckiest thing that ever happened to me," Brady corrected, shaking his head. "I'm dressed up—as a Christmas pudding, I think you said—because of her. I'm mincing about London, learning I'm not quite as lovable as I thought I was, because of her." He ran a hand through his hair in a very un-Gawain-like gesture. "God, Bram, I'm going in circles, even as I finally admit this much to you, even as I'm now admitting it to myself for the first time. That's what I'm doing, Bram. Going in circles until I'm dizzy. Round and round and round, not knowing if my head is up or down."

"Talk to Sophie," Bram said, putting his arm around his shoulder. "Talk to Sophie, my friend. She's very good at this sort of problem."

"Are you mad? Hand myself over to your matchmaking wife? I thought you were my friend."

"I am your friend," the duke of Selbourne said, laughing. "Good God, man, you're wearing lilac satin. If I weren't your friend, I wouldn't be within fifty feet of you. Now come on, it's time to rejoin the ladies."

Chapter Twelve

$\mathcal{S}$ophie says—"

"Sophie? She asked you to call her Sophie? Now that's dangerous."

"Why?" Regina handed her wrap to a footman and followed Brady into the drawing room. They'd come directly back to Portman Square after the theater, as they had no invitations to any private parties, a lack Sophie had assured her would be corrected by the morning thanks to Brady's outrageous behavior. In fact, the only disappointment of the evening was that the earl of Allerton's box was empty all evening, save for his son and his son's friend.

She watched as Brady went to the drinks table, poured himself a glass of wine, then a half glass for her when she looked at him expectantly.

"Why? Because, princess, if Sophie sees you as her new friend, she's going to stick her nose entirely too far into our business."

"Well, that's only what you think," Regina said, accepting the glass as she sat down on one of the couches. "I'll have you know that Sophie and her children are leaving the city tomorrow on an extended visit to my former employers, the viscount and viscountess of Willoughby. Much as she loves the Season, Sophie says her children need some time in the country."

"Really? Bram didn't say anything to me about any trip."

"Oh, he's not going. Sophie says he has to stay here, to watch out for you so that you don't do anything too silly."

"How the love of my friends and their high opinion of my abilities do comfort me," Brady said, tossing back the contents of his glass. "Would I dare to suggest that you accompany Sophie tomorrow?"

Regina resisted the urge to bite her bottom lip, that suddenly attempted to tremble. Why was he constantly searching for ways to be rid of her? Was her presence that terrible for him? "No, my lord. I really don't think you should. I'd just find my way back."

Brady sighed theatrically, then said, "Oh, the devil with it. Wadsworth! Get in here, if you please."

As if he'd been listening at the door for just such a summons, the butler entered the drawing room, bowed. "There is a bellpull in the corner, my lord, but if you wish to bellow, I suppose you are within your rights as earl. Although your mother wouldn't have approved."

"Thank you, Wadsworth," Brady bit out, walking toward the man. "Here, help me out of this damn contraption."

"I'll summon Rogers, my lord."

"You'll help me now before you see me fall on the floor in a dead faint for lack of breath," Brady said, turning his back on Wadsworth so that the man could help him shrug out of the tight-fitting evening coat. "Ah, that's better," he then said on a sigh. "Thank you, Wadsworth. I can't tell you how much better I feel."

"And I'd rather you didn't, my lord," the butler said as Regina giggled into her wineglass. "Now, if there is nothing else? Perhaps you'd like me to scurry upstairs and fetch your slippers in my teeth?"

"Would you do that?" Brady asked, winking at Regina as Wadsworth drew himself up straight and left the drawing room in a huff.

"Why did you do that?" Regina asked, as Brady unbuttoned his waistcoat and sat down on the facing couch. "You embarrassed him."

"Hardly. I shooed him away from the door without calling him a nosy, eavesdropping nanny," Brady pointed out. "Now, back to our conversation. Did you enjoy yourself tonight, princess?"

She looked at him as he stripped off his high neckcloth and opened the top of his pristine white shirt. He looked so relaxed now, hardly the dandy he played at the theater. And she did so admire the way that one errant lock of chin-length hair caressed his cheek. "I did. Are you comfortable? A better question—does Wadsworth think I should be here with you while you're being comfortable?"

"Actually, no, but I couldn't stand myself another moment, and I wanted to speak to you before you went upstairs. We barely had a moment to ourselves all evening, and I wanted to know if anything about Viscount Allerton seemed at all familiar to you."

She shook her head. "I already told you. None of the three men was blond. And they were all older by at least twenty or more years." Then she looked at him more closely. "Were you trying to catch me in a lie?"

"In another lie, you mean? No, princess, not really."

She tipped her head, arched one eyebrow.

"Oh, all right, all right," Brady agreed, getting to his feet, carrying his empty wineglass back to the drinks table. "I should just believe that you've told me everything, shouldn't I?"

Regina inspected her fingertips, thinking back on her last discussion with Cosmo and Thomas, and the hopes that conversation had raised in her heart. "That would be nice . . ." she said, her words trailing off.

"But not practical," Brady said, taking up a stance in front of the fireplace. "I didn't think so. Ah, well, shall we move on to other things?"

"Yes, my lord. Why don't we do that." Regina felt terrible, knowing that Brady was disappointed in her. Still, if he knew what she now hoped, would he keep her in London with him? No, he wouldn't. He'd made it very plain as to why he needed her, and if that reason did not exist, she would no longer be necessary to him. And if he wouldn't keep her here, then she had no chance, none at all, of learning whether or not her friends' notions had even a glimmer of being accurate. She was capable of many things, she was sure, but without the earl's support, she wouldn't have one chance in a million of success, not on her own.

Brady left his place in front of the mantel and began to pace, looking splendid in his shirtsleeves, his hair no longer bound by the lilac-satin ribbon, but hanging straight around his face, making him look like a drawing she'd once seen of a pirate walking his deck on the high seas—not, she felt sure, that many pirates wore lilac-satin breeches. She watched him, knowing that she fell deeper under his spell with every footstep he took. And she didn't care. She just wanted to keep looking at him.

"It's this ghost thing, princess," he said as he paced behind the facing couch. "Much as it pains me to admit it, I could do a lot worse than to apply for your assistance in just how best to carry it off." He stopped pacing, turned to look at her. "I suppose I could apply to one of your cohorts, but I think they already know enough of my business, don't you?"

Regina bit at her knuckle, considering his question. "None of them would betray you in any way, you know," she said at last, and smiled when he nodded his agreement. "That said, I don't think Cosmo would be your best choice."

"He's a little too substantial ever to have played a ghost in any of your productions?"

"That was tactful, my lord, but yes, you're right. David is too silly, and Thomas has already taught you how to seem to float as you walk. You do that quite well, by the way."

"I'd thank you, but I'm still trying to decide if I should be flattered by that compliment, or horrified."

"Be flattered, my lord. You were magnificent tonight. Half the *ton* hates you, and the rest think you're a marvelous oddity—and all of them are interested. So much better for your purposes than to be cold and aloof, or to fade into the background. Why, Sophie says you'll be served up for breakfast all across Mayfair."

"Including, we hope, in the Allerton household," Brady said, walking around the couch to sit down once more, his body leaning forward, toward her. "I want this over, Regina," he said with an intensity that momentarily frightened her. "I want to get on with my life—*my* life, Regina."

"Yes, of course you do, my lord," Regina said, her mood drifting dangerously close to self-pity, for when Gawain was gone and Brady got on with his life, she would have no part in it. "So it's best that we begin."

"By tomorrow, we'll have several invitations to choose from, and by tomorrow night we should have a good idea of just who Allerton's friends are. Being older, he travels in different circles, and I never paid that much attention to him."

"And then you'll make one of these friends a visit."

"Hopefully only one, but we may not be lucky the first time."

"You're still planning on sneaking into their houses, confronting them in their beds? I really don't think that's a good idea, you know."

"Oh, princess, I've already given that up as a bad job. I'll accost them on the street, just as they did with me. And I probably will include Cosmo and the others, since you're right, I do trust them." Brady sat back, gave a wave of his hand—Gawain and Brady melding into each other for a moment. She wondered if he realized how natural it had become for him to slip back and forth between the two roles.

"Not everyone is so foolish as to walk the streets of London alone at night, my lord," she pointed out reasonably.

"Oh, not to worry, I'm sure I'll be able to think of something to get around that small problem." Another wave of his hand followed that statement, this time one meant to dismiss her paltry concerns, and irrationally making her want to box his ears.

How *annoying* Gawain Caradoc could be. She wanted this over just as much as he did, for her own reasons now, and also because the man was probably making *new* enemies all over London, enemies who wouldn't soon forget that he'd made cakes of them all as he foisted the fictitious Gawain on all of them.

"Then let's get started, my lord," she said. "My friends and I will still have most of the traveling season ahead of us if you are successful."

Brady looked at her for long moments, so that her stomach did a small flip, then drawled, "Oh, my, yes. Must get the players back on the road, mustn't we? I'm sure you miss that life very much. Although, and you may most certainly correct me if I'm wrong, I thought you said you were done as an actress."

Regina gave her body a slight shake, then threw back her head and laughed. "Did I actually say that, my lord? My goodness, I tell so many fibs even I can't keep them straight. No, my lord, I would never give up my life, which is the only one I've ever known. I *live* to act, my lord. Why, remember, even now I am playing the role of your ward."

"Yes, you are, aren't you," Brady said, all traces of Gawain gone, his expression dark and rather forbidding. Then he slapped his hands against his thighs, stood up, and said, "All right, princess, let's be on with it. How do I become a creditable ghost?"

She rose as well, walking with him to the center of the room, where they stood only about three feet apart, facing each other. "First," she said, wanting this lesson over with so that she could retire to her chamber and kick something, "I think that now would be the time for you to be dangerous."

"I'm to be a ghost, princess. A spectre. A smelling, dripping, clanging, moaning apparition come out of the night, up from the depths, whatever. I doubt I'll have much trouble appearing *dangerous*."

"True, true," Regina agreed, "but you also have to be able to move, and move quickly, in case the man you accost takes one look and starts beating on you with his walking stick. So it's your dangerous appearance that we have to work on, your clothing, your chains. I think you should just have bits and pieces of the sack pinned to your clothing to keep your movement free, and the chains draped loosely around your shoulders, perhaps with a large, open lock hanging from one end?"

"That seems sensible enough," Brady said, nodding. "What about my hair? Only Gawain has long hair."

"A good question, my lord," Regina said, caught up now in the logistics of the thing, so much so that she stepped forward, reached up with both hands, and ran her fingers through his hair, pushing it behind his ears. "We could pin it all against the back of your head, I suppose," she said, then sighed. "No, that wouldn't work. You'd just look as you do when Gawain clubs his hair with a ribbon."

She went to step back, drop her hands from his hair, when Brady put his hands on her forearms, held her still.

"Don't," he said quietly, looking down at her.

Don't. Just that one word. Just that one word, his hands on her arms, and the look in his eyes. Regina couldn't move if someone set her hair on fire. *Don't.*

She swallowed down hard, tried to smile, failed badly. "What? Is something wrong?"

His fingers began to move up and down her arms, stroking her sensitive skin. "Do you remember that day at Singleton Chase, princess? Christmas Day?"

"I . . . I remember."

"Do you know why I left the next morning?"

She tried to lower her head, but he released her arm and put his fingertips under her chin, raising her head to his once more. "I think I know, my lord," she said. "And I think I'm glad you left."

He tipped his head to one side, as if repeating her words inside his head, trying to decide if she spoke the truth or had taken refuge in a lie. "Why, Regina? Why were you glad I left? Were you as frightened as I was?"

"I'm frightened now, my lord," she said, and she'd never been quite so honest in her entire life.

Brady smiled slowly, his lips curving, the skin around his eyes crinkling. "Oh, good. I'm not the only one . . ."

he said, breathing the words against her lips, then covering her mouth with his own.

White-hot lightning streaked behind Regina's eyes, shot through her body, all the way down to her toes. Brady's arms went around her, pinning him against her, trapping her arms between them for a moment before she could free them . . . wonder what to do with them now that they were free.

She slid them both up and around his neck and decided that she'd made a good choice, because now their bodies were melded together, and when they went up in flames they'd do so together. That seemed only fair.

Brady's mouth moved on hers, and she felt the tip of his tongue as he ran it along her bottom lip, tickling her slightly, so that her lips re-formed themselves in a smile that somehow seemed to double the sensations that had already rocked her to her core.

"Oh," she breathed, half in surprise, half in pleasure, and the next thing she knew Brady was drawing back slightly, only to come at her again, this time lightly sucking on her top lip, running his tongue along her soft, moist flesh.

He withdrew again, advanced again; each time coming at her mouth in another way, as if feasting on her, learning her, and all while driving her to the point where she finally clamped both hands on the back of his head and pulled him against her with all her might, holding his head still so that she could feast on him, learn him.

She vaguely felt his hands slide down her back, to her waist, clasping her to him for a few moments before his hands moved again, rising across her midriff, sliding up and over her breasts, settling there, cupping her.

It was wrong. It was right. It was what she wanted, what she had told herself she wasn't allowed to want. It was the last thing she needed, it was everything she needed.

"My lord, I'm coming in now to trim the wicks," Wadsworth announced loudly, the butler's words breaking through the sensual fog that had enveloped Regina, robbed her of every last ounce of common sense.

"Wadsworth," Brady grumbled, breaking off their kiss, burying his head against Regina's hair. "Thank God there's still one man of sense in this household." He ran his hands lightly down Regina's sides, gave her waist a quick squeeze, and stepped away from her. Turned his back on her. "Go now, princess, before he follows through on his threat. We'll talk again in the morning."

Regina nodded, realized he couldn't see her, but also knew that she couldn't speak if she tried. She ran her hands over her hair, smoothed down her bodice, and headed toward the door, stopping just in front of it to turn, look at Brady.

He was standing just where she left him, his head down, his shoulders still heaving slightly as he seemed to be trying to calm his breathing.

They'd made a mistake. She knew it, and obviously he knew it. And now nothing would be the same.

Regina gave herself a slight shake, straightened her shoulders, and opened the door to see Wadsworth standing there, a small brass scissors in one hand, a candle snuffer in the other.

At last she found her voice. "At least you had the good sense to bring props," she told him, her chin held high as she walked past him, toward the stairs. Her hand on the newel post, she hesitated for a moment, turned back to look at the butler. "Thank you, Wadsworth," she said, then mounted the stairs to her bedchamber.

The bell hanging above the shop door rang as David held open the door. Regina, deeply submerged in her role of bored lady of quality prepared to be unimpressed by the meager goods inside the *toniest* dress shop in Mayfair, entered the building, Mrs. Matilda Forrest trailing behind her.

"La, sir," she said to David, who was snapping his fingers to gain the attention of a young woman just then replacing a bolt of cloth on the shelves lining one wall, "I don't know what possessed me to believe I could find anything of any merit here in London. How many shops have we been in this morning? Four? Six?"

"Seven, Miss Felicity," David said, shooting the cuffs of his fine new coat of dark blue superfine, and his secret pride and joy, as the color so set off his eyes, his dark flowing locks, his perfect teeth. "Let us hope this one is not quite so inferior. Perhaps you'll be able to find at least one thing that pleases you and has hopes of being approved by your uncle Gawain."

David had said the same lines in each of the shops, following hard on Regina's lines, and in each establishment those lines had produced the same effect. Heads went up, noses sniffed the air—the ladies of the *ton* all seeming to go on point, like hunting dogs who'd just scented the fox.

Which had been the entire object of the exercise: gaining attention. Or at least that's what Brady's note delivered along with her breakfast tray had directed her to do. "Get out and about, show your face, spend my money, draw as much attention as possible." That's what the note had said. What the note had *meant*, Regina felt sure, was, "I'm sorry, it shouldn't have happened, and it won't happen again."

Regina, after sulking in her chamber for an hour while Maude told her that only a brainless looby would give up the chance to spend someone else's money, had decided to take His Lordship up on his offer, but not for the reason he'd suggested it—ordered it.

Oh no. Regina wasn't in Bond Street to shop. She was in Bond Street, traveling from shop to shop to shop, hoping to get lucky, hoping to locate a certain young woman by the name of—

"Lady Bellinagara, if you were to step back here, through the curtain," a rather portly woman with shocking pink hair said, "I'll have Mary bring your gowns for their final fitting."

Regina looked at Cosmo, one eyebrow lifted, and the man smiled around the last bit of meat pie he'd just popped into his mouth. "You know, David, I do believe this establishment might have *just* what I've been looking for, don't you?" she asked, picking up a small, pearl-encrusted reticule that probably cost more than the wagon she'd called home for all of her life.

A clerk came up to her, and Regina shooed her away

with a single sharp look, then softened her rebuke with a smile, saying, "I'll just putter about on my own a little longer, my dear. Perhaps if you could tell the owner that the earl of Singleton's ward is here, to consider a purchase?"

As the clerk tiptoed away and Regina pretended to inspect the reticule, she also watched Lady Bellinagara, the woman Brady had referred to as Belle, put down the bolt of palest green satin she'd been inspecting and walk across the room toward the curtain the proprietor was holding back for her.

Gorgeous. The woman was gorgeous. She had absolute *masses* of hair the color of honey, all of it piled high on her head save for the ringlets caressing her long, slim throat. Her eyes were huge, green as emeralds, in a small, heart-shaped face that also held a perfectly straight, small nose, and a Cupid's bow of a mouth. She moved gracefully, her palest grey-silk gown whispering around her feet, her small, high bosoms, narrow waist, and slightly flaring hips all so perfect that Regina suddenly realized she'd been grinding her teeth together, and quickly looked away.

So this was the woman with whom Brady was once "romantically involved." Exactly how had he phrased it? As if Regina hadn't committed every word to memory. She knew what he'd said. He'd said, "I pursued her, she eluded me, and that's the end of it."

Regina motioned for Cosmo to join her at the small table as she pretended an interest in other reticules. "Are you thinking the same thing I'm thinking, Matilda?"

"You were right to worry. She could be a problem,"

Cosmo said, nodding as he adjusted the bodice of his gown with a little too much energy. "His Lordship has a tender heart, I do believe. Tears in those huge green eyes would give any man pause."

"He'd give up our plans to see Allerton and his cronies punished for what they did to Mama and Papa, to him?"

"If she were to get wind of them before we can announce everything to the world, and beg his mercy, yes, I think he might. You were right in what you said this morning, my dear. We have to get this over with, quickly. Too much time could bring complications. Her Ladyship is a complication, unless we can find a way to use her for our own benefit."

Regina sighed. "Oh, Cosmo, if only we could do this without him. If only we could break down the walls without his help."

"If only we could be sure that our faith in a kind Providence, and the greed of our fellowman, have any merit. Yet I still say we shouldn't raise our—"

"I know what you say, Cosmo, and what Thomas says, and what David says—well, nobody pays any mind to what David says, do they? And yet, the more I think about it, the more I run that night over and over, through my head, the more my hopes grow. But first we need Allerton out of the way, and then we need His Lordship to broach the gates before—"

"Please don't allow your hopes to fly too high. I wouldn't want to see your dear heart broken yet again, sweetheart," Cosmo said, handing her a pair of softest kid gloves, and trilling loudly, "Have you ever seen such work? You must have them made for you in every color, Miss Regina, you just *must*."

The pink-haired lady, her ears fairly quivering, approached, all but rubbing her hands together. "I'm so sorry for my clerk's boorish behavior, approaching you that way, miss. She'll be let go at once, of course."

"Do, madam," Regina said, eyeing the woman icily, "and I'll have my uncle buy this shop and see *you* turned out onto the streets." Then she smiled, held up the pair of gloves. "In every color?"

"Oh, yes, yes, that's possible, but I do not sell gloves here. These are only for display, lent to me by the shop next door, just as I display some of my own work there. But surely I can interest you in a new gown? Not that what you're wearing isn't exquisite—exquisite! I have a few here fresh from Paris which I'm sure will delight you."

"That would be remarkable," David said even while admiring himself in a nearby mirror. "Miss Felicity is rarely delighted. Amused. Mollified. But rarely delighted. His Lordship, the earl of Singleton, has tutored Miss Felicity in fashion, so that she is loath to wear anything that hasn't been shipped here directly from France. That said, let me see these gowns, if you please, madam, and *I* will decide whether or not they're delightful."

"Yes, please do that, David, while I retire to the dressing room and someone helps me out of this gown. You will need my measurements, will you not?" she asked the proprietor.

"Oh, yes, yes, indeed. Your measurements, for I do not sell the gowns I receive from Paris, you understand, but use them as samples. Each of my customers has her gowns specially made by myself, personally." The woman motioned toward the curtain with her out-stretched arm. "And we have refreshments in the dressing rooms. Cakes. Tea. Comfits."

"How lovely," Cosmo fairly gushed, never one to turn down food.

"Please, Miss Felicity, if you and your . . ." she looked at Cosmo, who was picking at his teeth with his thumb-nail, ". . . er, your *companion* were but to accompany me?"

"Oh, that's all right," Regina said as Cosmo made to follow after her. "Mrs. Forrest is more than happy to wait here." She turned, glared at the man. "*Aren't* you, Mrs. Forrest?"

"Oh, yes, yes. What *was* I thinking?" Cosmo asked, flushing, then waggled his fingers at Regina. "But if you were to see that a few of the comfits were—"

"I'll be sure to have someone send some out to you, Mrs. Forrest," Regina said, rolling her eyes at her friend, then turned to follow the proprietor through to the dress-ing rooms.

Regina hid her disappointment when she realized that, instead of one large room she would share with Lady Bel-linagara, she was being led to a private room separated from the other one by a thick floor-to-ceiling curtain. Still, it was only a curtain. Anything Lady Bellinagara said would be heard by her, and vice versa.

Within moments, the clerk she'd first spoken to joined her in the dressing room, asking her permission to undo her buttons, help her undress, a permission Regina granted, hoping she sounded as if she did this sort of thing twice a day, and had done so for years.

"I'm new to London," she said conversationally as the clerk helped her out of her gown, "and know so little of the city. It compares well to Paris, my guardian tells me, but I'm still very much alone here, as my dearest late guardian kept me quite secluded at Singleton Chase. He did have the good sense to send to Paris for my wardrobe, as I was to make my debut this year, although his exemplary taste in fashion is, I believe, the only similarity between that poor, dear man and my new guardian."

Regina mentally reviewed her last statement, thinking she had managed to keep her lies straight, believable. They were piling up now, those lies, and that was one very good sign that it was time to end this charade.

The clerk looked at her curiously. Obviously she wasn't used to her customers speaking to her about anything other than bows and seams and button sizes. "Yes, miss?" the clerk said as she wielded the string she was using to take Regina's measurements.

Regina raised her arms to shoulder level, so that the clerk could measure her bust. "Oh, yes, indeed. It was so sad, too. I was there, all alone, when they brought his body from London. Not that I knew him well, and not that he was *really* my uncle, but it is sad to think about how he was murdered. Drowned, you know, in the Thames. Ah, poor, poor Uncle Brady."

Success!

Regina hid a smile as the dividing curtain parted and Lady Bellinagara walked into the room, also dressed only in her undergarments. "Excuse me," she said with a smile, "but I could not help overhearing you. You were ward to Brady James?"

"I was," Regina said with a slight nod, willing to answer, but definitely not willing to elaborate, which was probably what the lady wanted. She lifted her chin, looked down at the smaller woman from her perch on the fitting stool. "Is this your concern, madam?"

"No, no, naturally it is not," Her Ladyship said quickly, "but I did have your late guardian's acquaintance, and I wished to offer my condolences on your loss. I haven't met the new earl as yet, but I have heard about him. Is he really as—well, I shouldn't ask."

"Is he really as silly as they say?" Regina offered, motioning for Lady Bellinagara to come completely into the dressing room. "Madam, you don't know the *half* of it." She waved the clerk away and stepped down from the small, raised platform, a wave of her arm indicating the cakes and tea on a nearby table. "Would you care to join me? I'd so like to be able to tell my guardian that I've made at least one new friend here in London."

"I'd be delighted," Lady Bellinagara said as the eager fly willingly entered into the spider's parlor.

But which one was the spider?

Chapter Thirteen

$\mathcal{B}$rady spent the day with Bram, wandering about Mayfair, stopping in at some of the duke's clubs—that had once also been Brady's clubs—being introduced to people he'd known for years.

At least he'd thought he'd known them. Apparently, he had not.

He had been surprised by the very real expressions of sorrow he'd heard expressed over Gawain Caradoc's sad loss of his cousin, most especially from the sources of those condolences. These were men he knew, but never had known, never taken the time to know, for he'd been too busy rushing about, gaming, drinking, playing at life. These were men near in age to him, but all of them, he realized, were married, a little more sober in their habits, and interested in government and the world at large. Good men, all.

Brady had once thought them boring, but now he began to understand his friends Bram and Kipp, and the changes that had overtaken them since their respective marriages. Having a wife, having children or the hope of children—well, it seemed to change a man. Change him for the better.

Certainly they were better than the "friends" he and Bram encountered, the jolly, laughing, turf-and-table cronies he had believed to be his very good friends. These were the men he'd played cards with until dawn, ridden out to see mills with, rode with in the Four-in-Hand Club, drunk and laughed with, ofttimes at the expense of those more sober gentlemen who had, every last one of them, offered their very sincere sympathies over the tragic death of Brady James.

Those jollier "friends" had offered their condolences, yes, but often with a wink and a smile, even a pat on the back, congratulating Brady on having come into the title—even hinting that perhaps he'd had a hand in pushing the late earl into the water that fateful night.

Brady understood most of it. He was dead, and now Gawain Caradoc was here—alive, a sensation in the *ton*, apparently a near idiot, and with deep pockets that drew these men to him like bees to honey. How many offers had he received to join any of these men at the gaming tables in just a few hours of being out and about the town? Too many.

He'd been particularly struck by the reaction of Mr. Henry Finley, who had pumped Brady's hand up and down as he told him, not once but twice, what a "good man" he had been, what a "splendid man" he had been— all while sizing up Brady like a racetrack tout.

Finley thought he was an easy mark, a sure source of

funds if he could get him to the card table. Brady knew how to recognize the signs, for he'd known Finley for years, and had often played at this same not so friendly game with him, more's the pity. Still, he had really believed Henry Finley to be his friend.

"A good man?" he'd asked. "Really? I never knew him, you understand."

"You never knew him?" Henry Finley's grin nearly caused him to lose his two front teeth, not that he knew it. "Oh, well then," Henry had said, "I imagine it's safe to tell you. Brady could be awful. One of those know-it-all types, you understand. Always poking his nose into everyone else's business. That's probably what did him in, you know. Nosiness."

Brady had felt his face freeze around his smile, and politely withdrew his hand, taking out his snuffbox, tapping it open with one hand, and daintily taking a pinch to each nostril. "Really? Is that so? How very interesting. Would you care for a dip, Mr. Finley? My own sort, you understand. Very mild."

Leaving Henry Finley reeling from a paroxysm of sneezing, Brady had promised to meet Bram at Lady Sefton's ball later that evening, the first stop in a well-orchestrated plan to hunt down and speak with the earl of Allerton.

He'd dismissed the carriage that he'd used due to the slight mizzle that had kept the skies grey and the flagways wet, and walked all the way back to Portman Square, feeling more than a little sorry for himself.

Still, every cloud did have its silver lining, for he realized as he mounted the steps to his mansion that he hadn't thought about Regina for at least three hours. That was a good thing, because thinking about Regina led to thinking that he was probably the lowest, most base creature in nature, taking advantage of a young, innocent girl who certainly didn't know the rules of society.

The rules of society? What *were* the rules of society, he wondered, pulling a face. Be friendly to someone's face, then barely wait until the body is cold before revealing your true feelings? Were there *any* true feelings in society? Or were there only moves and strategies, plots and plans meant to keep oneself at the forefront of the *ton*, moves and strategies that included chasing after an obvious idiot such as Gawain Caradoc, merely because he had a title, money—or was just unique enough to lend cachet to those who could call him friend?

From somewhere deep in the back of his mind, a poem learned by rote at the insistence of one of his tutors dusted itself off and presented itself to him for his edification—Richard Barnfield's poem to one of his friends: "Everyone that flatters thee is no friend in misery. Words are easy, like the wind; faithful friends are hard to find. Every man will be thy friend whilst thou hast wherewith to spend; but if store of crowns be scant, no man will supply thy want. He that is thy friend indeed, he will help thee in thy need."

Brady had a few good friends. Bram. Kipp. A handful more, most of them living near Singleton Chase, friends since boyhood who either chose not to travel in London society or were too busy with their lands and families to do so. They'd all been at his funeral, Wadsworth had told them, wearing black armbands, a few of them weeping—

while most of his London friends had drunk his wine, eaten his food, and chased the female servants.

"Smart man, that Barnfield," Brady grumbled to himself as he handed his curly-brimmed beaver to one of the footmen, to have it taken to Rogers, let to dry, then carefully brushed.

He walked into the drawing room and pulled the crystal stopper from a decanter, pouring himself a drink he carried with him as he walked to a window and looked out over Portman Square.

His friend Bram had the right of it, as did Kipp. Find a woman you love, a woman who loves you, and the devil with the rest of the world, with the cock-eyed rules of society. Sophie and Bram had, together, conquered all of Mayfair, made it their own, because that's what they wanted. Kipp and Abby had turned their backs on London for now, caught up in the first flush of their happiness, but when they did choose to return it would be on their own terms, Brady was sure of that.

Bram and Sophie had succeeded, Kipp and Abby would succeed. And what if they hadn't? What if the *ton* had turned its back on them forever?

"No great loss in that," Brady said, tossing back his drink, then giving an involuntary shiver as its heat burned its way down his throat. Hadn't he already been bored with society? Hadn't he already begun to see the whole mad dash of it as silly and pointless, and begun longing for something different, something better. Something more substantial and lasting?

Yes. Yes, he had.

And when had he been happier than he'd been these

last months—once his body had healed, that was? He'd read, he'd ridden the fields near his hunting box, he'd taken an interest in the running of his estates. He'd played in the snow, and laughed over dinner conversation that didn't have to be cutting to be witty. He still hadn't bought a hound to lay at his feet, but he still wanted one.

Less than a year ago, Brady would have thought himself mad to be thinking the way he was now. But less than a year ago, he'd been playing at life, believing he was enjoying himself, only to realize, as he sank into the Thames, that he had never really *lived* at all.

The first thing to have interested him in much too long had been Regina Bliss's mischievous grey eyes. The first time he'd been truly content was when he'd wakened after a fever, to see her at his bedside. The first time he'd known a passion so overwhelming that it had nearly unmanned him was last night, when he'd held Regina in his arms. . . .

"My lord, if we might speak with you for a moment?"

It took Brady several seconds to clear his head, as he'd believed himself close to a revelation, but then he turned, nodded. "Thomas. Cosmo. Of course, of course. Come in. Would you care for a drink? Ratafia for you, Mrs. Forrest, as I quite naturally don't press strong spirits on my female guests."

"I think not, my lord," Thomas said stiffly. "We are here, you see, to ask your intentions as they pertain to Regina."

"That's what he's here for," Cosmo said, strutting toward Brady in his petticoats and whalebone stays. "I'm here to bloody your nose."

Brady looked at the two men—Thomas with his pale, thin fingers drawn up into fists, Cosmo with his stuffed bodice badly listing to one side. "And where is David? Isn't he included in this confrontation?"

Thomas sniffed. "Regina, in her determination to beggar you today in Bond Street, bought him another mirror, one he can hold in his hand. He's upstairs now, trying to maneuver it about so that he can get a good look at his own backside. If you'll recall, my lord, I did tell you that he's harmless."

"And so am I. Relatively," Brady said, motioning for the two men to sit down. "I suppose Regina told you about the kiss?"

Cosmo, who had been about to lower himself onto the couch, put out his arms and waved himself upright once more. "A kiss? Oh, that's it! A bloody nose, Your Lordship. At the least."

Thomas, who had sat down, crossed one long, skinny leg over the other and rested his hands on his knee. "Oh, sit down, Cosmo. It wasn't as if we hadn't guessed as much ourselves."

"I think my intentions are honorable," Brady said, sitting down on the facing couch, then amended that statement. "No, I'm convinced they're honorable. But, that said, I will agree with you that I've behaved badly. Regina has every reason to hate me."

Cosmo and Thomas exchanged looks, then Thomas said, "That's true, my lord. But Regina was already fairly disenchanted with men of your stature, considering the rough treatment her family has endured at the hands of what are supposed to be the Quality."

"Allerton," Brady said, nodding.

"Yes, my lord," Cosmo said, looking at Thomas rather than at Brady. "It would probably be best to keep your distance from Regina until that is settled, and then begin to court her, if that is your intention."

"Which you don't believe *is* my intention," Brady said, at last picking up on the meaningful looks being exchanged between Thomas and Cosmo. "Why not?"

"Are you using Regina now, my lord?" Cosmo asked.

Brady lifted his glass in salute. "*Touché*, Mrs. Forrest, *touché*. I see I will first have to earn your trust, before I can begin to earn Regina's."

Thomas tipped his head to one side, and said, "About that, my lord . . ."

"Yes?" Brady asked, instantly on the alert. "What? What's going on?"

"Cosmo, your turn, I believe," Thomas said, concentrating on inspecting his shirt cuffs.

Cosmo took a deep breath, at least deep enough that his whalebone creaked. "We traveled to Bond Street today, my lord," he said, then frowned. "I believed, at first, that Regina was just going to spend your money, see and be seen, as you had requested. However, it didn't take me long to realize that Regina was on a mission."

Brady looked at his glass, saw that it was empty, but made no move to refill it. "I'm not going to like this, am I, Cosmo?"

"I don't think so, sir, no," the man told him. "It would seem that Regina has struck up a friendship with one Lady Bellinagara, daughter of—"

"I know damn full well who she's the daughter of,

thank you!" Brady said, hopping to his feet. "I told her not to do anything like that. *Warned* her!"

"Well, that explains it then, doesn't it, Cosmo," Thomas said reasonably. "She tried to wave us off with some farradiddle about deliberately getting close to Lady Bellinagara in order to more quickly ferret out Allerton's friends, possibly even get inside the Allerton household and do some snooping of her own; but we weren't put off by that, were we, Cosmo?"

"Not for a moment. Especially when she began grumbling, and very downpin she was as she spoke about how the young woman was so delicate, so beautiful, so highly acceptable."

"That's when we finally realized that our dearest Regina is caught somewhere between wishing to avenge her parents and wanting to please you, my lord. We decided, Cosmo and myself, that Regina's heart is now involved, and concluded that, as you two are in such close company, and have been for quite some time, that it would be best that we, as her guardians, of sorts, ask your intentions."

"My *intentions*, at the moment," Brady said, refilling his glass, "are to wring your dear Regina's lovely white neck!"

Cosmo looked at Thomas. "Oh, good. He does love her. Well, my friend, we've done what we could. Would you care to join me in the kitchens? I'm sure I caught a whiff of cinnamon as we passed through the foyer, and Cook is always quite delighted to have me sample her creations and give them my approval."

"Just a moment," Brady said, rubbing at his forehead,

trying to stimulate his stunned brain. "Three more days, gentlemen. It can't go any longer than that, not if we're to keep Regina from putting herself in harm's way, or if I'm to retain my sanity. I know we only spoke of this for a few minutes this morning, but we have to move quickly. The ghost of Brady James walks tonight."

"But where, my lord?" Cosmo asked. "We've yet to figure out who other than Allerton is involved, remember?"

"That I hope to find out tonight, as Gawain Caradoc puts on his little production at Lady Sefton's. But if I don't, then I go straight to Allerton, and beat the other two names out of him, if I have to. Agreed?"

"Agreed, my lord," Cosmo said, as Thomas waited for his companion's opinion. "We'll be ready. Including David, if we can pull him away from his mirror."

Regina had spent part of the afternoon congratulating herself on her brilliance, part of it looking into her mirror and deciding that Lady Bellinagara's beauty cast her firmly in the shade, and the remainder of it wondering how she'd ever have the courage to look at Brady again after what had happened between them the previous evening.

She'd solved part of the problem, delaying the inevitable, by taking her dinner in her chamber, as she had postponed her bath until it became obvious that her freshly washed hair would never be dry in time to join His Lordship in the dining room.

But now she could no longer delay, not if she was going to accompany Brady to Lady Sefton's. The thought that he might think her absence a good thing, and leave without her, had her rushing down the stairs to the foyer the moment she heard Rooster bringing around the carriage.

"Ah, punctuality, something so rare in the ladies," Brady said from the doorway to the drawing room, striking a pose in yet another outrageous costume, this one in varying, and all rather shocking, shades of aqua, and with three pink tulip buds stuck in his buttonhole. He stepped forward, offered her his arm. "Shall we go? I believe your new friend will be waiting to see you."

"My new—oh, why did I think Cosmo could keep a secret?" she said angrily. She looked back at Cosmo, who was carefully descending the stairs, holding on to the banister with both hands as he tried to balance in his new, heeled slippers.

"You had me purchase these on purpose, didn't you, my dear, just so you could amuse yourself," he pronounced, finally reaching the last step, and sighing in relief at a safe journey. "The mirror for David, the bolt of green taffeta for Thomas, and these invitations to death for me."

"They were the only ones that fit, Mrs. Forrest," Regina pointed out, smiling at the memory of the clerk, rushing about, all a-twitter, trying to find something, *anything* that would fit Cosmo's fairly small, but also remarkably chubby feet. "But now I'm glad I bought them, and I hope they pinch you unmercifully all night. How could you tell His Lordship about Lady Belle?"

"How could I do otherwise, my dear?" Cosmo, asked, looking to Wadsworth, who nodded his agreement. "At least you and His Lordship will have enough conversation to fill the time we'll spend sitting in that carriage out there, waiting to arrive at Lady Sefton's door. Just in case you'd been worried about that, my dear. Were you worried about that?"

Regina, who had been about to say something else, snapped her jaws closed and said nothing, absolutely nothing, for the next hour, as the carriage crawled along in line behind fifty other carriages all waiting to disgorge their well-dressed passengers in front of the Sefton mansion.

They met the duke of Selbourne on the crowded staircase leading up to the receiving line, and after breaking her silence to say hello to Bram, Regina lapsed into silence once more, too nervous to speak, too angry to speak, too worried about the outcome of this very important evening to do much of anything at all.

Once they were in the huge ballroom, and Cosmo had taken up his seat with the dowagers—offering the women on either side of him peppermints he'd brought with him in his new reticule—and Brady and Bram had wandered off to find refreshments, Regina went in search of Lady Belle, locating her within moments.

"My dear Miss Felicity," Lady Belle said, kissing the air beside Regina's left cheek, "how very good to see you again. I've told Papa and my brother all about you this evening, at dinner, with the most amusing results. It seems Boothe—that's my brother, you understand—is upset that you and I have cried friends. Something to do with your guardian, although when I pressed him for details, he was remarkably unforthcoming. My papa, however, is most anxious to meet you. Well, everyone in society is anxious to meet you, aren't they? But, for tonight, you are my coup."

"And you, Lady Bellinagara, will be my introduction to the cream of the *ton*. Isn't it wonderful how that works out. Or were we supposed to pretend we're really attracted to each other's finer qualities?"

Lady Bellinagara's emerald green eyes glinted with anger for a moment, but then she smiled—a smile more crafty than amused. "How delightful. Honesty. I suggest you use it sparingly, my dear. Now, introduce me to your guardian, and I will return the favor by presenting you to the patronesses of Almack's. Fair enough?"

"More than fair, my lady," Regina said, not liking Lady Bellinagara at all, but beginning to respect her. "My guardian will be delighted to meet you."

Regina didn't know what she thought she'd both see and feel when she saw Brady and Lady Bellinagara together, but Brady's behavior didn't give her a clue, as he hid most effectively behind the mask of Gawain Caradoc.

He had been deep in conversation with the duke of Selbourne as she and Lady Bellinagara approached, but turned to her with a smile, then gracefully bowed over the other woman's hand, not quite touching his lips to her glove. "Ah, Lady Belle—surely that is what you are called? The *belle* of the ball, I'm sure. Perceive me prostrate before you, madam, both in awe of your beauty and in thanks for taking my dearest ward under your wing this evening, as Her Grace, the duchess of Selbourne, is unavoidably out of the city. I know so few people, you understand, and I wish for Miss Felicity to swim the seas of society without fear of sharks."

He leaned closer to Lady Bellinagara, smiled. "You do understand my meaning, don't you? There's quite a large dowry involved."

"Along with Miss Felicity's quite remarkable beauty, my lord," Lady Bellinagara said. "I'm honored to think that you trust me with your ward, whom I've found to be a delightful companion."

"Have you really?" Brady said in obvious disbelief, looking at Regina. "Imagine that."

Regina wondered if anyone would notice if she brained Brady with the nearest potted plant. Still, she joined in the silliness, eager to get to the point of the evening—almost as eager as she was to prove that she could be of help to the dratted man. "Lady Bellinagara has told me that her father, the earl of Allerton, my lord, is very desirous of making your acquaintance. Shall we seek him out now?"

Brady raised his quizzing glass to his eye and looked out over the crowded ballroom in dismay. "What? In this crush? Would that even be possible? Perhaps another time."

Regina gritted her teeth, longing to kick Brady in the shins. "But I did rather *promise*, my lord," she said tightly.

"Oh, very well," Brady returned, sighing. He allowed the quizzing glass to fall to his waist on its black riband, then offered an arm to each of the ladies. "I say, Bram," he called out to the duke of Selbourne, who was speaking to a rather overheated woman in a yellow turban, "have a look at me, if you will, positively surrounded by beauty. Neither of them clashes with my coat, do they? That would be too bad."

"I think you're safe, Gawain," Bram said, shaking his head. "And I think I'll head for the gaming room. You can join me there later?"

"If I can tear myself away from the ladies," Brady said, smiling down at Lady Bellinagara, so that Regina took the opportunity to pinch the tender flesh inside his elbow. And then they were off, in search of the man who had turned both hers and Brady's lives upside down.

They found him standing with a small group of similarly aged gentlemen, a not so tall and faintly portly gentleman with greying hair and the coldest brown eyes Regina had ever seen. Four of the gentlemen moved away, taking their discussion with them, but three remained.

Regina resisted the urge to turn and run when the earl of Allerton spoke and she recognized the voice she'd heard that fateful night. His Lordship acknowledged his daughter's introductions and then introduced the gentlemen with him—Sir Randolph Tilden, Mr. Samuel LeMain, and Baron Stanley Thorndyke.

Her father might have been a dreamer, and sometimes silly, but he had done at least one thing that showed his care for his daughter—he had never let her come out of the wagon when Allerton visited. Not in the three years they'd been traveling to Little Woodcote. He'd been afraid, her mother had said, of Allerton or one of the other gentlemen taking too great an interest in their only child and, believing her to be fair game, deciding to take a dead set at her virtue.

Protecting her virtue, Regina knew, had actually protected her life, so that although she still harbored a small fear that Allerton might somehow recognize her from the one time he'd seen her on the stage, she felt fairly certain she was safe. The problem that remained was that Allerton might know she existed at all.

"Allerton, Allerton," Brady was saying as he struck a pose, one hand on his hip, the other rubbing at his chin. "Now why is that name so familiar?" Then he brightened, snapped his fingers. "Of course! I saw the name in my late cousin's papers at Singleton Chase. George Kenward, isn't it? George Kenward, Earl of Allerton? You must have been great friends."

"No, actually—"

"So wonderful that my dear Miss Felicity and Lady Bellinagara have met, don't you think? And now we have met, and we shall all be great friends. Do you need friends, my lord? Perhaps you have enough? I don't know that my cousin had enough."

His Lordship didn't so much as blink. "I barely knew the man," he said, flicking at an invisible bit of lint on the sleeve of his evening coat. "Surely you're mistaken."

"Oh, no, no. I'm never mistaken, my lord. I saw your name among my late cousin's papers. I remember it quite distinctly, as he'd written it down three times in succession, then underlined each one. But, not to worry, I'm sure there was nothing mysterious about it, as I understand my late cousin was always involved in some mad start or another. Perhaps he was considering approaching you for some reason—for the hand of your beautiful daughter, for one." He smiled at Lady Bellinagara. "Is that it? Have I supposed correctly?"

"You flatter me, my lord," Lady Bellinagara said, but her green eyes, far removed in color from her father's dark brown, momentarily took on the same hard stare. "Although I will say that he did ask, several years ago. I refused him."

"Oh, gad! I'm sure he was crushed. *Crushed*," Brady said, as Regina debated whether she should kick him in the ankle or the shin.

Lady Bellinagara smiled. "Not really, my lord, if we're to be truthful about the thing, as you'll probably hear the story at some point. It's my understanding that he walked away with his head high, and with five hundred pounds of Sir Henry Cox's money, for he somehow learned that I did not wish to marry and he had wagered the man that I would refuse him. For an entire Season, everyone believed I wish *never* to marry. Your late cousin, my lord, could be a heartless man."

Brady put his quizzing glass to his eye, turned to look down at Regina, who refused to meet his eyes. All right, so she had her answer now, and she was probably happy with it, but he *had* told her he'd been "romantically involved" with the woman, hadn't he? She'd content herself with believing that he'd thought saying he had been attracted to Lady Belle would be enough to keep *her* at a distance from the woman. She'd have to remember, and never forget, that Brady James was deeper than he let the world believe.

"Sir Henry Cox, did you say?" Brady was asking Lady

Bellinagara. "Why, I believe I met the good gentleman the other night, at the theater. He was with a delightful woman, Lady Jersey. I understand from my friend the duke that I am to petition the woman about a voucher for Almack's for our dear Miss Felicity here. I must do that soon, mustn't I? After all, my late cousin was quite fond of the dear girl, and I wish to do right by her."

Lord Allerton, who had been looking quite bored by this conversation, suddenly seemed to be paying attention. "Miss Felicity was your late cousin's ward? I never heard of that."

"Yes, and isn't it strange? That's exactly what the duke of Selbourne said, when I spoke to him about her— pardon me, my dear, while we speak of you as if you aren't really here. But it's true. My cousin had her sent to Singleton Chase, just weeks before he was murdered as it turns out, with instructions to keep her safe until he could petition the courts to become her guardian. Didn't he, Miss Felicity?"

So much for refusing to use her as bait. But what else could she expect from him, having jumped in with both feet herself, which she'd done by disobeying him and making Lady Bellinagara's acquaintance. He'd just dangled her as bait as, at the same time, he'd also set himself up as a target. Brady must have been serious when he said he wanted this over, and as quickly as possible. He'd probably have her tied up and driven to the safety of the Willoughby estate before morning—if she let him. But perhaps, if she showed him how very *good* she was to have near him, how helpful she could be . . . ?

Regina gave a slight shiver, then rearranged her features into one of slight panic. She cast her eyes around the room, as if everyone was listening, and said quietly, "I really don't think it wise, my lord, to repeat what I've told you in confidence. Not when we don't know who—"

"Oh, now, now," Brady drawled, lifting the lapel of his evening coat, to sniff at the tulips in his lapel, "you're not going to start with that outlandish story again, are you? As if I believe a word of it, because I don't. Honestly, my lord," he said, looking at the earl of Allerton, "one would think Miss Felicity and my cousin were involved in some grand mystery, wouldn't one? I refuse to listen to her when she gets like this. Why, if I were to do otherwise, she'd soon have me checking for monsters under my bed."

"Fanciful, is she?" Sir Randolph asked, at last joining in the conversation. "Had a sister like that. She had a whole regiment of monsters under her bed."

"Really?" Brady said, looking at Sir Randolph as if mightily impressed by his words. "But, please, don't be put off by her missish ways. I've settled a fine dowry on her, frankly, because I would rather she become someone else's problem, dear as she is, dear as she must have been to my late cousin. Any takers, gentlemen? I vow, she could be like Scheherazade, telling a different wonderful story every night—although she does seem to be stuck on one particular tale. Pity. Miss Felicity, are you quite sure you wouldn't care to tell our new friends your marvelous story? Come, come now, don't be shy. It's truly fascinating."

Now Regina willed herself to pale, and blinked a tear into her eye. "Oh, why won't you believe me? But, no—

no. I don't want to talk about this anymore," she exclaimed in a voice trembling with terror. "Please, my lords, my lady, excuse me. I wish to return to my chaperone."

As she turned to push her way through the crowd, heading for Cosmo, she grinned as she heard Brady say, "Well, if that don't beat the Dutch, my lords. I'll never understand women, will you? Snuff, anyone?"

Chapter Fourteen

"You're hateful," Regina declared, sitting back against the squabs of the carriage with a small thump. "Absolutely *hateful*. Cosmo, cover your ears. I'm going to tell the earl *exactly* what I think of him."

"You mean, the way you've been telling me for the past two hours, the expression on that lovely face of yours so fierce that not a single gentleman present was brave enough to ask you to dance? Why? Have you something new to say?"

Brady watched as Regina opened her mouth, then shut it again. "No. No, I'm not going to say another word. Except for this, my lord—if you think you're sending me away now, you'd better have another thought. Is that clear?"

"I wouldn't even consider it, my dear," Brady said, giving a delicate shudder. "I like my enemies where I can see them. I read that in a book, I believe."

"I'm not your—oh, bother! I *hate* Gawain, so I'm definitely not talking to *him*!" Regina said, turning her head to look out the window.

"Did you hear that, Mrs. Forrest?" Brady asked, keeping to his role of Gawain because his playacting was all that seemed to be needed to keep Regina so angry with him that there would be no opportunity to discuss last night's indiscretion. Or to repeat it. "Miss Felicity is, I believe, overset at something I said this evening. I can't imagine why."

So much for the passing scenes of London, as Regina whipped her head back to glare at him. "You can't imagine why? For one—and just to get it out of the way so that we can get on to how you just put us *both* in danger—you made a *fool* out of me tonight, and you damn well know it!"

"Ah, I believe we are discussing Lady Belle now, aren't we? If you'll recall, my dear, I did most specifically ask you not to draw her into this."

"Yes, but then you *dangled* that farradiddle about having been *romantically involved* with the woman, and I've now had two long hours to try to figure out if you did that so I'd stay clear of her, or because you felt handing me that pack of lies was the one way to get me to go chasing after her. Either way, I'm insulted, and I doubt she'll ever speak to either of us again. Do you know how difficult it was even to *find* her, yet alone make her acquaintance so that I could wrangle you an introduction? Which was it, *Gawain*? Were you trying to protect me, or were you just angry that I succeeded?"

"She's a woman, my lord," Cosmo put in helpfully.

"No matter what answer you give her, I believe you'll still be in trouble."

Brady bit back a rueful smile, believing Cosmo was right. "Oh, very well, I suppose I should tell the truth now, though, and take my chances," he said, gaining himself Regina's full attention. "One, I merely told you to stay away from her, and it was *you*, Regina, who asked how well I knew her, at which point I said something I regretted the moment the words were out of my mouth. Trying to take them back at the time, or later, would only have made matters worse. Two, having grown suddenly older and wiser, I am now at least slightly ashamed of the small prank I played on her a few years ago and didn't want you to hear about it, which you would do if ever the two of you were in conversation and my name should crop up at some point. Three, now you tell me if you think Lady Belle is a nice young lady, or if you sensed something . . . *darker* in her."

Regina was silent for some moments, then nodded. "Her eyes can go very *hard*. I did notice that. And she was quite frank with me—as I was with her—telling me that she had sought me out only so that I could introduce her to you, and to bolster her own popularity, because everyone wants to meet you. I didn't like that. She's . . . ambitious."

"And beautiful," Brady added, then held up his hand before Regina could go on the attack once more. "It's her beauty that fools people, Regina, that's all I'm saying. A few Seasons back, she let a friend of mine believe that she would be agreeable to his suit, and then when he offered for her she turned him down flat. Well, not quite flat. She let him know that she was much too good for him, and that she had no plans to marry anyone under the rank of duke. He was devastated, as you can imagine, and bought himself a commission before anyone could stop him, then went off to get himself killed. He was successful, unfortunately."

"That's terrible," Regina said, reaching over to squeeze Brady's hand. "So you went after her?"

"Made a dead set straight at her," Brady agreed. "And she did with me exactly what she'd done with my friend—pretended to be flattered by my pursuit. For a few rather terrifying weeks, I thought we'd be hearing the banns read before I could wiggle my way free."

Regina grinned. "That must have been terrifying, I agree. But then, when all of London was expecting a match, you asked for her hand, she turned you down as she did your friend—and you very publicly collected on the bet with Sir Henry?"

"*Extremely* publicly," Brady agreed. "At which point an enraged Lady Belle began telling everyone she never had the slightest thought of accepting my proposal. Even the *ton* is not entirely brainless, and within days she had the reputation of a tease, and a woman so sure she would marry a duke that a courtship by anyone of lesser rank was already doomed to failure."

Brady adjusted the lace on his cuffs. "She hasn't had an offer since, for all her beauty. Oh, and one more thing. That was how I knew the cowardly Viscount Allerton would not allow me to call him out the other night. The man didn't even have the backbone to defend his own sister."

"Remind me never to cross you, my lord," Cosmo

said, as they arrived back in Portman Square. "And now to rouse Thomas and have him get me out of this corset. You will be wanting us within the hour, won't you, my lord?"

"You're going out?" Regina asked, as he escorted her into the mansion and toward the stairs. "You promised to take me with you, remember? You owe me, my lord, for setting me up as bait tonight after promising you wouldn't."

"I only did what you were going to do, the moment you had the chance. Correct me if I'm wrong."

She stopped at the landing and turned to him, smiling. "You're not wrong. Only I was going to concentrate more on the tulips in your buttonhole than on myself, right up until the point where I asked you to please, please remove them from your lapel because a tulip had been the death of my papa."

"Oh, you see? Much too heavy-handed, my dear," Brady said, walking with her to the door of her chamber. "My way was decidedly better. Allerton now knows that the ever-inquisitive Brady had you under his protection, undoubtedly after hearing your sad tale, and that Gawain—who has also heard your sad tale—believes you to be a necessary obligation but a bit high-strung and prone to fancies. And now, while they're still under the misconception that Gawain is as dangerous as a dandelion—to keep to the flower theme, you understand—the man foremost in their thoughts tonight, Brady, will pay one of them a visit."

"You're very impressed with yourself, aren't you?" Regina asked, shaking her head. "But all right, I admit yours was the better plan. Or perhaps you didn't notice that slight twitch under Allerton's left eye as you told your fibs?"

"He twitched? Really?" Brady grinned. "I must have missed that. I was much too busy watching the other three gentlemen for their reactions. We can rule out Sir Randolph Tilden, by the way, although all three of the gentlemen stayed with Allerton throughout the evening. Sir Randolph yawned partway through those fibs of mine, which I considered very telling. So we have our men, or at least I'm willing to bet that we have. Samuel LeMain and Baron Stanley Thorndyke."

"Yawned? I didn't notice," Regina told him, one hand on the door latch as she looked at him. "But I did see Lady Belle watching her father. I don't think she likes him."

"Lady Belle is rather like David, enamored only of herself. However, unlike David, she has a great love of money, just the thing her father and brother have been frittering away these past years. I don't think Her Lady-ship approves, especially since eligible dukes have been fairly scarce on the ground these past few years."

Regina raised a hand to her mouth, bit on her knuckle. "I'm beginning to wish I'd listened to you and hadn't gone looking for her."

"Well, we'll have to see, won't we?" Brady said, pri-vately sharing Regina's opinion. "I'm driving out with her tomorrow, you understand. I think her expectations may have dropped a notch or two, and the silly, obviously manageable, and quite wealthy Gawain Caradoc—who has no knowledge of her humiliation years ago and her rather tarnished reputation—could have a certain appeal."

Regina shook her head. "You think of everything, don't you?" she asked.

"I try," Brady said, stepping back a pace, for he suddenly realized how close he was standing to Regina and how he longed to be closer. He couldn't believe how easy it would be to simply lean down, kiss her. How natural. "That said, you'll find some of David's clothing in your chamber, all of it black. If you still wish to go with us, please be downstairs in, oh, two hours."

"If I still wish to go? I'll be downstairs waiting for you, my lord."

And she was as good as her word, for she was sitting on a velvet-topped bench when Brady came back downstairs, dressed in the more sober (and comfortable) evening clothes of Brady James, bits of burlap sacking hanging from his black evening cloak.

She stood up to greet him, and Brady swallowed down hard as he saw the way David's pantaloons hugged her curves, accentuated the length of her very straight legs. How would they feel, wrapped around him?

Brady gave a quick shake of his head, banishing his traitorous thoughts, knowing that he had no time for them until this madness was over, behind them, and they could get to know each other better. As people, not just as co-conspirators with the same objective. And with all the lies straightened out, all the truths told, including the truth that there was something between them . . . something they needed to explore.

"I thought we might have to wait a while longer, but we have our destination now."

"Where are we heading, my lord?" Regina asked, falling into step beside him as he turned, heading for the secluded rear door that led out to the mews. "Mr. LeMain? Baron Thorndyke?"

"Thorndyke," Brady told her curtly, averting his gaze, which had been too readily captured once more, this time by the way David's thick black sweater hugged Regina's upper body. "LeMain has a brain. Thorndyke doesn't, so I thought we'd begin with him."

"Well, yes, I can imagine how that would be helpful," Regina said, settling into the carriage.

Brady followed after her once he'd double-checked the doors, saw that his orders had been obeyed and the shiny golden crests had been covered with black cloths. "Thomas is at the reins, and Cosmo will be joining him on the box in a few moments. Then we'll be off."

Regina nodded. "And David?"

"He's already in position. Cosmo, Thomas, and I put our heads together this afternoon. We've had a very well orchestrated plan already in place, and it worked to perfection. Once I'd pointed them in the right direction tonight, David and Thomas followed Thorndyke over half of London as the man went from ball to party to gaming hell. Thomas returned less than ten minutes ago, to tell me where the man is now. He's in a hell on a narrow side street on the fringes of Mayfair, which is perfect for my plans."

"How organized you are, my lord. I'm impressed."

"Yes, so am I," Brady said, grinning as he reached

down to the floor, picking up a length of rusty chain and draping it over his shoulders. "Now, reach into that pocket attached to the door and remove the bottle you'll find there. I thought you might enjoy dousing me with its contents."

Regina uncorked the bottle, sniffed at it. Her nose wrinkled as she pulled a face and peered into the neck of the thing. "Are you sure there aren't a few dead fish in here?"

"Anything's possible, as I sent Wadsworth to retrieve that small sample of the Thames, and he may have added his own touches, just because such a chore was beneath him. He keeps forgetting that he's offered me his help," Brady said. "Now put the cork back until we've arrived at our destination. If we spill any of it on the squabs, I'll have to order the carriage burned."

They rode in silence for a few minutes, and then Regina said, "Brady?"

He smiled in the darkness, hearing his name on her lips.

"Yes?" he asked.

"I want to apologize," she said, pleasing him even more.

"Really?" Brady amazed himself with the even tone of his response. This playacting must be seeping into his bones.

"No, I'm serious, I want to apologize. I shouldn't have gone chasing after Lady Bellinagara. It was stupid. And I don't blame you for stepping in the way you did, making me look silly while at the same time setting me up as bait, and yourself as a possible target as well. Yours was by far the better story, and I was bound and determined to do it my way until you started that business about monsters under my bed."

"I may have gone too far with that," Brady admitted. "Still, from here on out, I believe we have to put our heads together, and tell each other exactly what we're doing. I did not appreciate seeing Lady Belle tonight."

"I know you didn't. She knows you better than Allerton, and might have recognized you."

"I run that danger every moment," Brady pointed out reasonably, "although the blindness of people I've known for years is but one of the disappointments and revelations that I've been banged over the head with since my return to London. Do you know, my dear, that except for Kipp and Bram, who would have done so if they didn't already know that I'm alive, no one has so much as *peeked* into the reason behind the attack on me, tried to find my murderers?"

Regina cocked her head to one side, looked at him. "You were not as well liked as you supposed, my lord?" she offered. "I'm sorry."

"I was not as well *anything* as I supposed. Except for being a rather long-nosed, high-living, fairly shallow man." He gave a Gawain-like languid wave of his hand. "Well, not to worry. I'll be liked even less once everyone finds out I've been teasing them with Gawain Caradoc. I can already think of several people who are going to cut me dead the moment that news is out."

"The duke and duchess of Selbourne like you," Regina pointed out to him. "And Lord and Lady Willoughby. They think you're quite wonderful."

"But a bit of a loose screw," Brady added, grimacing.

Regina shrugged. "Well, that's true. But if you hadn't been so long-nosed, as you say, perhaps the viscount and the viscountess would never have met. Had you thought about that?"

"You know that story?"

"Oh, yes. Abby—that is, the viscountess—told me all about it. So you see? You are a nice man, and a good friend. You're my friend."

Brady leaned into the corner, covered his mouth with his hand, and just looked at her in the darkness as a dozen questions tumbled around inside of his head. "And the other night?" he said at last, the most unfortunate question having beaten its way to his mouth first, then spilled out before he could stop it.

He watched as she wet her lips with the tip of her tongue, and he succeeded in smothering a groan.

"Do you regret it?" he asked, unable to allow the tense silence to go on any longer.

"Do you, my lord?" she asked right back at him, just as the carriage drew to a rather abrupt halt, at which time she all but tumbled over herself in her anxiety to drop the shade and look out into the street. "We're here," she then said, quite unnecessarily.

The small trapdoor above their heads opened and Thomas's head appeared in the space. "My apologies, my lord, Regina. I've never before driven horses so obedient to my directions with the reins. They did stop quite nicely, though, didn't they?"

The side door opened and David stuck his head inside. "He's still in there, my lord, but he'll probably be leaving soon, now that I'm not losing hand after hand to him with your money. And it wasn't easy, for if there's a man who knows less about whist, I haven't met him. Oh, and he's three parts drunk, also at your expense. He's started calling me his pretty boy, however, and I can't say I like that."

"Thank you, David, and my apologies," Brady said. "Where's Thorndyke's carriage?"

"Cosmo is climbing into it about now and loudly ordering his driver to take him home, as he's closer in size to the baron than either Thomas or myself. Thomas went with him to open the door for him, the both of them staggering, so that no one came down off the box to help. We know our stage directions, my lord. Have no fear that we'll not keep to them."

"Amazing," Regina said as David withdrew his head and went back to the corner, to watch for Baron Thorndyke. "The man will come outside, find his carriage gone, and—and what? What comes next?"

"David comes next, of course," Brady said, feeling the thrill of a plan going well and the anticipation of it going even better. "He'll offer Thorndyke a ride in his own carriage, then say he has to go back inside the hell for his gloves, and send him ahead around the corner, where I'll be waiting."

Regina clapped her hands together. "Oh, aren't you glad we met up with them on the road? How much easier this all is with their help."

"*Their* help, Regina," Brady pointed out, adjusting the chains around his shoulders. "You, however, are here only to watch, and because you would have found some way to follow me if we'd left you behind. Now, because you've been so very good—or perhaps because you've not—I do believe you could consider this carriage your front row seat to my debut."

"Your debut, and your very last performance, if this works," Regina said feelingly, following him out of the carriage, the opened bottle in her hand.

"You're forgetting Gawain Caradoc, Regina. I'll be playing that role for at least a few more days, not that you'll be in my audience."

"And just what is that supposed to mean?" Regina asked, holding the bottle in what he could only consider a threatening position. "You don't really think you're going to send me away, do you?"

Brady cursed under his breath. "I should have shut my mouth about two sentences ago, when I was still doing rather well. And, no, Regina, I'm not going to send you away, much as I want to, much as I should. But you won't be leaving the mansion until this is over, even if I have to tie these chains around you and bolt them to the floor. Understood?"

"Understood," she said. Then, before he could move out of the way, she stood on her tiptoes and dumped the contents of the bottle over his head.

❧

Regina carefully dropped the heavy leather shade by a third, then knelt on the squabs and looked out through the uncovered window.

Brady's back was just about plastered against the damp

brick walls of the side of the gaming hell, so that he was all but invisible, even though she knew where to look.

By turning her head, and pressing her cheek against the glass, Regina could just make out the turning in the flagway that denoted the corner, and she held her breath as she waited to see Baron Thorndyke approach.

This wouldn't work. It couldn't work. Nobody would believe the ghost of Brady James was haunting London, dragging bits of chain and sacking with him, smelling of the Thames. Only an idiot would believe such a thing.

Or a man with a guilty conscience, which was probably what Brady was counting on, Regina decided. That, and the man seemed to be enjoying himself, as if he'd been planning this revenge for a long time and the moment was finally at hand.

Regina remembered the way Brady had been when she had first seen him at Singleton Chase. Sick, weak, and frightened. He hadn't been anywhere near the carefree, perhaps even faintly silly man he'd been when she'd first met him in London. Not smiling, not at all brash, and definitely not quite as satisfied with himself as he'd been the first time he'd looked into her eyes, when she had been merely Regina Bliss, maidservant—although he had seen much more.

Being beaten and thrown into the Thames could probably rob a person of quite a lot of his brashness, his confidence.

But there was something else. Brady seemed to be learning lessons since his dunking, and it was clear to Regina that he didn't much care for many of them.

So what if all of London hadn't loved him? Had he really thought it did? Or was it even more than that? Had he learned that he did not necessarily love all of London? All of his life as he had lived it thus far? That's what Cosmo had told her, and Cosmo was a very smart man.

Cosmo had explained to her one of the reasons behind Brady's convoluted revenge. Fear. That's what Cosmo had said. He'd told her that Brady had been so crushed by his bad experience that he'd been afraid to come back to London as himself, not until he was sure who had tried to kill him. And Regina believed this was probably true, that Brady was hiding behind Gawain Caradoc as much as he was using his "new" self to ferret out his murderers and make them confess.

Of course, that didn't explain tonight, and dressing up like a ghost to frighten Baron Thorndyke into saying something stupid, doing something equally stupid. That part, Regina had decided, was just for the fun of it as, once Allerton was confronted, he would probably sing out the names of his cohorts before anyone could ask him to do so.

"A little boy," Regina whispered in the darkness. "Part of Brady is still a mischief-loving little boy. And thank God for that, after all he's been through. Thank God for that."

Her musings came to a quick halt just as her mind began its inevitable swing from thinking of Brady as a little boy and remembering his kisses, because someone had just lurched around the corner and begun staggering up the flagway.

"Curtain up, my lord, as the dastardly villain enters,

stage left," Regina whispered, lowering the window itself, the better to hear the farce as it played out.

She watched as Brady pushed himself away from the wall, his chains clanking, a large section of burlap draped around his head to hide his hair, and took two steps in Thorndyke's direction before raising his hand, pointing at the man. "You-u-u-u," he groaned. "I see you-u-u-u."

Thorndyke staggered to a stop, rubbed at his eyes, hit a hand against his right ear. "What? Who? *Where?*" he questioned, his words slurred with drink.

Brady took another step, so close to Thorndyke now, and so close to the carriage, that Regina could smell the brackish water of the Thames clinging to his costume.

"Why?" Brady asked, his voice sounding hollow somehow. The man must have been practicing. "My soul knows no rest. Every night I walk this city, and I ask *why . . . why.* Why? *Who?*"

Thorndyke gave a shake of his head. "Don't ask me," he said, obviously too drunk to understand that he was looking at a ghost in evening clothes, burlap, and chains, and Regina stuffed her knuckle in her mouth to keep from giggling. Nothing was worse than a drunken audience, although their aim with the oranges was usually just as impaired, which was often a good thing.

Brady's hand shot out, clamping down on Thorndyke's shoulder—probably in hopes of gaining the man's attention that had just wandered to the sole of his evening shoe as he lifted his left leg to inspect it. "Stepped in somethin'," the baron said to himself. "Must have. Stinks to high heaven, don't it? You smell that?"

Brady shot a quick look toward the carriage, and

Regina saw the frustration in his eyes, as well as a quick flash of humor. Well, wasn't it nice that they were all enjoying themselves?

"Baron Thorndyke," Brady groaned, rather loudly for a ghost, but he did need to bring the baron back to the moment. "It is I, Brady James, Earl of Singleton. You killed me-e-e-e. Why did you kill me-e-e-e?"

Well, it may have been heavy-handed, in more than one way, but that did it. The baron put down his foot and leaned his head toward Brady, squinting in the darkness. "It is you, ain't it? Singleton? You stink. God, man, and you look just awful. You should do somethin' about that, you know. Another tailor for starters—right after your bath. Have some respect for yourself, man. Juss' because you're dead don't mean—"

It was amazing to see the transformation in Baron Thorndyke's expression as he finally realized what he was saying, who he was saying it to.

"Singleton?" he asked, putting up his hand to remove Brady's hand from his shoulder, then obviously deciding that might not be a good idea. "No, it can't be. I'm drunk. That's it. I'm bloody drunk."

"So drunk, Thorndyke, that you don't remember the night you beat me, stuffed me in this sack, tied me up with these chains? The night you rowed me to the middle of the Thames and dropped me into that dark water? I saw you, Thorndyke, through the sack, in the light from the lantern on the bow of the boat. You killed me, then you went off to play cards."

Thorndyke shook his head, violently, although his fear didn't seem to sober his drink-clouded brain. "No! No, tha's—tha's not true! It wasn't my idea! I *told* him not to do it, to juss let it go . . . but he said . . . oh, *God*!" He bent his knees, nearly fell to the flagway, as he tried to get out from under Brady's strong grip, then began to shout: "Help! Ghost! Ghost! Help me!"

"Oh, now that's clever," Regina said out loud, unable to control her mirth. "Just what would make the whole world come to your assistance—telling them you need help to get away from a *ghost*."

"You did it," Brady said loudly, the tone of his voice sending a shiver down Regina's spine. "You killed me! Let me hear you say it. Tell me! You killed me, didn't you?"

"Yes, we killed you, but—"

Just as Regina thought Brady would ask him for the names of the other two men, Brady removed the chains from his shoulders and wrapped them around Thorndyke's neck, drawing him close, lifting the terrified man's feet clear of the flagway, so that their faces were now only inches apart.

"Afraid, Thorndyke?" he asked, his voice now so low Regina had to strain to hear him. "Do you feel your heart pounding? Have your arms and legs gone numb?" The chains tightened around the baron's neck. "Are your bowels turned to water, is your piss running down your leg? Do you want to *cry*, Thorndyke? Cry for me, Thorndyke. I want to hear you cry."

Regina's smile faded as she realized that there was suddenly nothing amusing about watching Brady, listening to him. Should she stop him? Would he choke Thorndyke if she didn't? And then, just as she was about to hop down from the carriage, calling to David and Thomas to help her, Brady released the man with a hard shove, sending Thorndyke to the flagway. The baron turned onto his stomach and retched.

"No," Brady said as Thorndyke coughed, choked, rubbed at his throat. "No, I'm not like you. My God, I'm *not* like you!"

Regina wasn't quite sure of exactly what she'd just witnessed, but she did know that it was time to get Brady out of there, for he was just standing there now, his arms at his sides, shaking his head in denial of something.

"David!" Regina called out as she opened the door to the carriage. "Get that drunken idiot out of here. Just take him back around the corner and leave him there."

Never late for a cue, David appeared, Thomas with him. Within moments Thorndyke was being led away, sobbing, and Thomas had shoveled Brady into the carriage.

He sat in the corner, pulled the burlap sacking from his head and looked at something Regina couldn't see. "I need a drink," he said at last, as Thomas and David returned to the box and the carriage lumbered through the streets.

"You need a bath, my lord," Regina told him. "And then, Brady, I think we need to talk."

He looked up at her, then nodded. "Yes, Regina, I think we probably do."

Chapter Fifteen

$\mathcal{R}$egina paced the carpet in her bedchamber for a full hour, but as the clock struck four the last of her patience fled. Gathering her dressing gown about her, she slipped into the hallway, just in time to see Wadsworth leaving Brady's bedchamber.

"Pssst! Wadsworth!" she hissed, tiptoeing down the hall. "Is he all right?"

"He, miss?" Wadsworth said. "Would you then be standing here, dressed completely inappropriately, to inquire as to Lord Singleton's health, a matter that is none of your concern? How very kind, I'm sure."

"Oh, stubble it, Wadsworth," Regina said, unimpressed. "He looked terrible when we got back here, and I could see him in a good light—and not just because of the costume, or the fact that he was all wet and smelly. Something happened tonight, Wadsworth, and I want to know what it is."

"Something happened months ago, miss," Wadsworth

told her, suddenly wearing the look of a man with a worried mind. "He was nearly murdered. And not a quick bullet, or the stab of a knife. He was beaten, tied up in a sack, made to listen for nearly an hour, helpless, as his attackers planned his death, then spoke of their plans for the remainder of the evening. He had time to consider the fact that he was about to die, miss. War is kinder."

Regina bit her lip, nodded. "The nightmares."

"Yes, the nightmares. Living with the realization that, no matter how dashing and brave he might have thought himself years ago, during the war, he had come face-to-face with a terror he didn't know existed, at least not inside him. That's part of it, miss, and I think you already have realized this. The rest, I fear, is not quite so easily explained or understood, as I believe His Lordship has decided that he's a rather base, unlovable fellow."

"But that's ridiculous! He's the most lovable—that is," she amended quickly, "he's a very nice man, Wadsworth." she looked down at her toes. "A very nice man."

"I suggest you tell him that, miss. In the morning, miss," Wadsworth said, once more looking her up and down, and making her feel as if she were standing there naked, which she most certainly wasn't. Why, her night rail was modest enough all by itself, and her dressing gown covered her from her neck to her toes. She'd often sat in company with Cosmo, Thomas, and David, and never given a thought to the fact that they were *all* in their nightclothes.

Besides, she'd already seen Brady's knees.

"Yes, of course, Wadsworth," Regina said, knowing

her arguments wouldn't move the butler a single step from in front of Brady's door. "In the morning. Good night, Wadsworth."

She felt his eyes on her as she walked back down the hall, entered her own chamber. Then she counted to one thousand, and opened the door once more. The hallway was clear in both directions.

Running nearly on her toes, Regina flew down the hallway, opened the door to Brady's chamber, and ducked inside, closing the door behind her and leaning against it, trying to catch her breath.

"That's twice," Brady's voice said from somewhere in the darkness, and Regina looked toward a small brace of candles, to see Brady standing there in a white shirt, open at the neck, his shirttails hanging loose over a pair of tan pantaloons. His hair, still damp from his bath, hung freely to his shoulders. "I've been expecting you. Not that you should be here, as Wadsworth already told you."

"You heard us? Out in the hallway?" Regina asked, slowly walking toward him.

"Wadsworth is exemplary in all things, save one. He's never quite mastered the discreet whisper. Or perhaps he has. Have you thought about that, Regina?"

She tipped her head to one side, considering Brady's words. "You mean, do I think perhaps that Wadsworth was trying to alert you that I might be breaking down your door sometime soon? I imagine it is possible. But why would he do that?"

Brady turned away, headed for a small table holding several decanters. "Now there's a question I'm in no great hurry to answer, although I'm willing to gift Wadsworth with the purest of motives. A glass of wine?"

"Yes, please," Regina said, walking over to the fireplace and seating herself in one of the pair of dark green leather chairs that flanked it. "I thought we were going to talk."

He walked toward her, a glass in each hand, the look of Gawain about him even in his simple clothes. "Dear me," he said, handing her one of the glasses, "and here I thought the nighttime was for sleeping, and the daytime for talking. Shame on me, for not keeping up with the latest fashion in our marvelous society."

Regina curled her upper lip slightly as Brady sat down, crossed one leg over the other, and sipped at his wine, the last finger of his left hand pointed toward the ceiling. "If you're quite through being an idiot . . . ?" she offered at last.

Brady drained the contents of his glass, put it down on the table beside him. "You don't like Gawain, do you, princess? Neither do I. Although he does have his moments."

"And his uses," Regina agreed, nodding. "But it's time he left, isn't it?"

Brady rubbed at the back of his neck, then grinned. "I think I might miss the hair. Cosmo says I'd make a wonderful Hamlet when I don't tie it up. What do you think?"

"I think I want to know what happened tonight, my lord," Regina told him honestly. "You were rather enjoying yourself, I believe, until Thorndyke admitted that he was one of the three men who tried to murder you. Then you changed, right in front of my eyes. I thought you might kill him."

Brady gave a toss of his head, so that his hair was off his face. "So did I, princess, so did I. I'm not sure what it was . . . his confession, or the bits of burlap and chains, the smell of the river . . . something. Suddenly I was lying in that boat again, being rowed to my watery grave—to be melodramatic about the thing." He spread his hands, palms up. "I wanted Thorndyke to suffer, princess. I wanted him to feel what I'd felt, what I'd lived through at least two dozen times in my nightmares."

"But you couldn't *be* him, could you? You couldn't kill him."

Brady slowly shook his head, then looked at her, smiled ruefully. "No, princess, I couldn't, not if I wanted to be the better man. And I do so want to be a better man."

Regina's heart ached, watching Brady, listening to him. "You *are* the better man, Brady," she said with some force. "Don't you know that? Wadsworth knows it, Cosmo and Thomas and David know it, your friends know it . . ." She took a deep breath, let it out slowly, ". . . I know it."

Brady stood up, and Regina twisted in her chair, watching him as he began walking around the room, touching a figurine on a table, trailing his fingers over the items lying on his desk. "Do you know, princess, I think my dunking did me a world of good. I'm not the same man I was last year. Oh, not that I went into the Thames in that sack, some sad caterpillar, and emerged a butterfly—nothing quite so miraculous. But I have had time to look at my life, at myself, and realize that things that once seemed important to me now mean nothing, while things I once laughed at are more dear to me now than my own life."

He walked back over to her, sat down once more. "Am I making any sense?"

"Yes, my lord, you are," Regina told him quietly. "And if you're telling me that you want to give this up, walk away from it, I understand."

Brady's head came up with a jerk. "Give it up? Oh, no, princess. No, no, no. But I won't be the one to punish them. I'll leave that to the courts. I hated them, Regina. I've hated those three men with a passion that frightens me now, when I think of it. I allowed my judgment to be clouded by that hatred, allowed myself to put you in danger. Everything I've done these last months, the nightmares, this Gawain nonsense, my ghostly incarnation tonight—I've done it all because of that deep, abiding hate. That hate kept me locked in that sack, princess, drowning in it. But now I'm out. I'm free. I'm free, and I just want this *over*."

Regina used the back of her hand to wipe tears from her cheeks. "I understand. I hate them, too, Brady, and for a long time I've wanted them dead for what they did to me, to my parents. But now Cosmo says—"

Brady hopped to his feet once more, slapping a hand against his forehead. "My God! Me! What a selfish bastard I am. I'm talking on and on—about *me*. When it's you, Regina. You had the greater loss."

"Yes, but I've also had more time to come to grips with my grief," she told him honestly. "Oh, I still want those men punished, just as you do, but I have reconciled myself to the fact that Papa brought most of his troubles on himself. He was in water as deep as the Thames, my lord, when he began lying to Allerton, taking his money that way, tricking him with that ridiculous, false black tulip. And, besides, now Cosmo says that he thinks—"

Brady reached down and took her hands in his, raised her to her feet. "Princess, nothing your father did warranted both he and your mother dying for it. But that's not really what I'm talking about now. I'm talking about you, the way you had to beg in the streets, be in fear for your life every waking and sleeping moment. If I've never told you how in *awe* I am of your courage, please let me tell you now. The day I met you I thought I saw something special in those lovely grey eyes of yours. Mischief. Intelligence. But it wasn't that. Oh, the mischief and intelligence are there, don't ever doubt that. But it was your courage that drew me, I know that now. You stood there, looking straight into Kipp's eyes, and told him one great whopping fib after another. You never flinched, you never lost your courage."

Regina smiled wanly. "You couldn't see my knees knocking, my lord. You wouldn't have been half so impressed if you could have seen my knees knocking together."

"Your knees?" Brady said, laughing. "I was too busy cursing the fact that Kipp had said you were a child." He ran the back of his fingers down her cheek. "I didn't see a child when I looked at you, Regina. I saw a woman, a woman with a secret. I've always hated secrets."

"You were always nosy, you mean," Regina said, knowing she should step away from him, also knowing that she couldn't. "But my secret nearly got you killed, and still might. I should have told you the truth the first time you asked."

"I didn't *ask*, princess, until after I'd gone for my swim, remember?"

She blinked, cocked her head to one side, then looked up at him. "Why, you're right. You *didn't* ask me, did you? You just went to Little Woodcote and got yourself into trouble." She lifted her shoulders, let them drop. "Ah, well now I feel better."

"Now you feel . . . ? Oh, God, Regina," he said, pulling her into his arms, "what a piece of work you are. What a piece of work we both are."

She pressed her cheek against his chest, suddenly overcome with the same feelings she'd had when he'd kissed her, except that now they were more intense, and even more frightening. "I . . . I should go now," she said, pushing away from him. "It will be dawn soon, and I know you plan to be waiting outside Thorndyke's town house to see whom he visits this morning."

"More like noon, as I'm fairly certain Thorndyke will be nursing an aching head in his bed for some time yet. But you know that I'm planning to watch his town house? How? I didn't tell you that."

"You didn't? Then perhaps I'm just brilliant. Did you tell me that, as you're sure Thorndyke will go to Allerton, and Allerton will call in LeMain, that this whole thing could be over by nightfall?"

"If I did, princess," Brady said, not attempting to touch her again, "then *I* would have been the one spinning tales. No, Regina, I'm afraid it will take at least one more day to have everything arranged as I want it. In the meantime, you'll be staying here. Understand?"

"I can't even go along to watch with you outside of Thorndyke's town house?"

"No, princess, you can't. You'll go nowhere at all, unless you're in my company."

"But you're going to Thorndyke's," she reminded him, just as another thought hit her. "You're *not* going to Thorndyke's. You're sending Thomas or David—because *you're* going out driving with Lady Belle!"

"Gawain is going out driving with Lady Belle," Brady reminded her, although that small distinction didn't make her feel the least bit better.

"So you say," Regina said, turning toward the door before he could see the jealousy that must have sprung into her eyes. He could say what he wanted about Lady Bellinagara, but the woman was still beautiful. "Well, good night, my lord."

"Regina?" he called after her, and when she turned around he was standing right in front of her. "Weren't you going to tell me about something Cosmo said to you?"

She looked at him, looked down at her toes. "No. No, I wasn't. It wasn't important. I'm sure I can take care of it myself, once you've shown Allerton and his friends for what they are. As a matter of fact, you don't need me at all anymore, do you, now that you aren't quite as dedicated to seeing those three men hang for what they did to you."

"They'd hang for what they did to your parents," he reminded her, and she kept concentrating on her toes, refusing to look at him again.

"I know," she said, measuring her words carefully. "But maybe they wouldn't. Maybe it would only be Papa who'd be condemned—the memory of him that would be condemned—for taking Allerton's money when he couldn't possibly give him a black tulip."

"Regina," Brady said, putting a finger under her chin and lifting her head so that she had no choice but to look at him. "Regina, I *know* we discussed this. If I can't mention your parents, I have little hope of exposing Allerton at all. Is that what you want? Do you want Allerton to escape justice?"

She pushed his fingers away, gave herself a small shake as she launched into what she knew to be part lie, part truth. "You said yourself that you're probably a better man for having been thrown into the Thames. And I'm alive, and I'm back with Cosmo and the others. We're both all right, my lord. So yes, yes. I want this to stop now, not tomorrow, not with Allerton exposed and punished. I just want it all to go away so that I can leave here and get on with my life."

She pressed a hand against her mouth for a moment, then ended, "The sooner I'm gone, Brady, the better it will be for the both of us."

She watched as Brady stabbed his fingers through his hair, thought she heard him say something fairly rude under his breath. "You want to go? To leave?" he then asked her. "Do you really think that would be better for both of us?"

"I do," she said quietly. "I'm an actress, my lord. I can't . . . I don't belong here. You're all right now. You told me so yourself, and I'm glad for that. I'm sorry that you got hurt trying to help me, and I'm glad I could help you, even a little bit. But I want to leave here now."

That last was a great exit line, and if her feet would only move, Regina would have whirled about dramatically and gone out the door. But her feet wouldn't move, and she wasn't going anywhere. Not as long as Brady kept looking at her that way, his expression so intense, his eyes so full of questions.

"What did Cosmo tell you, Regina?" he asked at last. "Is that why you're suddenly in such a hurry to leave? Because of something Cosmo told you?"

"No," she answered quickly, then winced. She'd answered too quickly to have her denial be anything except a lie.

"All right," Brady said, nodding. "I believe you."

Regina looked at him owlishly. "You believe me? Why?"

He took a step forward, and her traitorous feet still wouldn't move. "Do you have to ask? Isn't it enough that I believe you?"

"No, I don't think so . . ."

"Really?" he said, reaching for her hand, squeezing it. "Then to quote you, princess—why?"

Her hand was on fire, her arm ablaze. His thumb moved against her palm and the heat exploded past her arm, filling her entire body. "Because I'm lying," she admitted, closing her eyes.

He stepped closer, still holding on to her hand as he gently bent her arm, took it behind her back so that he could pull her against his body. "I know."

Regina's chest rose and fell rapidly as her breaths grew quick and shallow. "You know?"

He bent his head, whispered his next words against the side of her throat. "I know, princess. But if you want me to believe you, I will."

"But . . . but why?"

His free hand cupped her chin as he traced kisses across her cheek, toward her mouth. She looked up at him, saw him looking at her, saw his eyelids droop slightly as he concentrated his gaze on her mouth. "I'd do anything, princess, say anything, believe anything, if it meant you'd let me take you to my bed right now. Right now, Regina. Tomorrow, all the tomorrows after that, will be time enough for other plans."

Regina swayed on her feet, Brady's words, his tone, turning her knees to water. She should say no. She should push him away.

But he wasn't holding her anymore. When had he let go of her hand, her chin? She hadn't noticed.

He wasn't touching her at all. Except with the feather-light brushes of his lips against her skin . . . and the strong-as-iron-bands power of his words and the way he'd said them, that and the look in his eyes.

Did she want this? Did she want to take this memory with her when she left London, left this life that wasn't hers, couldn't be hers?

Yes. Yes, she did. She'd be a fool to deny it.

Slowly, barely realizing that she was doing so, her arms snaked up and around Brady's neck, and suddenly he was kissing her, kissing her full on her mouth, lifting her high into his arms, and carrying her toward his bed.

He laid her down on her back, and she buried her head against his neck as he joined her on the cool sheets, his arms going around her as he spoke to her, soothing her, gentling her as she opened her eyes and looked up at the dark silken canopy over her head.

"Don't be afraid, princess," Brady told her, moving slightly so that he could undo the satin ribbons holding her dressing gown closed. "If we're both afraid, this could end in disaster."

She smiled at that, adoring him for the way he knew how to reach her, tease her, make her laugh even as she allowed him to ease her dressing gown from her, moving her one step closer to the point beyond which she could not turn back.

And then, with one hand now resting on her waist, against the thinness of her night rail, he began to kiss her. Long, drugging kisses that sent her ears to buzzing, her mind to reeling . . . her hands to traveling up and over his shoulders, to press against his back.

More . . . more . . .

She knew there had to be more. More than this feeling of wanting, *wanting*.

Brady's hand closed over her breast, and she sighed into his mouth, rising up to meet him, wanting more. More.

His hand left her, gliding down over her body, reaching for the hem of her night rail, which had ridden above her knees. His hand was on her flesh now, her burning flesh. Moving upward again, tracing a path of fire along her as he pushed the night rail ahead of him, his mouth leaving hers only long enough for him to take the gown up and over her head, so that she was now totally naked.

Regina felt a sudden need to cover herself, but that need was fleeting, because now Brady was kissing her again, caressing her again, moving his hand over her breast and . . . oh! His fingers, his fingers. How they touched her, lifted her, molded her.

She held her breath as he rubbed the pad of his thumb over her nipple, sending a shiver completely through her, making other parts of her jealous for his touch, hungry for his touch.

Again she moved against him, straining for something she had never felt but knew existed, had to exist, or else she'd have nothing . . . nothing.

"Do you know how long I've wanted this?" she heard Brady ask, his voice coming to her as if from a distance, and she looked up, surprised to see that he had moved away from her, that he was standing beside the bed, looking down at her as he quickly stripped out of his clothing. "Do you know how much I want you?"

She didn't answer, couldn't answer, and he said nothing more, but now he was with her again, kissing her again, taking her higher, yet again higher . . .

Just when she felt that one more kiss would be too many—while still not being enough—Brady's mouth left hers and he began kissing her throat, then moved down so that she felt him close around her taut nipple, felt his tongue move against her wildly sensitive skin.

Regina began to sense the tension in Brady, in the way he moved, in the way his touch remained slow, and gentle, even as his breathing grew more rapid, even as he moved his body closer against hers and she could feel his hardness straining against her thigh.

With that realization, oddly, came power. The power to stir him, to move him, to make him want her as she wanted him. She wouldn't just take. She could give. She wanted to give. But *how*?

"Brady," she said as she bent her legs at the knee, pressed her thigh against him. "Tell me. Tell me what to do. Teach me . . ."

He lifted his head from her breast and looked at her, smiled at her in the near darkness. "You're incredible," he told her, even as he moved his hand lower, lower, moved it between her legs.

Her eyes widened as a new sensation gripped her. No, not new. Just better. More . . . and more . . . and more. Giving, taking. Sharing. With hands and mouth and body. Not thinking, not needing to think, or to learn, or to ask.

He was here, with her. She was here, with him. This was right, this was good, and there were no cues, no stage directions, no lines to recite. What would happen would happen, without prompting, without rehearsal.

And when it was over, she would leave, let him go back to his world, his life, while she went off to do what she had to do. *Romeo and Juliet* without the deaths in the last act, but still a tragedy.

Regina felt tears stinging behind her eyes, and moved on the bed, trying to recapture the feeling while she banished her thoughts, told herself that it didn't matter, that nothing mattered. None of her tomorrows mattered, as long as she would always have tonight.

"You're crying," Brady said, and Regina looked at

him, amazed that he was now somehow above her, looking down into her face. "Am I hurting you? I would never hurt you, princess, I promise. If you want me to stop, I'll stop."

"No!" She lifted a hand to cup his cheek. "No, please, Brady. I want this. Don't you want this?"

"Even if it damns me to hell," Brady told her, lowering his body between her legs, easing himself against her. Kissing her, whispering to her, holding her close when she cried out as a small pain surprised her.

"Now you know all my plans, princess, even if you've only begun to learn what it is we have now, what I always knew we could have, even when I lied and told myself it wasn't true. You can't leave me now," Brady whispered against her ear as he filled her, began to move inside her, took her beyond rational thought, so that she heard the words, but really didn't hear them. "I won't let you go. I can't . . ."

Nearly two hours later, as dawn crept into the city, Brady carried a sleeping Regina down the hallway to her chamber, gently laying her down on her bed. It wouldn't do to have the household know he'd taken her to his bed. He covered her, then watched as she sighed, turned on her side, and smiled in her sleep.

Leave? Did she really think he would let her leave him?

He hadn't said words of love to her, because they had

so many lies between them that he wouldn't expect her to believe mere words.

So he'd done the unspeakable; he'd taken her to his bed. Told her with his hands, his body, with the way he'd held her, filled her, shown her . . .

She'd know, soon. She'd know that it didn't matter to him that she was an actress, that she told a fib with every second sentence if the spirit moved her, that her father did something that would have had him thrown into prison.

She'd know that his life had changed from the moment he'd first looked into her wonderful grey eyes, and that he wouldn't change anything that had followed that first look, even the worst parts, if it meant never knowing her, never holding her, never learning what it truly meant to be alive.

He pressed two fingers against his mouth, then laid them lightly on her hair. "I love you, princess," he whispered, then turned and left the room.

Chapter Sixteen

Regina awoke slowly, one arm going out, stretching across the mattress ... encountering nothing. Her eyes opened, and she blinked in surprise as she realized she was in her own bed, in her own chamber, and very much alone.

"Brady?" she murmured, sitting up, pulling the covers along with her to cover her nakedness. A quick glance at the mantel clock told her it was only eight o'clock in the morning. She saw her night rail and dressing gown lying at the bottom of the bed and quickly threw them on before Maude could arrive with her morning chocolate, then jumped back into bed once more.

Her bed. "As opposed to Brady's bed," she whispered in the quiet room, "which is where you were last night." She slid down on the pillows. "Oh my. You've done it now, Gina. You've really done it now."

She deliberately lost herself in a daydream, remembering the way Brady had held her, the way he had kissed her . . . the way her bones had melted and her heart had sung and her world had changed forever. If she could live in that moment, that daydream, then all would be right with the world.

But she couldn't. Nobody could live in a daydream, not for long, and within a few minutes Regina's pleasant bubble of memory burst, leaving behind only the problems. The problems with no solutions.

They still had to expose Allerton and his two companions for what they'd done to Brady, without involving her father.

They still had to explain to the *ton* why Brady had deliberately played with them, teased them with Gawain Caradoc, and make it all reasonable and believable enough that the *ton* would forgive him.

She still had to tell Brady the truth, *all* of the truth. Including the notion Cosmo had put into her head.

She still had to face Brady this morning, after all that had happened last night. She had to pretend she hadn't heard what he'd said, how he'd sworn never to let her go.

She knew that he felt somehow grateful to her for having made him realize certain things about himself, about his life, that he now wanted to change. He was even kind enough to pretend to forget that her secrets, her lies, had nearly meant the death of him.

But that didn't mean that he loved her. Gratitude was not love. Desire was not love.

What mattered was that she was an actress, a person totally unsuited and unsuitable to be a countess. An actress, in the eyes of society, was no better than a streetwalker who could quote Shakespeare. There was no future for them, not if Brady wanted to continue to move in society. Brady knew that. She knew that.

If she could be as daring as she pretended to be, she would become his mistress, as actresses often did, and take the crumbs he could give her until he had put his life back together again and no longer needed her. Thought he needed her.

But Regina wasn't that daring, that brave. She couldn't be his mistress, because she loved him. She couldn't put the final touch on destroying his reputation by becoming his wife—if he asked her, which he just might.

He just might.

"Good morning, miss," Maude said, interrupting Regina's muddled, unhappy thoughts as she entered the room, carrying a small silver tray holding a fragrant serving of hot chocolate and two small biscuits. "Mrs. Forrest asks that you join her downstairs as soon as possible."

Cosmo? Of course, *Cosmo*! She wasn't alone. She had Cosmo, and Thomas, and David. Well, perhaps not David. He wouldn't have any suggestions for her, not unless she was asking him what colors went best with his eyes.

She needed a plan. She needed to find a way to help Brady finish the scheme without once mentioning her father's less-than-laudable actions. She needed his help in Little Woodcote, if Cosmo was right. And then she needed a wagon, some horses, and a way out of Brady's life.

Regina picked up a single biscuit, waving away the tray as she pushed back the covers and got out of bed. "Is my bath ready, Maude?" she asked, already rummaging in drawers, pulling out fresh underclothes.

"It is," Maude answered, putting down the tray. "Are you and Mrs. Forrest going out again this morning, miss? To Bond Street? I'd dearly love to see Bond Street."

Regina, the biscuit clenched between her teeth, stopped rummaging through the drawer, closed her eyes for a few seconds, then turned to look at her friend. A promise was a promise.

She took the cookie out of her mouth. "I did say we'd do that, didn't I, Maude?" she said, knowing that if she didn't take Maude to Bond Street today, the chances were that she never could. "All right. First my bath, then Mrs. Forrest. And then, Maude, we're going to show you Bond Street, and the devils on every corner. How's that?"

Maude's plain, country face lit up in a wide grin. "Cook will be *so* jealous!" she said, grabbing underclothes from Regina and laying them out on the bed. "I want to get her some lace to trim her nightcaps. And something special for Mrs. Gaines. Some ribbons, do you think? Oh, and my sister Bertha told me she'd dearly love a . . ."

Regina smiled and nodded, no longer listening, her mind fully occupied by thoughts of how she would live after today. She had to think about that, and about the future, because thinking about Brady would only make her cry.

Brady watched as Bram sat in the drawing room at the Selbourne mansion, reading a letter from Sophie that had just arrived from Willoughby Hall in the morning post.

He'd come to see Bram not twenty minutes earlier, and had spent those twenty minutes as Gawain, speaking of inanities, all while trying to bolster his courage so that he could ask Bram a few questions. A few very important questions.

Just when he'd sat himself down, still reluctant to speak but knowing that Bram was beginning to look at him oddly, the butler had brought in the letter on a silver tray.

It was amazing to see the duke of Selbourne transform from urbane gentleman of the world to anxious husband and father as he broke the seal on the letter, barely excusing himself before he began to read.

Brady busied himself looking about the large room, seeing Sophie everywhere he looked, from the dramatically flowing draperies, to the comfortable couches, to the small jack-in-the-box sitting on a table in front of one of the windows. The toy, he knew, belonged to Sophie's pet monkey, Giuseppe. Sophie had come into his friend's life, unbidden, definitely unwanted, and forever turned that life upside down. It was amazing. It was wonderful.

And Brady envied his friend's happiness more than he'd like to admit. Because Bram and Sophie had made it work. They'd survived scandal, they'd overcome gossip, and they were now two of the most genuinely happy, deeply and completely in love people he'd ever known. And what Bram could do, Brady could do. At least he hoped he could.

"Listen to this, Brady," his friend said now, reading the second sheet of the letter. " 'Constance sat her first pony the other day, and our lives will never be the same, my darling husband. All she has been saying ever since is *horsey, horsey, horsey,* until Kipp finally got down on all fours yesterday and took her for a ride on his back, because it was raining and we couldn't go down to the stables. Now Constance demands pony rides around the entire downstairs at least once an hour. Poor Kipp. He may never walk upright again.' "

Brady smiled, even as he felt another stab of jealousy. It was hard to believe that a year ago he would have made some joke at Kipp's expense and been done with it. Now what had once seemed silly had become something he desired with all his heart. His own wife. His own children. Regina calling him "my darling husband."

"Kipp on all fours, neighing. I think I'd like to see that," he said, as Bram went back to his letter, finishing quickly and then folding the pages, tucking them beneath his waistcoat. "Anything else you want to share? Does your Sophie still love you?"

Bram patted his pocket. "She misses me," he said, "and promises to be back to town within the week. That's a good thing, Brady, because no matter how much I've enjoyed watching you prance about in society, if Sophie wasn't coming home soon, I'd be going to her. I miss her, I miss the children. And I missed seeing Constance sit her first pony. You're amusing, Brady, in your satins and lace, but I would much rather have been watching Constance bouncing on that pony."

"My most sincere apologies, Bram, but I still very much need your help, and your advice," Brady said, going over to the drinks table to pour them each a glass of wine. He carried the glasses back to the facing couches, handing a glass to Bram before he sat down on the other couch. "I think I've gotten in over my head, old friend."

"Over your head? Well, that is how this all started, didn't it? With the Thames closing over your head?"

Brady put away all of Gawain's affectations as he leaned forward, holding the wineglass between his cupped hands. "You know what I wanted to do. What I've been planning for, working toward, all these months."

Bram nodded. "Very publicly unmasking the men who tried to kill you, then watching them being led away to hang."

"Sounds so simple, doesn't it?" Brady asked, shaking his head. "Well, all right, not exactly *simple*. I had everyone believe me dead so that I could hide behind these silly satins until I knew for certain who was trying to kill me. I involved Regina, first because I felt sure she knew why I'd been attacked, and then because . . . because . . ."

"Because you felt sorry for her, learning that her parents had been killed? Realizing how courageous she was to have saved herself any way she could? Wanting to show off for her as you punished the men who killed her parents?"

Brady waved a hand at his friend. "That last one," he admitted, because there was no more reason to lie, not if he was going to be honest with himself. "That last one was rather important to me. All the reasons you stated were important to me, including one you didn't mention. Regina was my best hope for success, and I wasn't above using her, putting her in danger, to make my plan work. But that's all changed."

Bram took a sip of wine. "Has it? How?"

Downing his wine, Brady stood up once more, walked over to the table holding the jack-in-the-box, picked it up. "I'm thinking of letting it go, Bram," he said quietly. "Walking away without doing a damn thing about Allerton or the others." He wound the toy, flinching slightly as the lid snapped back and the puppet inside popped up.

"Do you really mean that? You'd give it up? After all the planning, all that they did to you? I saw you, remember. You were half-dead. And you're thinking about walking away, forgiving them? Letting it go?"

"Never forgiving them, Bram," Brady said tightly. "I just don't think my revenge is worth the price I'd have to pay."

He put down the toy, returned to the couch. "I could do it, you know. Gawain could be called away for some reason, and then a few months later I could surface again with some story about having been set upon by thieves, robbed of my purse—and the ring you found on that body. I'd been hit on the head, my bones broken, my memory gone—"

"I think I get the idea, and Lord knows our dear friends in society are more than willing to swallow any ridiculous tale as long as it makes for good gossip. Gawain disappears, you reappear. But that would leave the problem of Allerton, remember? He might still wish you dead."

Brady rubbed a hand across his mouth. "I know. I thought of that. I'd be constantly watching my back."

"So why do it? I don't understand."

Brady tipped his head, looked at his friend. "Because I can't expose Allerton without exposing Regina, or her fa-

ther's involvement in all of this. Regina is highly—
highly—protective of her father's memory. Everyone
would know about his scheme, and everyone would
know she's an actress. Not that it matters to me, damn it,
because it doesn't."

The duke of Selbourne rested his chin in his hand and
looked at Brady. "I wish Sophie were here," he said almost to himself, then continued: "Why is it important to
you that no one learns that Regina is an actress?"

"An actress, Abby's maid—it makes no difference. Sophie may have had to steel herself to the gossip over her
mother, but she was wellborn, her mother and father had
been in society. Regina grew up in a wagon, traveling
around the country, performing onstage. You do see what
I'm saying, don't you?"

"I do. But only if Regina were to *remain* in society,"
Bram said reasonably. "She's already been accepted as
your ward, although there hasn't been enough time for
too many questions to arise over that. Our small world is
still too titillated by Gawain Caradoc to ask too many
questions. So, is Regina going to remain in society,
Brady—with *you* in society? Is that what this is all about?
Because, if it is, I owe Sophie a new ruby bracelet."

Brady stabbed his fingers through his hair. "I took her
to bed last night," he said at last, looking Bram straight in
the eyes.

"Really," Bram said after a slight pause.

"Really," Brady repeated. "It was wrong, I know that.
She was innocent and I took advantage of her."

"Really."

"She's going to leave me. I can sense it, I can feel it.

She's still holding something back from me, still lying to me. She was going to run away before I could expose Allerton, expose her father for his part in this whole thing. I couldn't allow that. I couldn't allow her to leave me. So I took her to bed. I compromised her. Totally. You would probably be doing Regina a kindness if you were to have me taken out and shot for the opportunistic bastard that I am."

"Really," Bram said yet again, this time with his fingertips blocking his mouth, so that Brady didn't know if his friend was smiling or simply trying to keep himself from saying something other than "really."

"Would you please stop saying that? You're not being very helpful, you know. I did a terrible, an unforgivable thing," Brady said in exasperation.

"Forgive me," Bram said, adjusting the cuffs of his coat. "Are you done now? Or is there something else you want to tell me? As it is, I probably won't be able to remember every word, the way Sophie would expect me to when she comes home. So let's see if I have this right. You've decided to give up your revenge, walk away now that you're so close, and all because Regina would be hurt if you didn't. Is that right?"

"Her father tried to foist a fake black tulip on Allerton and took money he didn't deserve," Brady said, nodding. "Without that piece of information, there's no reason for Allerton's attack on me. I'd have to expose Regina's father if I want to see Allerton and the others punished."

"Yes, I understand that. Kipp would be mightily impressed, you know. He'd probably say you're a true

Aramintha Zane hero, dashing and honorable and all of that sort of thing."

"If he dares to use this whole mess in one of his books, I'll—"

"No, he wouldn't do that. He's fond of Regina. Although obviously not as fond of her as you are."

"I'm in love with her, as you well know," Brady said, wondering when he'd turned into a silly, sighing, romantic ninny, but not upset that he had. "I think I fell in love with her the first time she looked straight at Kipp and lied her lovely head nearly straight off."

Bram stood up, walked straight to the door of the drawing room, and ordered that he be given the earl of Singleton's hat and cane. He brought them with him as he walked back across the room, unceremoniously pushing them at Brady. "Go home," he said shortly. "Go home, tell Regina what you're telling me. It's the only answer, Brady. The only answer."

Brady took the hat and cane, but didn't move. "I can't. I'm supposed to be driving out with Lady Belle in less than an hour."

"So?" Bram asked, raising one expressive eyebrow. "Send a note, tell her you're ill."

"That won't work, I'm afraid. Belle's already got her sights set on Gawain, no thanks to Regina, or to my big mouth. She'd just show up in Portman Square to inquire about my health. I don't want her talking with Regina again until I've convinced Regina to marry me. Belle's too eager to ask questions, and Regina's too willing to tell whopping great fibs. I can't chance that." He stuck his curly-brimmed beaver on his head at an exaggerated tilt and stowed his cane under his arm. "It's better that I take Belle for her drive, then go home and explain everything to Regina."

"I'm going to assume that Regina loves you, Brady. That said, she may not like the idea of you coming back to society as yourself as long as Allerton and his friends are still walking free. You had considered that, hadn't you?"

Brady smiled ruefully. "Why do you think I want Belle out of the way first? I have a feeling Regina and I will be talking for most of the night."

Bram patted his friend on the shoulder and Brady headed for the door. The duke called after him, "Just remember, if she throws something at you, don't step out of the way. They hate it when you do that."

⌀

It had just gone noon when Regina watched Maude climb down from the carriage, her arms full of packages, and walk toward the Portman Square mansion. Then she turned to look at Cosmo, who had put away his corset before the trip to Bond Street, and was dressed in his old but well-brushed dark blue jacket and a pair of dove grey pantaloons.

"I thought she'd never decide between the yellow ribbons and the green," Regina said, sitting back against the squabs as the carriage moved out of the Square. "But a promise is a promise, and I did promise."

"You're that sure we're not coming back?" Cosmo asked her. "I only said it was possible, remember. I could be very wrong. Besides, even if I'm right, I think we'll have to come back. We'll need the earl, definitely."

The carriage stopped at the corner and a moment later the door opened and Thomas and David piled in to join them.

"Thomas," Regina said, looking at the man who was fussing with his neckcloth, "do you think we'll need the earl? Because I really think it would be better if we didn't have to come back."

"Not come back?" David looked at Regina, panicked. "But we have to come back. All my new clothes . . . my mirror . . . oh! We have to come back!"

Cosmo reached over and patted David's knee. "We're coming back, I promise. Unless Gina thinks we're going to be stealing His Lordship's fine carriage?"

Regina sat forward, startled. "But . . . but I thought we were only using the carriage to drive to wherever it is you've put the wagon. That was the plan, wasn't it?"

"It was *your* plan, my dear," Thomas told her, sighing. "But with our own Hector and Hecate in the shafts, we'd be lucky to make it to Little Woodcote before nightfall. This way, we can be there and back before dinnertime, with the earl none the wiser. As far as he'll know, unless we have something to tell him, we've just all gone for a long drive."

Tears stung at Regina's eyes but she blinked them away. "What if we're wrong?"

Cosmo looked up from the muffin he'd been happily pulling raisins out of and said, "No, no, he's right, my dear. We can be there and back before dinnertime. Rooster assured me, and he'd better be right, because we're being served roast pork tonight, and a lovely cherry pudding."

"No, that's not what I meant," Regina persisted. "What if we're wrong about what we'll find in Little Woodcote? The mere thought that you might be right has had me driven nearly to distraction these past three days."

"I never said I was right," Cosmo reminded her gently. "Still, we need to know for certain, don't we, before you let the earl tell his story tonight."

"If we're right, he definitely *can't* tell his story, tonight or ever. Oh, how he'll hate me." She sank into the corner of the seat and closed her eyes, sighed. Part of her wanted to be gone, forever gone, and another part of her—by far the larger part of her—couldn't imagine where she could go that her memories of Brady wouldn't follow her.

How she loved him. How very much she loved him. She loved him enough to not want to see the day dawn when he'd look at her and realize that his gratitude—or whatever it was he felt for her—was *all* that he felt for her. Gratitude, pity, possibly some admiration, which would be nice. But love? Oh, no. He couldn't love her. He had enough problems in his life right now, without loving her.

"Regina?"

She opened her eyes, looked at David. "Hmm?"

"Don't you trust the earl? I mean, we could have told him, you know. Told him what Cosmo thinks? It isn't as if it's a bad thing.

Regina sat up straight, looked at her friend. "Trust him? Of course I trust him."

"So you've told him the whole truth?" Thomas asked.

"You told him everything that happened, and just how it happened, just the way you told us? I've wondered about that, you know, because the earl is a very smart man. I would have thought he'd think what I thought when you told me. I grant you, it took me a few days to think it, but it is a logical conclusion. Now, why do you suppose he didn't come to that same conclusion?"

"Because I didn't tell him everything," Regina said in a small voice, then tipped up her chin defiantly. "Now don't you all look at me that way. I barely told him anything at first. I didn't know him that well, and I needed him to believe me, help me, and keep me around so that I could help him. And I could hardly tell him that I was . . . that I was *relieving* myself in the bushes when everything happened, now could I? It was a much better story the way I told it. Very dramatic, with Papa telling me to run, run like the wind! Besides, what difference does it make? They never came back, did they? They would have come back."

Thomas looked at Cosmo. " 'Oh, what a tangled web we weave . . .' "

"I was *not* trying to deceive him, Thomas!" Regina protested. "I told him the truth."

"Some of it," Cosmo, said, popping another raisin into his mouth.

"Close to all of it," Thomas amended, nodding.

"Wouldn't want to have her embarrassed with that business about being off in the woods doing . . . you know . . ." Cosmo added.

"But it would have helped him if he'd known. Probably wouldn't have had to dress himself up like some popinjay and prance about . . ."

"Although he does it well. I'm a fine teacher."

"Could have thought what we think, gone back to Little Woodcote, sneaked about to see what he could see . . ."

"Never come to London in his satins at all. Never had Regina here playing at society miss, being in his company all those *long* months. Not that she *knew*, you understand, for she most certainly didn't know . . ."

"Couldn't have known. Too filled with grief, too busy trying to survive out there on her own. But, still, she did land in a deep gravy boat, didn't she? And she could stay there, too, I'm fairly certain. Don't you wonder why she's in such a hurry to hop out of it?"

"Embarrassed," Thomas declared, nodding his head. "It's never fun, being caught in a lie, now is it? Why, if she'd told the truth from the beginning, before His Lordship went snooping about in Little Woodcote, none of this would have happened—whether we're right or we're wrong."

Regina bit her lip, that had begun to tremble. "All right, all right! So I should have told the earl of Willoughby when he asked. I should have told him everything, at least once they'd been so kind to me. But I didn't tell Lord Singleton to go poking his nose into my business, now did I? That was all his idea. It's *his* fault that he was nearly killed."

Cosmo, who had been smiling as he and Thomas teased Regina, sobered, saying, "That terrifies you, doesn't it, my dear? That His Lordship could have been killed. And you've been blaming yourself all this time. Do you really think *he* blames you?"

Regina shook her head."He . . . he says he's *glad* it happened, that he's learned so much, that his whole life has been changed for the better. But I saw him when he was so battered and bruised, Cosmo, and I saw him last night when he was choking Thorndyke with those chains . . ." She closed her eyes, leaned her head against Cosmo's shoulder. "Oh, Cosmo, you're right. If I had only told the truth from the beginning, then perhaps none of this would have happened."

"Yes, and you'd never have been in his lordship's company, would you, my pet? He would have gone on with his life as he had lived it, never knowing a different life. And you would have gone on with yours—never meeting him, never meeting up with us again, never even considering what we're considering now. It's a strange and wonderful world that goes round and round, isn't it, Gina? Now, tell me again that you don't want to be back in Portman Square tonight. Tell me that you don't love His Lordship with all your caring heart. Tell me so that I can believe you."

Regina sat up, wiped at her eyes. "Never, Cosmo. I won't say that. I'll never tell a lie again."

David looked at them all in turn, his brow furrowed. "Then I'll be able to retrieve my mirror?" he asked, just as the carriage turned sharply onto a bumpy dirt road and pulled to a stop.

"We're as close as we should be for you two," Rooster said, opening the square door cut into the top of the carriage and sticking his bright red head inside. "And within the hour, too. I told you I could do it."

"Isn't he wonderful?" Cosmo asked, as Rooster withdrew his head, shut the door. "A good man, Rooster, but not very fond of Gawain, as his loyalties still lie with the late earl. If only he knew! Oh, did I mention that we owe him ten pounds? You do have ten pounds, don't you, Gina?"

"I do, but it's nearly half of what I possess. Couldn't you have gotten him for less? Oh, never mind, I'm just babbling." She looked out the side window at the trees lining the narrow roadway. "Are we really here? Oh, Cosmo, what if we're wrong?"

"If we are, we won't find that out sitting here, now will we? Now, do you remember what you have to do?"

Regina rolled her eyes. "When have you ever known me to forget my lines?" she asked, pulling a small mirror out of her reticule and checking her appearance in the glass. "David, are you ready?"

"As ready as you are, *sister* dear," he said, straightening his neckcloth. "We'll meet you back here in twenty minutes, is that right?"

"Twenty minutes," Thomas agreed, already half out of the door. "Just do your best to keep all eyes looking at you, and pray we find what we hope we'll find."

Chapter Seventeen

$\mathscr{L}$ord Singleton to see Lady Bellinagara," Gawain said, stepping into the black-and-white-tiled foyer. He handed his gloves, hat, and cane to the butler who'd come running from the depths of the house to escort him into the drawing room. "Oh, don't tell me. Her Ladyship has been detained. I'll be sitting here, cooling my heels—lovely heels, aren't they? I so adore red—for at least an hour, ladies being what they are. I don't think that's good, do you? Having my horses standing out there all by themselves? Send someone out, if you please, to keep them company."

"Your Lordship, there is a groom standing at their heads," the butler told him.

"Yes, but does he sing?" Brady asked, lifting one eyebrow, the better to stick the quizzing glass to his eye.

"My lord, I have no idea if the boy sings."

"Really? Do *you* sing?"

The butler, a rather starchy sort—and weren't they all,

Brady's own Wadsworth included—pulled himself up to his full height and replied, "I don't know that it matters, my lord, but yes, I do sing."

"Oh, good, good. Splendid! I'll wager you have a most stunning baritone. Do you know that lovely ditty—'In the Month of Maying'?"

"I do, my lord, but—"

"Splendid! Again, splendid! Now go, go. Outside with you, man, at once," Brady said, making shooing motions with his hands. "Sing 'In the Month of Maying' to my horses. I vow, it's their very favorite. Don't stop until Lady Bellinagara is tripping down the steps to my curricle with me."

The butler's eyes narrowed to slits. "Lady Bellinagara will be down in two minutes, my lord," he said coolly.

"Yes, I rather thought she would be. In that case, just be kind enough to put your head outside and tell the groom to *hum*. That should be sufficient."

"Yes, my lord," the butler said, then bowed, turned on his heels, and left the room.

"Being a twit does have its advantages," Brady commented to himself as he walked to the drinks table and lifted a crystal stopper out of a decanter, frowning as he sniffed the contents. "Inferior, definitely inferior. Allerton must be counting pennies," he decided, then poured himself a glass of water—which, in London, could do more to injure his insides than the worst wine.

He already knew that Allerton wasn't at home, because Thorndyke—obviously still suffering badly from his night of drinking, among other things—had sent round a note that had quickly summoned the earl to his friend's lodgings. Brady knew this because David, who had been cooling his heels outside Thorndyke's lodgings, had come and told him so as he'd been leaving Bram's household shortly before noon. Now David was back at Thorndyke's with Thomas, to see who else might arrive.

So Allerton was with Thorndyke, and soon, if things worked out as planned, a third man would be summoned to Thorndyke's rooms. Then Brady would know the names of all three men . . . for all the good it would do him.

"Singleton! What are you doing here?"

Brady turned slowly, moving his head first, pointing it toward his left shoulder, and then followed with his body. His tutor used to do that—skewer him first with his eyes, then with the rest of him—and Brady knew just how intimidating being on the other end of that stare could be. He'd have to tell Regina about it—maybe she could use it on the stage. No, not on the stage, because she would never tread the boards again. She'd use it on him, in which case it was probably better not to tell her.

"Ah," Brady drawled, blinking and smiling. "If it isn't the viscount. How charming to see you again."

Boothe Kenward, Viscount Allerton, didn't seem to share Brady's joy. "What are you doing here?" he asked baldly.

"At the moment? Why, at the moment, I'm taking my life into my hands, sipping water. The only thing more dangerous, I believe, would be to drink it straight from the Thames." He put a hand to his mouth, giggled. Regina would have been very proud of his giggle. "Oh, my, that *was* naughty, wasn't it? My dear and departed cousin *drank* from the Thames, didn't he? Copiously. I'm so ashamed, please forget I said a word."

The viscount brushed past Brady, heading for the drinks table. "I never liked your cousin above half, but I'm beginning to think the wrong one drowned," he said, pouring himself a nearly full glass of port. "Don't think you'll get anywhere with my sister, sir. She didn't accept your cousin, and she won't accept you."

Brady now pressed his splayed fingers to his chest. "Dear God, man, you're not talking *marriage*, are you? With your sister? Don't you think she's a little long in the tooth? Why, I imagine she'll be putting on her caps any day now. Sitting with the dowagers, knitting, raising cats—that sort of thing."

The viscount threw back his head and laughed out loud. "Oh, I can't wait to tell her you said that!" He stepped closer to Brady, so that it became obvious that the glass of port wasn't his first strong drink of the day, for his eyes were faintly blurry and his posture was unnaturally stiff, as if he had to concentrate on remaining upright. "Tell you something," he said, slipping an arm around Brady's shoulders. "She ain't raising cats yet, but m'sister has her claws out for you. I think she wants your late cousin's money, which seems only fair, since he's the one who ruined her chances of landing a duke. Do you know about that? Let me tell you about that."

"I've already heard the story, as a matter of fact, but thank you anyway, I'm sure," Brady said, then bent his knees slightly and neatly stepped away from the viscount, who staggered a step or two before blinking, shaking his head, then wisely heading for the nearest chair.

"Heard it, have you?" The viscount took another sip of his drink. "Then what are you doing here?"

Obviously the man wasn't *that* deep in his cups. "What am I doing here? Why, I hoped to see you, of course. I want to apologize for the other evening. I didn't really mean it when I called you a bug."

"You didn't? Well, then, that's all right," the viscount told him graciously, and most probably because, even drunk, the cowardly man knew not to cross the earl ever again. "So we're even now, aren't we. You apologized for calling me a bug, and I warned you off Belle. We can cry friends, right?"

He hopped rather unsteadily to his feet. "Tell you what, *friend*. Let's leave Belle to her cats and you can come with me. There's a cockfight to start in less than an hour, and my money's on Cocksure. He's *sure* to knock off the favorite, if you take my meaning, but no one knows that but me, so the odds are magnificent. All I need is a neat fifty pounds, and I'll be able to fill my pockets. Fifty pounds, Singleton. I'll be able to pay you back yet today."

Brady hid his disgust at the viscount, a man who would endure any insult—to either himself or his sister—in the hope of borrowing a few pounds from the man who had levied those insults, one as Brady, the second as Gawain.

"Between allowances, are you?" he asked, reaching into the small pocket in his waistcoat and pulling out a fat purse.

"Between them, without them. Same thing," the viscount said, eyeing the purse. "But not for long. A few more days, and we'll make Croesus look a pauper, that's what m'father says." He tore his avid gaze away from the purse to look at Brady. "Are you going to be my banker, or what?"

Brady held up the purse, doing his best not to grab hold of the viscount's lapels and shake the man sober, shake him into answering the questions now burning in Brady's brain. "Rich as Croesus, you say? Imagine that. How?"

The viscount was staring at the purse, now swinging from its strings held loosely in Brady's fingers. "I don't know. Don't know. Who listens? I only know there's been a bunch of foreigners tramping in and out of here, talking in their foreign tongues. Something to do with posies"— he waved his hand in front of him—"posies and colors and—thank you! Thank you! Wait—aren't you going with me?"

Brady grabbed his hat, gloves, and cane, and was heading out the door when the viscount called after him. "What about Belle? Aren't you taking her with you?" He turned away from the door, hefting Brady's purse in his hand. "Oh, this is wonderful, wonderful. I'll go tell her. About time I had some fun . . ."

CB

Cosmo and Thomas climbed onto the roof of the carriage, and from there to the high stone wall running entirely around the perimeter of the Allerton country estate. After giving them about ten minutes to move through the trees, get into position, pick their targets (plus five more minutes to account for the amount of time it would have taken Thomas to talk Cosmo into jumping down from the wall), Regina nodded at David, who then tapped his cane against the roof of the carriage.

Rooster had already turned the carriage at a spot farther along the small dirt road and returned them to the more traveled roadway, so that within a few minutes they were turning off that roadway again, then almost immediately stopping at the small gatehouse at the edge of the estate.

"What do we do if they don't let us in?" David asked, nervously peeking out the side window as a rather burly, mean-faced man approached the carriage, looking up at Rooster.

"Don't be silly, of course they'll let us in," Regina said, then sat biting at her knuckle until she heard the heavy iron gates groaning as they were pushed open, and the carriage began to move once more. "See, I told you so," she then said, vastly relieved. "It's an unspoken rule that visiting earls and such are never turned away from a peer's household."

"You didn't know that. You couldn't have known that for certain," David pointed out, dabbing at his perspiring forehead with his handkerchief. Poor David. Much as he loved to perform, he always worked himself into a state before stepping on stage.

"All right, so I couldn't have known that for sure, but Thomas said so, and Thomas knows just about everything."

"I hope he knows how to rescue us if it goes badly," David said, sighing. "I still don't know why we have to do this."

Regina rolled her eyes. Some romantic figure of a hero David was—as long as someone else put a wooden sword in his hand and the words in his mouth. "I've already told you twice, David. We are a diversion. Allerton's in London, so there are probably only a few servants about, not counting anyone working in the fields, which are on the other side of the stone wall in any case. We're to keep attention on us, so that Thomas and Cosmo can feel free to move about the outbuildings, peeking in windows, and that sort of thing. Now, we'll be here and gone in less than an hour, so please try to be brave."

David's head went up, and his smooth cheeks flushed a hot and angry pink. "I *am* brave!" he protested. "But it would have been better if I'd gone with Thomas. Cosmo is probably making enough noise to rouse the dead, crashing his bulk through the trees."

"True enough, but you're the only one with such a pretty suit of clothes. Besides, you're so handsome, all the female servants will be crowding around, swooning, just to look at you, and all the men will be watching the females watching you. It's simple, really, if you just think about it. I suppose you could look at it as a curse, your being so pretty, but there it is."

Her words had the desired effect, as David sat up straighter, patted his hair to be sure of its perfection, and then bared his teeth, running a finger back and forth across them as if polishing their surfaces. Regina turned her head, rolled her eyes.

The carriage bumped along the long drive that had not seen a fresh layer of gravel in quite some time, and finally drew to a halt after traveling up a long, slow rise to the front doors of the rather modest country mansion.

Regina peeked out the window to see the front door opening and an older woman dressed in black and wiping her hands on a large white apron coming down the granite steps. "See? Not even a butler in residence. This is going to be simple. Here we go, David. Just keep smiling, all right?"

Rooster was already hopping down from the box, waving his hands and talking a mile a minute to the woman, and to two footmen who had followed her out of the house. As he talked, he opened the door of the carriage, pulled out the steps, and then stepped back as David, in all his glory, hopped down to the ground.

The sunlight hit his magnificent head of hair, caressed his smooth skin, glinted off his mouthful of straight white teeth. The woman, who had been looking at Rooster with some question in her eyes, opened her mouth and began staring at David, who smiled at her, then gave an acknowledging nod in her direction.

"Oh, my good woman," David said, holding out his hand as he approached the housekeeper, so that she first half dropped into a curtsy, then held out her hand, then quickly retracted her hand and finished her curtsy. Within a moment, Regina thought, making a face, David would be ensconced in the drawing room, shoving cakes into his mouth as the housekeeper offered to slay the fatted calf for him.

"I cannot," David was saying, "simply *cannot* tell you how fortunate my sister and I are that I recognized the crest on His Lordship's gates. We've been traveling in circles for *hours*, my dear lady, thoroughly lost. My sister vows her stomach will absolutely *drop* to her toes if she isn't allowed a few moments to sit, to sip some tea, to collect herself."

"Your sister, sir?" the housekeeper asked, looking past him, directly at the carriage.

"Your cue, Gina," Regina whispered. She gave herself a slight shake, then pulled out her handkerchief, holding it to her mouth as David came to assist her down the small steps to the ground.

"Oh, David, how good it is *not* to be moving," she said, holding the handkerchief to her mouth as she leaned heavily on his arm. "I vow, I would cheerfully murder for a cup of tea."

Regina peeked out of the corners of her eyes, watching the housekeeper as that woman came to a decision. "You," the older woman finally said, pointing to one of the rather scruffy young boys who had come from the stables to see what all the commotion was about, "get this carriage away from the door. Tend to the horses."

The housekeeper then looked at Rooster, who was standing quietly now, his hat in his hands, and realized that although the young gentleman was pretty, the coachman—a fine, strapping man—was more within the reach of her dreams. "And you, sir, may then go around to the kitchens. There's cakes and beer there for you, I'm sure."

"Yes, ma'am," Rooster said, remounting the box, then following after the young boys, who ran ahead of him toward the stables.

"If you'd like to come inside now?" the housekeeper

asked, motioning for Regina and David to precede her into the house. "The young miss can go right upstairs, to freshen herself, and you, sir, can join the others in the drawing room."

Regina stopped dead, her foot on the first step. "The *others*?" she whispered to David. "What others? God, David—what *others*?"

David, now that he was on stage, now that he had his audience, responded splendidly to this unexpected complication. "Others? Oh, dear, are we intruding? We most certainly wouldn't wish to intrude, Mrs.—?"

"Mrs. Cooper, sir," the housekeeper told him.

"Ah, yes, Mrs. Cooper. Please excuse my sister, but she feels she is not looking or feeling at her best at the moment, and she'd rather travel on to the nearest inn, rather than to *barge* in on your master. Is it your master who is here?"

Mrs. Cooper nodded. "The earl of Allerton, yes, and his guests. But I can have your sister taken straightaway upstairs, so that she doesn't have to worry her head about not looking at her best."

"Get . . . us . . . *out* . . . of . . . here," Regina whispered, digging her fingers into David's forearm.

But David had the bit between his teeth, God help them all. "Splendid!" he said, all but dragging Regina up yet another step. "My sister will go with you, and I will meet with the gentlemen, share a drink, whatever. Just please give me a moment to talk to my sister, and we'll be right there."

"Are you out of your mind?" Regina asked him as

Mrs. Cooper shrugged, reentered the house. "Allerton's in there."

"Yes, but you're heading straight upstairs, and he's never seen me. Oh," he then said, dragging at her once more, "your name is now Rose, all right? I'm David . . . Manners, and you're my sister, Rose Manners. You'll see, Gina. We'll be fine. Just fine."

"Not if you call me Gina," Regina reminded him tersely. Then, as the two footmen watching them had begun to look at them with more interest than she would like, and with Rooster and the carriage already gone, she took a deep breath and headed up the steps. "Ten minutes, David, and then we're gone, understand?"

"Yes, yes," David said absently, looking around the foyer as if he had just stepped onto the stage at Covent Garden. "Drinking with the gentlemen. Ah, you know, *Rose*, there are times I really believe I was *born* for this."

"And I worried that he'd be too nervous to say a word," Regina grumbled to herself moments later as the door closed behind Mrs. Cooper and Regina surveyed her surroundings.

She walked over to a white-skirted dressing table, lifted a small blue glass bottle and sniffed at its contents. This must, she thought, be Lady Bellinagara's chamber. How odd that she'd been shown into this chamber, unless the rest of the house was in Holland covers.

Holland covers. Holland. Tulips. How could she have forgotten?

Racing from window to window, she searched the grounds, looking for any sight of Thomas or Cosmo, any sight of a building that might be used for—there it was!

A long, almost completely glass-paned building behind the stables. It looked fairly new, raw, and it was the first bit of solid hope Regina had allowed herself since the horror of the past spring.

As she watched, Thomas appeared from the line of trees, running in a sort of crouched position until he plastered himself against the side of the building, sitting on his rump, his back to the glass.

"Stand up, stand up," Regina urged him quietly, and she held her breath as he did just that. He turned around, cupped his hands on either side of his eyes, and pressed his nose against the glass "Yes? Yes? What do you see? Oh, Thomas, what do you see?"

Brady paced the Selbourne drawing room, slapping his fist against his palm, cursing under his breath.

"Brady?" the duke of Selbourne said by way of greeting as he slowly walked into the room, still chewing on a bite of the apple he held in one hand. "I've been told that you came barging in here, demanding to see me. Twice in one day, I'm flattered. But shouldn't you still be out driving with—"

"She's gone," Brady said, interrupting his friend. "Damn it, Bram, she's gone!"

Bram frowned. "Lady Belle?"

"No, *Regina*. She's gone." Brady stabbed a hand through his hair, turned his back on Bram, and paced some more—not the slow, measured pace of a man deep in thought, but the quick, tension-filled back and forth of a caged lion.

"Gone? Gone where?"

"That's the thing—I don't know," Brady said, throwing himself into a chair. "They're all gone, so there's nobody to ask. Regina, Thomas, Cosmo, the twit. And that's not all—the twit left a note for me. He and Thomas were supposed to watch Thorndyke's, damn it."

"Not a note telling you where Regina has gone, I take it," Bram said, putting down the apple and pouring them each a glass of wine. "Here, drink this. You look like hell."

"I feel like hell," Brady said, downing the wine in one long gulp. "I can't believe it, Bram. I can't believe she just *left* like that. Oh, God, I've handled this all wrong—all of it—start to finish."

Bram sat down, looked at his friend. "Are you sure she's gone? She took her clothing?"

Brady shook his head. "No, but that doesn't mean anything. Regina wouldn't take the clothing. I bought it for her, remember?"

"All right," Bram said, nodding. "How did she leave? Did she take a hack?"

Brady looked up, stared at his friend. "No. No, she didn't. She—they—took my carriage. With Rooster in the box, now that I think about it."

Bram sat back, spread his hands. "Well, there you go then, don't you? If she wouldn't take the clothes, she wouldn't run off with the carriage. And I highly doubt she'd run off with Rooster. They've gone out for a drive. Lord, Brady, you're a mess. They went for a drive."

Brady rubbed at the back of his neck, considering this. "I imagine it is possible, but she wasn't supposed to leave the house. I distinctly told her—"

Bram's bark of laughter interrupted him. "Oh, well, then, there you have it. You *told* her not to leave the house. If I ever said anything like that to Sophie, she'd be halfway to Dover before I could find her. There, now that we've settled where Regina must be, tell me what was in the boy's note. Were you right? Is LeMain the third man?"

"What?" Brady asked, still not happy with Bram's conclusions. And he knew why, although he'd never tell his friend. He'd gone to his chambers, to ask Rogers if he knew of Regina's whereabouts, and found the pearl necklace neatly laid out on his bed. Even if she had only gone for a drive, even if she did come back—she'd made it plain that she wouldn't be coming back to *him*.

"The note, Brady. What was written in the note? Pay attention, please."

"Oh, yes, of course," Brady said, going back to his pacing, feeling that he should be someplace else—he didn't know where—but that he definitely shouldn't be here. "The third man isn't LeMain, as I'd supposed. It's Sir Randolph. A footman was sent to fetch him to Thorndyke's lodgings not five minutes after Allerton arrived."

"Tilden? Really? Well, then it's a good thing you didn't try haunting LeMain. He probably would have shot you."

Brady stopped, held up his hands. "Yes, yes, but that's not all of it. I went to take Lady Belle out driving, remember?"

"I remember. I remember telling you to go home. I think you should have listened to me."

Brady shook his head, vehemently. "No, no, the best thing I could have done was to go to Allerton's mansion. I had a talk with Kenward."

"The viscount? What could possibly have been good about any conversation with him? The man's an idiot."

Brady squeezed his hands together, tapped his knuckles against his lips. "An idiot. Yes, he is. But he said something, Bram, he said the last thing I would ever have expected. He told me that foreigners had been running tame in his father's house these past few days, and that Allerton had told him they'd soon be rich as Croesus."

"He told you that?" Bram said, getting to his feet. "How odd. I wonder if Allerton knows his son's tongue runs on wheels. Go on. There is more, isn't there?"

"Oh, yes, there's definitely more. According to the viscount, Allerton's coming fortune has something to do with *posies*. Think about that, Bram. Think about that for just about thirty seconds—and then tell me what conclusion you come to, a conclusion I'm fairly certain will match mine."

His friend didn't disappoint him. "The black tulip. It's the only answer."

"The only answer, yes, but not the only question," Brady said, still feeling something nibbling at the edges of his brain, something important, something he'd missed. And then he knew. "That's it! That's it! Allerton wasn't at home!"

"So?" Bram asked, going over to the wall to tug on the bellpull. "You said he was closeted with Sir Randolph, at Thorndyke's."

Brady shook his head. "No, no. David's note said he'd

followed them, the three of them, back to Allerton's mansion in Allerton's coach. But they weren't there when I came to get Lady Belle. If they aren't there, Bram—where are they? And where's Regina?"

"You rang, sir?" one of Selbourne's footmen asked from the doorway.

"Yes, George, I did. Have my carriage . . . no, my horse . . . have my horse brought round in ten minutes, if you please. That will give me time to change." Then he turned to Brady, who looked resplendent, but highly unsuitable, in his palest blue satin. "First to Portman Square, for your horse and a change of clothes, and then to Allerton's. Somebody should know where's he's gone."

"I didn't want to get her hopes up," Brady was saying, shaking his head. "The moment I realized what Kenward was saying, I thought—but I wasn't sure if I could tell her, you know? I wanted to think about it, consider it, and probably go back to Little Woodcote, do some more checking . . ."

"Understandable, understandable," Bram told him, putting his arm around Brady's shoulder and leading him toward the door. "Oh, and I just thought of something else. You can't be seen here in town in anything but those satins, not without giving yourself away, so I'll go to the Allerton mansion on my own, and then come to you. I'll meet you in Portman Square as quickly as I can. Let's just hope that Regina is there when you get home."

"If she is, I may wring her neck," Brady said feelingly as he headed through the foyer, on his way to his curricle.

"Ah, young love," Bram said, heading up the stairs to change into his riding clothes. "I remember those days . . ."

Chapter Eighteen

Regina stayed at the window, biting her bottom lip, watching as Thomas made his way toward the corner of the building, then disappeared. Where was he going? What had he seen?

She started counting, timing his disappearance, and had gotten all the way to five hundred by the time he appeared again, running from behind the building, straight into the trees.

Five hundred. She thought about that. He must have been gone—what? Just above five minutes? Only that long? It had seemed like hours. Still, whatever the time, Thomas had seen something, and now he was safely back in the cover of the trees.

It was time to leave, if David could bear to tear himself away.

Regina looked around the room, searching for a bellpull, but there was none. She couldn't chance going down the stairs to search for anyone, because Allerton might see her, recognize her.

Recognize her? Now that was a thought!

She ran over to the dressing table, pulling open drawers, praying that the flush in Lady Bellinagara's cheeks had been as false as she'd believed it to be when they'd met. Because where there was one paint pot there would be more.

Sitting down at the dressing table, Regina began pulling the pins from her hair, ruthlessly ridding herself of the lovely upswept style Maude had fashioned for her that morning. "Go away!" she then called out as someone knocked on her door. "I cannot *abide* interruption when my stomach is unwell. Please just have the carriage brought round and tell my brother I wish to leave in . . . in fifteen minutes. Thank you!"

"But, miss—" a maid said, opening the door.

"Don't come in, don't come in!" Regina shouted, her tone frantic as she hid her face in her hands. "I'm so afraid. There are these . . . *things* . . . all over my face. Oh, God, oh, God, oh, God help me! What if it's small-pox?"

Regina grinned at her reflection as the door shut with a bang and she heard the maid running down the hallway in search of Mrs. Cooper.

She got up, turned the key in the door, just in case Mrs. Cooper was more curious than she was terrified of small-pox, and went back to the dressing table. She had work to do . . .

Brady was looking out one of the drawing-room windows overlooking Portman Square when Bram rode up on his large bay mare, and was already in the foyer when his friend entered the mansion. "Well? What did you learn?"

The duke started to answer, but then just stood back, pointed at Brady. "What in God's name is *that*?"

Brady looked down at himself. He was dressed in tan buckskins, but there were bows at his knees. Lace foamed at his throat and cuffs, his yellow waistcoat was embroidered with horses' heads, and his bright green jacket had so much buckram padding at the shoulders that the moment he stepped outside half of London's pigeons could roost on them. "Watkins's idea of what the Continental gentleman should wear while out riding," he said, dismissing his ridiculous outfit. "What did you learn?"

"Well, first I learned that Lady Belle knows words I thought no lady knew," Bram said, brushing past Brady to enter the drawing room, going to pour himself a glass of wine. "It's a good thing Gawain Caradoc is going to do a flit soon. Otherwise, the earl wouldn't be the only one in the family looking for a way to slip a knife into his back."

"I'd send round flowers and an apology, but I'm not a nice man," Brady said, his tension easing, just for a moment. "What else? What about Allerton?"

"He's gone to Little Woodcote," Bram told Brady, downing the rest of his wine. "He often goes out there, Lady Belle said, just for the day. You know, I've thought about purchasing some sort of quaint country cottage closer to the city, so that Sophie and I could do just that . . . get the children out of town for a few days, seek a little respite from the—"

Brady held up his hands, so that the duke stopped talking. "He went to Little Woodcote? Alone?"

"Well, now, Brady, how was I going to ask that question? I'm a duke, I have consequence and all that sort of thing. But how odd would it look for me to interrogate Lady Belle about her father's comings and goings? I don't know if he went alone. But he'll be back in town by this evening."

"So will Regina, if you're right," Brady said, picking up his gloves and curly-brimmed beaver. "What do you want to wager that Thomas and David learned where Allerton was going, and then came back here, told Regina, and now they're *all* following the man? Possibly all three men? Does that sound logical?"

Bram pursed his lips, nodded. "It does, it does. Sophie would do that. Not the sort of woman to sit back, let someone else have all the fun. Do you remember me telling you about the night the two of us went skulking about, trying to return something my dear aunt had—"

"My horse should be out front by now," Brady interrupted. "Are you going with me?"

"Gawain, my dear," Bram said, tapping his own hat back onto his head, "I wouldn't miss it for the world."

Regina was just putting the finishing touches to her now vastly altered appearance as another knock came on the door. "Rose? Rose! Open this door. Mrs. Cooper says—my God—"

Before David could say anything else, like: "My God, *Gina!*" Regina pulled him inside and shut and locked the door behind him.

"What in bloody blazes are you doing?" he asked, looking at her, bug-eyed.

"I'm getting us out of here in one piece, that's what I'm doing," Regina told him, going over to the bed to pick up her bonnet, fortunately one with a large brim, that partially hid her face.

"But why? I was having a perfectly wonderful time down there," David protested, obviously having lost sight of the reason he and Regina were here in the first place. "The room is chockful of very interesting people, not that I could understand more than every second word. But Mrs. Cooper brought in these small cakes—all drenched in icing, and with little candy flowers on them—"

"David!" Regina exclaimed, grabbing his arms. "Try to remember why we're here. I saw Thomas through the windows, and he's seen something, and now he's gone back into the woods. They'll be waiting for us, but if Allerton sees me, they'll be waiting forever, because you and I will be dead. Do you understand now?"

David frowned, nodded, then pointed at Regina. "But . . . this?"

"Necessary, believe me. Allerton will want to come out, bid us farewell. I can't let that happen, now can I?"

"Yes, but—"

"David," Regina said, fighting down the urge to slap him senseless—which would have been a fruitless exercise because he most certainly was *already* senseless, if he didn't recognize the danger they were in as long as they remained under Allerton's roof. "David darling," she said, keeping her temper under control. "You were wonderful. Splendid! But now it's time for you to take your bows, and leave the stage. Are you up to a last scene?"

David looked toward the windows, then back at Regina. "All right, all right. I'm sorry, Gina. I believe I must have gotten a little carried away. What do you want me to do?"

"Just go back downstairs, order our carriage brought to the door, tell everyone that your sister is quite ill, and then come back upstairs to get me. Nobody will protest, I'm sure, especially if they think I might have smallpox. Take my arm, keep your body between mine and Allerton's, and get me out of here, all right? Can you do that?"

"Certainly I can—smallpox? You have smallpox? Gina, do you have any idea what that would do to my *face*?"

"David, do you have any idea what lying under six feet of *dirt* would do to your face?" Regina asked, longing to shake him. "Now go, go!"

Regina went back over to the dressing table, to inspect her appearance one more time as she tied the bonnet strings under her chin. She allowed her posture to slump, dropped her eyelids to half-mast, worked her jaws together until she had enough saliva to push some of it out of her mouth, to drool down onto her chin. "Perfect," she said, then took a deep breath and waited for David to come back.

She didn't have long to wait, but when David returned

he wasn't alone. Mrs. Cooper was with him, her apron held up in front of her, covering her nose and mouth. She stood just outside the opened door and peered in at Regina, who was leaning heavily against the chair in front of the dressing table.

"Oh, please, stay back," Regina pleaded, raising one arm as if to ward the housekeeper off, then covered her mouth as she began to cough. Loud, terrible coughs that racked her body, shook her shoulders. She moved her hand away, and drool was running down her chin. "So sick . . . so sick . . ." she said. "David . . . David, help me. I want to go home. I need Mama . . . I want Mama . . ."

"My stars!" Mrs. Cooper said from behind her apron.

"Rose, darling, you can't leave here. You're too sick." David turned to Mrs. Cooper, put a hand on her arm. "You'll nurse her, won't you?"

The housekeeper shook off his hand and stepped back several paces. "Me? But the child wants her mother. You heard her, sir. And your carriage is already outside. Just get her out of here, sir, before His Lordship sees her. As it is, I'll have to burn everything in Lady Belle's room. Oh, how will I explain this? Get her gone, sir—get her gone!"

David made a grand scene out of crossing the room, reluctantly taking Regina's arm, very reluctantly allowing her to lean her weight against him.

Regina wondered if the man was an even better actor than she'd supposed, or if she were the better actor, and David half believed she did have smallpox.

It didn't matter, really, and within moments they were heading down the stairs, Regina hard-pressed not to break into a run as they passed by the closed doors to the drawing room.

And then they were in the carriage, and Rooster was driving them back to the gatehouse, to the roadway, to the dirt road where Cosmo and Thomas would be waiting for them with news that would either swell Regina's heart . . . or break it yet again.

Brady and the duke rode in silence once they'd gotten beyond the confines of London streets, not galloping to the rescue without a thought to their horses, but with a controlled urgency that would get them to Little Woodcote in under an hour and still leave their mounts the stamina to *leave* Little Woodcote in a hurry if that became necessary.

This left time for Brady to think about all that had happened since his first trip to Little Woodcote. The mistakes he'd made, the lessons he'd learned. And time to work on his plan to make Gawain Caradoc disappear while at the same time convincing Regina that if *she* disappeared, his life would have no meaning at all, the lessons he'd learned would have no value.

He even had time to contemplate the lovely sight a bonfire of his Gawain clothes would make, and reason to contemplate that sight, because his bow-bedecked buckskins were definitely not fashioned for anyone who wanted a comfortable ride in the country.

"Brady—look up ahead," Bram called to him just as Brady was trying, yet again, to find a comfortable seat on his mount. "Isn't that your coach coming toward us?"

Brady peered into the distance, instantly recognizing his coach, and Rooster on the box. He pushed his horse forward, riding to the center of the roadway, and raised both his hands, waving them so that Rooster saw him, brought the coach to a crashing halt not ten feet from horse and rider.

Brady was off his mount in an instant, and running toward the door of the carriage, pulling it open—just to have Cosmo come tumbling out at him.

"That's it," Cosmo grumbled as he picked his bulk up from the ground. "I'll keep to our wagon, and our peaceful Hecate and Hector. Man drives like a madman, and then stops without warning." He stood up, began brushing himself down, and then realized to whom he'd been talking: "My lord Singleton?"

"Matilda," Brady said, tipping his hat. "I think you've misplaced your corset."

"Yes, my lord," Cosmo said, stepping away from the opened door, so that Brady could see the tangle of arms and legs still inside the carriage. "We've good news, my lord."

"You mean you left her alive so that I can kill her?" Brady asked as Thomas, his long legs exiting first, also disembarked from the carriage. "How very kind."

Brady's heart was beating so quickly that he was surprised it didn't burst from his chest—although the snugness of his horse-head-covered waistcoat would most probably prevent that particular embarrassment. "She is in there, isn't she?" he asked as David, looking a little less handsome than usual, exited the coach.

The duke had also dismounted, and now stood beside

Brady, looking at the three men who had accompanied Miss Regina Bliss to Little Woodcote. "You know, Brady, it wasn't as if she was unprotected." He looked again . . . at Cosmo, who was, for some reason, stuck all over with briars. At Thomas, who was busily patting at his cheeks with a lace-edged handkerchief. At David, who was actually running both hands over his face, as if taking inventory, making sure he still had two eyes, one nose, one mouth, and that none of them had been damaged when Rooster stopped the coach and sent the four occupants to tumbling about like dice in a box.

Bram sighed, added, "Well, maybe not *protected* exactly. But she wasn't alone, and she is safe. So don't shout, Brady. Believe me, you'll get nowhere if you shout."

Brady turned his head slightly, looked at Bram with one eyebrow arched high on his forehead, then turned back to peer into the dimness inside the coach. "*Regina!*" he bellowed. "Get out here—*now!*"

"Why is it that people listen to Sophie, when *she* gives advice?" the duke grumbled, walking back to the two horses before they could wander off.

Brady had just enough time to reconsider his demand when he was suddenly attacked by a robin's-egg blue gown and matching cape, a straw bonnet whose brim gave him a sharp poke in the eye, and a pair of arms that nearly strangled him.

"Regina!" he exclaimed, wrapping his arms around her and holding her tight as her feet remained at least six inches off the ground. "My God, Regina, I thought I'd never see you again." All his anger forgotten, he whirled about in a circle, squeezing her to him. "But you're here, I've found you . . ." He reluctantly put her down, stepped back to look at her. ". . . and you're covered in *spots*? What in bloody blazes—?"

"That's what I said, my lord," David piped up, confident now that his pretty face hadn't suffered any damage in his unexpected tumble onto the floor of the coach. "She said smallpox, but I say she looks much more like measles. What do you say?"

Brady was still looking at Regina. Her hands, her entire face were dotted with red bumps, the complexion beneath those red bumps a pale, sickly white. He lifted a hand, rubbed his thumb over her cheek—and the red bumps smudged. "Do I want to know about this?" he asked her.

She shook her head, smiling through tears that streamed down her face, washing away that sickly complexion. "No, I don't think you do, my lord," she said honestly, and then launched herself into his arms once more. "They're alive, Brady! Mama and Papa—they're *alive!*"

"Yes, I thought they might be," Brady said, closing his eyes for a moment, wondering how and where this would all go now, with this added complication—a delightful complication, but a complication just the same.

"I have a suggestion, Brady," the duke said, as if able to see inside his mind. "One of these fine gentlemen can accompany me back to town on your horse, and the other two can keep Rooster company on the box. Or am I wrong, and you and Miss Bliss don't feel the need for some private conversation?"

By way of answer, Brady picked up Regina and, with a dexterity that amazed even him, got the both of them inside the carriage, the door closed behind them, and the shades drawn tight . . . all within the space of a heartbeat.

C&

Regina clung to Brady's neck, unwilling, perhaps unable, to let him go. "I didn't see them, but Thomas talked to them . . . and they're just fine, fine. They've been prisoners, with Papa forced to produce another black tulip. Oh, Brady, Papa's promised success this time, and they have only a few days left before the blooms open. We've come to the rescue just in time! Of course, not just now. We should probably go back to London now, and come back later because . . . well, never mind about that. You probably already know, don't you?"

She lifted her head slightly, looked at the smears of makeup on Brady's jacket. Inanely, because her mind was still having trouble thinking in anything resembling a straight line, she said, "Oh, dear. I've ruined your coat."

"Ah, such a pity." Brady pulled her close once more. "Come home with me, Regina, and promise me you'll ruin the rest," he told her, and she smiled as she felt his chest rise and fall as he laughed out loud.

Oh, how she loved this man. And, oh, how she must have disappointed him. Leaving Portman Square after he'd specifically told her not to, going off to Little Woodcote, nearly getting herself in some very, very bad trouble. . . .

Regina put her hands against Brady's shoulders and

pushed away from him, even if she remained seated in his lap as the carriage moved toward London. "*How?* How did you know that Mama and Papa are still alive?"

He cupped her cheek in his hand. "Can't we talk about this later?" he asked, moving his head closer to hers.

"But . . . but we've got to do something. We have to rescue them . . . get them out of there tonight. We are agreed on that, aren't we?"

Brady untied the ribbon at her throat. "Tonight. Definitely."

"Yes, tonight . . . before the tulips can . . . and I must look *terrible*. . . ."

She was probably going to say something else, but when Brady's lips touched hers, and her eyes closed, and her stomach did this rather odd little flip inside her . . . well, Regina seemed to forget exactly what that something else might have been.

"Oh, Brady." She sighed against his shoulder, as he broke the kiss, began nibbling at the side of her neck. "We shouldn't be doing this."

"I shouldn't have taken you to my bed last night. I shouldn't have left you this morning," Brady said between kisses, as he ran his hands over her body. "I should have told you that I love you . . . told you how much I love you."

Regina didn't notice the tears that ran down her cheeks. "I—I returned the pearls," she said, tilting her head so that he could continue to kiss her throat, press his lips against the skin of her chest where it rose above the low neckline of her gown. "I thought it would be better for you if I left London. I thought you were only grateful to me. I thought—"

"You think too much," Brady told her, raising his head to look down into her face. "You talk too much, and you think too much, most especially if you thought it could possibly be better for me if you left London. The only thing that would be better for me, princess, is to never again wake without you in my arms. I love you, princess. I love you so much."

"Oh, Brady, and I love you. I love Gawain. Mama and Papa are alive. I love *everybody!*" Regina told him, then gave herself over to his kiss once more.

C&

"You know, old friend, you should be careful, walking around with that smug look on your face. Someone might want to wipe it off," the duke said, as Brady entered the drawing room just as the clock on the mantel struck the hour of eight.

Brady, fresh from his tub and dressed now in his own familiar—and comfortable—clothing, grinned as he poured his friend a glass of wine, then another for himself. "Now you know how I felt each time either you or Kipp looked at your lovely brides. Amazing, isn't it, how one small woman can barge in, change your life."

Bram accepted the glass Brady offered, then sat back, crossed one long, muscular leg over the other. "Thomas and I had a very interesting discussion on our way back to town. So it's true. The mother and father are alive. I know we'd thought so, what with Kenward going on about fortunes and posies."

"And colors," Brady reminded him, sitting down on the facing couch. "Of course, if you've spoken to Thomas, you now know that we all came to the same conclusion by traveling along entirely different roads."

"Yes," Bram said, smiling. "I heard."

Brady shook his head. "Regina has finally told me everything. I don't believe it—I still don't believe it. She didn't want to tell me she had gone off into the bushes for . . . personal reasons, and then when she came back, the wagon, and her parents, were gone. Her parents just left her there, almost as if they'd forgotten she existed, or at least that's how Regina sees it. I'm not so sure. To me, I think her parents didn't want anyone to know Regina was with them at all—that they were protecting her. Anyway, she didn't want to make her parents sound uncaring, so she lied to us. She never woke to shouts, her father never told her to run—"

"Run like the wind, I think is what Thomas said she'd told him. Highly dramatic words. You should have suspected something then, old friend."

Shrugging, Brady said, "True, but in my own defense, they are a family of players. I saw nothing too strange in the melodrama of the thing. I think I'm only surprised she didn't say her father spouted some Shakespearean quote to warn her."

Bram put a hand to his heart. " 'Over hill, over dale, thorough bush, thorough brier—' run, run, my dearest child."

"Yes, something like that," Brady agreed, smiling.

"But it wasn't like that at all. Her parents went off willingly enough with Allerton, they just didn't come back. And, since Allerton never saw Regina, he had no idea that she was out there, waiting for them to return. The rest of it is pretty much the same, with Regina going to the estate, seeing her parents' wagon. She waited, for days, a week, perched on the stone wall, watching for them, but they never appeared, and on the third day, the wagon was burned.

"I believe I would have come to the same conclusion Regina did," Bram said, sighing. "Why burn the wagon if there were people to ride in it? Thomas told me they'd waited for Regina and her parents for nearly two weeks, but then moved on because they had to earn their supper and couldn't do it where they were. They followed the usual circuit, the one they'd traveled for years, hoping that Regina and her parents would catch up with them, but they didn't. Because the parents were locked up in Little Woodcote, and Regina was in London with Cast-iron Gert, then with Kipp and Abby and, finally, with you."

"But when Regina met up with Thomas and the others again, and she told them her story, Cosmo got it into his head that even Allerton wouldn't be so stupid as to kill the golden goose—that as long as he believed Blissington could produce a black tulip, he'd keep them alive. And he was right." Brady looked into his empty glass. "I suppose Thomas also told you what he learned from Regina's parents today?"

The duke nodded. "After at least another half dozen failures, Mr. Blissington has promised that, this time, he has done it. There will be at least one hundred black tulips going from bud to bloom before the week is out. That's why Allerton has his foreign guests, and that's why he's told his son they'll soon be rich as Croesus."

"But if Blissington fails this time, he will be dead. Allerton's desperate, in part because of me. I waved Regina under his nose, wore those damn tulips in my buttonhole, went after Thorndyke. He has to know something has gone wrong, that someone—either Gawain or myself—is on to him. Now that I think about it, even if those tulips turn out really to be black, the Blissingtons are already as good as dead. Allerton can't afford leaving any evidence around, just in case I decide to tell the world what I know. Still, we're lucky in one thing. The Blissingtons have been prisoners for so long that Allerton has gotten careless—or doesn't have the funds to hire more than a single guard. A tap on the guard's head, and we're in the greenhouse, then out again with the Blissingtons."

"You're right. It's barely a challenge. So we go back to Little Woodcote tonight, get them out of there," Bram said, standing up, signaling his readiness to be off. "And Allerton, if he hears that they're gone before we can do anything to expose him, will probably bless his luck, because then he won't have to worry about disposing of them. As long as we leave the tulips behind, that is."

But Brady shook his head. "I've already involved you enough, my friend. Sophie would have my head if anything happened to you."

"Brady," the duke said, grinning, "Sophie would have your head if you spoiled my fun."

"We'll be leaving in about five minutes," Brady told

him. "As soon as Thomas joins us. I thought it best that the Blissingtons saw a familiar face when we break down the door to rescue them."

"Good point. And Regina? What about her? Surely she wants to go along."

Brady smiled. "Regina is quite content to stay here in Portman Square and allow me to effect the rescue, thank you very much. She trusts me, you know."

The duke looked at him curiously. "My God, man, you may be full leagues ahead of either Kipp or me, if she already listens to you like that. My compliments."

"Accepted," Brady said, shooting his cuffs. "I don't see why you and our friend Kipp had so much trouble. I explained the situation, pointed out that she'd simply be in the way, and she agreed. I'm the man, she's the woman. I effect the rescue, and she waits here, ready to serve tea or whatever when we get back. Where's the problem? Perhaps you'd like lessons . . . ?"

"Very amusing. Now come on, let's go. I'd like to be back in town before morning—because we'll need a full day to plan exactly how you're going to make this all come right."

"Oh, I've already worked that out in my head," Brady said, following his friend to the foyer. "Didn't I tell you that? Regina says I'm brilliant. And I think she's right."

"There they go," Regina said, peering out the window overlooking Portman Square. "With any luck, they'll be back before midnight, Mama and Papa with them."

"Or even earlier, as the night is fine, the moon will be full, and the earl's horses are the finest, even if Rooster is in the box." Cosmo, who had been sitting at his ease in one of His Lordship's chairs in front of the fireplace, looked at David and said, "Are you going to be all night? The pawn, boy, the pawn. It's your only move."

"But then you'll have my queen," David protested, shaking his head. "I'll never win at this game."

"Then it's a good thing you're so pretty, isn't it?" Cosmo said, as Regina came up behind his chair, leaned over it, kissed the top of his head as she slid her arms down and over his shoulders. "The key isn't in my pocket, dearest, but with the earl. We're as locked up tight in here as you are. I think we're only here to make sure you don't tie the bedsheets together and go out the window. That would be your alternate plan, I suppose?"

Regina hit her palms against the top of the chair, muttered something unlovely under her breath, and went back to the window. "I can't believe he locked us in here. I did say I'd stay, didn't I? I even promised him. Anyone would think he didn't trust me."

"Yes," Cosmo said, winking at David. "Anyone would. I really like that young man." David sighed, finally made his move, and Cosmo leaned forward, picked up the black queen: "Checkmate."

Chapter Nineteen

$\mathcal{K}$ipp Rutland, Viscount of Willoughby, had ridden hell bent for leather all the way from Willoughby Hall after a loud pounding on his front door in the middle of the night had awakened him to a scribbled message from Brady. He'd dressed quickly, penning a note for his wife, Abby, who still slept soundly, then kissed her forehead and slipped out of the house, mounting the horse that was already standing outside.

He'd stopped at his London house for a bath, a meal, and a change of clothes, and arrived at Lady Jersey's ball after the first crush of guests had already mounted the stairs, been greeted by their hostess, and then moved into the crowded, overheated ballroom.

Walking through the press of bodies, snagging a glass of wine from a passing waiter, he kept moving until, at last, he saw the duke of Selbourne standing near a Grecian column, talking to a squat, fat lady with ostrich feathers sticking out of a hideous purple turban.

"Good evening," he said, bowing to the woman, and then frowning at Bram. "I don't believe I've been introduced?"

"Mrs. Matilda Forrest," Bram told him, "dearest Regina's chaperone. Mrs. Forrest, may I present the viscount of Willoughby, just arrived from the country."

Cosmo looked at the duke. "What do I do now, Your Grace? Curtsy? Offer my hand for him to kiss? He may not like that, once we tell him. I know I wouldn't. Not above half. Now, if it was Thomas rigged out like this, *he'd* like it, because His Lordship is a fine specimen, but I'm not Thomas."

Kipp looked at Bram in confusion, then looked at Mrs. Forrest once more. "It's been a long day, Bram. Explanation, please."

"Mrs. Forrest is really Cosmo, one of Regina's troupe of players," the duke told him as if he was explaining something simple, then turned slightly and gave a small inclination of his head. "Over there, that pretty boy being ogled by half the women here tonight—and no less than three men, or at least that's how many I've counted so far—is David. Disgusting, isn't he? Michelangelo would have used him for his *David*, if he'd seen him, and none of the ladies would have even noticed the lack of a fig leaf. He's another player, in case you were about to ask."

Kipp shook his head. "How did you get them in here? Sally Jersey is such a stickler."

"Simple. We promised her a show that would have people talking about her ball for the next six seasons," Bram explained. "But I'm not quite done yet. To your left, wearing the rather ill-fitting lilac originally fashioned for our good friend Brady, is the third player, Thomas. At the appointed time, and on cue—as Regina terms it—all three will position themselves at the exits closest to the scene of action. You and I will serve in a similar capacity. We wouldn't want anyone leaving early, you understand."

"I don't understand *anything*," Kipp pointed out tersely. "I only know I received a note from Brady, asking me to be at the ball tonight, ready for anything. I spent my entire ride to town trying to think about what *anything* could be," he continued, looking at Cosmo, "but obviously I never even came close. Is Brady here? Is there time to tell me what's going on, or am I simply supposed to stand at one of the doorways, turning back anyone who wants to leave? That ought to make me popular."

"Mrs. Forrest? If you'll be so kind as to excuse us?" Bram said, taking Kipp's arm. "Come along, Kipp. We'll go out on the balcony, and I'll explain everything. And introduce you to two more players who are, for the moment, safely stashed there out of sight—we're hoping it won't rain. They very much want to meet you, by the way, and thank you for your great care of their daughter."

"Their—what in *hell* is going on here?" Kipp asked, walking with Bram, but still looking back at Cosmo, who was waggling his fingers to him in farewell.

CE

Brady stood at the edge of the ballroom, waiting for Regina to return from the balcony, where she had gone to check on her parents. She seemed unable to allow them out of her sight for more than five minutes at a time, as if fearful they'd disappear on her again.

He could still smile as he recalled their tearful, immensely joyful reunion. His smile broadened, however, when he remembered the way Regina, once the first hugs were gotten out of the way, had begun sternly to scold her parents "for being such sillies, and worrying me half to death."

Clearly, in this little family, Regina was the parent.

Edward and Cecilia Blissington were quite a pair. Regina had obviously taken her looks from her mother, who was as petite and grey-eyed as her daughter, except that Cecilia seemed to prefer dressing in layers of filmy draperies and wore her long burnished curls flowing down over her shoulders. Beautiful, with a rather dramatic manner, the draperies and hair and gracefully fluttering hands wonderfully disguised the fact that her left leg was badly crippled—the result, Regina had told him, of an accident with the wagon the year before she had been born.

And yet Brady hadn't really noticed the limp, just that Cecilia was always holding on to her flowing draperies, waving them about like half-folded wings as she walked—floated, from spot to spot. It was fascinating to watch, and also explained why Edward Blissington had never tried to escape from Little Woodcote. Cecilia couldn't run, wouldn't be capable of climbing the high stone wall around Allerton's estate house, wouldn't be able to keep up if they had to flee from a chase.

What was also clear was that Edward Blissington

adored his Cecilia. When Brady and Bram had broken through the door to the greenhouse, then smashed the lock on the small room where Thomas had told them the Blissingtons stayed when not working with the tulips, Edward had thrown his body in front of his wife and dared them to "harm a single hair on this good woman's head and it will go badly for you, sirs!"

You had to like a man who protected his woman. Especially a bespectacled, tall, thin, rather stoop-shouldered man who looked to be more than twice Brady's age, a man who was dressed in carpet slippers and a huge mud-stained apron, and wielded a small trowel as his only weapon.

Thomas had quickly stepped between Brady and the duke, and just as quickly explained that Regina had sent "these two fine gentlemen" to rescue them, take them to their daughter.

And that, Brady thought now, grimacing, was when the trouble had started.

Edward didn't want to leave his tulips, and Cecilia refused to leave Edward. Only a few more days, one or two at the most, and Edward knew he'd have his black tulips. He was sure of it this time, convinced he had succeeded. How could he leave his tulips to that dreadful, terrible *barbarian* who saw the work of a lifetime as nothing but money? It broke the heart, that's what it did. It broke the heart.

"Mr. Blissington," Brady had said to him reasonably, "there is no such thing as a black tulip. You know it, and I know it. The world knows it. You won't be able to talk your way out of it this time, sir. When those tulips open,

Allerton is going to kill you, you and your wife both. Whether they're black, or yellow, or green with white spots on them."

"Son, there are no green tulips," Edward Blissington had told him, shaking his head—the head covered with really remarkably thick and full shoulder-length, white-as-snow hair. "Any fool knows that."

Brady remembered gritting his teeth and turning away, saying to Bram, "Your turn I believe."

"Mr. Blissington," Bram had said, using his handkerchief to dust off a chair, then sitting down, carefully splitting his coattails. "I can understand how involved you have become with this . . . project the earl of Allerton has forced you to—"

"Forced? Oh, no, not forced. Well, perhaps at first, but I know I can do it, you see. I've already—"

Brady had whirled back to glare at the man. "Are you out of your mind?" he yelled, so that Bram had to remind him that they had sneaked in here and hoped to sneak out again without shouting at the top of their lungs and waking everyone for miles. "Are you out of your mind?" Brady repeated, still unable to speak without gritting his teeth. "Do you know what Regina's been doing since Allerton brought you here?"

"Why, yes, we do," Cecilia Blissington said, nodding. "Lord Allerton has taken Gina to London to be companion to his daughter, Lady Bellinagara. He's been most kind, even if we haven't been able to see her. She's been so busy, you understand, what with her new wardrobe, and going to balls and such. Lord Allerton has promised her a fine dowry once the tulips bloom."

"And you *believed* him?" Brady had pushed the fingers of both hands through his hair as he growled, ready to grab both the Blissingtons and bang their heads together until they understood the truth.

"Allow me, my lord," Thomas had then said, pushing Brady toward the door leading back into the greenhouse. "We'll be with you in a few minutes."

Brady had stood his ground, until Bram had taken his arm and led him away, just as he heard Thomas saying, "Now, Edward, Cecilia darling, let's take our heads out of the tulip pots and see what we can see . . ."

Smiling as he remembered the trip back to London, their mission accomplished—more than accomplished—Brady looked around the crowded ballroom and wondered who in that room would applaud him in a little while, who would cut him, and who would cheerfully wish him back at the bottom of the Thames. As Regina had told him, a lot depended on how well he delivered his lines.

"Measuring your audience?" Regina asked, walking up to him and slipping an arm through his elbow. "The wine is flowing freely, and that should be a help. Still, you have to be prepared to be praised for what you did, and condemned for the way you did it."

"Yes, so you've said," Brady told her, looking at her as she stood there in her heavy ivory-silk gown, his pearls around her neck. "As long as you love me, I'll be fine. How are your parents?"

"Mama can't wait to join the party, and Papa is worried about his tulips. He's sure they're opening even as we stand here. Thank you, Brady, for not hating them."

"I can't hate them, princess," Brady told her. "Although I have to admit that I'm still having a deuced difficult time believing that they truly thought Allerton was taking care of you all these long months."

"Papa always believes what is easiest to believe," Regina said, sighing. "But he's terribly remorseful now, poor thing. I don't think he's been this upset since he spent a year's profits on a machine promised to make dry rain."

Brady looked at her, one eyebrow cocked. "Dry rain?"

Regina nodded. "Oh, yes. Put water in this *huge* bucket rigged up in the rafters, turn the crank, and *dry* rain would fall on the stage, looking like real rain, but not getting the players wet while they spoke their lines." She sighed soulfully, shook her head. "Poor Cosmo. He nearly drowned in the middle of his soliloquy. And then there was the time—stop laughing!"

Brady stuffed a corner of his lace-edged handkerchief in his mouth and turned away, pretending to inspect the fronds of the potted palm standing behind him until he could recover himself. He dabbed at his eyes as he turned back to Regina once more, and said, "All right, I forgive him. I'll forgive him anything if you've got more stories like that one."

"Oh, I've got dozens, and Cosmo and Thomas have hundreds more," Regina assured him, grinning—and then her smile faded. "Oh dear, look at that. Allerton's here. He just came in, and Sir Randolph and Baron Thorndyke are with him. The duke and the earl are on the balcony, with Mama and Papa, but promised to come back inside when the music stopped, take their positions. Are you ready?"

"As ready as I'll ever be, I suppose," Brady told her, looking out across the ballroom, watching Allerton moving with his cohorts on either side of him, all three of them looking fairly well pleased with themselves.

Obviously word had not come to them yet from Little Woodcote. It was amazing how a few pounds put in the right pockets could slow a message traveling from Little Woodcote to London—and it certainly helped that Allerton had not paid any of his servants' wages for the last two quarters.

"Brady? You're still standing here," Regina reminded him. "Perhaps you've decided that this is too risky? If so, I wouldn't blame you. Really. I think it's so wonderful that you'd decided not to expose Allerton because it would mean telling the world about Papa's little deception. But I also agree that we'd never feel safe as long as Allerton is free to move about, plan a revenge. Still, maybe there's another way?"

"If all that was meant to bolster my courage, princess," Brady told her, "I'd hate to see you at the head of a troop about to go into battle. Now stay here and let me get this over with before I lose my nerve. It's not that I'm afraid to face my peers, you understand. It's that I hate the thought that I'll be speaking as Brady, and looking like Gawain. You're sure you parents understand what they're to—"

"Papa has *never* forgotten a line, and he's trod the boards since he was in short coats. Just ask him. Only not now.

We're never allowed to speak to him for at least two hours before he appears. He says it's bad luck."

"But I thought you said that Bram and Kipp were out on the balcony, talking to him?"

Regina pulled a face, then tried to grin. "Oh, well, Papa's been wrong before . . ." she said, her words trailing off as she gave Brady a slight push at the back of his waist. "Remember, I love you."

"I hope you love me more than you love being in society, princess, because, after tonight, we might never be here again," Brady said, then walked away, heading for Sally Jersey, who smiled as he approached, clearly ready to be "amused."

*

Regina fought the urge to gnaw on her knuckles as she watched Brady wend his way along the perimeter of the dance floor, heading toward their hostess.

What a day they'd had! She'd been waiting in Brady's bedchamber, looking out the window for what seemed like weeks, until the carriage had pulled into Portman Square, at which time the lying Cosmo had produced a key from his shoe and opened the door, then been almost bowled over as she'd ran toward the stairs.

So much hugging, so much crying, so much laughing! Mama had looked tired, and rather confused, but Papa had looked and sounded his usual unflappable self—calm, according to Thomas, born of a mind that didn't examine anything too deeply.

Someday, she might tell them how she'd lived during

the year they'd been separated. But she might not, probably wouldn't. Papa would be devastated, and Mama would cry for days. It was better that they be happy with the story Brady had told them on their way to London—the one she had crafted herself, and a lie just large enough for her parents to swallow.

She only hoped that Papa would forget his intention to seek out Mrs. Gertrude Iron and thank her for her kindness shown to his daughter.

After getting her parents settled, which hadn't been until nearly dawn, Brady had taken Regina's hand and led her down the hallway to his bedchamber, apologizing—his heart not really in it—for locking her in his rooms while he and Bram rode back to Little Woodcote.

She'd tried to be stern, to warn of retribution when he least expected it, but her heart couldn't be in it; she was much too happy to have her parents with her again, to have Brady back safely from yet another good-hearted intervention into her life.

He'd taken her to his bed, and they'd lain close together, talking about her parents, about the evening ahead of them, about the life ahead of them once this evening was over. They'd kissed, and they'd held each other, but they hadn't made love. They would not make love again, Brady had told her, until they were married.

It was a noble thought, but Regina privately concluded it had a lot to do with the fact that Brady had ridden to Little Woodcote twice in a single day, and he was too tired now to do anything more than hold her, kiss her, and then go to sleep in her arms.

How she loved him . . .

"Here we go," the duke said, having come up beside her, watching along with her as Brady and Lady Jersey walked to the center of the room just as a servant appeared above them in the gallery where the musicians were busily sawing away on their violins. The servant spoke quietly, the music grew to a sort of fanfare, and then stopped, leaving several dancers adrift, not knowing if they should finish their steps or just stand where they were, looking rather silly, actually.

Sally Jersey clapped her hands, then made shooing motions, as if she could push back the throng of dancers with her waving arms—which, it turned out, she could.

"Ladies and gentlemen," she called out in her surprisingly unlovely voice, "my dear friends. We have a treat this evening. Gawain Caradoc, the earl of Singleton, has agreed to tell us a story. Isn't that wonderful?"

There were some murmurings close to Regina, most of them male, most of them disparaging, but no one dared contradict their hostess, who was now holding out her arms to Brady, urging him to step forward.

He looked splendid, of course, if one was enamored of lightest blue-on-blue brocade and yellow-and-white-striped waistcoats. Longish hair tied back with a yellow ribbon. A huge silver-rimmed quizzing glass hanging on a matching silver chain. Clocked hose. Black patent evening slippers with large silver buckles. Dripping lace at both neck and cuffs, sapphire buttons, and a diamond bar pin holding not one but three small budding pink tulips to his wide lapels.

Brady sauntered to the center of the dance floor, chin

high, one hand braced on his hip, the other slightly out-stretched, holding a handkerchief by its corner.

All he needed, Regina thought, smiling, was a rose be-tween his teeth and a flowing satin cloak. And perhaps a monkey on a leash.

He bent over Sally Jersey's hand, holding it to his lips just long enough to titillate his audience, and then turned, made an elegant leg to everyone else.

"Forgive me, please, for interrupting your evening," he began, his voice clear, slightly drawling his words. "But Lady Jersey is correct. I do have a story for you. A story . . . and a revelation. I begin with the story."

Bram had left her, heading for his post at the door. Regina looked around the room, saw that most everyone was watching Brady, some with interest, some with barely disguised boredom. A few were laughing, one young buck was imitating Brady's pose for the delight of his friends.

"Count to ten," Regina whispered, repeating the advice she'd given Brady earlier. "No more, no less. Give them time to settle, not enough time to unsettle again."

She looked toward the doors to the balcony and saw Cosmo and Thomas, already in position. Behind her were two sets of doors leading to the stairs. Bram was at one, Kipp in front of the other.

". . . three . . . four . . ." She searched the crowd for Allerton and his two companions, locating them standing three pillars away from her, on the same side of the dance floor. Good. Good. Everyone was in place.

". . . six . . . seven . . ."

"What's he up to?" Lady Bellinagara asked, startling Regina so that she nearly dropped her fan.

"Lady Bellinagara, hello," Regina said, looking at the woman, smiling as she recognized the rouge on the woman's cheeks, her lips. "How very good to see you again."

"Good? Is that what you call it? I wish I'd never met you. Your guardian, madam, is a low, unprincipled—"

"Shhh! He's about to speak," Regina interrupted. "You'll want to listen to this. It will explain everything, I'm sure."

Regina nodded as Brady looked at her, and then took one step forward. "Oh, and by the by, this is a *true* story. You see, I want to tell you all about my cousin, Brady James, the late and lamented earl of Singleton. Of course," he added, grinning, "if he were not the late earl of Singleton I would not be the current earl of Singleton, so you will know that my gratitude to the man knows no bounds."

"Cheeky," a man behind Regina commented. "Not even wearing a black armband, is he?"

Regina bit her bottom lip. The man was right; Brady had forgotten the armband. Oh, well, that would soon be explained. Perhaps not forgiven, but definitely explained.

"I want to tell you that I have learned that my cousin was murdered," Brady continued, holding out his hands as people began to murmur. "Yes, yes, you all know that. I, myself, had believed his death to be an accident, perhaps even a suicide, until it was brought to my attention that seldom do gentlemen beat themselves *up* before lowering themselves *down* into a watery grave."

Brady took his snuffbox out of his pocket, neatly opened it with one hand, and sniffed a "pinch" up each nostril, finishing by lightly touching his handkerchief to his upper lip. "Forgive me, but I must build my courage at this point, because I am here tonight, dear ladies and gentlemen, to tell you that my cousin's death was not the result of a mere robbery, or at the hands of any of the local cutthroats. Oh, no, no, no. I have learned that my cousin was murdered—beaten, tied up in a sack, weighted with chains, and tossed into the Thames—by someone in this room."

Regina watched and listened as lady turned to gentleman, lord turned to lord, and several cries of "No! That can't be true!" could be heard around the large room.

Holding up his hands for silence, Brady said, "Oh, but it *is* true, I fear. My cousin, you see, had a terrible failing. He was a nosy, nosy man. Always poking that nose into other people's business." He shrugged his shoulders, sighed dramatically. "It was only a matter of time, I fear, before he stuck that nose into quite the wrong business."

"Whose business?" someone called out from behind Regina, and she recognized the duke's voice.

"Ah, so very glad you asked," Brady said. "But before I can tell you that, I fear that I must tell you yet another story, this one about an innocent young girl left alone in the world, penniless and afraid, when her parents were ripped from her life, made prisoners of evil men intent on creating a private fortune. Her parents, you see—more specifically the father—had something these men wanted. Rather than purchase that something, which would be the *honest* way to do business, they locked up the man and his wife and demanded he give them what they wanted."

"What's he talking about? The man makes no sense, does he?" Lady Bellinagara asked Regina, who ignored the question.

"But enough of the parents for the nonce," Brady said, beginning to pace the center of the dance floor, directing his words first at one group, then another. "Let us return to this poor, innocent girl. Cut adrift. No parents, no roof over her head. Not a penny to her name. Where could she go? What could she do?"

Brady paused for effect, brushing a bit of lint off his waistcoat. "I'll tell you what she did, my friends. She *survived*. Young, yes. Innocent, yes. Miserable with grief and fear, most definitely. But unbowed, ladies and gentlemen. Proud, and resilient, and with a mission, to find the murderers of her parents and wreak her revenge."

"Dead? You say the parents are dead?"

Brady looked at Lady Jersey, who had asked the question. "No, my lady, I did not say that the parents were dead. But the young woman *believed* they were dead. Which is worse? To believe yourself orphaned, or to know that your parents are captives and you can do nothing to rescue them? Perhaps believing them dead was a kindness?"

"I still don't understand," Lady Jersey said. "What does any of this have to do with your cousin? Oh, and by the way—you're right. He *was* a nosy sort, but he was never mean. I rather liked him. Young, and silly, but never mean."

Brady bowed. "Thank you, madam. But to continue!"

He began walking in a large circle, speaking as he passed by some of his audience, stopping occasionally as he spoke to one person in particular. Everyone's eyes were on him, most of them blank with confusion, but all of them interested, still hanging on his every word.

"Picture if you will, ladies and gentlemen, this lonely, unhappy, *desperate* girl. Picture her alone here, in London. Walking the streets, hungry, with nowhere to go, no place to rest her head. We all know what happens to innocent girls in London, don't we?"

He stopped, turned, held up his hand. "But not to *this* one! Oh, no, not to this one. Because, ladies and gentlemen, this one met the viscountess of Willoughby, an angel of a woman, and she was taken into the viscountess's household, to work as a maid." He lowered his voice slightly, and Regina watched, smiling, as several people took a few steps forward, so as not to miss a single word.

"It was there, in the home of his friends, that my cousin saw this young girl. It was there that he saw in her an indomitable spirit, a *purity* that drew him to her, made him ask *why*. His heart *needed* to know why because, for the first and last time in his life, my cousin was in love. Deeply, wonderfully, frustratingly in love. He had to know. Why was this clearly extraordinary creature working in his friend's household? Where had she come from? And so, just as you might already have realized, my cousin began asking questions. The girl was evasive, afraid, her tragedy ill preparing her to trust another gentleman of the *ton*."

"He said it again. It's one of us," a voice called out—

this time definitely the viscount of Willoughby's voice. "Tell us! Tell us!"

"Goodness! A little patience, please. My cousin traveled out of the city, to the place the young woman said she had come from, a village not far from London. He asked questions, he left his card, he hoped for an answer. That answer, ladies and gentlemen, came one night last spring, when my cousin was accosted by three men, beaten into a jelly, and tossed into the Thames. Never to know *why*, never to see the young woman again, never to love, to marry, to know the happiness he'd sought."

"What utter nonsense," Lady Bellinagara said in a carrying voice. "As if an earl would marry a nobody—a *maid*! He'd be laughed out of society."

"Why, my lady?" Brady asked, walking over to peer down at her through his quizzing glass. "*You're* still in society, and there is *no one* to offer for *you*."

Regina grabbed at Lady Bellinagara's arm as the woman tried to raise her hand, slap Brady's face. "No one heard but the three of us, my lady. Sympathy lies with His Lordship at the moment. Let it go."

Lady Bellinagara looked at her for a few moments, then turned on her heels and headed for the back of the ballroom. The viscount Willoughby looked at Regina, who nodded, and he stood aside, allowing Her Ladyship to leave. It might be kinder if the woman weren't here when Brady finished his story.

"So now," Brady said, returning to the middle of the dance floor, "let us learn what my nosy cousin could not. Let us learn *why* he was killed, why the young woman's parents were taken prisoner, why the young woman was left alone, to live or perish without family, without friends. Let me tell you, my dear friends, about . . . *tulips*."

"Tulips?" Sally Jersey lifted a hand, flicked at the three budding tulips on Brady's lapel. "You mean—*tulips*? Like these tulips? It was an interesting tale, my lord, but it's no longer amusing. Tulips? What could possibly be so dangerous about tulips?"

"Dangerous, my lady? A good question. Flowers should not be dangerous. However, in this case, they were, they are. Because I'm speaking of *black* tulips. Black as ebony, black as coal, black as a starless night, a killer's heart. An impossible color, an impossible creation." He walked over to where Allerton was standing, Allerton and his two friends. "Do you agree, my lord? Aren't black tulips an impossible creation?"

"How would I know about that?" the earl shot back at him, his expression blank, his eyes cold with rage. "You don't tell a very good story, my lord, and I think everyone here agrees. None of what you say makes any sense."

"Ah, but bear with me, my lord, for this is where it becomes interesting, I promise. Here is where it all comes together."

He turned from the earl, speaking to the company at large once more. "Tulips, my lords, my ladies. Once so rare, so treasured, that a single root could fetch the same price as twenty acres of standing corn. One root! Those mad days are gone, of course, but they would return in a heartbeat—less than a heartbeat—if a black tulip could be created. Why, the man able to produce such a *rara avis* would be the richest man in England—possibly the world. Surely this is a treasure worth anything . . . even murder. Do you agree with me now, my lord? Baron Thorndyke? Sir Randolph?"

"Allerton?" David called out from across the room, his hand over his mouth but his elocution, his projection, still excellent. "Are you saying Allerton murdered the earl?"

"And the other two? What about the other two?" Thomas asked, his voice coming from yet another area of the room.

"This is preposterous!" Allerton said, as more voices were raised, more questions were asked. "I will not stand here and be insulted in this way. How *dare* you, sirrah!"

"I *dare*, sir, because the young woman my cousin loved has become my ward. I dare, sir, because I listened to her story, and then I took it upon myself to drive down to Little Woodcote, where my cousin had been, and see what *I* could find. Miss Blissington? Please join me."

Regina felt all the eyes in the room concentrated on her, and lifted her chin, walked to the center of the floor, put her hand in Brady's.

"Almost over, princess," he whispered to her.

"Yes, but please hurry. Or haven't you noticed that our audience isn't quite in charity with either of us?"

"I noticed," he told her, then addressed Allerton once more. "You ask how I dare accuse you? I dare, sir, because what I found was the esteemed botanist, Professor Edward Blissington, and his wife, Cecilia, locked inside a greenhouse on your estate, *sir*, with hundreds of pots filled with tulips. Deny it, sir, if *you* dare."

"I do deny it—I deny every word!" Allerton blustered, as Sir Randolph and Baron Thorndyke edged backwards, intent on disassociating themselves from their friend. "And where do you two think you're going!" he called out, turning to glare at his friends.

"Do you also deny, my lord, that these two good people were locked inside your greenhouse for a year, your prisoners, your slaves?"

Regina bit her lip as her parents entered from the balcony, the gentlemen and ladies of the *ton* parting to let them through. Her father, his wild mane of white hair tied at the nape, walked slowly, his head held high, his wife's arm through his as she leaned on him, her limp accentuated.

Baron Thorndyke, who had already seen one ghost in the past few days, yelped, turned, and started running toward the door, only to be stopped by the duke of Selbourne, who turned him about like a top, then pushed him back toward the dance floor.

"Oh, don't rush off, dear Baron," Brady said, as Thorndyke, Bram walking right behind him, was herded back to his place. "There's still more to come. Lord Willoughby, if you were to open the doors behind you?"

"My pleasure," Kipp said, pushing both doors open, then standing back as Wadsworth—the epitome of grace in astonishing circumstances—wheeled in a small, two-wheeled cart holding one hundred pots containing one hundred open tulips.

Dark purple tulips.

"Yours, my lord?" Brady asked, as Wadsworth maneuvered the cart to the center of the dance floor.

Thorndyke, who belatedly realized he'd said enough,

and Allerton, who seemed to refuse to say anything, just stood there, looking at the sea of dark purple tulips.

Sir Randolph, however, was another story. "Purple!" he exclaimed, running over to the cart and picking up one pot, then another, shaking them under Allerton's nose. "Bloody purple! Do you know what this means? We're ruined, Allerton. All of us—ruined!"

"Shut . . . up," Allerton ordered tersely, as the lords and ladies of the *ton* gathered round, picking up pots, obviously eager to have a memento of this extraordinary evening.

"Shut up, is it?" Sir Randolph said, raising the pot he held high over his head. "This was all your idea. You'd seen one, you said. The professor here showed you one, and—"

"He's *not* a professor," Allerton gritted out, being jostled by the crowd, everyone intent on getting a tulip, hearing the end of the story, watching as three of their own were carted away to the hangman.

"Brady, do something!" Regina exclaimed as she felt herself being pushed toward the cart, caught in the midst of the mob of wellborn, well-dressed idiots.

"Right," Brady said, picking her up at the waist and lifting her into the cart, following after her. "Ladies and gentlemen!" he called out loudly, trying to be heard. "My story isn't over."

"Yes, it is," someone yelled out. "Allerton and Sir Randolph, and Thorndyke here—I've got him by the arm, so he can't run away—killed your cousin. Now toss me one of those pots!"

"And it all worked so well in rehearsal," Regina said,

holding on to Brady so that she wouldn't tumble out of the cart. "I fear, my darling, that you are not destined for the stage."

"I could let them hang, you know," Brady told her. "They all still think I was murdered." He looked around at the people he had called his friends, the people who had, when you got right down to it, all the manners of Cast-iron Gert and her crowd as they dived for pennies on the flagway outside Covent Garden.

"You can't do that," Regina told him. "I know you can't."

"Oh, very well," Brady said, then put a finger in each corner of his mouth and whistled—a piercing sound that at last called the scrabbling, greedy *ton* to attention.

"I told you all that I was here to tell you a story," he said loudly as the mutterings died down—except over to his left, where Sally Jersey was fighting Matilda Forrest for the last tulip pot. "You now know that the earl of Allerton, Sir Randolph Tilden, and Baron Thorndyke had hoped to line their pockets—and empty yours—by coercing the good professor into producing roots for true black tulips. You know that Miss Blissington was left alone, believing her parents were dead, and forced to fend for herself. You know that Brady James stuck his nose into Miss Blissington's life, prompting Allerton and the others to accost him, beat him, and throw him to his death in the Thames.

"But there are still a few things you *don't* know, and I ask your indulgence while I tell you what they are. First, Professor Blissington *did* create a black tulip. *One* black tulip, which he foolishly showed to Lord Allerton, which he foolishly promised to reproduce in quantity for Lord Allerton, which he and his wife ended up being imprisoned over, until those one hundred roots were produced.

"The black tulip that had been created died because of some fatal flaw within it. Or perhaps nature itself destroyed the tulip, knowing of the tragedy it would bring to the world. Who can say? What we can say is that it could not be reproduced. The professor has tried, countless times, to duplicate his great feat, but to no avail. The world has seen one black tulip, but it will see no more."

Regina squeezed Brady's hand, thanking him yet again for the genius of his story, an explanation that saved her father from being deemed a charlatan who was at least partially responsible for his own troubles.

"Allerton and his friends did wrong, my friends. They kidnapped a decent man and his wife. They left a young woman abandoned and penniless. They tried to kill the earl of Singleton . . ."

"They *tried*?" Lady Jersey asked, clutching a tulip pot to her beaded bosoms. "They succeeded!"

"No, my lady, they did not. What they did, my friends, was to *save* the earl of Singleton. They tried to send him to his death, but ended by showing him life. What life should be, what it can hold, what it can mean. They gave him the opportunity to return to London as Gawain Caradoc, and learn that Brady James had *not* been the best friend, the best gentlemen. They blessed him with the opportunity to learn from his mistakes, to find love, and to be able to stand here this evening in front of all you good people and say, from the bottom of his heart, I promise to be a better man."

Halfway through Brady's confession, the duke of Selbourne and the viscount of Willoughby had climbed into the cart, to stand beside their friend. "Well done, Brady," the duke told him, patting him on the back.

"I would have written it better," Kipp told him, "but, yes, well done."

Regina watched, tears streaming down her face, as Brady took a deep breath, let it out slowly, and then climbed out of the cart, to face the people he had duped, either to be welcomed back from his watery grave or given the cut direct as the *ton* turned away from him.

The silence that had fallen over the crowd was finally broken when Allerton said, "Then it's you? You're not dead? We didn't murder anyone?"

"No, you didn't. I forgive you. I can do that, you know. I forgive you. The professor and his wife and daughter forgive you. But I can't speak for everyone else here tonight, or those who will hear about all of this tomorrow."

Allerton grinned, straightened his jacket and turned to his peers, the people he had known for all of his life. One by one, they turned their backs. One by one, they walked over to Brady, slapping him on the back, calling him "you old dog," shaking his hand.

Allerton and his friends were finished, done. For years all three had lived on their family names, going deeper and deeper into debt, but able to keep the duns away because of their exalted positions in the *ton*. Now, shunned by society, their creditors would begin appearing on their doorsteps before dawn the next morning, demanding payment for all their debts, because a man who'd lost the backing of society had lost everything. Within the month, Allerton, at least, would be in the Fleet, imprisoned for his debt, and his friends would soon join him there. Their positions, destroyed. Their houses and lands, taken from them. In some ways, a hanging would have been kinder.

"It's going to be all right, isn't it?" Regina asked Bram, as he helped her down from the cart. She watched Brady, saw his smile, the sparkle in his eyes. "I really think it's going to be all right."

Bram motioned with a slight nod of his head, so that Regina turned to see Lady Jersey approaching her, a tulip pot in one hand, the other held out to take Regina's hand in her own, to welcome her to society. "Oh, yes, my dear. I'd say it's going to be quite all right."

Epilogue

$\mathcal{B}$rady never did get his bonfire, unless he could count (and he did) the blaze burning at Allerton's estate the night he and the duke had rescued the Blissingtons, as Lady Bellinagara's bedclothes, draperies, and such were put to the torch by the efficient Mrs. Cooper.

As it turned out, however, Thomas was much enamored of Gawain Caradoc's outlandish rigouts, so that Brady made the man a gift of them all, right down to the last lace-edged handkerchief and shoe buckle.

Not so easily settled was the disposition of Edward and Cecilia Blissington. Regina wanted them to stay with her, travel to Singleton Chase, take up residence, raise tulips. But the sweet and kind and remarkably strong-willed Cecilia had declared with some vehemence that she'd seen quite enough tulips, thank you very much, and longed to be back on the road once more.

Most certainly, they could winter at Singleton Chase. Most certainly the troupe would avail themselves of the earl's hospitality—but she longed to play Lady Macbeth, she longed to hear the applause, she longed to sleep under the stars and see her beloved England from the seat on their very own wagon.

That part was easy. A new wagon was purchased, outfitted and painted. New costumes, scenery, and anything else Edward and Cecilia desired were loaded on that wagon, and within a month of Brady and Regina's wedding, the reunited Blissington Traveling Players were off, promising to write, promising to be at Singleton Chase in time for the Christmas holidays.

Allerton, the door to his private study bolted from the inside, to keep out the men sent to remove all the furniture from the house to help satisfy his debts, did the world a great service by turning his dueling pistol on himself a week after Lady Jersey's party. His cohorts chose the Fleet, and would be residents there for some time, as nobody in the *ton* seemed willing to come to their assistance.

Brady and Regina remained in town, Brady mending fences with those he had duped in his role of Gawain Caradoc—at times no easy chore. There were still people who refused to speak to him, which would have bothered him more if he'd liked those people more. But since he didn't, he was content.

More than content. He saw the world—his world— through new and enlightened eyes. He recognized its silliness, he accepted its foibles, and, for the first time in his life, he could say that he truly enjoyed his fellowman.

That didn't mean that he wished to spend the majority of his life in London. Not anymore. Singleton Chase now held an allure he hadn't noticed in many years, and he'd enjoyed his months there with Regina, as they lived, as they loved, as they tumbled more deeply into love with every passing day.

He bought a dog. Two dogs; one for him, and one for Regina. Gawain still did not sleep with his head on Brady's feet, but he had chewed up his master's second best boots. Caradoc followed Regina everywhere like a lovesick puppy, which was pretty much what he was.

Brady was amazed, and said so, to learn that he could think he'd been happy, then be shocked into realizing how empty that happiness had been, how unrewarding, how meaningless. He knew the difference now, in his new happiness, and believed with all his heart that the difference was love. Loving. Being loved.

He knew now what Bram had found, what Kipp had found. If, as at that moment, he sometimes amazed himself by realizing that he'd actually sat silent in the drawing room at Singleton Chase for a full hour, a smile on his face, watching his wife put infinitesimal stitches in yet another gown meant for his son or daughter, he also knew that he was more fortunate than he had any right to be.

"You're smiling again, darling," Regina pointed out as she lifted the small white gown to her mouth, bit off a length of thread. "What are you thinking about?"

"Nothing, really," he told her. "About Kipp's letter, telling us of his son's birth. Of our visit with Bram and Sophie next month, and how Bram will say 'I told you so' at least a dozen times, and I'll forgive him each time. Of how much I want to make love to you . . ."

Regina smiled, tipped her head to one side. "You're

only *thinking* about it? And here we are, with at least two full hours before the dinner gong."

Brady considered this for a moment, then decided he'd been issued an invitation. Perhaps a challenge. He put down his wineglass and walked over to his wife. "You know, princess, I promised myself that I would never again have to look back on my life and regret those things I hadn't done."

She gave a slight shiver, then put down her sewing, stood up, ran her hand down Brady's chest. "La, sir, am I then to believe you do not wish this afternoon to be listed under your regrets?"

"Yes, you might believe that," Brady said, reaching for her.

Regina braced both hands against his chest, holding him at arm's length. "But wait, good sir. I must think about this. Do I say that I am delighted, and show myself a wanton? Or do I deny my interest, and brand myself a liar?"

Brady grinned, rather wickedly. "Ah, but my dearest countess, I do believe I heard it whispered somewhere— perhaps even into my own ear—that you vowed never to lie again."

She lowered her head slightly, then looked up at him through her eyelashes. "Well, there is that, isn't there, my lord? Poor dear thing—it appears you've wed a wanton," she said, then laughed as he scooped her up into his arms, carrying her out of the drawing room and across the foyer.

"Delay dinner an hour, Wadsworth, if you please," he

said to the butler, who was emptying the mail packet on the large, marble-topped table under the chandelier.

"My thoughts exactly, sir," Wadsworth said, rolling his eyes. And then, as Regina giggled into Brady's shoulder, the butler smiled, turned sharply on his heels, and headed toward the kitchens, a happy man.